Praise for *Grabbing the*

"This book defies classification. It is at once a treatise on the nature of mankind and the role of government, as well as a fantastic voyage into the realm of visionary fiction – an exciting, prophetic, and fascinating heroic adventure."

"Beautifully written...imaginative and insightful."

"*Grabbing the Brass Ring* is an epic saga of an awesome man, Richard Mansan, who has a vision for the survival of the human race. It is a tale like no other."

"This story could very well be the future. Makes you wonder...can human beings destroy the Earth? Can one person make a difference?"

"Visionary fiction at its best, unique and thought-provoking."

"When I read *Grabbing the Brass Ring*, I was transported to a world just slightly different from our own...rich characters...intense drama...profound insights into the strengths and weaknesses of human nature."

"The characters become real. You feel as if you are there with them."

"This book is definitely ahead of its time. Nolan seems to see through history and propels us into the future."

"Amazing story...even more incredible biography!"

"I discovered years ago that the only place you'll find an interesting story is if it is written by an interesting person. Nolan *is* and *does*!"

Foreword

To be exceptional, by its very definition, is rare. Although the literal meaning of the word is merely that it is *different* from the norm, many of us infer or attribute a loftiness...a singular specialness...to the concept, as well as to the subject it designates.

It is a cliché to expostulate upon society's inclination to lower the bar of exceptionalism. By the original and untainted standard, if, in our lifetime, we have an opportunity to meet a single truly exceptional person, we are immeasurably favored. For that person will touch us...affect us...change us...by the simple reality of proximity and example. For we are who we are. Yet the exceptional individuals remind us, by the fact of their existence, of who we could be...*might be*.

If one is fortunate to meet an exceptional person, then I must be blessed because I have known three such men in my life. Each distinctly, uniquely, and profoundly exceptional. Each coming from a very different path of life. To be sure, each one amassed a lifetime of phenomenal accomplishment, while, throughout all of the years, demonstrating a pure and strong character. Let me tell you about them...

The first of my trio was found in the field of athletics. Inauspiciously, his story began his freshman year of high school. He tried out for the football team and was told by the coach that he was too slender to play the game. His reaction to this rejection defined his character and would for the balance of his life. Using homemade weights, he began to build himself up so that by his sophomore year, there was never any doubt that he would be on the team. Playing the positions of tackle, guard, and kicker, this young man quickly became known as a fearsome competitor for the next three years, earning a spot on the team of the university in his hometown.

During his high school years, he also competed in track and field, winning medals, setting records, and making a mark which lasted for decades.

If this young athlete became famous on the field during his high school tenure, it would not be an overstatement to say that he became a legend at the college level. He again filled the positions of tackle and kicker, and his freshman team not only went undefeated for the regular season, but none of the opposing teams scored a single point against them. His varsity years catapulted him into the arena of national attention and acclaim. He was selected first-team tackle on the All-Border Conference

Team and the *Phoenix Gazette* All-Border Conference Team, and named Honorable Mention on the Associated Press All-America Team and the *Liberty* magazine All-Players All-America Team.

The next year, he went to play professionally for the Chicago Cardinals and was the first from his university to play pro ball. His impact on the sport did not diminish with time. For an astonishing five decades after his last season of college football, he was selected by sportswriters to be among the eleven best football players of *all time* from the university.

His affection for other sports intensified in college. Joining the track and field team, he again broke and set records…one of which stood for over thirty years. He specialized in javelin, shot, discus, and the high jump. During this same period, he also won titles in wrestling and boxing, later pursuing a career as a professional heavyweight boxer.

One of the more remarkable stories occurred after calling an end to his sports efforts so that he could follow a different path. He found himself working at a major copper mine project in Peru. His past accomplishments preceding him, he was invited to participate in a Peruvian national track and field meet. At the age of 46, twenty years after his last competition, he became the shot put champion of the meet and placed second in the discus.

Throughout his sports career, he was known by his coaches and teammates as an affable, self-deprecating man who refused to tout himself, even when invited to do so.

The second man in my exceptional triad was – plain and simple – a war hero. Enlisting in the Marine Corps at the age of 30, before the beginning of World War II, he would later volunteer for assignment to the Marine Raiders. During the course of the war, he fought on Guadalcanal, Bougainville, and Iwo Jima. Entering the Corps as a private, he received a battlefield commission on Guadalcanal, finished the war as a captain, and retired with the rank of major.

A rare combination…he was admired by his superior officers and revered by the men under his command. The tales of his deeds were chronicled by newspapers, as well as lovingly portrayed for many years after the war by the men who served with him. The overwhelming mountain of anecdotes would be far too much to share in this introduction, but I would like to relate one:

He went to Iwo Jima as the CO of a DUKW Company charged with running supplies from ship to beach, a chore that was not his way to fight a war. He intimidated a Lt. of artillery out of a 75mm Pack Howitzer, got some of his guys to help him, dismantled the Howitzer, manhandled it to where the fighting was raging, reassembled it, and fired point-blank into Japanese caves. Indeed, he had turned over the operation of hauling artillery and supplies to a lieutenant, and joined the front-line action.

He was never one to seek a medal, believing that the Marines who served with him deserved the recognition more than he. Nor would he ever pin a single decoration upon his uniform, preferring only to wear his rank and the USMC insignia.

The third on my honor roll was, in many ways, a much lower-key individual. He was a civil engineer, as well as something near and dear to me – a novelist. And first and foremost throughout his life, he was a husband, father, and grandfather.

Abandoned by his parents at a very young age, he quickly learned two lessons he would never forget: the importance of self-reliance, and the importance of family.

Growing up during the Great Depression, this young man traveled around the country, hopping freight trains and moving from town to town to find opportunities to make money. He succeeded in doing so in some most fascinating ways. Characteristically, rather than spending his earnings on himself, he would give money to the families of friends in his hometown to help them get by during these difficult times.

His early life left another mark upon him which he would also never forget. Over the years, this kind and gentle man could not turn away from someone in need. Whether the person was family, a friend, or a stranger, he never hesitated to offer a hand. Whatever was needed – a meal, a job, a place to stay, or money – he always did what he could for anyone who might be down-and-out.

He did not marry until after World War II, and together he and his wife had a daughter. At this point in his life, he returned to college, acquiring a degree in civil engineering. After working for a time in the private sector, he joined the U.S. Forest Service and became the engineer responsible for the Coronado National Forest, a sprawling 1.875 million-acre park with almost 900 miles of trails – a position he loved and considered a sacred trust.

As the chief engineer over this magnificent park, he had an opportunity to put in place programs and mechanisms designed to safeguard the delicate environment, while building improvements which provided enhanced havens for the citizens to access and enjoy.

It was after his years with the Forest Service that he began to put ink to paper, creating vibrant, insightful, and dramatic fictional tales where he, with the stroke of a pen, populated stunning new worlds with spirited and dynamic characters.

Throughout it all, from his nuptials until his passing, he remained a loving, steadfast, and devoted husband to his wife and an almost magical and mythical father and grandfather to his daughter and grandchildren.

The reader may have guessed by now that the three men described above – each a phenomenal individual with achievements and a grace which would distinguish him – are all embodied within one man. Michael Earl Nolan. A man I am proud to have known. A man I am proud to have called my father-in-law.

His novels, as well as the astounding story of his life, are decades overdue.

I hope that you enjoy this first publication of *Grabbing the Brass Ring*. And I also believe that when you delve into the details of his complete biography – *An Extraordinary Life* – you will begin to get a sense of the kind of man he was.

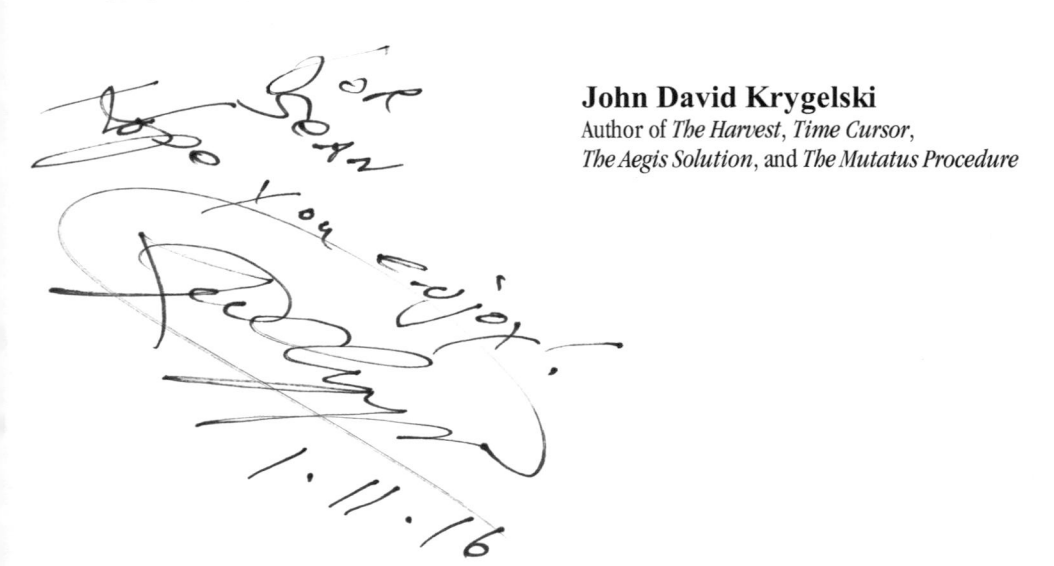

John David Krygelski
Author of *The Harvest*, *Time Cursor*,
The Aegis Solution, and *The Mutatus Procedure*

Grabbing the Brass Ring

Michael Earl Nolan

STARSYS PUBLISHING COMPANY

Grabbing the Brass Ring
and
An Extraordinary Life: The Biography of Michael Earl Nolan

www.starsyspublishing.com

Copyright © 2014 - by Jean Nolan Krygelski. All rights reserved

The name Starsys Publishing Company, the distinctive star logo and colors, are a registered trademark

Cover art - Michael Nolan — www.michaelnolanart.com
Editor - Jean Nolan Krygelski

The novel — Grabbing the Brass Ring — is a work of fiction. Names, characters, places, and incidents either are the product of the author's imagination or are used fictitiously. Any resemblance to actual events, locales, organizations, or persons living or dead is entirely coincidental and beyond the intent of either the author or the publisher.

All rights reserved, including the right to reproduce this book, or portions thereof, in any form.

Published by Starsys Publishing Company
www.starsyspublishing.com
526 N Alvernon Way
Tucson, Arizona 85711

ISBN 10: 0989652610
ISBN 13: 9780989652612
Library of Congress Control Number: 2014930196

First Edition - February 2014
Printed in the United States of America

Dedication

This book is dedicated to the eternal spirit who is Michael Earl Nolan, and who, we profoundly believe, is watching over us still.

May his legend live forever. May his legacy thrive.

And to all the Nolan family, and the generations to come…may you always feel his love.

Acknowledgments

This publication is the culmination of a long and amazing journey. Special acknowledgments are due along the way.

First and foremost, thank you to Michael Earl Nolan for writing *Grabbing the Brass Ring*, and for living a life so worthy of documentation in *An Extraordinary Life: The Biography of Michael Earl Nolan*.

Heartfelt gratitude to John David Krygelski for his passionate belief in this project and for his countless hours of dedicated attention to making it a reality; to Michael John Nolan for his masterful cover art, which captures the spirit of his grandfather's words; and to Starsys Publishing Company for fulfilling a dream.

And deep appreciation to the many contributors whose words are cited in the biography, adding the incredible details of a life well lived.

Part I
Richard Mansan

When asked the secret of life, Nolan replied,
"All power comes from within."
– Michael Earl Nolan, 1989

Chapter One

Could an act of stupidity be accomplished with any degree of intelligence? To put the same question in different text, was there a right way and a wrong way to cut our throats? Surprisingly enough, there were some people who would not only answer these questions, they would create the situations which made these questions seem logical. The word *logical*, however, was so far out of concept with the original situation that the entire affair assumed an Iliadic allure where tactic authors, activators, and even the results became forever engulfed in an impenetrable shroud of virtual idolatry, a veritable shrine which must never be desecrated by the prying eyes of mere mortals. The untold millions of human beings who had been sacrificed on these false altars showed that man still respected this last remaining stronghold of the ancient gods.

Today my role was that of an activator; and from what I could see, the plans were kind of thin, totally lacking in tangible substance. I was also learning that the final scene of each situation, hairy as it was, had to be completed without applicable props and script. And there was a fringe benefit, in a negative sort of way, assuring the audience of an ending, with or without the cast. This was in keeping with the Iliadic allure which had always managed to blind the audience with fantasies existing exclusively in the human mind.

The audience, as unlikely as it might seem, was the reason why such archaic productions were possible. The non-involved audience – each member in his or her own uncomprehending way, not knowing and caring even less – was every bit as responsible for the final scene as were the tactic authors. We could multiple-use a minor road construction job to death with our involvement, but when our lives depended on sound battle tactics, we divorced ourselves from this responsibility without giving our actions a thought. If our excuse was that our generals were more qualified to decide on a life-and-death battle than our construction superintendents were qualified to build a road, then our status as human beings needed an impact survey, as well.

Tonight our small company was on the road again. Our production number was also small, but it had all the usual potentials for getting smaller yet. A great deal would depend on the reception our first appearance would receive. The one firm part of this evening's offering was that we would drop by parachutes into enemy-held territory. I was not absolutely sure why we were doing this. The sole explanation I could come up with was that we were jumping because we had the parachutes. Someone could have decided that parachutes were a modern component of the latest battlefield tactics, and we had the chutes, so why not use them? This line of reasoning, of course, was ridiculous, and it was probably not the explanation, after all. No matter how hard I tried to find a logical argument for our actions, I repeatedly came up with the same answer.

I had to occupy myself with something, so I had been mulling over in my mind several of the thoughts I had about our *grand tactical plans*. Most of the plans would make Caesar's invasion of Gaul look like amateur night, and they were just as applicable. Regardless of how applicable our tactics were tonight, I would have to admit that the basis of the operation was sound. We needed parachutes if we were going to jump, and this was all that was needed to guarantee impunity for those authors who designed the battle plan. In the case of failure, it could certainly not be said the latest components of modern warfare had not been used. We had a tendency to go this route due to our surplus of manpower.

As I sat in the barn called a transport plane, I showed no emotions whatsoever. I was a few years older than the other men in our forty-man unit, and I could sense that the others in the plane felt the same way I did about the operation. This included our commanding officer, Lieutenant O'Riley. I also knew that the glances of the men were directed toward me. Perhaps I simply imagined that they were watching me, but those men I did look at smiled questioningly, almost as if they sought reassurance over whether we were indeed taking the most intelligent approach to the impending battle. They were willing to grasp at any straw. Since I was the oldest man aboard, they saw in me someone whose advanced years would surely not permit us to be part of a fiasco.

The plane droned on into the night toward our destination.

My name is Richard Mansan. Besides stupidity, I could think of no other reason for my being with this group tonight. We were at war, but that was not a unique position for us. I had only recently become adjusted to civilian life when this war broke out. It was possible I could have passed up this engagement, but I had a couple of ideas about involvement which needed a bit more exposure. At this very moment, I was not sure I had made a wise choice. Something about our battle tactics did not add up, and I promised myself I would keep an open mind about the part I would play in this coming operation.

Lieutenant O'Riley had asked that I be transferred into his platoon for this action, and I hoped the man's trust in my ability as a soldier would not prove to be a disappointment. Taking everything into consideration, it looked like a fun evening, and the happy hour was not far off.

My facial expression must have shown the humor that was on my mind. The kid sitting next to me would have taken my smile to mean I approved of this outing. As he spoke, his face actually showed the same enthusiasm of a schoolboy playing in the park.

"Mr. Mansan, you were lucky to get this detail on such short notice, weren't ya?"

"Yeah, kid, I guess I was."

What might have been the start of a long question-and-answer session was broken off when our sergeant gave everyone the word to get ready. We would be over the jump area in ten minutes.

Again, I had to smile as I watched the sergeant. He reminded me of an old land surveyor who had trained me several years ago. The old surveyor was a self-educated man who eyeballed-in all distances and bearings, except the final measurements. The final measurements were made with the most sophisticated instruments available, and the mathematic computation used to correct for Earth's curvature and temperature changes had me properly snowed.

Now, as I stood in line waiting for my turn to jump, I recalled the old surveyor's doctrine and noted the similarities between him and the sergeant in front of me. This man was also exceedingly meticulous with his final instructions and adjustments. I got the impression that no one would be allowed to leave the plane until every last-minute detail of decorum had been observed. However, I noticed that the sergeant had not even put on his own parachute. When I called this to his attention, his face turned white the instant he realized what had nearly happened. As I was the largest man aboard, I figured to be the first to land. I certainly did not want any scatterbrained sergeant beating me out of that dubious honor.

We had been at war for two years, and the date of this outing was January 19, 1986. Not too much for me to remember, but an old soldier once told me that anytime I got into a critical situation, what I had to do was remember the exact date. This would assure me that I had all of my mental faculties working and, in all probability, I would be several country miles ahead of everyone else. I was not thoroughly convinced this was enough. If our sergeant was any indication of the people I was supposed to be miles ahead of, I was in trouble.

○

As I floated down to earth, the full moon peeked through the scudding cloud cover, acting as nature's searchlight, focusing its beam of light across the landscape.

Somehow I got the feeling we were being watched. This was only natural, especially since millions of people would be living in the vast enemy-held land below me. It was just possible that at least one of these people would be in this area and witness our maneuvers.

The fleeting rays of moonlight did little to help me estimate the type of terrain where I would be landing. Most of the landscape I had seen was far away, due to the angle of the moon. The conditions of the earth immediately below me remained unknown.

Whatever those conditions were, I did not quite find out on my original contact. The tree I had fallen into snagged my chute. My feet, instead of being on terra firma, were dangling in the air. I realized that my present position was in no way meant to prolong my longevity.

By the time I had finally managed to cut myself loose from my parachute, I figured that about a half hour had passed. I spent another half hour getting the chute untangled from the top branches of the tree and wadded into a tight bundle, which I dropped in the direction of the ground. I was certain I heard a slight splash, so I checked out this bit of information right away by dropping my helmet. There was water below me.

The time was three o'clock in the morning, and I was literally up a tree. Granted, it was an unlikely place to be; but, under the circumstances, I climbed higher into the top branches where I could, at least, have a chance to take advantage of the moonlight which occasionally swept across the region. What I saw had a sobering effect on me.

As I looked in a northern direction, the pattern of white chutes in the treetops told me that part of the platoon had run into the same bad luck I had. The fact that the chutes were still in the trees was the part I did not like. I looked in back of me for several seconds until the moon lighted up my surroundings once more. There was nothing. I returned my attention to the north and climbed even higher in the tree, stopping as the branches started to give way. The moonlight took forever to again light up the area. When it did, I counted as many chutes as I could. There were nineteen, and then darkness.

I thought briefly about the whole scenario. Our mission was in keeping with the entire operation: vague. The direction of our advance was to be north. Our plan of action would depend upon what we encountered. I had to admit, it took a lot of brains to get people into a jackpot like this. My mind started to go blank, and I realized that the material I had been working with, and trying to piece together, actually did not exist.

Once again, I concentrated my attention to the north and waited for the next sweeping moonbeam to illuminate the far tract of land. This time I had no desire to count the chutes. My animal instinct told me that it was in this direction I was needed, and only another view of my field of action was needed to implant the picture firmly in my mind.

Before the next beam of light had run its course, I was on the ground. The water came to my knees, but my feet were on land.

The distance to the first chute appeared to be about five hundred feet from where I stood. It was impossible to determine the distance of the chute farthest from me, and at such a distance I was virtually guessing I had truly seen a chute.

Within minutes I was climbing the tree to the first stranded paratrooper. It was the sergeant, and he was dead. His neck must have been broken. I cut the chute in two and lowered the sergeant to the ground. The procedure had taken barely fifteen minutes. As much as I wanted to, I could not even afford to use that amount of time if I was going to check all the chutes I had seen.

I continued north, directed by my mind's photo of the chute pattern. The next man was O'Riley. He was alive, and he told me he could make it all right.

I hurried on to the next location, only to find that this soldier had been impaled by a broken branch.

The wind had blown the early morning sky clear, and the moon lighted up the floor of the swamp with a weird speckled stenciling which I found appropriate and totally in keeping with the entire operation, from its conception to this very minute.

The sequence of the parachutes was still fresh in my mind. I estimated I had probably traveled a mile by the time I reached the next man. The time was four o'clock in the morning. This meant I could not possibly reach the last man before eight o'clock. So far, I was not having much luck. This man was also dead.

I must have hesitated for a second to allow the reality of the situation to sink into my mind. Rifle shots rang out far to the north. I hurried forward.

The next man was alive. It was the young fellow who had spoken to me on the plane. I cut him down and continued my race northward. Another shot rang out, closer this time.

The next man was also alive. I told my young friend to cut him down and then follow me. The rifle fire was getting closer, and it was not ours. I figured I might have another hour left to work before I had to face up to the hard, cold facts. The enemy had started on the other end of the parachute line, and we were working toward each other with very different intentions.

As I was cutting down the next man, the other two men joined me. I quickly gave them instructions and then continued on my way.

By five-thirty, I could go no farther. The enemy had just shot the next man in line for rescue. I now had ten men, and I could tell that the preceding few hours had somehow shortened the span of the years between us. They were all armed with automatic rifles, and I told them to take up their positions in the swamp south of me and about fifty feet apart. I would hold the position nearest the approaching enemy.

The cold morning air pressed close to the earth, entrapping the swamp vapors. As the long line of enemy infantry snaked through the misty swamp, their eyes looked upward, ever intent upon finding their next human target.

I counted exactly one hundred soldiers before I cut down the last ten enemy in line. In their close formation they did not have a chance.

I left seven men to make sure all of the enemy were dead. The other two men followed me back to get O'Riley.

O'Riley had a broken leg. Other than that, he looked in fair shape. It was a simple fracture, which I padded and splinted well enough to get him back to the spot where the others were waiting.

Without hesitation, O'Riley put me in command.

I told the men to spread out and cut down each of our men and haul down the parachutes. The first man to finish was to follow me. I took a minute more to tell everyone that from now on, if we lived or died would depend only upon our own actions. We were soldiers and, under the conditions we found ourselves at the moment, our duties were very simple. All we had to do was fight. The fun hour was over.

Then I took off as fast as my legs could carry me, heading north.

○

It was seven o'clock before I reached dry land. I could easily tell that the enemy had entered the swamp at this exact spot. There had to be an enemy camp in the area.

I did not have long to wait for the first of our men to arrive. It was my young friend. His name was John Martel. I told Martel I wanted him to go back into the swamp and bring one other man back with him. "Yes, sir" was all he said, as he plunged into the swamp like a runaway stallion. I had to smile at the "sir" part of Martel's response. It must have been the age difference. Whatever it was, he was back within minutes with another man. I told this fellow to find as good a spot as possible and have the men rest. I wanted half of them on security guard duty at all times, and I wanted every one of them hidden, sleepers and guards alike. Martel and I were going to do a little reconnaissance and get acquainted with the countryside.

"Martel, I want you to stay in back of me about one hundred feet, and keep your eyes and ears open."

"Yes, sir."

"One other thing, I don't want to hear you say 'sir' again."

Martel remained quiet. He nodded his head, and we took off in a northern direction.

The ground was fairly well covered with shrub oak and juniper, and there were scattered pine and walnut trees. The fruit from these last two species of trees blanketed the ground around them. I made a mental note of this. The possibility always existed that we would have to eat nuts and seeds until a better alternative turned up.

We had traveled about two miles. The ground was smooth, and the grade we had been climbing was not excessive. I approached the top of a hill, and crawled toward the underbrush which grew on the very crest. In front of me, no farther than five hundred feet away, was the enemy's camp. There was not much to it, but I did see six large canvas-covered trucks, a field kitchen, and five people. As far as I could tell, this was the kitchen crew, and they were civilians. One man and four women.

Since I had found the location, I was no longer in a great hurry, so I watched the camp for about an hour. No one else was in the vicinity. I could see that the trucks had entered the area from the north. From what I could see of the surrounding landscape, the terrain did not appreciably change. There were some sheep and cattle, and I could see two houses about five miles north of my position. Taking everything into consideration, the place looked like a quiet countryside.

There were just two items on my mind that were not compatible with this peaceful scene: the dead men in the swamp and our missing men. Twenty men were accounted for – eleven alive, and nine dead. Only half of the men had been hung up in the trees. There were twenty more men, and they had to be in this immediate area. They would have landed on dry ground. In fact, they would have landed on the very ground Martel and I had walked over.

Backing away from my lookout position, I motioned Martel to me. There was a very good chance our men had been captured and were still nearby. I had Martel follow me as I took off in a western direction. We looked the area over thoroughly for any sign of our missing men. I repeated this action for two miles north, and then Martel and I turned east. When I estimated we were opposite and two miles north of my original lookout position, I stopped and made my way to the small hill a short distance to the south. Premonition told me that my search was over even before I saw the carnage below me.

Martel and I worked our way around to a point directly south of our men. I left Martel in a lookout position at that point, and I slowly walked down to take a closer look. The men had all been shot at close range, and their bodies had been mutilated.

This should never have happened. They were very young; war had been just another game for them to play one day, get captured the next day, and then play again. The people ultimately responsible for the fact that these men were lying here today remained safe many miles away, and they would probably live out their useless lives without ever knowing the results of their stupidity. I walked back to where Martel was stationed.

"Martel, I want you to go down and take a long look. Later today, I want you to be sure that all of our men see. Afterward, I want these men buried. And, remember, I want security guards posted."

As I waited for Martel, I thought about my own personal rules of warfare which had guided my actions in the past. No doubt my actions could stand a little improvement. To be honest, I found it most difficult to agree with anyone's line of thinking regarding war.

○

When Martel returned, we accessed the enemy camp from the north side. The five people were eating lunch as I walked into the tent. I motioned at them to remain seated, while Martel searched the area for weapons. After that, I had the people step over to me one at a time, and searched them thoroughly. There were no weapons in camp. I then pointed toward the location where I had found the bodies of our men. This, seemingly, did not sit very well with the five people, and it was obvious from their reactions that the same enemy troops I had killed earlier were responsible for capturing and killing our men. When they understood that I wanted to know where the men's weapons and parachutes were, the five people immediately showed me the spot where these items had been buried.

The enemy soldiers had ordered the cooks to bury the weapons, the chutes, and our men. The women had refused to bury the men.

I figured I had settled the score with the enemy for killing our incapacitated paratroopers this morning. The killing of our twenty other men presented an entirely new offense.

When I sent Martel to bring the rest of the men, I instructed him briefly on their approach march and where I wanted the men placed after they arrived. O'Riley would be brought here to the camp.

Martel took off on a dead run. Knowing him as well as I already did, I guessed he would probably be back in a half hour. Meanwhile, I had the five people remain in their seats until he returned.

Silently, I watched our men approach. We had been hurt badly by stupidity. If we were to survive, there were a few more facts we would need. I knew that this situation would be a complete change from what these men were used to, but the last hours should have made them a bit more aware of what war actually was.

Martel stationed his lookouts and placed a guard on the cooks. Half of the men headed for the erosion ditch where their buddies lay.

O'Riley's leg was swollen and discolored. It was impossible to tell what would develop in the next day or two. I took off the crude bandage, cleaned and then re-bandaged the leg. This time I came closer to doing a professional job.

Food had been cooking for one hundred men, so we would not go hungry. By four o'clock, I had started and driven all of the vehicles, the men had eaten...and we had buried our dead.

It was about time I came up with a solution to our predicament, if there was one.

I took the male cook away from the camp area. He undoubtedly thought his time had come, and I spent several minutes getting him quieted down sufficiently to comprehend the meaning of our little get-together. To begin with, my sign language was generally aimed at the man's family life. We both knew a handful of words in common, so the conversation did not turn out to be as difficult as I had expected. The women were his wife and daughters. They lived in a small village named Morea, about thirty-seven miles away. He was a tailor, but the enemy had made a cook out of him.

Martel had just returned to camp, and I called him over. "I want you to take this man to the burial ground and get as much information as possible from him about the enemy in this area: how many, where they live, their relationship with the civilian population, the works. And, Martel, I don't want you to threaten or use any force whatsoever."

When Martel left with the man, I had our guard bring the women and their camp stools closer to me. The women were hysterical, convinced I meant to bury the man in the same place I had buried my own men. I made sure the women understood that it was the man's idea to go with Martel, and that he was visiting the graves to pay his respects. He was also a minister, and it was the least he could do.

This was too much for the oldest lady, and it did not take her long to inform me that the man was her husband and the girls' father. He was a tailor, a lousy one. And she was very emphatic about her husband's lack of credentials as a cook. He could not even boil water.

Minutes later, I could tell that the ladies were ready for a few questions which were definitely more along the lines of the information I needed. I drew an X on the ground, indicating our location. Then I drew a line from the first X to another one, the village. One of the daughters marked the distance on the line; it agreed with the distance the man had given me. I marked one hundred soldiers under the first X. The women had no way of knowing that I knew the number of the enemy who had occupied this camp. I moved to mark the number of enemy under the second X, when I noticed our guard standing about fifty feet away. I dropped the stick I was using to mark the ground, and left to talk with the man Martel had assigned to the cooks. When I returned, it was all written out. The ladies had added the two figures, giving me a total number of enemy soldiers in the area: two hundred. I had already taken care of one hundred of these.

After I escorted the women back to the camp, Martel reappeared with the husband. Both men were smiling. I was certain the cook's smile would change by the time his family got through with him.

"Mansan, another hundred enemy are stationed at the municipal building just north of town, and they are presently restricted to that building because of their recent trouble with the townspeople."

"Let's get this show on the road and pay our friends an overdue visit."

"I'm with you, sir."

"Martel."

"Sorry, Mansan."

"Assemble the men, and meet me here in ten minutes."

After Martel took off, I checked on O'Riley. He was lying on a canvas cot sound asleep.

When the men assembled, I talked with them briefly about my plans. One man would stay with O'Riley and the cooks. He would have a truck loaded and ready to roll in two hours. The rest of us would proceed to the municipal building in two of the trucks. Martel would drive one truck with four men. I would drive the other truck with the remaining three men. Under no conditions did I want any civilians injured. Everyone was well aware what the rules of the game were with regard to the enemy soldiers. Martel would lead the way. He claimed he could get there with his eyes closed.

○

The first twelve miles were cross-country. All we had to do was follow the enemy's old tracks. For the next twenty-five miles we followed a one-lane wagon road. It was quite dark by the time we arrived at the outskirts of the settlement. Our rate of speed had been excessive the whole way, but I was sure no one noticed. Martel did seem to know exactly where he was going.

As for my own thoughts at the time, I had reached a saturation point. If I could have hated the enemy any more than I did at this very second, I would have exploded. I realized we should all be dead by now, and anything we accomplished was far beyond what we had reason to expect. The men were young, but in a few hours they had seen it all. They were no longer raw recruits.

Martel never hesitated. He drove like a man with a mission, a very young man in a hurry.

The large building in front of us, about a quarter of a mile away, was obviously our destination. It was the only structure in the area with lights in front. As we roared down the main street, the people stood well out of the way to let us pass. The strong headlights on Martel's truck were already focused on the municipal building at the end of the street. The enemy must have assumed that their trucks were returning, for there was a wild scramble to get into formation directly in front of their headquarters. I passed the word for the men to get ready on the left side of the truck. I knew that Martel would make as wide a right turn as possible so we could pass in front of the enemy's formation.

The first enemy soldier to raise his rifle was shot before the others could adjust their thinking to this rapid turn of events. It was doubtful that the entire one hundred enemy soldiers were able to get off ten shots before they fell.

Martel and I, with the seven men following, quickly entered the building. For a brief second my attention was drawn to the man with the enemy commander, and in that length of time the enemy officer fired his pistol point-blank at me. I was so enraged that I felt nothing. I did not even hear the men's rifle fire which riddled the body of the enemy officer.

As my thinking came back to normal, I noticed the other man again. He was dressed in a different foreign uniform; and when I questioned him, he informed me that he was on assignment to the enemy forces as an observer, and that his name was Tyron Jrcy. I figured the man to be about twenty years old, and he represented a real international problem as far as I was concerned. I quickly took off the small pack I was carrying and tossed it to him. The moment I pointed to the back door, he needed no other instructions, and left the building on the double.

After he ran out, I glanced briefly at Martel and the others. They were actually laughing. The strain of the last hours had given way to laughter, so letting the foreign officer escape had accomplished quite a lot.

When we came back outside the building, I noticed that the civilian population had gathered on the far side of the trucks, and I approached them unarmed. They did not seem to be alarmed over what had happened during the preceding minutes. One distinguished-looking gentleman stepped forward and spoke to me.

"You are wounded, sir."

I had felt a stiffening in my left shoulder. When I tried to raise my arm, it just hung limp. The enemy officer's shot had found its mark, after all.

The man spoke again. "I am a doctor, sir, and your arm needs immediate attention."

At the word *doctor*, I thought of O'Riley. I looked in back of me where Martel was standing.

"Are you okay, Martel?"

"Yes."

"Then send a truck back for O'Riley and the cooks. O'Riley is to be brought to this man's office as soon as possible.

"One other thing, Martel, check the men over. Those who need medical attention will follow me to the doctor's office. The others will remain inside the building until I return.

"And you be sure they post security guards twenty-four hours a day."

Martel left on the run, as I turned to follow the doctor. There was something wrong with me. I had been shot before, but this time I had a pinched feeling, as though I was drying up. My nostrils seemed to close, and even my eyesight was failing.

○

When I awoke, the room was quite dark. A small kerosene lamp had been placed on a table across the room from my bed. I lay still for what seemed like an hour, trying to fit the pieces of my memory together. I could get as far as my walk toward the doctor's office. Everything else was blank.

I must have fallen asleep again. When I awoke the next time, the first face I saw was that of O'Riley. He was smiling like a kid on his last day of school.

"Welcome back, Richard Mansan. You had us worried for a while."

There were other people in the room, but they were strangers. Then I spotted Martel. I smiled. At least I thought I smiled.

"Welcome back, sir" was all Martel said, but the smile on his face was enough. I made a mental note to have a little talk with him about that "sir" habit of his.

As I thought about the fiasco we had been through, I remembered I never had asked O'Riley what the master plan of the operation was. I had wanted to question him about this after I finished talking with the cooks, but he was asleep at the time. I was sure he knew less about what was on the agenda than I did. It was weird, to say the least. This time I must have smiled, because O'Riley noticed.

"What is it, Mansan? I know I missed the majority of the action, but from what I saw of it, nothing was funny."

The others in the room had remained quiet all this time. Finally, one of the brass

– a general, no less – started to talk. The next thing I remembered was looking at the small lighted lamp on the other side of the room. It was nighttime again, and I had fallen asleep during the general's speech. I lay for a few minutes before I decided to try standing. It was obviously just a thought. The next time I woke up, Martel and O'Riley were sitting by my bed, and the doctor was standing beside them. I did not remember seeing him since that first night. The doctor was the first to speak.

"Well, young man, how are you feeling?"

"Thanks to you, Doctor, I feel better. What was wrong with me, anyway?"

"Besides a broken arm, the artery in the arm was severed, and you lost most of the blood from your body. That was one month ago, but I am now very happy to tell you that you will live. It will take a while before you are up and around, and I must say, full recovery from this injury is a long, slow process. Do not become discouraged. The main thing is that you will live, and in time you will be completely well again."

The doctor left the room, and Martel and O'Riley got up to leave. I stopped them.

"Where are you two staying?"

Martel laughed when he answered, "In the room right next to you."

All I could do was shake my head.

The doctor was so right about the time it would take to regain my strength. It was another week before I even became conscious of the daily routine necessary to sustain me. The doctor must have been some kind of man. He had every one of our specialists at his beck and call. It was another month before I could stand, and then only for a matter of seconds. By the end of the third month, I could walk as far as the front door.

○

One spring day, O'Riley, Martel, and I left the doctor's office for the last time. I had grown very attached to the doctor, and it was with much reluctance that I parted from him.

The three of us were then taken by helicopter to a waiting ship, which took us far to the south. After seven days aboard ship, we arrived at the most beautiful harbor I had ever seen. In fact, the harbor was more than just beautiful. I immediately got the feeling I was dreaming. I had never seen such natural beauty before. It was like a picture. Nothing seemed to move, from the light blue sky with its fleecy white clouds to the contrasting green hills which reached down to an azure-colored sea. The setting had a hypnotic effect on me, and I must have fallen asleep in the deck chair. I could feel a hand on my shoulder. Then I heard Martel's voice.

"Wake up, Mansan. We're home."

Home, indeed, I thought. If this were home, I would never have been foolish enough to leave it.

As it turned out, it was Martel's home. The Martel family had some kind of a program going with our government. At the moment though, the details were all too complicated for me to understand.

As we were being transported from ship to shore, I noticed him standing in the bow of our boat, waving to the people who were waiting on the wharf. The Martel family were evidently people of great importance. From my stretcher I could see the family reunion. The last thing I remembered was Martel pointing toward me. The sea voyage must have taken a toll on me, and I seemed to lose the ground I had gained under the old doctor's care. It was another two months before I again found the strength to sit up in bed.

One evening, I awoke to see two very familiar faces by my bedside, Martel and O'Riley. I felt strong for the first time since I had been wounded. The nurse raised my bed so I could get a better look at my two visitors.

O'Riley was dressed in full uniform; he was returning home tomorrow. He was so pleased to see me sitting up that he actually jumped up and down like a young boy. O'Riley and Martel hugged each other, and I was afraid they would eventually get around to me. Both men were clearly not lightweights, and I knew they did nothing halfway. Luckily, the doctor entered the room right then and warned that it would be some time before I could hold my own with them.

O'Riley was leaving. I had mixed emotions about that bit of news. He somehow represented a quality in our officer ranks which I had found sadly missing. O'Riley was a regular soldier, no more stupid or brilliant than the rest of us. He made no effort to hide his stupidity, nor did he try to impress anyone with his brilliance. I found this quite refreshing, and I had confidence in the man. I could not help but tell him what was on my mind.

"Lieutenant, you stay with it, and one of these days you will be running the entire show."

"Lieutenant Manson, that compliment coming from you makes me feel as though I have already made the grade."

So, it was Lieutenant Manson now. I seemed to have made a rapid advance while I was in bed.

Martel had left the room as O'Riley and I were talking. When he returned, the doctor was with him and there was news from both of them. I was, at long last, to be discharged from the hospital in one month's time, and the Martel family had requested that I remain in the country permanently. They assured me that there would always be enough to keep me busy.

I told Martel I enjoyed his incredible country and I was certain he and his family were offering me such a fine opportunity that I would one day wonder why I could have been so foolish as to consider refusing it. Yet, at the time, I did not feel I had the dependability to give the Martel family an answer to their generous offer.

○

The war was over, at least for the time being. Although I hated to see O'Riley leave, he had undoubtedly chosen an Army career, and it definitely would not help him at this early stage of his life to become too settled in the present interlude.

As for my own fortunes, I was a civilian. The game I had just finished was an interim act which had already been played out on one previous occasion. I was hoping this was the final go-round. I did not like it the first time, and I liked it a great deal less this time.

One of these days, I was sure, we would carry our carelessness and stupidity too far. War was not a toy anymore that governments could pull out of their bag of tricks and use to get what they wanted. In order to stay on the winning side, a nation had to keep up with the latest developments in war materiels, materiels which would bring about the obliteration of the human race. We were sitting on a time bomb.

As it turned out, I did stay a while with the amazing Martel family, and any fool could have found more than enough right there to last a lifetime. I learned to manage the Martel fishing fleet. The business was enjoyable work, and the voyages along the coastal waters offered a never-ending scenic wonderland, unmatched anywhere in the entire world.

When I took my leave from Martel and his family, I promised them I would return.

Right now, my direction was north. This time no enemy would be waiting, unless wolves and Mother Nature could fit that category.

Chapter Two

John Martel's mother and father were the only people I had ever known who met each of the qualifications for greatness. Besides the fact that they were concerned parents and leaders of the highest caliber, their foresight, initiative, and actions toward a better life for all people were surely unique in our modern world.

My decision to leave the Martel family and their beautiful country could not be attributed to my well-known vagabond instinct. This particular time my emotions were governed by a stronger urge to take constructive action on my own. It might not be much; but then, if I did not try, I would never know if I could have made the grade.

No more battle assignments for me. As I looked back to my past performances on the front lines, I had to laugh at the absurd thoughts which had occupied my mind during the last ten years. I had actually thought the human race was coming to the end of the line. Even though I was certain that other crackpots were singing the same song, I differed in one respect from my fellow carolers. I had sold myself on the idea that the front lines would somehow lead me to the "Erewhon" which had long eluded the rest of mankind. Stupid? Not really. The front was, after all, the ultimate testing ground where man would see himself and his fellow man without any camouflaging veneer. The tests were many, and they were most difficult to pass. Only when the individual's character was laid bare, so everyone could see, was the final grade given. This should have been the first prerequisite course for all who aspired to the role of leadership, the very first obstacle in the "run for the purple robe," or whatever the road to leadership was called.

It might come as some surprise to the lay mind, but the percent of those failing to pass their tests under fire was very small. There was one main reason for the high percentage of front-line troops who made the grade. From our total civilian population, six percent were chosen to do the fighting in major wars. Of this six percent, one man out of every six made it as far as the front lines, and that one man came to fight.

I called my version of ascent to leadership "grabbing the brass ring." Although the method had long been out of style, until recently I had this crazy idea that history was about to repeat itself. I was still not thoroughly convinced my original thoughts were so far off-base. True, the latest war had produced nothing of a positive nature. Both sides seemed to languish in the vicinity of the old front lines, while endless non-applicable meetings were held.

Naturally, I hated to think that those ten years had been wasted, but I did not intend to loll like the others. During the time I spent with the Martels, I had experienced the good life, far beyond my fondest expectations. For this brief interlude, it might have seemed as if I had indeed followed the theme of enjoying my life without repentance for the past or concern for the future. This was not the case. In reality, I had taken months to give up something that others would have never relinquished in a lifetime.

Today I was headed north, just as far north as I could go. If I seemed somewhat off-center to the normal mind, I adjudged that I had plenty of company. We had bent all the way to live with our shortcomings, and most of the people saw nothing but their own little battles with their economic status. This was the way our leaders meant it to be. As long as we were wrapped up in making ends meet, our minds were not focused on the big picture.

Had we once taken into consideration that the totality of our actions polluted nature's irreplaceable resources, we would have realized that the atmospheric conductance, planetary reflectivity, solar-induced thermal action, and even the rotation of the Earth depended upon the world and its atmosphere remaining unchanged. A shift in the ocean and air currents would be our first step toward joining the other dehydrated planets of our universe. Whatever steps nature took would be unpredictable, insurmountable, velocious, and lethal. This was the big picture, and there was no more logical basis for it to happen than there was for the last war.

In all of the very sophisticated guidelines human beings enacted to govern their lives, scant thought was given to the effect man's actions had on nature. Rarely did man take into consideration the adverse impacts his activities would have upon the land, the sea, and the air which made up his home, and those rare occasions of recognition were possible simply because man was trying to gain a financial advantage over his competitors. Instead of basing his development upon what best agreed with nature, he had based his activities upon gold, a much overrated element with little or no natural value whatsoever.

○

It was a long three-week ocean voyage to the seaport of Valmy in the Northland, and I had plenty of time to make tentative plans. Much would depend on the reception I received at Valmy. I could be thankful for the long-established good relations which the Martel family had with the people of the Northland. It was John Martel's great-grandfather who first made a hydrographic study of the continental shelf off the north coastline, the widest in the world. Here man could actually raise and harvest vast quantities of fish, to ensure his survival through time. All that was needed was to supply those life-sustaining nutrients so necessary for sea life. The major rivers which flowed into the North Sea could, with a minimum of work on the part of man, furnish the nutrients needed. This was the Martel family's contribution to the people of the Northland, and it might have been the greatest gift ever from one nation to another.

The letter of introduction I carried from John Martel's father was just a bit out of proportion to the status of the bearer. A man with thinner skin would have suffered some degree of self-consciousness. However, I was a born opportunist, and the letter I carried was an advantage not everyone could have received. Fewer people yet would know how to use it. Today I could be thankful to the old surveyor; he had taught me decidedly more than surveying, and I had a hunch that my informal education was about to pay off.

If I could make the connections I needed at Valmy, I planned to explore the uninhabited peninsula one thousand miles farther north. As a fringe benefit, I could put my past behind me forever. This was a big order, and there were possible setbacks to my plans. The people of Valmy might want no part of me, definitely a chance I was taking. The part of the country I was heading for had proved to be a death trap for many of its previous visitors. As I was paying my own way, the government had nothing to lose. I might even be the person who could discover the full potential of that forbidden land.

Another possible setback to my disappearing act was the fact that O'Riley would learn from the Martel family where I was. I was certain of this. The port officials would also have a complete record of my future activities. Riding off into the sunset was becoming increasingly unlikely with each passing year. It was not that the members of the human species were gaining in value, only that the land available for their habitation had become difficult to find.

After ten days at Valmy, the government had enough personnel records on me to last a lifetime. The port officials did everything but measure the size of my head. There was no doubt in my mind that Richard Mansan was now a bona fide, registered member of the human race. Whether I liked my current situation or not, I was probably the best-known person in the government filing system. I was on record for applications covering land lease, timber and mineral permits, hunting and fishing permits, and home-building permits. To keep up to date on the necessary reports I would have to make out each month, I could have used an office force of at least ten people. Of course, not much of a chance existed that I would ever have an office force, and it would be a while before I knew if my resource applications had been approved, anyway. My final application was for citizenship, a rather sophisticated matter with a ten-year waiting period.

The way I felt at the moment, a ten-year waiting period was the least of my worries. I felt that my actions were caused by necessity. It was the low point in my entire life, a time when I had not determined if my plans were the results of frustrations or if there truly was some substance to my actions. Win or lose, the outcome of this forthcoming venture would definitely be with me a long time.

The whole affair was a gamble on my part. My resource applications could be turned down, and my citizenship application was still more uncertain. I needed a sponsor. The one person I knew in the Northland was Tyron Jrcy, and if I used his name, the government might question Mr. Jrcy's connection with me. I actually did not know him. The only time I had seen the man was that night at Morea, and the brief meeting we had did not exactly give me a good picture of his true potentials. A soldier hightailing it out of the action zone always left a little to be desired, even though he was told to get lost. No, I would have to come up with someone other than Jrcy.

It could easily have been said that I was out of place in this country. I realized the position I was putting myself in, and I realized something else. I had to make a go of it this time; there was no other place for me to head. My present actions for membership in the human race could very well be my one remaining chance. I had to laugh at my audacious thoughts of grabbing the brass ring. Obviously, a person who aspired to such prominence would make the run for the top when his position was the most favorable. Today I was an unknown in a foreign land, a hostile land at that. No, this was not what people would call "riding the gravy train" or "getting money from home." Anything I gained here would come at a very high price. I would have it no other way.

There was no chance that I had come to the Northland to retire. With all of the surveys I had to make on my resource permits, I planned to be busy night and day. It was up to me to make a good impression the first year. The land would remain under government ownership, and the government would receive one-half of any profit I made from the land. What might have appeared to be a brazen attempt by a foreigner to corner the resources in this one area of the Northland was, after all, simply the government's nonfinancial investment in my ability to open up the territory for settlement. It was common knowledge that we needed land for our increasing population, and we needed the life-giving atmosphere of our polar regions. Here in the far north was the last frontier of clean air.

I was amused by the efforts of the government officials to snow me during our repeated question-and-answer sessions. I was not quite as ignorant as these people thought I was. I was also aware that they made a great number of decisions based upon prior efforts to develop the far north. These prior efforts, as far as I was concerned, were made with no definite goal in mind. I did indeed want the land with its life-giving atmosphere. If I could find other natural resources, these resources would be used to develop the north country into a habitable area.

Yes, I considered myself a crackpot. Only a crackpot would leave the beautiful locale I had lived in during the past year, and only a crackpot would worry about some disaster which might never happen. However, as I said, even with my peculiarities, I was not as mixed up as these officials seemed to believe. The permit contracts I signed called for the government to reinvest in the land all payment made by the permittee during the first ten years. I was sure the officials considered this particular entry in the contracts merely as so many words. To me it meant that any payment I made to the government would come back to me in the form of transportation, communication, and power facilities.

It was evident I had to change my attitude toward people. Sponsors were people, and right now I was in need of a sponsor. I would be the first to admit that it was magnanimous on my part, but a few concessions regarding humanity could be made, if these concessions fit my purpose. Not only would I be needing a sponsor, but I had a hunch I would soon be needing other members of the community, as well. Under these conditions there was absolutely no excuse to let old frustrations stand in my way.

○

It was the first of March when I left Valmy for the north. I traveled by helicopter, and within hours I was over my touchdown area. The country seemed to have everything – rivers, lakes, mountains, open fields, timber, valleys, and wild animals. I realized that my new home was one thousand miles north of the nearest civilization, and that only a fool would ask why this region was uninhabited.

The peninsula was four hundred miles, north and south, and it was two hundred miles, east and west. Besides the fact that it was the coldest place in the nation, not much else was known about the area. It was just a tract of unexplored land which the government never had a use for, and had largely overlooked. Outside of a couple of hardy families who grazed livestock on the western side of the peninsula through the summer months, I would have the entire area to myself.

During the spring, summer, and early fall, I built a large living quarters with four bedrooms, a kitchen, and a living room. Each room had a rock fireplace. The building was the first step I took in my new location to impress people. If the weather was as treacherous as everyone said it was, I might be able to catch myself a high government official in my comfortable living quarters. I still needed a sponsor, and I could think of no better way to get one.

My winter food supply of cured codfish and salmon grew steadily until I had to enlarge my storage facilities. Wild cherries, grapes, blueberries, bilberries, and blackberries grew in abundance. Hazelnuts and beechnuts were also plentiful. I had my food supply gathered and stored long before I finished the building. I was quite proud of my living quarters, with its two-foot-thick flagstone walls set in natural lime mortar, and a gabled roof of hewed spruce logs, supported by trusses and covered with rough cedar shingles. Ventilation was a matter of opening the lee-side inlet ports. Wood and food storage sheds were built onto the back of the building.

I actually had only one enemy in this country, the extremely low winter temperature. There were a few minor obstacles like winds of one hundred miles per hour, as well as long hours of darkness, but the one major natural force I had to contend with was temperature. Of course, a bit of irony was involved in my struggle with nature's low temperature. It could very well prove to be the strongest ally we had, our consummate front against man's contamination spreading north.

Before I departed from Valmy last spring, I left word with the Governor. He was to assume that I had lived through the winter, and he would have another load of supplies delivered to me on the first of March. Included with this delivery would be a team of dogs, a small generator, an ample fuel supply, and a sunlamp.

Good fortune was on my side. I had weathered the first winter, and I did it the hard way, crossing the peninsula two times in the east-west direction. This was a journey of two hundred miles each way, and I spent most of the winter making a survey of my ski trails, building shelters at each ten-mile station, locating fishing holes in the main rivers, recording species and locations of animals, recording terrain features and vegetation growth, and keeping a daily record of the weather.

This coming spring I would make the journey around the north end of the peninsula, and at the end of that journey I should know what resources were available. As I mentioned, when I worked for the old land surveyor, he taught me everything he knew. He was without peer as a geologist. From gold to water, the man could find it all. He was invaluable, and yet he managed to get lost in the common herd of humanity. The old surveyor had died years ago, unknown and unwanted. However, even today I, who bled him for every bit of information I could get, particularly remembered my old instructor and boss for his unique method of making land surveys.

○

When my supplies arrived from Valmy, I noticed I received more than two times what I had ordered. The Governor's aide, Norman Lara, and the pilot would stay at my camp overnight. Two other passengers were also aboard the helicopter, Marina Costa and her son Janus. Lara had assigned the Costas the job of laying-in my winter's food supply. This meant I could leave for the northern end of the peninsula early tomorrow. If I decided to return south for the coming winter, the food supply would be waiting for me. Members of the Costa family were currently moving their herds into the area, and they could use my camps as their headquarters.

Norman Lara was quite an unusual man. He had already been in the government service ten years, and he had asked for his present isolated assignment. Many people would have found this odd, but Lara's approach seemed logical to me. The man could probably put in most of his time in Valmy without the usual political undercurrent. Later in his career he would have a much better chance for one of the top positions in the government. I had to smile as I realized that I was Lara's special responsibility; it was probably the first time in his political career when he had found himself out on a limb. My activities were strictly high-pressure, and they were loaded with great possibilities. A person could become over-enthusiastic, and although I meant to see my project through, there were a few tough obstacles I would have to overcome.

Lara proved to be full of surprises, especially when he asked me if I was the Richard Mansan who had fought in the battle of Morea. When I told him I was, he informed me that Tyron Jrcy was his cousin. Jrcy had recently contacted Lara and asked him to check on my identity.

I could never expect anyone to believe my real motives for permitting Jrcy to go free that night at Morea. International problems the brass would dump in my lap? Maybe, but if the truth of the matter were known, I was also suffering from a severe case of "rankitis." O'Riley had just put me in command of the people we had left, and I could feel my tenure in office rapidly coming to the end. My command was a one-shot deal, and once we left the Morea area, the name *Richard Mansan* was not likely to become a household word. I felt I had to do something while the power was still mine, so I magnanimously allowed Tyron Jrcy to escape. What had been done to satisfy a case of enlarged ego might have been the smartest move I would ever make.

Lara seemed almost patronizing for the rest of the evening. For reasons of my own I did not question Lara about Jrcy, nor did I, in any way, propagate discussions on the topic of Morea. I was certain Lara appreciated this. We were on thin international ice, and what had passed was best forgotten by everyone. Lara assured me Jrcy would be extremely happy to learn that I was, indeed, the Richard Mansan he had met in Morea.

I had a feeling my luck was starting to flow, and I was up early in the morning inspecting my dogs. They were busy giving me the once-over at the same time. After both man and dogs were satisfied with our original inspection, I harnessed the dogs to the sled, and we were on our way. Lara and Marina Costa accompanied me on their skis for about five miles. The only reason I could see for this patronizing gesture was that they were not yet sold on my ability to operate a team of dogs.

○

My plan was to follow the coastline north to the mouth of the Onque River. I would have the late spring and early summer to build a camp. By mid-autumn I planned to have explored the major part of the northern area around the end of the peninsula. There were three tributaries of the Onque River which I wanted to look over.

Originally, I had planned to return to my southernmost camp by early winter. Marina Costa and Janus would have returned south with their herds by the time I returned to my camp. If I decided to change my plans, my contact with Lara would be by way of the herdsmen when they returned south in the fall. However, I had informed Lara that I might stay in the northern part of the peninsula for a second year. A great deal would depend on what I saw this summer.

The peninsula was an old land formation worn smooth by ages of glacial actions. There was evidence of ancient volcanic eruptions, but to the untrained eye this evidence would have been mistaken for glacially formed terrain features. The ground cover was mainly spruce and birch trees. Smaller plants like the blackberry bush showed through the frozen snow. It would be another two months before the snow cover would be gone in the open areas. By that time I would have established my camp near the mouth of the Onque River.

My entire journey north was uneventful. After the first two days, I traveled every other day. This schedule afforded me the time to hunt, fish, and build shelters at all my campsites. Shelter and food were my main necessities, and nature had made provisions for both. I could net a hundred pounds of fish within an hour's time, and the supplies of building materials and dry firewood were unlimited.

Several species of wild animals called the peninsula home on a part-time or full-time basis. I was mainly interested in the two species which could offer me the most competition in this little game of survival, wolves and bears. Neither animal made a very compatible bedfellow with man. In fact, they did not even care too much for each other's company. The one I would have to watch out for was the wolf, chiefly during the winter. The bear was a fisherman par excellence. He could live off the fat of the land through the winter months. The wolf, on the other hand, could not have caught a fish if his life depended on it. Yes, it would be in my best interest to keep an eye on the wolf. He might be considering a new supplement to his bill of fare this winter.

My first job when I arrived at the mouth of the Onque River was to build a cabin, storage shed, and fenced-in shelter for the dogs. There were a few other chores that needed to be accomplished at the same time. The winter's food supply for one man and nine dogs, and the winter supply of firewood had to be given high priority. So far, I had spent virtually all of my time in this country building shelters, laying-in food supplies, and gathering firewood. This life was a great leveler. For a man who aspired to leadership, purple robe, brass ring, or whatever, I was having a hell of a time supporting myself and nine dogs. If I was ever going to do any leading, I would first have to be able to deploy myself and the dogs against nature's forces. If I could not win this initial conflict, it would be ridiculous to consider leading hundreds of millions of people in their quest for survival.

When I left Valmy the previous spring, I had instructed my pilot to fly over the headwaters of the Onque River and to follow the course of the river north to the peninsula. That trip now proved to be invaluable for me; I held a good picture in my mind of the geological changes that had occurred in the area between Valmy and the north coastline. The old land surveyor had been a wizard at reading nature's landscaping, and taught me quite thoroughly.

First, nature had plowed this land with volcanic eruptions. Then, for hundreds of millions of years, the disintegrating action of the changing temperatures, rains, winds, and glaciers prepared the land for its first vegetation. Again, millions of years passed while the ageless wind and water carried those seeds nature would ultimately choose as applicable for the northern regions. The cycle was completed when animal life migrated from other parts of the world. Whether the different species of animal life had evolved from a common ancestor, or from several common ancestors, was of no profound importance. Today it was much more critical to be able to solve international disputes between real people than it was to expound on some unmaterialistic, eggheaded theory.

We knew that a geological cycle embraced all of nature's known phenomena. From that point on, the eggheads basically dropped out of the picture and the crackpots took over. None of us, eggheads or crackpots, had the least idea what impact man's fumbling with the resources would have on the geological cycle, but it was an ideal time for somebody to sound off. As no one knew a damn thing about the courses of action nature would take to counteract man's pollution, the stage was set for the crackpots. This group, of which I was a member, had just enough knowledge of our fragile biosphere to make us dangerous. At least this was the classification that the general non-involved masses of people gave us. Our cause actually became a rallying point for all dissentients, and as we gained in number, we lost in strength. Most likely, the one positive movement in the history of mankind was dying because of over-patronization.

Crackpot, egghead, or non-involved, we were equally guilty for our past wars and for the pollution of our natural resources. This was the only attitude I could take as I walked across nature's landscape. I had seen the same terrain features quite often in my life. The difference this time was that none of nature's handicraft had been disturbed. Man had seen this part of the world many times, but he had never secured a beachhead. This was surprising. John Martel's great-grandfather had surveyed both the wide continental shelf that formed the north coastline, and the principal rivers that flowed from the south into the North Sea. More important, Martel had imported those nutrient-bearing plants that currently grew along the riverbanks almost two thousand miles south of the north coastline. Together, the water off the north coastline and in the great rivers teemed with salmon, char, codfish, and lobster. The Northland had not chosen to tap this prodigious food reserve, and the government would permit no other nation to fish in the North Sea area.

There were several reasons for the existing situation in the Northland. The country was rich in all natural resources, and it was an expansive land which would probably not suffer from overpopulation for years to come. The only trouble with the Northland today was the fact that the government had allowed a member of the crackpot fraternity to become entrenched. That member was now walking over the landscape, looking for those resources nature had provided.

At the headwaters of the Onque River there was potential power, sufficient to operate the largest generators man could build. In the vast Playa Lowlands there was additional power in oil and natural gas, and those areas of ancient volcanic action would be rich in minerals. Thanks to the Martel family, the ocean and rivers could supply the Northland with food for all time, if managed correctly. And, of critical significance, the cold atmosphere of the north would be the last to submit to man's polluting. Yes, this was, inarguably, our hope for the future, and nature was doing her best to protect the area. As long as nature could hold out, man would always have a sanctuary in this region of the Earth.

It was early in the fall when I met one of the families who used the peninsula as a pasture land. The family was getting ready to return south, and I gave them a message for Marina Costa. I would stay at my northernmost camp for another year. I also sent a message to Lara, requesting that he pay me a visit next September at my north camp near the mouth of the Onque River. This would give me another summer to explore the northern end of the peninsula.

I had been panning the mountain washes in my spare time, and if I was right in my estimate of the wealth in this country, the riverbeds were overloaded with gold and diamonds. I already had enough of both to buy a fleet of helicopters. This should make

Lara happy.

In the month of September, I enlarged my storage space and laid-in a winter supply of firewood. Two times a week I took the dogs on a twenty-mile run to one of my outlying camps. I cut these exercise periods down to once a week throughout the winter months and, of course, they did accompany me on my daily ski runs. I had to experiment with my ability to survive in this environment, and there was no time like the present while I was still young and could offset some of the mistakes I would make.

It was during the winter that I decided to return to the south camp in the coming fall and look for another section of land where I could build. My present camp was much too large for my needs.

○

By the time September rolled around again, I was pleased with what had been accomplished. True, I was a little eccentric, but I had an overall plan, with the natural resources to back me up and pay the bills. I had a good feeling that I had attained an impregnable position where my plans were not just a one-shot affair. They actually could cover any eventuality caused by pollution or by overpopulation.

I was all packed and waiting for Lara a week before the man arrived. During that week I reached one main decision, to step out of the picture and let the government take over immediately. I was never certain when I made decisions like this if I was acting intelligently, or if my actions were inspired by my fear of commonplace monotony. I called it "soaking the ashes after the fire was out." In reality, my actions probably were quite meaningful, but if I had to explain my line of thinking, I could only say that my thoughts today were the same as they were at the time I left Martel's country. I simply did not have the staying power to settle into a daily routine of predetermined events.

When Lara arrived, the Governor and Marina Costa were with him. This time, Costa was the pilot. She was proving to be a very unusual person. I knew very little about these people, but their modus operandi was interesting.

I had prepared a big meal of lobster and grape wine. The supper was not what you would call a seven-course meal, and the dishes were not of the finest china, but my guests all ate as though the habit would soon be going out of style.

We talked most of the night. After we had finished our business, it was decided that the peninsula would be developed over a forty-year period, beginning with the southernmost one-hundred-mile section. This would be a government-controlled operation, and the grazing rights would be retained by Costa's people.

Well, I finally found out who Costa was. Her people were the original settlers in this area, and Costa was the leader. She was also General Costa of the national armed forces. As she questioned me regarding my own ideas about the future of the north country, I gave the general my best pitch. We had, right in the far north, what amounted to the last frontier, a land that was rich in natural resources, and a land that could support our millions of people. We were undoubtedly the most fortunate people in the entire world. Our survival had been assured. All we needed to do was develop the northern region. The Valmy Peninsula was just the beginning, and the gold and diamonds would pay the bills. I had made my report to General Costa and the others with a rather broad and light-hearted approach, but the moment I mentioned gold and diamonds, my personality changed one hundred percent. I had opened the Pandora's box of mankind's troubles, past and present. For the first time in my life, I made a pitch for the top position. No, it was not a declaration of my final intention; I was merely gauging the controlled movement of the merry-go-round so that I would be in position to grab the elusive brass ring.

Costa, Lara, and the Governor were taken aback when I emphasized the necessity for strict control of the exploitation of natural resources, notably the recovery of the gold and diamonds. My instructions were very simple, and unless they were followed, the four of us tonight had sealed the doom of the human race. It was not fear I noticed on the faces of my three guests, but what I had to say made an impression. The Governor and Lara were not real leaders. Costa was, and she understood the reasons for my instructions. If my theory on worldwide destruction was not acceptable to Costa, my axiom regarding overpopulation was acceptable; and I was advocating the same cure for both ailments – strict environmental control of development in the northern part of the country. I was especially interested in the dredging of the rivers, the use of the land, and any pollution of the air, land, and water.

I was surprised to learn that my permits covered all resources on the peninsula, except grazing and water rights. The water rights I shared with Costa. No matter how I tried to explain my version of this and my decision to turn the operation over to the government, the Governor and Lara would not budge and kept restating my rights. I felt like a big clown, but I settled with them for one percent of the future profit derived from mining on the peninsula. It was a great deal more than I wanted, or than I had a right to expect. I was already a rich man, and one percent of future mineral development was beyond estimate.

The Governor was so pleased with my settlement that he gave me a lifetime lease on nineteen hundred acres of land in the southwestern part of the peninsula. The annual rent would be one-half of any natural resources I developed. There was no minimum annual fee. Communications and electric power would be installed, and I could pay the cost, which would be agreed upon for these utilities, over a twenty-year period. All of my holdings would revert to the government upon my death.

○

A kind of nostalgia came over me this morning as I loaded my dogs aboard the helicopter. I was leaving one of the few places where I had been happy. The rigors of the country had tied me to my northern campsite, and I did not look at the ground until we had been airborne for several minutes.

What I saw drew my full attention – a bear and a wolf traveling side by side, and heading in the direction of my old camp. I had learned months ago that the bear actually caught fish for the wolf. Now I wondered if the wolf was again using the bear, this time to break into my cabin. The pack followed at a distance of one mile behind their leader and the bear. We could definitely learn from these creatures. They were part of nature's alarm system, and I, for one, intended to watch their actions with much interest in the future. If they could survive man's viciousness for so many years, they might be able to make it all the way.

When we arrived at my south camp, I invited my three guests to spend the night. They surprised me by accepting. I might have been wrong, but I had the feeling that the Governor, Costa, and Lara wanted me to return to Valmy with them. This was out of the question although more than two years had passed since I was trying to hide from people. I had come a long way, but I was not ready for city life yet.

Marina Costa had sealed the storage sheds by nailing the doors shut. Even the bears were not able to breach the security. The food supplies were intact, and I was impressed by the amount of corn, cabbage, and potatoes that Costa and her son had raised during the short growing season.

Marina insisted on beginning the cooking while I hooked up the generator to a string of lights. The Governor had brought everything I needed to wire the whole house, and I soon had the electric plant in operation. Meanwhile, the Governor and Lara had fires started in all of the fireplaces. My improvised ventilators were opened, and the entire building gave out a deep forest scent of spruce trees.

I had never eaten food that tasted better than Marina's supper. If I could get cooking like tonight's, I would gladly live in Valmy or in Timbuktu, for that matter.

Morning brought the usual parting which always called for quite a production in this country. We had been together just a couple of days, but the four of us seemed to see everything the same way. This was unusual. Any one of these individuals should have been able to duplicate my recent actions in the north. Maybe I was wrong in thinking that those actions were not exactly characteristics of true leadership. I was not, however, wrong in my estimations of my three companions. Marina Costa was the only leader in the group. One out of three was not bad.

I had spent years on the front battle lines, hoping I had found the spot where it would all happen. I knew my own special philosophy would sound ludicrous to the normal mind, but I wanted to believe I could effectively propagate the front-line position into national leadership.

Now, for more than two years, I had walked over hundreds of miles of country that I was convinced could buy us a little extra survival time. Ridiculous? This was hardly the word. The crackpots and I were almost peas from the same pod. I said *almost*. In my own mind, I was certain that I alone was on the right track. With such a conviction, I would probably qualify for the leadership of the crackpots. In the back of my mind was the ever-present reminder that man's continual fumbling with nature's resources would destroy us. I did not think we would all just start dying. Such thinking would indeed be a waste of time. We were already dying from contamination, so it was time to take an educated guess on what nature's next step would be.

I did not believe in the classic statement that mankind would be smitten down. I did believe we would die in our own pollution. Overpopulation would also play a very important role, but we could live with that.

Pollution actually affected the rays of the sun which, in turn, affected all of the other natural forces, mainly the air and ocean currents. No one definitively knew what nature's reactions would be. There were all kinds of educated guesses to choose from, and if we cared to switch from the crackpot class to the egghead class, we could choose the reaction which best fit our hopes and aspirations. I did not know, but I was betting that nature's heavy cold air would be the one natural force which would remain intact for the longest time. I felt good. I was playing it both ways. Two problems, same answer. The problems were overpopulation and pollution. The answer was the far north.

Chapter Three

When I first came to the Northland thirty-nine years ago, I was desperate. I needed to get away from people, and at the same time I was looking for someplace where I could belong. I had considered the belonging part necessary simply because I needed help in order to survive. My hypocritical approach did not change my belligerent attitude, and the fact that I needed people only made me frustrated. My main trouble could have been that I was a nobody, and there was not a damn thing I could do to change the status quo. In reality, there was nothing anyone could do.

I tried not to overlook the chance that I was at fault. Marina Costa, Lara, the Governor of Valmy and, without a doubt, Tyron Jrcy had all been instrumental in my survival. Others had helped me as well, and I was probably allowing some of my previous experiences to sour me on the entire human race. It was seemingly impossible for me to accept anyone as a friend, and yet I was undeniably one of the more fortunate people in the world. In our over-sophisticated social systems, people would have to consider themselves lucky if real friendship ever entered their lives.

Today I had time to reflect on my early years in this country. It seemed quite simple to recognize the help I had received, along with the various sources from which that help came. My survival had been a very methodical thing, to keep myself alive as I proved that I could make a worthwhile contribution to society. In the end, I planned on being the big winner, so no magnanimity was involved.

In retrospect, my mind's reflections of the past made an unusual and melodramatic picture, with the center stage occupied by one of the scenes which I had always thought would be my starting mark, the battle of Morea.

Since I had been living in the past these last few years, I was not at all surprised by the imaginary scene before me. The old surveyor was there, and occupied a place of prominence on the far left side of my kaleidoscopic extravaganza. I was amazed at the clearness of Martel and his family, and I could tell by the fashions of their attire that I was looking at several preceding generations at once. Lara, Jrcy, the Governor of Valmy, Marina Costa and her family, and General O'Riley were in a group who made up the foreground in the picture. I could recognize every building I had constructed, and the piles of gold and diamonds I had found seemed to surpass what I had remembered. Nothing was missing from the scene. Even my dogs were present, six generations of them.

I could see everything my mind would accept in the left half of the scene. It was an awesome sight which had many implications for the past and present. The future was also there on the far right-hand side, but I would not look. I tried my best to focus my mind back to reality, but the harder I tried, the clearer the picture appeared in my mind.

John Martel's young sister, Nele, stood just to the right front of the Martel family. She was a beautiful girl, and the purple dress she wore set off her flaming red hair.

The purple robe Jrcy wore over his shoulders was a bit archaic, but he had been in a position to set his own fashion standards.

The one member of Marina Costa's family I had met was her older son, Janus. I did remember her telling me that she had another son and two daughters. The younger daughter's name was Lamira, and right now my attention was drawn to her. Like Nele Martel, Lamira Costa occupied a position to the right front of her family, and she was dressed in purple.

Again, I tried to bring my mind back to reality, this time successfully. The scene had been too much for me. Looking into either a factual or a fancied future had never been one of my stronger points. I had a habit of losing interest when my future became too well known. Maybe I had broken the habit of shaping the scene to my liking and then moving on to greener pastures. I had managed to slip out from under the big development programs in the north. I had also managed to leave Martel's country on some flimsy notion about getting away from people. At the moment, I was certain I had seen enough of my immediate future. Nele Martel and Lamira Costa had occupied a position in my vision just to the right of center, so they would grab the brass ring at a near future date. Jrcy already had that elusive bauble, and his position in my vision was just to the left of center. What I had seen was the imagination of a fool, but in case there was any truth in it, I had not looked at the right half of the scene. The positions of Jrcy, Lamira Costa, and Nele Martel formed the dividing line with past and present on one side and future on the other. I had yet to live through that part of my life as represented by the right-hand side of the scene, and wanted to enjoy the luxury of the unknown. I would cross my bridges as I came to them without the help of any clairvoyant nonsense.

○

Many changes had come to this part of the world. Whether the changes were good or bad had not been determined yet; hopefully, the time would never come when we had to make that evaluation. As I thought of those changes, I thought of others as well.

I had moved to my present location right after Lara, Costa, the Governor, and I returned from the northern end of the peninsula. My cabin was the only two-story building in the area, and the sleeping quarters were on the second floor. The building had double plate-glass windows with storm shutters, and all the latest facilities. I had built the cabin originally with the idea in mind that it would be the basic blueprint for future housing on the peninsula. Every detail had passed government inspection except the second story, and no matter how hard I tried to sell the two-story model, the people laughed at the idea. In this country a living room meant exactly that, and sleeping was an integral part of living.

My original flagstone home was currently the center of a settlement which had a population of five hundred people. The old building housed the government post office and general store. The name of the settlement was Mansan's Outpost. I had gained immortality, another way of saying I was growing old.

For some time I had known I was faced with a far greater enemy than I had ever faced before: old age. The rigors of the past year had proved to me that my adopted homeland was more biased toward the Richard Mansan of thirty-nine years ago. Even the fifty-five-mile trip to the settlement was becoming a chore which taxed my endurance, and I tended to put it off. I used to look forward to picking up my mail and groceries. The dogs could easily make the run in ten hours, but I had always made a big production of my visits to the settlement, camping out overnight at the midway point. It was a near ritual with me. I could almost relive the challenges that had faced me during my early years on the peninsula.

The country was made to order for young people, and I no longer fit into that category. I had recently passed my seventieth birthday, and as much as I hated to admit it, I was spending a great deal of time inside the cabin these days.

O'Riley and I corresponded with each other. Sometimes the letters were a year apart, but he seemed determined to keep in touch with me. He had been retired from the Army for two years, so I figured that it should be the end of his attempt to recruit me again. As I predicted a long time back, he had made it to the top in his profession. He was General O'Riley now, and until he retired, he was the ranking officer in his nation's armed services.

During my thirty-nine years in the Northland, O'Riley had fought in four wars. Each time, he did his damnedest to get me back in uniform. The man seemed possessed with some long-range plan which would change the entire order of events in the destiny of mankind. I must have represented an integral part of his plan. At the outbreak of the last war ten years ago, he had promoted me to colonel. What made this unusual was the minor detail that I was not even a citizen of his nation, and he knew it. Did O'Riley still have all his faculties? I would say *yes*, but only because I too had lived with the same impossible dream, a dream that led only to frustration and then despondency. I certainly had known frustration. Despondency I fought by throwing myself into a life-and-death struggle with nature. O'Riley was a quite different individual. The man directed his efforts in one direction and never varied. Undoubtedly, if trouble did come again, he would make the same pitch to get me in uniform.

I had no idea how O'Riley's correspondence affected Tyron Jrcy. I did know, however, that the government was censoring my mail. After ten years in the Army, I had learned to accept this invasion of privacy. I was never able to accept the arrogance and obnoxiousness of our elected and appointed officials who fell far short of representing the original intent of our government.

John Martel and I exchanged Christmas cards each year, but my main source of information came from O'Riley's letters. Ten years ago Martel's parents had died, and John and his sister, Nele, were busy managing the family affairs. Nele and John had each married and, in fact, they were grandparents. Nele's name was Moran, and she had seven grandchildren.

Tonight as I sat in my overstuffed chair facing the fireplace, I wondered what kind of a family man Richard Mansan would have made. The very thought of having a family made me restless, and I realized, for the first time in many years, that I was out of position. The action had passed me by. I was an old recluse who had long since outlived his usefulness. I actually jumped up from the chair, grabbed my parka, and almost ran out of the cabin.

The stars lighted up the valley and reflected off the crystals on the frozen snow. The fresh fragrance of the spruce trees saturated the cold night air. I had the feeling of walking into an elegant ballroom illuminated by thousands of crystal chandeliers. This would be my last night in the valley that I had called home for most of my life.

I had made up my mind to pay Martel a visit, and then, well, who could know?

It was as if I had just awakened from a deep sleep. I had plainly spent close to twenty years doing absolutely nothing. Occasional journeys around the peninsula with my dog team helped me recover the past. Those first years in this country had become my whole life. They were crowded years; I was a miner, hunter, fisherman, and builder, all rolled up into one. I appeared to have a driving desire in those days for wealth. If it had not been for my dog team, I would have spent every moment of my time mining; but I did have the dogs, and they had to be fed. It was not as though I had been all that wrapped up in wealth itself; I was totally wrapped up in the development of the peninsula.

Officially, Costa, Lara, the Governor, and I had agreed years earlier that the government would develop the peninsula, and I made sure the government had the financial backing it needed to start and finish the job. Today farming, fishing, mining, oil and natural gas wells, and power generation were the main improvements. There was more. The small, thriving settlement of Mansan's Outpost was connected to the seaport and railhead at Valmy by a thousand miles of all-weather road, and housing was being constructed throughout the interior of the peninsula. The gold and diamonds had paid for everything. I still had both, and so did the government, far exceeding what we could ever use.

Last year the government had finished the main development projects on the peninsula, and yet, the true wealth of the area remained unknown. Years ago I had been mainly interested in methods to widen the Onque River to control the heavy runoffs. I knew the riverbed was rich in diamonds and gold, as were the bordering alluvial fields which had built up over millions of years due to volcanic eruption and the disintegrating actions of other natural forces. As the intensities of the early weather conditions subsided, the Onque River slowly took the form it had today. To dredge or widen the riverbed at the present time for its wealth, or for any other purpose, would have a disastrous effect on the ecology of the area. We had to ensure ourselves against the possibilities of flooding, and we had to retain the nutrient balance and spawning grounds for the sea life in the area. Our lives depended on one as well as the other.

Through the eyes of the old surveyor and with the mind of a crackpot who saw the finale as something dry and wet, hot and cold, loud and silent, light and dark – I was able to see the ancient routes that the Onque River had traveled. If the rat could live through it all, so could man. I found those old riverbeds, and traced them from the headwaters to the sea. The removal of a slide area here and the construction of a new channel there gave me what I was looking for, a new riverbed. Well, not exactly a new riverbed, but we had reopened some very old ones, riverbeds that had once carried the torrential waters of a very young world. Oftentimes, only a landslide had slowed the waters long enough to build up and seek another route. As it turned out, we now had three auxiliary Onque River channels that would keep any future floods within bounds. The ageless wealth which nature had deposited millions of years ago along the old streambeds paid the bills, with a substantial amount left over to soothe the dissidents.

Yes, there had been many crowded years, and what I especially liked about the outcome of all those years of work was the fact that the impact on the land was small.

We had an area which could easily support twenty million people, and it had been developed without cost to the citizens and without disrupting nature's forces in any way.

People did not exactly rush to the newly developed Northland. That would come later *when* overpopulation became an issue, or *if* pollution made the move necessary. My venture could not lose. These were the odds I liked. When overpopulation became a reality, the name *Mansan* would assume the very essence of intelligence. If pollution eventually shoved us into a corner, the name *Mansan* would warm the hearts of my fellow crackpots everywhere.

At this point in time, my holdings included citizenship, a one-percent interest in mining operations on the peninsula, the cabin I lived in, several storage buildings, and a homestead of approximately nineteen hundred acres. I had built my cabin and lived here because it was the one place on the entire peninsula that had everything – water, trees, animals, hills, snow, and the coldest winters in the Northland. Tonight the country was giving me its final performance. If I were younger, I would have stayed.

○

Early in the morning, I was up packing the few belongings I would take with me. It was still dark when I blew out the lamp and left the cabin.

For just a brief second I hesitated outside the cabin door, and then I was following behind my dog team like a man with a mission in life. No more evenings by the fireplace, not for a while anyway.

I felt like a young man again, and this time I let the dogs have their way. We reached the settlement by mid-afternoon. The stage from Valmy would arrive in about one hour, and it would stay overnight. I rented a night's lodging at the inn, gave my dog team to the postmaster, and picked up my mail.

Tonight was the first evening in nearly thirty-seven years that I had spent in the same proximity with my fellow human beings.

After a breakfast which would have satisfied the hungriest teenager, I boarded the southbound stage.

In my rush to get my last-minute business out of the way, I had completely forgotten about my mail. Usually, it consisted of letters from the National Environmental Council and occasional letters from Lara, Jrcy, Marina Costa, the Governor, and O'Riley.

This morning there were letters from O'Riley and John Martel. The letter from Martel was truly a surprise. There had to be something big in the wind. I opened O'Riley's letter first.

January 19, 2026

Dear Colonel Mansan:

It seems I only write you when I need help. The international situation becomes more crucial every day. The sophistication of our dealings with each other allows no room whatsoever for logic between nations. On the home front, the situation is ever worse. Camouflaging tactics are used to keep the people's interest in those issues that, in reality, are not our main problems. We, among all of the countries of the world, are especially vulnerable to this form of attack. This, however, is no consolation for the other countries. We will all go down the drain together.

We have many problems today, but the one that must occupy our main efforts is the pollution of our environment.

The problems on the home front and the present international situation are tied closely together. The people cannot support the continual, increasing expenditures for the technical advancement of weapons of worldwide destruction, and the environment cannot stand the use of these weapons, or any of the residual negative benefits derived from their manufacture, maintenance, or disposal.

John Martel and Tyron Jrcy have agreed to a meeting with me, and they both expressed their wishes that you attend.

It would be like old times if we could get together again.

O'Riley

It looked as though he was still trying. I was a few years older than O'Riley, but I was certain the man was in his late sixties. This was not exactly the age for international fun and games. I had never taken part in the more genteel actions of international fiascoes, but I realized that they dealt with frustration and humiliation, two human deteriorations not compatible with old age.

One of the passengers woke me as we arrived at our first night's stop. O'Riley's letter had a negative effect on my imagination. There were just too many people involved. The wrong approach had become a way of life. I saw the impossibility of finding the key to the situation, specifically when the situation was very possibly merely a stigma of that same imagination.

The next four days of travel were somewhat similar, and it was not until the afternoon of the fifth day that I arrived at Valmy. I immediately phoned the Governor's office, but he was out at the time. I left a message requesting a meeting at his earliest convenience. I had not seen the Governor for several years. He and I were about the same age, and I guessed that he had slowed down a bit, as I had.

The following evening, the Governor visited with me at my hotel. I got the feeling he was not at all enthusiastic about seeing me leave. My traveling permit would need to be signed by Jrcy, and this would take a little time. Meanwhile, I would be the Governor's guest. Even Nele Moran would have to be notified of my approximate time of arrival.

So, it turned out that Nele was the leader of her country, and I was finding out that it was harder to leave my country than it was to get into it.

Instead of looking at the ridiculousness of the procedures, I enjoyed my stay with the Governor. I had always wanted to play a leading role in some master espionage plot. I felt this plot lacked in substance, but it was probably the only one I would ever have.

After all the *top-level* decisions had been made regarding my travel permit, I had confirmed my opinion that the human race would never make it. If I was wrong in my evaluation of human competency, then there was one other alternative: I was, indeed, a double agent engaged in acts of sedition against my government.

The day finally arrived when I was given a clean bill of health and allowed to board a southbound freighter. As far back as I could remember, I had enjoyed ocean travel. There was a mysterious aura about sailing to faraway places that reminded me of the fantasies I had in my youth.

Tonight as I stood on deck watching the southern horizon, I thought of Martel and his beautiful country. I assumed it was natural for me to wonder what my life would have been like if I had stayed there. My mind also recalled one other thing: I had completely forgotten about Martel's letter. I returned to my cabin and took the letter from the inside pocket of my topcoat.

As I opened the letter, I remembered a young man who seemed to be about two feet off the ground every time I spoke to him. His parents had the same mystical power over me. They were wonderful people, and I was always afraid I might do something that would displease them. Only Martel's sister, Nele, made me feel as if I had the situation under control. She was a holy terror, and she was accustomed to having her own way with everyone except me.

When I started to read the letter, I had to smile. Time had not changed John Martel.

This is an unorthodox beginning for a letter, but I never knew how to address you. I was certain after all these years that I would be able to sit down and write a normal letter to my oldest friend, but even forty years have not changed the first impression I had of you.

General O'Riley is planning a meeting with Chief Council Jrcy. There is nothing new about this technique. However, this time the main topic will be pollution, and not war. I get the feeling that war has, at long last, reached its final battlegrounds, the home fronts. The impacts of these new battle tactics will be worldwide and much more deadly than the old battle confrontations. We were sure to reach this stage sooner or later. Our big challenge today is to recognize our problem and not continue to camouflage the issue by the threats of a shooting war.

Nele and I are looking forward to seeing you in the very near future.

Martel

○

After reading it, I folded the letter and put it back in my coat pocket. It was astounding how alike the letters from O'Riley and Martel had read. These two men definitely had minds of their own, so there was not much chance that either one would sell the other on a particular line of thought. If the battleground was currently on the home front, we had a problem. As strange as it might seem, the strongest nations would be the most vulnerable. To the normal mind, home-front battles were inconceivable. We had a tendency in wartime to think in terms of traditional battles, those actions that had changed so little throughout the centuries, the two lines who faced each other over a stretch of real estate which had long been appropriately called "no-man's-land." The home front would have no such telltale designation. Everything else that the human mind could imagine was present, but there was no vast array of marching men. Nor was there even a need for such a display of might. We had once labeled home-front actions as sabotage, sedition, propaganda, fifth column, depression, inflation, recession, oppression, anarchy – calling them decadent, acephalous, and a great many other names that became most difficult to pronounce and impossible to understand. At this point, we could add an additional name to our imposing list of home-front components, without adding to or subtracting from its influence on the thinking of modern mankind: pollution.

I had always thought our blueprint for international relationships was not in the best interest of all people. As our past fumbling was coming home to roost, I was more certain than ever that we were slipping into oblivion. Unlike the exploits of the ancients who passed this way, today was a markedly different ball game. Either we all survived, or we all went down together.

Tonight it seemed like a long time since I had last taken part in a wartime operation that was designed for oblivion. The planners of our destinies had thought nothing of dumping forty of their fellow countrymen into the unknown. Whether we lived or perished would never have caused the normal flow of events to be influenced the slightest bit. I was fortunate enough now to be able to look back on that night, and I could see for myself if forty lives had honestly made a difference. There was a difference, but not the kind of difference we would choose. The planners were still fumbling, but they were fumbling big. No more forty live-units. Fourteen billion was more like it. And this time, the touchdown area would not be a swamp. *Hell* was a more appropriate name.

In a negative sort of way, we had improved, and we had done it by the sweat of our brows. By war or by peacetime actions, we had tried to exterminate ourselves every inch of the way. Probably only the common rat could rival us in the world of survival. I found my comparison interesting. These very creatures, which we had used to test our own possible survival potentials, could one day truly inherit the Earth.

Whether the human race had evolved from another form of life, or if we had indeed appeared on Earth in our present form was not the important question at the moment. Whatever our method of advent had been, we had one or possibly two irrefutable weaknesses from the very start. Both the lack of human values and the prevalence of greed could be connected with man long before he left a written history of his life behind him. When man did start leaving a record of his actions, it covered nothing else but war, war spawned by the same lack of human values and by greed. As counterproductive as it might appear, at times those wars were brought about by man's efforts to correct the very weaknesses that he was propagating.

Today we had extra things going for us, and they were all real killers. Besides war, we had accepted mismanagement of our resources; killing and maiming types of transportation; mentally and physically deteriorating habits; pollution of our land, sea, and air; and an attitude toward each other that allowed no room whatsoever for even the slightest spark of human dignity to exist. To pick the key killer from among our frailties was not much of a problem, if actual survival was in the balance. The very obnoxious and arrogant way we went about polluting our natural environment was the one luxury we could not afford. Our resources were all irreplaceable. The few handfuls of gold we traded for our heritage would buy us nothing when nothing was available. If gold blinded our leaders, then we should look toward the wild animals for the leadership we needed. They, at least, were in tune with nature and could recognize pollution.

I was convinced we would give the rats a run for their money; we were not bad at adjusting so that we could live with our faults. We were producing synthetic foods, desalting sea water, harnessing solar energy, streamlining our governments, and we managed to get increasingly resourceful as our ranks thinned. In some ways our weaknesses were our strong points. It did not need to be this way; however, if worse came to worst, we would eventually get down to one fighting unit with an overall command. We were only fighting ourselves, so the overall commander should be able to do the job.

The rats, of course, had several strong characteristics which could also keep them in contention. They could eat anything. Pollution could not kill them. They already outnumbered us, and they could live through the very same technical weapons of destruction we had designed for our own demise.

It was all very complicated. I thought of the rat simply because the very name we had given this creature was synonymous with contempt and ridicule. It seemed that the rat and mankind, with our own fumbling mode of life, would make ideal actors to bring down the final curtain.

There was no doubt about my qualification for membership in the crackpot class. There were only two other groups of humanity – eggheads and non-involved. As I always occupied a minor role in the action, I could not say I was non-involved. Nor could I classify myself as an ardent supporter of the status quo, so that kept me out of the egghead class. I was not quite sure what all the defining variables were between my three classes of people. If I could forget my conviction that we were about to join the other lifeless planets in our universe, then I could say I was non-involved. If I saw war as a culling process to keep our population down, or even if I could see war as a cure for our economic depressions, then I could say I was an egghead.

○

On my tenth day at sea, Crackpot Mansan was treated to one of my long-cherished dreams come true. We took two other passengers aboard from a passing freighter, Martel and O'Riley.

The way it looked, on this voyage I was entering into the true inner sanctum of intrigue. I had always wanted to be a part of the inner circle, that small but very select clique, the veritable planners of world destiny.

As I watched Martel and O'Riley start up the gangway, my suspicious mind told me that Jrcy was deeply mixed up in this action somewhere. It seemed to me that people like Martel, O'Riley, and Jrcy should have a distinct advantage over the rest of humanity. After all, the sum total of human knowledge at this juncture was only a huge bomb drifting through our polluted atmosphere. This was it. There had been a beginning and those interim years with our unreasonable approach to life. Now, just maybe, I was watching mankind's first step in almost five hundred thousand years toward a life that was meant to be, but never was.

I met my two old friends halfway down the gangway, and this time I was not convalescing from a battle wound, and could handle their roughhouse tactics quite easily.

By the time the three of us were seated on the foredeck, our ship was under way, and I had a strange feeling that somehow the years which separated today from our last voyage south existed only in my imagination. The sound of O'Riley's voice brought me back to reality.

"Well, gentlemen, the three of us are together once more. It took almost a lifetime to accomplish, but here we are."

He was literally rubbing his hands together with satisfaction. Martel was smiling. Even I began to see some of the odds that made this reunion quite unusual.

O'Riley was speaking again, and this time he handed me a book titled *MOREA*.

"This is a book I had published about twenty years back. It's an account of our action during the battle of Morea, and I think you will find it quite interesting. Jrcy also has a copy, but I didn't mention his name in the book. I assumed you would want it that way."

The book evidently played a part in O'Riley's long-range planning. He had a meeting coming up with Jrcy, and that meeting was, beyond question, in his mind long before Jrcy reached the top. O'Riley was not the type of person to take the usual steps. The coming meeting had taken him years to bring about. Whatever happened in the future would actually have had its beginning during the battle of Morea.

When I looked at O'Riley, my eyes must have shown the wonderment that was in my mind. The man had set his plans around characters he had believed would one day have leading roles. There would be a pivotal drawback to his plans. He was a member of the most politically oriented society the world had ever known. It did not know the meaning of the words *absolute leadership*. O'Riley, the author of the world's seemingly perfect survival program, would himself pass through the portals of time unrecognized. It would not be the first time this error had been made.

At this point, my eyes must have shown the doubt that was on my mind.

"Cheer up, Richard. You started this whole affair forty years ago when you made sure Jrcy, Martel, and I would be around today. My plans are looking better all the time.

"In reality, it is very simple. Only a few heads of state need to agree on what the main issues are. From that point on, sophistication goes out the window, and we will all enjoy our life on Earth."

After he spoke, I remained quiet, not because I disagreed with him. His words were true, and his ideals were beyond reproach. O'Riley did not fit neatly into any of my three predetermined categories of humanity. I was also certain he could see the same negative actions of mankind as well as I could see them. He might not have noticed that nature had already taken a hand.

I had lived with the wild animals so long that some of their instincts had brushed off on me. The air and sea currents were changing. I had mentioned this to the ship's captain several days earlier, and the man had his nose buried in his navigation books ever since. I did not want to insult the captain's intelligence, but all he had to do was watch the creatures of the air and sea. They, along with the land animals, were nature's first-alert mechanism. I had noticed the land animals over the last years, and more of them were taking up yearlong residence in the far north.

And yet, I could not have brought myself to believe that nature was ultimately getting into the act if we had not continually polluted our irreplaceable air and water supply. In the past ten years we had five major nuclear explosions, and fifteen major nuclear waste and plant fires. We had polluted the sea with our disposal of nuclear waste, to a point where even the evaporation in the tropical zone was contaminated.

Numerous things were on my mind as I sat with Martel and O'Riley on the foredeck of the old Northland freighter. Forgetting all of my convictions about mankind's inherent negative characteristics, there was a gray zone in my mind, regarding how much degradation our atmosphere could stand, and what action nature would take to counteract man's pollution. Another question I had, and this one should have been answered long before this, was how internal security was handled these days.

Finally, I got up from the chair I had occupied for the past hour. The damned suit I had worn was baggy at the knees and butt from years of wearing without pressing. I was seventy years old, and I must have presented a ridiculous figure. When I looked at Martel and O'Riley, I realized that they were still depending on me. Their faith in my judgment was something which had started many years ago, and the intervening years had somehow added to my overinflated stature.

Of course, I was expected to respond; and from the looks on the faces of my listeners, I could have told them that black was white and that the moon was made of green cheese. I had to assume a neutral attitude until the novelty of my presence wore off. I did not think my attire added to, or even sustained, my image. A great deal would depend on my first statement.

"Gentlemen, I hope that all countries have tightened up on their internal security. The old battle tactics have changed considerably. We still have national forces-in-being, but from now on, the main fronts are in our own backyards. There can be no justification for pollution – not gold, national security, technical advancements, construction, ignorance – nothing.

"Unless each country can maintain its own discipline, we are beaten."

So far, my outburst was just confirming the philosophies of O'Riley and Martel, but I was warming up to a subject which was the hallmark of my personality. I turned my back on my small audience so they could not see the disgusted look on my face. I quickly turned back and faced Martel and O'Riley. This time there were much more valid reasons for my action. First, the wind was hitting me in the backside, and the thin, sagging fabric of my trousers offered no protection whatsoever. We were already traveling south, so I needed no further omens to tell me I was standing on thin ice. Richard Mansan, with his butt out in the wind, was heading south.

Naturally, I had another reason for looking directly at the two men in front of me, and for an instant I almost said exactly what was on my mind. I had long ago come to the conclusion that a well-defined dividing line separated the oral and the action approaches. Once the two were mixed, the cause was lost. I had just arrived at the dividing line, and to have said anything else would have only defeated what had been said so far. I did not want to do that. I thought that all of our problems today could be solved on the home front. That was where the action was. I was also aware that both O'Riley and Martel thought the same way I did. What I had to do was get out from under the present line of conversation at once, and I could do it very easily; at the same time I could get the answer to a question which had been bothering me ever since O'Riley and Martel came on board.

"Who the hell thought of this meeting out in the middle of the ocean, anyway?"

"Jrcy."

O'Riley had a big smile on his face as he answered me. When he finished giving me the details, I could see that everyone had worked overtime to make my voyage south look like something out of Mata Hari's diary. According to Martel, Jrcy had set up the entire affair, coordinating it with the Governor of Valmy and Nele Moran.

All I could say was "Damn it, and the whole time I thought the cloak-and-dagger routine was top-level international intrigue."

Chapter Four

TODAY WAS THE FINAL DAY OF OUR VOYAGE, and at five o'clock in the morning I was already out on deck, watching our landfall take shape in the early dawn. This was a view I had waited a very long time to see. It was my own private price I had paid for the last forty years. As I recalled each landmark that I knew so well, I realized what a rare privilege I was having. The fact that I was older did not seem important. I was seeing a very pleasant setting in my past life and, for some reason, I was actually enjoying feeling sorry for myself. I did not figure anyone else was involved, so my feelings were not encumbered with any limitations. If I had indeed been stupid enough to allow this veritable paradise to slip through my fingers, I felt I could now enjoy my full return to sanity. It was as though my mind was a component apart from my body, and it was telling me that the best was always saved for last.

The scene before me almost seemed unreal. Even my rationale for being here lacked all of the Mansan logic which I usually seemed to have in an inexhaustible supply. If I could accept either one, I could accept the other. Miracles had never played a very important part in my life, but this morning, for a very brief period, I had a feeling that I could have gone forward or backward in time. As I was afraid of losing the fleeting moments I had captured, I chose to settle for the reality of the present.

"Welcome home, Richard Mansan. This time, please stay with us."

Martel had come up behind me, and my mind followed every word that was spoken. The transition in time again flashed before me. I could see Martel start to put his hand on my shoulder, but he must have changed his mind.

Home. I was positive Martel had used that word years ago, and he had used it in this exact location of the bay.

"It is beautiful, John, just as I remembered it. I never realized how much you sacrifice by being away from home."

I looked toward the shore, and those disconcerting emotions which were plaguing me began to fade from my mind. Martel interrupted my reverie.

"O'Riley chose this city for his coming meeting with Tyron Jrcy. We are hoping that Jrcy will arrive within the month, so you have no excuse for ever leaving this country."

I was back to normal, but the beseeching tone of Martel's voice reminded me of a concern I had all but forgotten. I was not the essence of stability when I could see my future laid out in an orderly sequence before me. Since I was back in the part of the world where nature offered no challenge, there was a chance I would never again be content to stay in one place.

Early in my life I was convinced I could set my own standards and go all the way to the top. The world, as I saw it, was nothing other than a large area governed by a few people, people who, for the most part, could not punch their way out of a wet paper bag. I was thoroughly sold on the idea that I must never permit myself to settle into the dull routine of existence and consign myself to soaking the ashes.

At this stage, I was not sure if my approach had been right, nor was I altogether sure if there was a right approach anymore. Our very lives were governed by a written set of non-applicable laws, laws that could work as easily in favor of the nonconformist as against him or her. In truth, it was a mixed-up world. We had gone so long living our regulated lives that we did not notice when everything changed. War, as we had known it for thousands of years, no longer existed, and in its place was a more deadly game which would tax our leadership to the maximum. In my mind I was thoroughly convinced we were living in the past. We seemed to lack the reasoning power to see the present and adjust to the future. Only the ability of certain individuals to position themselves would extend our survival.

My own positioning action had been dormant for several years. Even when my efforts were at their heights, I was a nobody, a person who had the same chance as a snowball in hell. If I had followed O'Riley's or Martel's approach, would either of those paths have made the difference? We could forget the small successes we had each experienced. Those short periods of personal satisfaction were preliminaries fought while the hall was filling for the main event, the brass-ring bout, the one for all the prizes. It was this brass-ring extravaganza which brought my mind back to O'Riley. As I thought of him, I realized that the man was standing by my side. The smile on his face made me wonder if he had been reading my mind.

○

Martel called our attention to the small yacht coming toward us. Our ship had stopped as soon as the yacht was sighted, and Martel was busy pointing out the members of his family to me. There was his wife, Patty. I had met Patty years ago before she and John were married. Their children, five daughters, were all married with families of their own. By the number of people aboard, every member of the family was present this morning.

Then Martel called my attention to the pilot of the yacht, and I trained my binoculars on the woman at the helm. Before he spoke again, instinct told me who this person was. Her name was Nele Moran, and her family was also on board.

I remembered Nele as a ten-year-old girl with a king-sized temper. Nele's parents seemed to have everything under control except their daughter and, predictably, the girl always wanted to sail with me during the time I was captain of the Martel fishing fleet. At the beginning of each voyage, I would go through the same solemn ceremony for Nele's benefit. She had to stand before me on the foredeck and read the articles of war, as they applied to the discipline of a ship's crew in wartime. I smiled when I remembered how she used to put her small hand on the Bible which our cook, Mrs. Revin, held. This was the most solemn moment of all as Nele, with tears in her eyes, would promise to do exactly what she was told. Nele's duties on those voyages were to help Mrs. Revin with the galley work, and it was the one program in Nele's early life that her parents endorsed a hundred percent.

I was never sure how Nele's mind worked. She seemed to look forward to the ritual I put her through before each voyage, but she was evidently deathly afraid of me. On those occasions when Nele did get out of hand, the one thing Mrs. Revin had to do was tell the young culprit to report to the foredeck for the captain's punishment. It was as if she had waved a magic wand. On the majority of the voyages, I never saw Nele; she avoided me like the plague. Now, as I looked through the binoculars at the pilot of the approaching yacht, I could see no resemblance between the woman at the helm and the young girl I had known.

After the Martel yacht came alongside the freighter, I followed Martel and O'Riley down the ship's gangway. It was impossible for me not to notice the emotional reunion of Martel and his family. He and O'Riley had left here only a few weeks ago, but the reception was nearly a mob scene. This breach of ship's discipline brought some very specific instructions from the skipper of the yacht, and I chanced a look in her direction. She was addressing her instructions to the younger members of the family. Their duty was to hold the yacht in place until we had boarded. Once discipline had returned and the young crew members were back at their posts, Nele turned her searching eyes to me. I smiled and then directed my attention to Patty Martel who had come toward me as soon as I stepped on deck.

In my memory, Patty Martel was a very beautiful girl, and the years had made her more beautiful than ever. As she started introducing me to her daughters and their families, I did my best to cut down on the formalities which had always been the mark of my relationship with the Martel family. This tension probably started with John Martel during the battle of Morea. Later I was certain that young Nele Martel was convinced I intended to feed her to the sharks. At this moment, a second and a third generation of the clan must have had me pictured as a monster, and in baggy pants at that. Speaking of baggy pants, before I was halfway through meeting Patty and John Martel's family, there were at least five kids hanging on to the seat and legs of my trousers. If this kept up, I would lose a great deal more status than I bargained for. I still had Nele Moran's family to meet, and I noticed that she had come down to the foredeck and was waiting directly in front of me.

"Richard, you remember my sister, President Nele Moran?"

John Martel was right beside me when he spoke, and I looked at Nele who had a firm grip on my old coat sleeve. It came off as the yacht rolled slightly. In my effort to support her, I forgot about the kids holding on to my trousers. I fell flat on my face with half of the Martel family on top of me. This was not quite the entrance I had planned, but I could feel almost assured that any inflated image these people had of me was lost forever. If my future problems could be solved as easily, I would consider myself most fortunate.

○

Afterward, I did manage to meet the Moran family, and I even survived the trip to the boat dock. If we had, just for a few minutes, forgotten the troubles which faced us, we were brought back to the world of reality when a messenger handed O'Riley a report from his national headquarters.

O'Riley seemed stunned as he read the message, and without saying a word he handed it to me.

One of our western nuclear waste pits exploded and burned tonight. Sabotage suspected. Damage unknown at this time. Will keep everyone informed on an hourly basis.

I handed the message to Martel, and I could only guess that nuclear waste was our weak link in technical advancement. We evidently did not know much about nuclear waste disposal, so we tried to hide it in the earth and in the sea. This was a weakness we should have recognized. Now it was too late, and regardless of how well we weathered this latest disaster, we would never recover from it. Our atmosphere kept permanent records; we would always keep this pollution. We had gained nothing and we had lost nothing since the beginning of time. The sole difference was that we changed nature's elements by mixing them into compounds which caused pollution, and these pollutions had a permanent home in our land, in our water, in our air, in the food we ate, in the clothes we wore, in our bodies, and in our minds. Pollution covered it all. Whatever we did, we were both the recipient and the propagator. Pollution was the enemy, and everyone was on the front; the non-involved, the eggheads, and the crackpots alike were front-line fighters. The difficulty lay in the fact that there really were no front lines and no traditional enemies. Recipients and propagators were interchangeable. When a recipient rebelled against a propagator by saturating his own body with deadly drugs, he, in turn, became the propagator without losing his identity as a recipient. In reality, we were all full-time recipients and full-time propagators. Our first job was to recognize the enemy and determine the extent of the front.

The time had come, and we had to make changes; but if we stopped polluting, we covered everything, even greed and human degradation.

A few questions remained on my mind. However, I was out of position, and questions under those conditions were of no importance to me. I saw a connection between all national disasters. Disasters represented the new enemy we had to face; whether or not it was a premeditated attack by a foreign enemy, or by an enemy from within, did not make much difference to me. I was concerned that we would be going down because of our lack of intelligence, or because there were those among us who did not give a damn. Internal security needed to be tightened up immediately. If some of us could not stand our toes being stepped on in the process, this was the first lesson we would have to learn. Everyone was involved. Pollution made no distinctions between people. Today we were no longer dealing with a neighbor's barbecue fire; we were faced with a disaster which would probably kill millions of people. Perhaps it was the saturation point that nature's atmosphere must one day reach.

"We will undoubtedly receive accurate reports on the extent of this disaster. It will be something that will affect a great many people."

O'Riley was speaking to no one in particular, and I knew he was only voicing his own thoughts about reports on crucial happenings under censored conditions. Hundreds of acres of burning and exploding nuclear waste could cause a catastrophe unequaled in the history of mankind. Censoring would be impossible. Other nations would have instantly taken a stand; and, for one thing, the air would be monitored night and day.

The VIP treatment which had been planned for our arrival had to be postponed. I was not feeling too "fortissimo," and any exposure I had to the general public at this time did not exactly appeal to me. If my true thoughts were known, I was not overly

Grabbing the Brass Ring   49

enthused about my present location. I wished that I could be back in my overstuffed chair, sitting in front of the fireplace. How misaligned could one person be? Days ago I did not have a worry in the world. Now I felt as though the world was against me. It was probably a toss-up between O'Riley and yours truly as to who was the most unpopular man in this country.

O'Riley called a meeting with Nele Moran, John Martel, and me as soon as we arrived at the Martel residence. The latest report had just come in, and conditions were starting to get black. The old waste pit was located in an isolated area, so there were no known casualties. One small town within fifty miles of the explosion had been evacuated. Highways were already jammed with traffic within a radius of five hundred miles from the epicenter.

As O'Riley read the report, I got the impression that the same leaders who had been responsible for this disaster were no better equipped to handle the results of their incompetency. The stampede toward individual efforts for survival had started, the sure prelude to the chaos that would follow.

Nele, as chief of her country's security, assumed complete leadership during national emergencies. Her nation's forces had taken up their battle stations years ago. No sign of panic could be observed among these people; they accepted their daily routines without any adverse show of emotions whatsoever. What a difference a little self-discipline and good leadership could make. The two were inseparable and seemingly most difficult to come by.

I stayed up all night listening to the news bulletins as they came in every few minutes. So far, no significant details were reported that we had not guessed beforehand. The wind had remained steady in a northwest direction, and the contaminated front was expanding with each passing hour. The traffic on every highway within a radius of one thousand miles from the original blast area was getting out of control.

Finally, I decided to go to bed and get some sleep. I could not change the course of events which had already been set in motion, and if I continued to listen to the reports, I could easily become a casualty of a battle that was taking place on the other side of the world.

○

It was nighttime when O'Riley woke me. I could tell that the man had not rested, and this disturbed me as much as the report he put in my hands.

The traffic conditions were in utter chaos, and widespread panic had broken out in areas far from the original disaster site. Hospitals were no longer able to care for the people. In sum, a complete breakdown had occurred in internal security and in the medical profession.

"What the hell is happening, Mansan? I had planned to call the Chief Council's office and check with him about concentrating our air and sea power on the contamination as soon as it cleared the mainland. I'm very glad I didn't. They can't even handle a traffic jam."

O'Riley was not as excited as he seemed to be. The man was mad, and justifiably so. Whoever was running the show, if anyone was, would have to get on top of the evacuation problem. There was no excuse for the people not knowing exactly what part of the country had been contaminated, as well as the direction and speed that the contamination was spreading. If the existing government could not even control the traffic, I would have to concede that the prognosis was hopeless.

Many actions had to be taken immediately. Of course, most of those actions should have been taken years earlier when there was time to calmly think everything out. Now, due to the lack of good planning, fast and decisive action was the order of the day. The study period was over, and so was the efficacy of those officials who were still trying to justify their existence by calling for more "in-depth" study time.

Whatever O'Riley's shortcomings were, they did not impair his ability to handle crucial situations. I was well aware of his ability. The only unknown area in O'Riley's makeup was his approach to power, the capturing of the old brass ring. It was this approach to power which prompted my answer to his question.

"General, do you think you can possibly get your foot in the door?"

If I had to explain my response to O'Riley, this would prove he was not a contender. But I did not have to explain anything to him, and he seemed to be deep in thought. If O'Riley was indeed thinking of his chances of assuming the reins, his mind would be carrying a heavy load. Government might have been man's overriding weakness. It, at least, ranked a close second to greed. The great leaders of this human race were mainly products of accident and not design. The usual roads to leadership covered the ballot box, inheritance, and revolution. Real leaders were spawned so seldom by these methods that the odds stood at approximately two billion to one against it happening. Nor was a curriculum established which guaranteed true leadership qualities. As no known prerequisite route existed to ensure the necessary characteristics, everyone was a self-styled leader. This human phenomenon made the advent of the true leader during crucial times an impossibility. In normal times, the ability was not tested; we never knew the character of our leaders until it was too late. We further compounded our weakness by jealously guarding the attainment of power. None except a chosen few, whose credentials covered everything but leadership, were allowed to enter the captain's quarters.

O'Riley had a problem, and this problem had nothing to do with the chaotic

Grabbing the Brass Ring

conditions in his nation; it was the impossibility that he would be chosen to lead the people. If O'Riley was silent after I asked him about getting his foot in the door, the man had a reason to remain silent. A premature lunge toward the brass ring could result in permanent failure. It was not a light undertaking, and the method I personally recommended was the savoir faire approach. If conditions were right, and if a person was in the right place, he or she would get the brass ring, with no trouble whatsoever. This route might be impossible for anyone except me, simply because I was probably the one person in the world today who believed it could happen. I knew there would be some people who would consider my theory to be that of a pompous ass. Before such an accusation could be made, however, they would have to thoroughly understand my definition of what those conditions actually were. Currently, the term "right conditions" in my book meant that we were on our way to join the other dehydrated planets in our universe. With this in mind, I saw my ascent to power as only a scraping of the bottom of the barrel. Pompousness could hardly be connected with such modesty and unpretentiousness.

After a while, O'Riley picked up the telephone, and then he hesitated. The voluntary approach to leadership was the most popular of the routes to the top. It was also the most certain to fail. O'Riley knew this as well as I did. Had I offered to lead our remaining men at Morea, he would have laughed at me. Now the shoe was on the other foot, and he was within seconds of being humiliated.

General O'Riley had weathered well during his forty-year military career. These days he was retired and on special assignment for the Chief Council of his country. His present job was not generally known, so it was not looked upon with any degree of envy by anyone. In other words, the name *O'Riley* was not a household slogan, and even his past deeds had faded somewhat since his retirement. The general public was notorious for its fickle attitude toward yesterday's heroes.

The man was well aware of his present status, but long-range planning could take several different tacks. His plan was, in many ways, similar to my own. O'Riley was a "situation" leader, and the market for this type of person was normally so small that the job, the person, and the necessary characteristics thereof were all but lost. The idea, as I saw it, was to wait on the sidelines and jump in at the most opportune time. Surprisingly enough, there *was* such a time, a time when the existing regimes would welcome a reprieve from their responsibility, a time when it would look as though the leadership had been forced upon a seemingly reluctant recipient.

The leader had to follow only two criteria in his or her final bid for the brass ring. First, the word *volunteer* and any of its derivatives were strictly taboo. If help was needed, it would be asked for, or ordered. Anyone could and would offer to help, and it would be accepted up to a point. That point was a very well-defined line which separated anonymity from acclaim.

The second criterion was, to be precise, a characteristic of the leader. He or she needed the animal instinct that smelled the weakness in the opposition. Right now, O'Riley was out of position. He was on the opposite side of the world from the action, and he did not have a chance.

I looked at O'Riley as he started to dial the telephone. The slight negative motion I made with my head caused him to put down the telephone like a hot coal.

There had to be an answer to O'Riley's problem; more accurately, it was everyone's problem. Whether the time was right for his final move depended on the character of his government. It alone held the key to the future, and that key was O'Riley.

In a subtle sort of way, I had pointed out to him where the action was. He had two choices: to call the Chief Council and volunteer his services, or to go home and wait on the sidelines for his opportunity. If that opportunity never came, O'Riley would, at least, have saved himself the humiliation of having his voluntary offer refused.

○

The human race had never understood government. Somewhere in our advancement up through the different units of togetherness, we had lost sight of the very characteristic which should have put human beings above the other creatures that occupied our planet: reasoning power. We had made grave mistakes in the past, mistakes which actually devalued us to the lowest level among all animal species. We enslaved each other. We limited the number of people who could take part in government. We killed and maimed each other. We caused starvation, physical and mental degradation, and so much more. I had to admit that some of us were trying to rectify our prior mistakes, but the errors we had singled out for amelioration were few, and they were always corrected in a retrospective sort of way. This avenue took no reasoning power whatsoever. Now we were blowing a simple evacuation maneuver which would not have taxed the mental capacity of the wildest animals.

I saw a great many self-evident examples of human incompetence, and the latest one was the chaotic situation in O'Riley's country. If we were not able to look for leadership from the government in crucial times, I failed to see the need for the current over-sophisticated governments we supported in normal times. Their only efficiency ended when their own needs were met.

Had we forgotten the meaning of the word *leadership*, or was it more valid to say that we never knew it? Did we really know so little about leadership qualities that we thought we could get by with anyone who passed through the standard election procedures? Could it be that government was the Achilles' heel of the human race, and the people chose not the most competent, but the least dangerous form of government?

Today it was doubtful if any of our past or present forms of government would be capable of stemming the tide which had turned against us. For any government to survive this newest disaster, there could be no dissentients. This was a simple and logical rule to follow. Even the family unit could not survive with internal dissension; nor could a nation survive. In fact, no nation would ever win a war when torn by internal dissension.

○

O'Riley would leave for home within the coming hour. I knew that he wanted me to go with him, and I also knew that he was aware of my feelings in this matter. My returning with O'Riley would have given his position away, and he was not in any condition at this time to commit himself one way or the other. I was a crackpot, and at this stage of my life, I was a well-known crackpot. There were a few other small details which the "Simon Pures" would dig out. I was sure these small details would impress the lay minds in a negative sort of way. Some of my previous actions even snowed me.

It was after midnight when John Martel and I returned from the airport after seeing O'Riley off, and I went right to bed. Although this action might have appeared strange to Martel and the other members of his family, I already knew the worst that could happen. The last thing in the world I needed was to stay up all night and get a slow blow-by-blow description from countless conflicting reports.

○

O'Riley had said that we could expect accurate reports about the disaster, but he overlooked man's ability to prey upon his fellow man, to take advantage of those misfortunes which befell people in crucial times. Like our hindsighted actions to make amends for our past mistakes, we would slowly learn of the atrocities which had been committed during this hour of need, atrocities which should have been averted by a reasoning government. It would seem that after nearly five hundred thousand years in residence here on Earth, man would have learned of his potential reactions to all human situations. From the peacefulness of a family picnic in some pastoral setting to the final charge of a fanatical enemy against the last starving bastion of national defense, the human animal was quite capable of playing many roles.

Part II

Jrcy, O'Riley, and the Martels

"Impossibilities are the inventions of the human mind.
Possibilities are the results of human effort."
– Michael Earl Nolan, 1975

CHAPTER FIVE

Tyron Jrcy

TYRON JRCY, LIKE O'RILEY AND RICHARD MANSAN, was a product of the era of "limited warfare." To offer an explanation for this period of strange human behavior was impossible. It was much easier to see what had happened than it was to understand why it had happened.

Limited warfare was very simple, hardly worthy of rating as one of man's ultra-sophisticated accomplishments. It amounted to promoting war between two small countries under the guise of political and economic stabilization. These small countries were capable of manufacturing nothing more deadly than bows and arrows. Their food supply was marginal, and their wardrobes could be wadded up into a pillow at night.

All of the locales selected were without doubt the least likely scenes imaginable for actual war. The countries, the people, and their way of life were better suited for roles in a classical operetta, where music and pageantry stirred only the emotional fantasies. The fact that such settings could be used for some of the most brutal acts which man had ever perpetrated was far beyond rational thought.

In many respects these idyllic settings for the limited-war games must have been exactly what man wanted, and governments seemed content to supply the people with an inexhaustible amount of free materiels and other commodities. A few of the truly enthusiastic nations even sent human sacrifices. However, it was problematic at best to arrive at any reasonable justification for limited warfare, because the entire concept had a shallowness about it which would not have been expected from a five-year-old child.

The basic concept of the limited action had several props that rivaled it for weirdness. The use of nuclear weapons was taboo; and unlike the so-called illegal criminals, mankind trusted one another implicitly to honor this gentleman's agreement. The possibility of worldwide destruction never entered the more feeble minds, and any thought of pollution was considered ridiculous.

There was absolutely no room for a budding Napoleon Bonaparte. All battle tactics required a certain staticness about them in order to ensure a lengthy war. It seemed to be a prime concern that the war should go on as long as possible, and heads could roll for being too competent on the battlefield, just as easily as they could roll for being incompetent. It always became difficult to draw the line.

A great void developed during the era of limited warfare, a kind of nothingness that left the individual soldier in limbo. It almost seemed as though the only non-questionable conclusion was to get killed. If there were fringe benefits to be derived from the limited warfare, they had to be, in some way, connected with the unending amount of supplies that flooded the war zone, supporting both friends and enemies. In short, it was a very amateurish staging of the old production starring good versus evil. The limited wars had one dubious honor. They were mankind's most expensive pastime, in every respect.

It was hard to tell how long this obnoxious tactic would be used, but it eventually did go out of style, along with "flushing 'em out with cold steel," and numerous other gems. What might have sounded its death knell was the proliferation of unexplained disasters on the home front, disasters which caused hundreds of thousands to die from nuclear radiation and other contaminants. In reality, the limited wars were so ridiculous in concept that they might have been used solely to camouflage the location of the big battles on the home fronts.

○

Regardless of the reasons behind these past actions, Tyron Jrcy had used the last forty years to his advantage. His government did not furnish the warring nations with manpower, but it did furnish supplies. A few men like Jrcy were detailed to see that these supplies were used and neither sold to the enemy nor wasted.

His career spanned nearly a lifetime of observing his government in action. This was the route he had chosen to reach the top; and after a very shaky beginning at Morea, he never faltered again. Where some people were blessed with natural leadership qualities, he had learned to be a leader, the most difficult of all human accomplishments. Jrcy's ability to outlast others in a world governed by intrigue and deception had made him an equal to the man who ensured his career forty years earlier at Morea.

He had first read O'Riley's book on the battle of Morea several years ago, and he had carried the book with him ever since. Something about O'Riley's story stood out in Jrcy's mind. There was nothing whatsoever in the book about out-thinking the enemy. The impossible had been accomplished by physical strength and by instant decision-making. Certainly none of Mansan's decisions had been brilliant. Jrcy thought he had the answer: *Impossibilities are the inventions of the human mind. Possibilities are the results of human effort.* Tyron Jrcy would remember this.

Two years ago he had reached the top, and he did it with the complete approval of the National Council. During forty years of government service, he had weathered well. His apprenticeship had been completed without attachments or commitments to anyone. From the very first day as Chief Council, he went quietly about initiating his new programs without the usual ado which had always characterized the changing of the guard. Years of practice had made him into a distinctly effective human machine, with the cunning of a wild animal. From Mansan he had learned how to attack the impossible. It might be the combination he needed to do the job.

A comprehensive engineering survey had already been completed of the natural resources in the entire northern part of the country. This vast northern area was the Northland's last frontier, and Jrcy was of the opinion that his people would need all the help from nature they could get. He did not believe, as Mansan did, that the human race would exterminate itself. Not that it made any difference, but Jrcy believed in the old theological prediction that man did not have the power to destroy the Earth; nature would have the final say. As there was probably no escape, there was no consolation either way. There was, of course, the probability of a postponement. What was even more important to people everywhere was the fact that Jrcy had dedicated himself to making the postponement a reality.

His transition into the top office was accomplished with his full knowledge of the strength and weakness he would find. Governments were expensive, and the officials' salaries amounted to a mere fraction of their other expenses. It was a staggering burden which the people in the production forces had to bear. If those people could be thankful about one thing, it would have to be that they did not get as much government as they were charged for.

Jrcy was quite unorthodox in his approaches to the status quo. In the government he now controlled, he made no impact changes. The old guard would remain until their retirement dates. At that time most of the personnel would not be replaced. The government was undeniably overstaffed, and a large number of the employees were in nonproductive agencies which needed no more than skeleton forces. However, to phase out four of every five government employees at one time would have ruined the country. To phase out the positions after retirements and deaths took a while longer, but it left the old employees independent and, at the same time, the burden on the taxpayers decreased. The phased-out government jobs should never have been created in the first place. Once they had been created, the jobs, like the original officials, entailed untold added expenses.

Undeniably, Jrcy's government had not cornered the world market on inefficiency. The weakness was worldwide, and it simply took the erroneous caption of "government." There was actually no cure which could be applied to all systems, nor could one cure be applied to one system all of the time. Mankind's world was the perfect planet in a universe of long dead and dehydrated bodies, their existence betrayed only when the sun lighted up their bleached surfaces at night. It was too bad that Earth would one day have to join those inert masses solely because man had never learned to govern.

Several situations required Jrcy's immediate attention. Additional people were needed in agriculture and its related industries, and additional people were needed in ocean-connected industries. Present government expenses would be cut in the cloud-nine adventures and channeled into the agriculture and ocean projects, where the effort and production were necessary. The Army engineers were being used to do a majority of the engineering development work in the northern region. A surplus of working capital was already piling up from Mansan's program, and by gradually eliminating some of the government agencies, Jrcy had watched the effects of this phasing-out schedule very closely to determine if any impacts were involved. Government was a highly sophisticated organization which was interwoven into the lives of the people. Due to this circumstance alone, a textbook approach was impossible. If the officials were unaware of the true living conditions of the people from day to day, they could not possibly pass and enforce applicable laws.

Jrcy's programs were popular, mainly due to the conclusion that there appeared to be no added impacts. He did have a dissentient problem which had surfaced in the first year of his administration. To say that he caused the problem was probably wrong. To say that he caused the problem to surface was probably right. To say that the problem was crucial and belonged entirely to him was the one hard, cold fact Jrcy faced. The presence of so many dissentients was one of the components which made government impossible, and on more grounds than the original issues involved.

If he had committed himself in any way during the past two years, it had to be that he was concerned about the living conditions of all people. Everything he had done so far pointed in that direction, and the scale had started to tip in another direction which also made government impossible: too much public participation.

Jrcy realized that he would have to handle the dissentient phenomenon himself, and it would not be easy. If he became too involved on the side of the dissentients, the movement would grow and slow down government activities. He could suppress the movement, but this approach would result in resentment and frustrations, two other well-known enemies of government. Frustrations especially caused a serious physical and moral deterioration that propagated crimes against the social system. The battle was now on the home front, and another of man's individual and uncoordinated fights for survival had to be headed off. Like all other individual efforts inspired by frustration or panic, the end product was disaster.

With the major problems today that needed immediate answers, Jrcy wondered why he had been foolish enough to set his sights so high. While Mansan was sitting on his butt in a cozy cabin far away in the north country, Jrcy had been busy running errands for imbeciles, and for what reason?

There was a worldwide food shortage, and the problem was getting worse. Contingent supplies could no longer carry any nation in the world through one poor harvest. Overpopulation, threats of war, incompetent governments, and pollution were only a few of the more popular problems on the agenda. At the moment, the problem which worried the Chief Council the most was air pollution.

He was a firm believer in single-person administration during crucial times. The astonishing fact about human beings was that they seemed to be well read on the evil of one-person rule. Those same history books were just as clear on the disadvantages of the overstaffed system, yet invariably the people leaned toward that top-heavy form of government. It could be that one lone individual was considered too dangerous. Jrcy had nothing to worry about. His nation now had the best, or the worst, of each form of government: the single ruler and the overstaffed system.

○

For the past week Jrcy's air and sea forces had been monitoring the polluted air current which was coursing toward the northern part of the country. This current covered a front about five hundred miles wide, and it was staying very close to the surface of the North Sea. Jrcy's forces had been watching the movement of the front closely, with the hope of using the atmospheric conditions to help eliminate the potential disaster before it hit the Northland. There was a chance of washing the air clean by causing rain. If atmospheric conditions were favorable and this operation was successful, the next effort would be made to neutralize and clean up the contamination on the surface of the ocean.

Jrcy was furious, but retaliation against the people responsible for this disaster was out of the question. All efforts were needed to correct what had been done. It was common knowledge that nuclear waste could not be destroyed with any degree of certainty; because of this, Jrcy's nation was freezing its nuclear wastes.

This latest disaster was stirring up discontent across the world. It made Jrcy's internal dissentient problem look like child's play. The most vocal members of those groups were advocating a much greater form of air pollution; and if they had their way, the big weapons would be readied for immediate action. If Jrcy's efforts in the next few days did not bring positive results, his leadership would be tested to the limit. One slight mistake in his use of the atmospheric conditions and he could lose the whole ball of wax. It was too bad that worldwide existence now depended upon the frailties of human actions. Without nature's help, man was not sufficiently competent to shoulder such responsibility, and it was doubtful that he would ever be.

Since the world was about to have its first real battle for survival, people turned their attention to the man who led his forces into the very eye of the gathering storm. What they found was very surprising. He was an unknown. The glitter which usually surrounded the marshal of human destiny was missing. A common man had made it all the way, without publicity, oration, promises, or previous deeds of valor – a common person, theoretically no more intelligent or stupid than millions of others.

Jrcy personally harbored some strong feelings about his own chances. Years ago he had sold himself on the idea that he would one day occupy the exact position he held today. A career in government, which should have ended in Morea, had actually been blessed with good fortune from that day on. Seemingly, there was a special aspect to the battle of Morea. Although he was on the losing side, he could truthfully say that he came out of the battle the only winner. Jrcy's country had considered his escape of more importance than Mansan's country had considered his victory. Had acting Lieutenant Mansan decided to turn him over to the people of Morea, Jrcy would have been killed. If Mansan had turned him over to higher authorities, Jrcy's career would have been ended. As it happened, Mansan's actions that night were highly irregular; it was almost as if he had saved Tyron Jrcy for a pivotal role in the future.

Mansan had recently returned to the scene. He was, in fact, right now waiting in the wings to see if his investment in Jrcy's life had been worth the effort.

○

Jrcy was already at sea, watching a huge black cloud as it moved in the direction of his country. Its boundaries had been marked several days earlier with a purple dye which united with the radioactive particles. Time was running out on the Chief Council and on a great many other people, as well. The approaching dark mantel of death covered the entire horizon. So far, half a million people had died, and millions more would probably die as a result of this man-made catastrophe. Even the color of the sky, which was meant to help Jrcy locate his enemy, gave the looming disaster an enlarged fearfulness which could very easily bring panic to the mere humans who were trying to stem the tide that had turned against them.

Every known and unknown method for starting rain would be used on a twenty-four-hour schedule each day, beginning at three o'clock the next morning. As of now, Jrcy was blasting the atmosphere high above the dark cloud with explosives. This action was considerable, and if he did not start a chain reaction of total destruction, he should at least cause it to rain.

By three o'clock in the morning, carbon dioxide shells saturated the atmosphere just above the contaminated air. The dark cloud was bombarded with shells containing silver iodide, and all the time the air high above was vibrating with two-hundred-pound charges of high explosives.

By six o'clock in the morning, the planes were ordered to return to their carriers. Visibility was rapidly closing in on zero, and all units in the Northland's forces had to be guided by radar. By twelve o'clock noon, the task forces were a hundred miles south of the danger zone and enjoying somewhat better visibility. Jrcy gave orders to continue the same bombardment pattern over the contaminated area. The operation would proceed around the clock without letup. The sea forces would be joined by the larger land-based planes as soon as the contamination came within their range.

Jrcy estimated that he would see results within the next twenty-four hours. The land-based planes would be in the act by then, and they would each be carrying several tons of explosives. Monitoring reports showed that the air around the contamination had definitely reached the normal saturation point. Heat or some unknown reaction within the polluted front was causing the moisture in the air to be absorbed beyond the normal saturation limits.

He had issued orders days ago to evacuate the northern region, and he doubted that his orders had been obeyed. The people were all helping with the incoming supplies which he was using in his fight.

Even nature might turn against Jrcy, but he could not believe that it would happen. If nature's winds did shift in direction or speed, then he was certain the end would come, sure and fast. His people were furious, and the big weapons had been manned for action.

The coming day would be crucial. The polluted front would be within range of the land-based bombers, and Jrcy meant to pour it on. The general area of the battlefront had been enveloped in a heavy mist ever since the operation began. Now he planned to step up the attack. In addition to larger amounts of chemicals and explosives, he would use the fine-powdered clay that was mined in the north. The clay would be spread throughout the contamination. This operation would be followed by more and larger quantities of chemicals. With the five-thousand-pound explosive charges which the land-based planes carried, Jrcy was convinced that nature would give up something besides mist.

The clay would be parachuted into position above the contamination and released from containers by small explosive charges. The powdered clay was light, and each plane carried a supply to cover a square mile. Jrcy was hoping that the absorbent qualities of the dry, powdered clay would attract enough water out of the moisture-laden air to form normal-sized raindrops. This could start a chain reaction of rainmaking throughout the polluted front. If this did not work, he was planning on doubling his efforts on the upper atmosphere. Vibration of the atmosphere caused rain. This was not an accepted theory, mainly because the only time the needed components were available for a test of this kind was during certain battle conditions. After forty years of battle-zone duty, Jrcy was sold on the idea that prolonged periods of vibration caused rain or snow, whatever the case might be. Like the approaches he had to government, he did not give a damn what the eggheads thought.

After eight o'clock in the evening, the Northland's planes were already dusting the contamination with powdered clay. This operation would continue throughout the night, while the Navy lighted the area with their slow-burning chemical shells. Maybe it was the reflection from the burning chemicals filtering through nature's mist that caused the cloud to take on a golden-brown color. It could also have been Jrcy's imagination, but brown was the exact color he wanted to see. It meant that the orange-colored clay powder had mixed with the purple-colored contamination. He could see the possibility of the massive front falling into the ocean with a big splash. In order to ensure that it would happen, early morning would bring the big planes with their five-thousand-pound explosive charges. Jrcy was so confident of victory that he left the bridge of his flagship and retired for the night.

○

When the Chief Council woke up at noon, his planes were still pounding the atmosphere above the polluted front. The excited aide, who informed him of the latest development, failed on the first try to tell Jrcy what he most wanted to hear. The aide quickly corrected his statement. The planes were indeed bombing the atmosphere – only now they were bombing the atmosphere above where the polluted front had been. The latest reports showed that the air had been washed clean. The last visible trace of the big brown cloud was a blackish flux on the ocean surface.

Even so, Jrcy was not out of the woods. It would take months to clean up the mess on the water's surface; then the residue would have to be transported to the north country and put into the deep freeze.

As Jrcy thought of the north country, his old friend Richard Mansan came back to mind. They were fellow countrymen; at least, they had been for thirty-nine years. Jrcy had been largely responsible for Mansan's stay in the Northland. Not many people knew about this. There was another matter no one knew about. For years Jrcy had the

Grabbing the Brass Ring 65

idea that he would one day have Mansan on the National Council. It was a long shot, not quite as long as O'Riley's plan for a meeting which would solve the world's problems; but the possibility of Mansan grabbing his elusive brass ring in his adopted homeland did stretch the imagination.

Mansan had recently left the north country, and according to his business settlements with the government, it looked as though he was not planning to return. Thirty-nine years was a long time, and Jrcy could only hope that Mansan had found what he was searching for. Today, Jrcy felt content that he had, in a small way, paid something on the account he owed Mansan.

○

Jrcy was so right about the time and effort it would take to clean up the mess at sea. It was very dangerous and frustrating work. A person with an egghead's approach to the problem would have let nature assimilate this last dose of man's pollution, but Jrcy's morale was a bit higher than that. Both the atmosphere and the oceans were non-rejuvenating bodies. They worked closely together with their original issue of elements, but once mankind fouled these elements, they remained forever fouled. Man had been polluting his home for hundreds of thousands of years, and especially during the past one hundred years. This very complacent attitude toward pollution was based upon his total lack of knowledge, and upon his desire for gold. The land, sea, and air which made up his ageless planet must have represented a certain boundless infinity that no one in his right frame of mind would consider as nonexpendable. Man did not even consider his own species as nonexpendable. The elements of his surroundings only occupied the minds of the demented.

Tyron Jrcy, Chief Council, had done the best he could to buy the people more time, and at a very high price. It would not be known until later just how high that price had been. Man was dealing with a virtual unknown, and the eggheaded approach did not cover all the necessary counteractions he needed to harness the adverse effects of his own inventions. Jrcy and his task forces had been exposed to these adverse effects.

In reality, man's greatest battle ever had now been fought and won. A possible total disaster had been turned into an additional entry in his long list of warnings. The world's leaders could go back to their head-roaring forms of chin music, and the rest of the people could once again continue with whatever it was that justified their existence. After all, man believed that he lived in an infinite organic world, and the mute testimony of its sister planets told him nothing. They were merely bodies of inorganic dust, the setting for science fiction writers. What these planets had once been or how they had reached their final resting places was of no seeming importance. Man, on his own infinite planet, was firmly entrenched. The main front was securely held by billions of non-involved human beings, all staunch defenders of the status quo; and they presented a most formidable-looking array indeed, a veritable force-in-residence.

Chapter Six

O'Riley

THE SOPHISTICATION OF REALITY WAS CATCHING UP with ex-General O'Riley, or maybe it was the other way around. Probably the major question which should have been answered today concerned one small, insignificant human being. What if everything actually did depend on whether O'Riley grabbed the brass ring? The human race had worked long and hard to ensure the devaluation of its own species. Not that it would make any difference at this late date, but could any individual possibly be capable of stirring up the chain of human emotions which could unite all people? And, crucially, did any man or woman retain enough dignity to find the compassion necessary to do the job?

O'Riley, a strict company man and a leader, was not too optimistic. He was not the elected leader of his country, and to make his case even more hopeless, the bottom had just fallen out of his last official assignment. It would be some time before the Northland would be willing to sit down at the conference table with him, or with anyone else. Only a very efficient effort on the part of Tyron Jrcy and his forces would prevent man's possible final act of destruction from becoming a reality.

After forty years of plugging along the route he had chosen to reach the top, O'Riley was a nobody. He realized this. He also realized that Mansan's standby policy was not limited to standing by, but embraced a great many more supporting props than O'Riley himself could ever muster.

The groundwork Mansan had laid during the past forty years was very much in evidence in the Northland. Although he seemed to be a social dropout, his real hang-up was his inability to cope with the dull routines in human affairs. Mansan was a doer, and he was a person whom other people thought of when they needed help.

The life of O'Riley varied appreciably from Mansan's. O'Riley had completed all of the mundane routines in human affairs; the glitter that surrounded those who dared to be different was missing in him. Although glitter was merely man's main personality trait, it was looked upon by the people as a reflection of true character.

No, the standby policy would definitely not work for O'Riley; there was not the requisite amount of glitter surrounding the man to keep him before the public eye. His sole alternative was to join the already overpopulated group called "volunteers."

If he was indeed that one person who could make the difference, he was likely to have an uphill climb, the whole way. If he volunteered his services for the good of his country, he would certainly run into a stone wall. A particular human phenomenon was connected with every act that encompassed any degree of volunteering. It could only be explained on an individual basis; but, fundamentally, the infinite space of anonymity, in which the volunteer worked, awaited all members of the human race who would dare to offer their services in return for food, gold, revenge, compassion, acclaim, or whatever else motivated them. In most cases the route to the top was jealously guarded; even those minor plateaus above the ditch line were out of reach. And for the very few who ran the entire gauntlet, the credit for their best efforts was denied them.

O'Riley thought he understood Mansan's approach to government. It was simply the complete disrobing of sophistication from national and local agencies, and the creation of a small and efficient government whose members must first have occupied a front-line battle position, as would the future industrial leaders. O'Riley determined that there could be no automatic exemption from that front-line battle assignment, including gold, religion, or political ties; and whether the individual considered the cause right or wrong could make no difference in the procedure. Everyone would be called for service. If war was what people thought they wanted, they should all become acquainted with its stark reality. Other problems would then be much easier to solve.

At present, he knew of several minor problems which needed action instead of study. It was evident that one of these was the gradual reduction of government forces. The way it was now, no front battle line could possibly accommodate the untold legions of nonproducing government employees. Another serious drawback to good government, and one which needed correcting, was the nature of the people's involvement. Any similarity between the original intent of the election procedure and what currently existed was accidental. What was called "freedom of choice" today was limited to voting for a very few handpicked candidates. If there was a choice, it did not entail the human qualities that the people were searching for.

What would O'Riley find when he returned home? The first criterion of leadership was to recognize leadership qualities in others. The man was well acquainted with his government, and for this reason more than any other, Mansan wondered why he would seriously consider going home.

When O'Riley landed at the capital airport, his arrival was known in advance. It was also unprepared for and unattended. In fact, the only accommodations the man could get for the night consisted of a canvas cot at his old headquarters, hardly the red-carpet treatment, and definitely not the treatment given to recognized leaders. His long route to the top, which had its beginning in Morea forty years ago, ignominiously ended on a government-issued canvas cot. If he was looking for an omen of things to come, he needed to look no further.

O'Riley spent one day looking for a place to stay, and one day listening to the National Council. More accurately, he spent only a half day listening to the Council. The third day after he arrived at the capital, he requested and received permission to tour the disaster zone. He himself would make all the arrangements for the tour, and he would pick up the tab for all expenses.

It was improbable that any member of the National Council could accuse O'Riley of making a play for recognition, but he became suspicious of the Council once he learned that the recent disaster was being treated as a political issue. Four million people would probably die as a result of this fiasco. The atmosphere and oceans would be permanently polluted. Even the finale of the human race was a possibility, and the National Council still continued to play "political chairs."

As O'Riley embraced no political doctrines, there was absolutely no chance for him to improve his status. His fight from here on would be to protect what little reputation he had. This was called "politicking." Under the guise of government, and playing upon the people's weakness of believing everything they read in the newspapers, the officials could make anyone into a king or a tramp. O'Riley knew that the Council had no intentions of making him a king. He would, therefore, be extra careful to stay on guard and watch for the little game called "character assassination." In order to ensure against the possibility of any hanky-panky occurring, he placed himself under the protection of a competent private surveillance organization, one of the many such companies in the capital.

There were small breakthroughs which O'Riley managed to fall into as he readied for departure. The main one was an invitation from the Council to discuss his coming tour of the disaster area. Actually, this was a major breakthrough if the Council's intentions were on the up-and-up. However, he chose to look upon their actions as strictly political, and might have lost his chance at the first firm step upward. Invitations were derivatives of volunteering, and this time he was on the other side of the fence, the winner's side.

The pervading atmosphere of the capital was unreal. O'Riley could not quite put his finger on the trouble. It was a physical thing which slowed the breath and quickened the pulse at the same time. During the first days after his arrival, he was certain that his feelings were emotional; but after a few nights of troubled breathing, he began to notice the actions of the people. O'Riley foresaw untold casualties before this mess was cleaned up. The country was already defeated, and he was satisfied that the real enemy lay within the national boundaries.

Tyron Jrcy had stopped the disaster from circling the Earth and mixing with the pre-existent polluted atmosphere. Questions remained regarding how much of the contamination had escaped into the upper layers of the atmosphere, and how much of the contamination had fallen to the ground, to be picked up later by wind, groundwater, animals, and insects.

Jrcy was trying to clean up the surface of the ocean, and it was more than doubtful that the ocean would ever be the same again. Radioactive particles took hundreds of years in dormant surroundings to lose their effectiveness. In the open air they took a while longer to reach the docile stage.

As Jrcy led his forces in an all-out effort to stem the tide, O'Riley's government held meetings. It had been a time to take decisive steps, and the erstwhile general was astounded to discover that his nation was altogether knocked out of the action. If this latest disaster was indeed the work of a foreign enemy, all O'Riley's homeland had to do now was wait for the arrival of the foreign courier with the stack of documents he would want signed.

The fall of the mighty was a very simple matter. The only thing simpler was for the mighty to avoid that fall. The secret in both cases was to work toward either the gold or the goal desired.

○

O'Riley's career had started to ebb. Maybe it had never cleared the starting blocks. He had won several brilliant victories in his forty years of service, but this was not always looked upon as the criterion for acclaim. Winning assured survival. The events that followed determined the type of survival. If the designers failed to follow the unselfish standards of those who gained the victory, all was lost.

At this time, the man was virtually unrecognized in his own country. There were other facts involved which added to the very bleak picture of internal affairs. The people were suffering from shock, and there was something physically wrong with them. Even O'Riley had a tendency to become disinterested. This caused him to feel sorry for himself and to develop the predictable sour-grapes attitude that went with any form of disregard. This was not a characteristic trait of a true leader; yet, it was one of

Grabbing the Brass Ring 71

the luxuries of self-indulgence which everyone was exposed to at one time or another. No doubt was in O'Riley's mind that Tyron Jrcy and his people were similarly affected by the unknown impacts of the recent disaster. Leadership qualities would win out if they were strong enough, regardless of the known or unknown forces. If the support from the top echelon of a nation faltered, the leader could not enjoy the luxury of self-pity.

Today's troubles seemed to differ from many of O'Riley's problems in the past only in the respect that he was not now in a position to do anything about those troubles. Of course, this was not technically true. His previous problems did include those times when he could do absolutely nothing to influence the outcome of the battle. In Morea he was bleeding to death in a swamp, and his men were being killed like flies – a most impossible situation, also a situation that he could do nothing about.

There were other times when his star shone just a bit brighter. Several years ago one of the limited-warfare actions had blown up into a major conflagration, and General O'Riley was faced with an instant choice, either to make a stand or to throw in the sponge and take a "country beating." Again, it had been an impossible situation. That time, a nation had committed its armed forces on the field of battle without a total commitment to their victory, a sure sign of disaster, but a true test for leadership.

Twenty years had passed since the day O'Riley and his forces were backed up to the sea by an enemy who overwhelmingly outnumbered them. His land force, numbering under forty-six thousand men, had been pushed into an area of less than thirty-seven square miles. This relatively large section of real estate became appreciably smaller once it was taken into consideration that five million non-involved civilians had crowded into the area, seeking the protection of O'Riley's forces. Evacuation was the impossible order given to him that day, and he solved the impossible by the least complicated approach he could envision. As simple as his tactics had been, he indisputably set the predetermined course of man's great sophistication back at least thirty years.

The word *evacuation* was, in reality, merely a catchall or filler script. Too often words were used for sound effects without a precise knowledge of what they meant, without the faintest realization that they had vastly different meanings in different situations. The word *evacuation* was a component of O'Riley's final orders, but its meaning under the conditions which existed could have filled volumes. Words like *sacrifice*, *suicide*, and *exploitation* could have been used in place of *evacuation*.

To make the word *evacuation* fit the situation as it existed on the battlefield twenty years ago, the general, with the help of his small supporting Air Force and Navy, attacked an enemy force of more than eight hundred thousand men. The tactics used that day would never find their way into the classics, but with two lone battleships, thirty-seven rocket-carrying planes, and forty-six thousand men, O'Riley changed the course of human events. The action was not the usual repulse of an enemy's attack. It was a complete annihilation of an enemy who was caught within the twenty-mile firing range of O'Riley's two battleships. If there was a factor during the battle where superior reasoning set the stage for the final scene, it was his use of the Air Force to destroy the enemy's air power on the night before. Even this would not have ensured victory if the enemy had not driven him into such a congested area. He occupied the best position possible for the battle that followed.

The impact of this sudden victory was felt on every home front around the world. The war had not been a survival contest in the strict sense of the word. There had been an extensive sophistication to it, and many predetermined events had been disrupted. O'Riley's future remained in limbo for years after the war, and it was still extremely doubtful that the people saw the relative aspects in their true perspective. Maybe the future orders to some beleaguered commander would be written with victory in mind. Catchall and filler script were used only by those make-believe leaders who would shape human destiny. War was the last resort to ensure national survival. It was not a game to be won or lost for any other reason.

Quite a bit more than the definition of the word *evacuation* was changed by O'Riley's actions on the battlefield. The ultra-sophistication of limited warfare also changed, affecting the very economic structure of every nation in the world. It was a noticeable change, but a change which the leaders must have found difficult to accept. Limited warfare continued like an obnoxious cancer until the increasing number of disasters on the home front changed the entire complex of war. And yet, as a whole, the human race would not allow itself to be completely divorced from its past tinkering with nature's elements. If there was a way to destroy the world, the leaders seemed dedicated in that direction, and the people supported them wholeheartedly.

The scene as it appeared to O'Riley could be easily summed up by the words *limbo, void,* or whatever else could be derived from the infinite nothing. Historically, limbo had always been a way of life for more than half of the world's population. Now it seemed as if the other half, the pacesetters, were tiring rapidly. All people were slaves of their own system, and the endless table where they sat day after day existed in an atmosphere of sameness, without an emotional stimulant of any kind. Each person was no more than a body without emotions and without the means to make even the smallest wish come true.

The existing atmosphere of human behavior had just been brought home to O'Riley, and the one antidote he could think of to cure his own languorous condition was to inspect the disaster area. His star was definitely setting, but he refused to take his place at the endless table. He would remain in the action zone until he started to sink; then he would run. It was much too late to try Mansan's cure. Besides, Mansan had long since broken ground in the world's last habitable region.

○

O'Riley would begin his inspection at the site of the explosion. He then planned to cover the approximate seventy thousand square miles which had been affected. The ground would be contaminated for some time to come, and there was a good possibility that the wind would spread the contamination in the air and over a far greater area of land. He would travel by helicopter, and he would make sure that the air was monitored on a twenty-four-hour basis.

Meetings would be scheduled with the people who had lived in the vicinity, and nothing would be overlooked, regardless of how minor it appeared to be.

Although O'Riley might have been at the end of the trail, he had risen from the ashes of defeat before. He was now in control of his faculties, and even the touch of sour grapes he might have experienced in the past was gone from his mind. O'Riley was a leader with the confidence and the inflated ego that go with a leader's characteristics. It was hard for the man not to express his feelings. He also realized that if he had to expound on his own virtues and on his country's need for his services, he could sing like the proverbial pigeon and each note, however sweet, would fall on deaf ears.

It was obvious O'Riley could not initiate the action that was needed. Unsolicited help had a long record of failure; it was part of the same package which housed all volunteer actions. He was getting close to the end of a long career, and the only action he could take was the simplified version of fading out of the picture without any show of emotion whatsoever. He had missed his chance somewhere along the way, and he was not a contender for Mansan's pet bauble. O'Riley realized this on the first day of his return. His meeting with the National Council had been a stalemate, neither side able to recognize leadership qualities in the other.

He started his inspection with seven other people – his pilot, his secretary, a photographer, a representative of the people who lived in the immediate area, the Chief of the National Monitoring Service, a medical doctor, and a member of his protective agency. Reporting on air conditions was a continual operation. Visual and general inspection of the disaster area included the body count of humans and animals; a survey of wildlife activity, vegetation type, water bodies, and runoff patterns; the collection of air samples; and chemical drop-tests for land and water contamination readings. If possible, a sufficient number of samples of earth, air, and water would be taken to work out antidotes. And there would be substantially more information that O'Riley himself could read from the disaster area.

Each day's operation was concluded by a thorough decontamination check of aircraft and passengers. The inspection time was set up so that meetings could be held with the available survivors of the disaster, and then a daily report was sent to the National Council.

The inspection trip was the perfect tonic for the entire party. O'Riley had been right. Every individual felt as though he or she was contributing something toward easing the effects of the disaster. Leadership always brought out the best efforts in people.

The first days of the inspection were spent over the original blast site: one square mile of contaminated land which might prove to be a death trap for generations to come; one square mile of poison to be picked up and scattered by the wind, water, insects, and wild animals; one square mile of perpetual destruction.

Of foremost interest to O'Riley were the nearest residential buildings, and he spent several days looking over the ground that spanned each house site and the old waste area. Possible connections were noticed between two of the homes and the waste area; both excessive and not enough camouflage served as equal giveaways to his sharp eyes. Names of the home owners and their life histories were recorded. Information that was not available was requested at once. The nation was at war, and whether the people liked it or not, many of the liberties they enjoyed in the past would come in for scrutiny until their survival was assured. The government would have to learn how to most effectively carry on this type of operation, and the people would have to learn how to allow their toes to be stepped on for a while. It would be a very small price when compared to what some of them had already paid.

There was not much that O'Riley could learn from the people. Generally, their input was too emotional, and it covered those facts he had known, or had guessed. The government was not exactly popular among the individuals he spoke with, but then, this was an indictment that the citizens would need to share with the government. The leaders under discussion had been endorsed by the people O'Riley interviewed. If the leaders overlooked certain crucial components of their job, the people would have to share the guilt for voting them into office. In his mind, this lessened the validity of the static he was receiving. The man was not an authority on voting procedures. He was positive, however, that the government did not make anyone vote for the candidates on the ballot. Nor was the ballot closed to all but the select few whose names appeared on it. If voters could recall a candidate from office, they could as easily add another name to the ballot.

O'Riley was reluctant to leave the site of the old waste dump. The answers to the majority of his questions were right there, and he recorded in his recommendations that teams of investigators should inspect the area on the ground as soon as possible. He was particularly interested in the connection, if any, between the individuals who lived in the houses nearest the waste dump. The whereabouts of these survivors should be known at all times until the investigations had been completed. The names of the government officials responsible for the location of the waste area should be made known to the people who elected them. In his frustration, O'Riley considered that even the names of the people who elected the officials should be made known. Government was a heavy responsibility, and it was time that everyone became involved. The fun-and-games period was over.

Along with O'Riley's first report and recommendations, he requested detailed information on the protestors who had marched on the other energy plants and installations throughout the country. There was a question in his mind about those actions, and it was only fair to all citizens, protestors and non-involved alike, that the question received an answer.

Protest marches did not bring out the most affluent members of a society; and at the isolated locations of the several energy plants and waste areas, great expense was involved in setting up these demonstrations. Who financed the demonstrations, and how? The people had a right to know how their government officials were financed, and it was just as important for the government to be aware of any financial arrangements made for the people, and why.

As O'Riley flew north along the long axis of the destruction, he always managed to have an informed representative of the people with him. The disaster area was very revealing, and it told O'Riley true stories that the normal human mind would never imagine. The area was totally contaminated, and no one knew how long it would be before the land could be used again. Domestic and wild animals had died. Human beings had also been caught in the area. Now, wild animals were eating the bodies of both man and beast. This fact did not seem to visibly distract O'Riley to the degree that it did the other passengers. At the moment, his eyes were focused on other pressing problems on the ground, portents of further desolation.

Natural drainage and the rivers which flowed through the area were contaminated. This would affect everyone who used either the groundwater or the surface water.

Wind would play an active part in spreading the contaminated soil particles and vegetation.

Wildlife and insects would spread the contamination.

O'Riley recorded his thoughts and sent them to the National Council, along with his recommendation that the government mass the scientific expertise of the nation on the front lines immediately. Evacuation would be necessary in many areas, and this time it should be controlled.

The scenes of the disaster area recalled to O'Riley's mind one of the country's main weaknesses: control of internal affairs. The delinquencies had been allowed to develop to the point where only punishment for a crime was a possibility. Crime prevention was unheard of, and the crime rate had soared.

As he viewed the scene below him, the numerous different licenses on the vehicles and the cargo each vehicle carried told a sordid story of total social collapse. If this was not conclusive enough, the telltale signs of murder were very much in evidence. Looting was among the lowest forms of depravity. The word itself did not adequately describe the crime. Taking advantage of a fellow human being in his hour of need was hardly an aspiration worthy of human classification.

O'Riley's final convictions regarding these delinquencies were confirmed by the ever-present area representative. It was difficult to imagine that such a polluted social system had arisen so quickly from the ashes of defeat.

Combative measures had to be taken immediately and a front had to be established. True, the contamination was fairly widespread from border to border, and all the people could have trouble later in their lives, but much of the people's trouble was mental. The main front was still the contaminated area where the dark cloud of destruction had passed. O'Riley was able to fly over that area, sometimes at a height of fifty feet. Since the soil, water, vegetation, and air samples had been taken for neutralizing experiments, the next step was up to the government to marshal its forces and justify its existence. The foreign courier had not yet arrived with possession papers, and it was highly doubtful that the country could find a sponsor of any description at this late date.

○

The inspection tour continued for five months, and it took a great deal more than financial stability out of O'Riley.

Now he knew what frustration actually felt like. It was a rotten feeling which affected the individual proportionately to the size of his or her ego. In O'Riley's case, he was sick.

No doubt remained in his mind that the country was defeated. At least, to the standards of past battlefield results, it had already suffered the third largest man-made disaster of all time. The signs of utter chaos, panic, and broken morale were everywhere. Never had he seen such conclusive evidence of social collapse. The entire scene was so monstrous that it was impossible to believe. Had it happened because of a defeat on the field of battle, O'Riley could have accepted what he saw. This defeat was the country's own fault. Even if the explosion had been caused by a foreign enemy, in truth the people killed themselves by not having the leadership necessary to head off the panic. Only half the effort expended in the panic would have been needed to ensure the safety of the many lives which had been lost. It was officially estimated that four hundred people lost their lives. Four million would be closer to accurate, and millions more would die long before their allotment of years was reached.

Subhuman acts were so prevalent that the main disaster was almost forgotten. Thousands of citizens had used what few faculties they had retained, in order to prey upon the panic-driven hordes of humanity. Whatever the human mind could imagine had indeed happened.

O'Riley was sixty-six years old, and he had been retired for nearly three years. His chance of ever meeting with Tyron Jrcy was a thing of the past, and his chance of grabbing the free-ride token had never existed. He was just another human body, a free commodity of no recognizable value beyond any other. As he passed through the portals of his country for the last time, he could be thankful that he was still alive and able to retain his own self-respect.

In fact, O'Riley's swan song was not exactly unique. In the world's very sophisticated societies, the theme was repeated uncounted times during the course of each day. The consequences on the individual took varied forms, from criminal to ecclesiastical. The impacts on the people seldom, if ever, had reached above the local level. As for O'Riley, there was no outward effect on the stoical personality of the old battlefield commander. However, the very probable repercussions for the people would this time extend far beyond the local environs.

Chapter Seven

The Martels

For years it looked as if John Martel would be the heir apparent for the leadership of his country, but John's interests lay elsewhere. He was a man of high intelligence. Although his early training on the field of battle would seem to have prepared him for a more drastic approach to survival, Martel chose to focus on natural resources and the environment. As it turned out, he was without peer in his chosen professions. He was one person who could have made a lasting and positive difference in the affairs of the world, if the world had been looking for such a person.

Nele Martel married James Moran when she was nineteen years old. Moran was a magnetic person who could have made a fortune selling empty pop bottles. The man chose politics as a career, and within ten years after he and Nele were married, Moran was elected President.

What might have appeared to be just another victory based on a charming personality quickly turned out to be quite unlike what had been expected. James Moran, in his short tenure as President, set some noteworthy precedents. No longer did the people have to be upstaged when they took their problems to the Capitol. Moran took the government to the people. The voters had elected him, and if they had any ideas of losing another politician behind one of those ten-foot doors at the Capitol, the people were due for a revelation. The citizens would pay Moran a high salary for the rest of his life, and he meant to give something in return: leadership. They had elected a man with a great personality, and by accident they had a leader instead.

In many ways the human race had to be on an unswerving path of destiny. James Moran died one year after he was elected to office.

The world was probably full of potential leaders, champions who could do the job if they could once gain the enclosure of the lists. Moran had made it inside those lists, but the script of destiny read very differently from what he had planned.

For several years after Moran's death, Nele helped John manage the Martel business empire; and after their parents died, they brought a younger generation of Morans and Martels into the business. For the first time in their lives, Nele and John had time to pay attention to the problems of the national government. It was actually not surprising that Nele eventually took dead aim at the nation's top office.

One year after Nele assumed her political role, the woman, for the second time in her life, had to place her hand on a Bible and swear to carry out all duties as prescribed by the laws of her country. The ceremony was not as solemn as the rituals Richard Mansan put her through years before, but the job carried a bit more status with it. Nele Martel Moran had become the new President by an overwhelming majority vote.

The quest for the purple robe had taken undeniably strange pathways during man's presence here on Earth. The modern day political procedures, which jealously guarded the portals of the throne room, were definitely easier to pass through than some of the earlier obstacles had been. Nele Moran demonstrated how ridiculously easy it could be.

○

The government President Nele Moran led was unsophisticated in the respect that it was small and organized in a way allowing it to be enlarged with knowledgeable personnel in times of emergency. Moran's government had a few different wrinkles in it, but the basic idea was typical of stable nations that were rich in natural and human resources. There was no limit to the country's internal spending power during national emergencies. This simple fact permitted economic stability without internal or international impacts. Only a strict and intelligent government was necessary to administer the action.

The number of candidates that Moran had to beat out for the Presidency was unlimited. There were no handpicked candidates' names on the ballot. Virtually all citizens within a specified age limit were eligible to be voted into office, and voting was compulsory. In effect, the list of candidates was unlimited, and the people could vote for anyone they chose to vote for, so there was no compelling excuse not to vote.

Each member of the President's Cabinet represented a certain division of the country's industries or services, and each member was voted into office by those people directly connected with that sector of the economy.

Elections were held every year in conjunction with the voters' compulsory reports to the President and Cabinet. Those reports were then published for everyone to read.

Government was a highly responsible undertaking, and hanky-panky in politics was a serious crime.

So, in some respects the government led by Nele Moran was different from the other governments of the world. Whether Moran's system was right or wrong depended upon its ability to serve the people without undue negative impacts. This was why the laws were passed which made public involvement in the actual formation of the government a compulsory action. If the people made a mistake in their choice of an official, it was their duty to go on record, admit their error, and correct it.

Additionally, Moran's government routinely considered the impacts of its actions on the other nations of the world.

On the whole, the actions practiced by Moran and her staff officers were basic. If a unique feature was involved, it had to be the stripping away of all camouflage from government processes and undertakings. This approach to national and international stability was possible only when the gold standard was set aside. Most stable societies took this avenue in times of national emergencies, but general acceptance seemed to be incredibly difficult because of one word, *greed*.

The system accommodated national emergencies by realizing the potential of the people, and by using them as administrators in their specialty fields. This way, the citizens had full confidence that their leaders were knowledgeable, and also that the people's interests would be protected. During emergencies, the government would lead, supply, and support the people. It was the simple case of a nation using its resources, natural and human, to survive.

Maybe Moran's approach was the way the human race was meant to live. If it was, a great many people were on the wrong trail. The world's natural resources were being used as though there were no tomorrow; they were largely wasted or polluted. And the saddest case of all was the debasement suffered by the most important resource of all, human beings. Although some general opposition to this degradation did surface, it was based mainly on frustrated oratory and negative action.

○

Briefly then, Nele Moran's government started by compulsory and general voting for the top position. From that point the election procedure worked down the ladder with fewer voters involved. By contrast, Tyron Jrcy's Northland government started from the bottom, with the people of each state voting for their choice of National Councilman or Councilwoman. The National Council then chose the Chief Council from the nation at large. The major difference would have been the staff of officers led by each head of state; unlike the specialized members of Moran's Cabinet, Jrcy's Council did not come anywhere close to meeting those qualifications.

Other differences between the two governments were not particularly unique. Typical along this line was the fact that Jrcy's government was still extremely heavy at the bottom, with many overstaffed minor agencies in operation. Customarily, all governments had embraced this overstaffed structure, at both top and bottom. The proliferation of expensive and unnecessary leadership had a wide variety of justifications; everything from the convenience of the people to the convenience of the government was used as an excuse. In reality, most of the governments achieved the same goals; and if the negative results could be overlooked, it could be truthfully said that their accomplishments added up to zero.

Jrcy's country did recognize the existing national emergency, and this action, in itself, was commendable. The Northland was rich in natural and human resources, and it knew exactly how to use these resources without any interference from the gold standard.

How much Jrcy would change his government remained to be seen. In Manson's estimation, government was man's weakest accomplishment, and, generally, people propagated this weakness by allowing their governments to stay perpetually overstaffed and uncoordinated. This proclivity was looked upon as the best method of ensuring a type of government that would have minimum impact on the civil liberties of the people, expensive but not dominative. There were several drawbacks to this line of thinking.

During normal times, the chain reaction of events which led to economic depression; the chain reaction of events which led to morale and social breakdown; and finally, the resulting impacts on the rest of the world, including war and other disintegrations in international relations, were the outcomes of poor government. At this point, it looked as if another problem had been added, a problem which made the rest look amateurish.

Pollution of the environment was the finale of all adverse human actions. Unlike the very elements man mixed to form pollution, the end product remained forever unchanged with a catalytic quality which contaminated the air, water, land, and every form of life. Even the air and ocean currents, which spread the contamination, could change in direction and intensity.

The human race had a problem, only if its educated estimate of the future would permit recognition. However, estimates of future situations had always played second fiddle in the symphony of human life, sometimes degenerating to the pretense of actual playing. Under the direction of a competent leader, there could be no faking of instruments whatsoever; the people paid for sound and not pantomime. One fact was crucial: the future must be given equal billing at all times.

Tyron Jrcy and his forces had recently been caught up in a situation which could have been avoided by an intelligent estimation of the future. Now Nele Moran was using the time that Jrcy had purchased for her.

○

Nele's first step was to close the borders to all immigration, and her next step was to develop what she had to work with, in order to prevent disaster from engulfing her country. The sounds of Nele's actions were loud and clear. In a way, a certain show of panic was involved. Such a grave situation should have worldwide coordination, and not just individual national effort. However, if the world leaders had come out from behind their ten-foot doors long enough to have managed such a cooperative effort, there would have been no adverse situation to deal with in the first place. World coordination between nations was an almost mythical action which had eluded the human race, and yet the answer was so close to home that its simplicity would not allow belief.

On a national basis, governments had a tendency to display a high profile. This was ideal during countrywide emergencies. During normal times, a much lower profile was desired, and the family structure took center stage. The family leaders reacted as would be expected to the norms and emergencies of daily living. If, for any reason, the emergencies were far out of proportion to the norms, the family would have a noticeably more difficult time coping. It could not possibly go off the gold standard. Failure of the family unit to adjust would need to be recognized as the first crack in the national foundation. The governments which recognized the importance of the family unit only in terms of the support it rendered were starting the long chain of reactions which led to economic depression, social decline, and international war. It was essential for the family unit to remain firm; that was the very foundation of any country.

Nele Moran was not personally bothered by a weak family unit, and as the leader of her country, she considered her main job to be ensuring that other family units were not bothered.

She looked toward the sparsely inhabited western section of her nation for development space. Most of man's past activity in this region had been limited to extracting nature's riches from the land. As nothing had ever been done to improve the land rather than deplete it, the western area had remained virtually unsettled.

After the disaster with air contamination, the possibility existed that the people in the eastern section of the nation would have to be evacuated in an attempt to take advantage of the air currents which flowed north over the western section. Thus, the western land would prove ideal if evacuation was necessary. If evacuation was not necessary, the nation needed room for growth, anyway.

Water and electrical power would be needed in great quantities, and nature had very generously furnished the basic components for survival.

The western region was an expansive area of semi-arid land, bounded on the west by two thousand miles of coastline. It was this coastline that drew Moran's attention, especially the many sheer rock-walled inlets which funneled the ocean water inland at an ever-increasing rate of pressure. At some of these locations, the powerful surf rose into the air for two hundred feet above the ocean level.

It took three months to blast the first tunnel through three hundred feet of solid rock. The tunnel was twenty feet in diameter and emptied into a vast natural interior basin, eighty feet above the elevation of the ocean level. The experiment was a complete success, and approximately three million gallons of water a minute gushed into the interior basin in a nearly continual flow. Solar evaporators and electrodialysis cells were installed which produced fresh water, totaling millions of gallons each day. Part of the salt water was returned to the ocean through turbines which operated huge electric generators.

There was the possibility of developing nineteen similar water and electric plants on the west coast, and Nele Moran would lose no time breaking the ground for construction at all nineteen sites.

Currently, the small number of highways leading west could possibly turn any evacuation into a nightmare. When Moran explained this problem to the people, they came up with a tentative answer to the problem by holding evacuation drills, using every available watercraft and aircraft to relieve the congestion on the western highway.

At the time Nele Moran started the development in the western part of the country, this action was looked upon as a possible escape route from atmospheric pollution. However, in her proposed five-year plan, the west would one day rival the east in development. She wisely planned to build two new highways connecting the eastern section with the west.

○

Throughout the world, substantial time had been wasted by the usual nonessential bickering. It was the same old story of man's inability to recognize and activate a worldwide survival program without the usual human frailties surfacing. As long as disaster was not knocking on the front door, business as usual was the order of the day.

Governments appeared to know better than to start a war, but the arms race was something out of science fiction. National defense budgets had eventually arrived at a new word in human vocabularies, *trillions*. The different nations could not even agree as to how much money a trillion of any monetary denomination actually represented.

The impact on the family unit in most countries was so monstrous that the traditional family structure was changing. Birth rates had dropped, and the age-old ceremonies which bound man and woman together were becoming obsolete.

Many nations had fallen to a point where they could no longer control their death rates. Starvation and disease were already affecting the fragile economies in the world, and per the usual chain reactions which govern all human affairs, the trouble was spreading.

Nele Moran had closed the borders to immigration. What did this mean? The answer was very simple. The panic was on, and people were scattering like quail. Survival had become an individual effort for them, and they saw Moran's country as their last frontier, a sanctuary where a few more troubled years of life could be salvaged. In reality, it was too damn bad. People deserved a better break than they were getting; they did not deserve what was happening. Nor should any animal on Earth ever have been subjected to such degradation.

Part III

Richard Mansan

"They were genuine leaders not only with the ability to do the job themselves, but with poise enough to involve each human being to the point where responsibility became a personal thing, and the final outcome or accomplishment became a component of each individual's destiny."
– Michael Earl Nolan, 1976

Chapter eight

I LOOKED UPON O'RILEY AS A PARADOX, a staunch defender of the status quo, who had an ear for what the crackpots were saying. He was not the usual pretentious ass who changed beliefs to best fit the company he found himself in. He was just the opposite. To the crackpots he appeared to be a defender of the system, and to the system he was all crackpot. The combination just might have worked, except for one slight flaw. O'Riley appeared to be a neutral, and ordinarily that would work. It would not work, however, in those crucial hours when an issue was in doubt.

He had missed his chance when he met with his National Council. The very fact that he was not taken into their confidence told the entire story. Leadership qualities had to be existing in both O'Riley and the Council; otherwise, one party could not possibly recognize the other. This did not mean that the members of the Council were beyond help. It simply meant that they had no confidence to share with O'Riley, nor among themselves.

The general had returned home without being asked. Once he was home, there was no recognition of his arrival or of his continued presence in the capital. Those hours he spent with the Council produced nothing.

I thought a great deal of O'Riley as a friend and as a leader. It was astonishing, but the very personality and character traits which made the man outstanding, in my opinion, were not visible to the government he served.

He had made one sizable error in judgment during his years as a soldier, and that error culminated in his last visit home. I knew there would be quite a bit of retrospective thinking about his final hours in the capital, but the main fault in those hours lay with the National Council. What O'Riley should or should not have done was of no importance now. He had chosen to inspect the disaster zone and make recommendations to the Council. This was probably the best decision he could have made.

The tip-off to his one error happened about twenty years ago at the time he chose to write about the battle of Morea. Even renowned leaders could not afford to cast others in the leading roles, and Morea was definitely not one of his better parts.

I was probably one of the very few people in the world who saw the logic of O'Riley's actions. He wrote about the battle of Morea because it was part of his long-range plan for a meeting between himself and Tyron Jrcy. Admittedly, such a meeting was not as impossible to imagine as it might have appeared. Jrcy was already closing in on his nation's Chief Council job when the book was written to remind him of the debt he owed. The account of the battle was worded in a true allegorical style which fit only the period of time we were passing through, and the main characters in the book had been preserved for their later appearance on the actual scene. The book was a masterpiece of metaphoric literary skill, and I was certain that O'Riley had accomplished much beyond what he imagined. The writing style, and not the content, had caught the imagination of people throughout the world.

Maybe time would prove that I was wrong about O'Riley's schema for the future, but I could not see any benefit to his long-anticipated meeting with Jrcy. O'Riley's first step should have been to ensure his own advancement up the political ladder, instead of wasting half of his life planning a meeting.

Meetings between national representatives were strictly components of the status quo. They had accomplished nothing during the known history of the human race. Solely by example could we bridge the gap of greed and human degradation, and the beauty of example was that the stage must be set on the home front. Until our own national problems could be solved, it was more than doubtful our leaders could solve the problems of the world. We had overlooked this one great weakness to such an extent that we failed to recognize a very sad fact: many of our leaders could not manage to hold their own family units together. They should never have been allowed to meddle in government at any level, but again we appeared to sanction the weak approach to government.

At times, it seemed ridiculous to even consider the possibility that one person could have a constructive impact on the future of human events. To foresee such an impact, we needed only to consider those people who were capable of leading. In this group we needed only to consider those few who would try for the brass ring. O'Riley had spent the better part of a lifetime trying to establish what he determined to be his best position before he made the final move. He never achieved the position he sought, and in this respect he probably typified the leader's role in our modern society.

Tyron Jrcy had spent more than half a lifetime on the trail of the elusive bauble as well, and he had won.

Nele Moran had achieved the goal within a year's time, with nothing more going for her other than a famous name. This did not mean that Nele was not a leader; it meant that she had won the Presidency because of the name *Moran*. How she subsequently handled the job had nothing whatsoever to do with her name.

O'Riley had returned home of his own free will, and any voluntary action which approached the exalted area of acclamation was most certainly doomed for failure. As might be imagined, there were several variations of this procedure, but failure was the one constant which was always present. I, personally, would not volunteer for a damn thing, and yet, I was surprised to learn that the man had failed to be recognized by his Council. I guess I was totally wrapped up in O'Riley as a leader. I had been convinced he would accomplish the impossible and be recognized, regardless of what method of approach he used.

○

I was also returning home, and like O'Riley's, my actions could be considered as voluntary. I needed a ruse of some kind, something that would change the entire complexion of my endeavor. My gimmick would have to disrupt the thinking pattern of the government and the people. I could, basically, set my own time limits on my future actions, and I had several thousand miles of room between the beginning and terminal points of my journey. In that distance, if I could not appear in whatever guise I chose, then I was not qualified for any role.

My journey to the capital of the Northland would have to assume the proportions of an odyssey. Unlike the ancient epics, the record of my actions had already been written before I started for home. The written account of my travels did not deal with the usual prosaic impacts long associated with the human race. The elysian foundation of my script merely expressed my mind's ideal of the fantasy lands I would pass through. I could thank O'Riley for this stylistic bent. His book about Morea was indeed a work of art.

President Nele Moran had been my collaborator, and the series of articles I had written of my coming journey would have worldwide distribution. For some unknown reason, human beings had always accepted what they read as the very acme of veracity, and I meant to stretch their imaginations to the limit. As I said, my writings were elysian in content – no ax to grind, no politics, no sour grapes, no insurmountable obstacles to overcome, not even a fair maiden to rescue or a dragon to slay. I was the veritable "Mr. Goodbar" who had all but passed into legend before he ever made the scene.

I would not return to the Northland this time by way of Valmy. My route would be across the southern nations which lay between Moran country and the Northland capital. My itinerary in each of the ten nations I would pass through would be lengthy, pleasant, officially approved, and published. If I accomplished nothing else, I planned to be the most talked-about person in this part of the world. People were curious by nature, and I was willing to bet that every scrap of information about me would be dug out and enlarged many times. I was finally making my bid for a leading role.

People were also afraid of leaders, and for a person to be in the right position when he or she was needed would be almost impossible. In the history of the human race, the few accepted leaders were great showmen who played various roles, from the slogging foot soldier to the elegantly robed head of state. They represented the potential within all human beings, the highest symbol of human dignity.

In fact, we had most likely divorced ourselves from leadership to a point where real leaders could no longer emerge from our sophisticated social systems. Only in our imagination could the dazzling robes of leadership be visible. I was about to use the props I had, in order to set the stage for my first and final appearance. The more dazzling my entrance could be, the better chance I would have.

As much as I hated to leave Nele Moran and John Martel, I could not allow myself to accept such an easy way out. My ideas were based upon certain unconventional convictions I had. Our lives were exactly what we made them. I could not accept the status quo as set by others, and I did not give a damn about political procedure. There had to be more to life than following some accepted mundane form of existence.

The first leg of my journey would be a three-thousand-mile ocean voyage. I would then have ten countries to pass through before I reached the southern boundary of the Northland. At that point in my excursion, I would make up my mind what my next move would be. This would definitely be an odyssey which could take months, years, or a lifetime to complete. Yes, I could actually close the book on my affairs by just traveling for the remainder of my life. This was not as unusual as it might seem. Thousands of people throughout the world followed similar routes every day, and we heard nothing about them. If the truth of the matter were known, we did not give a damn either.

The countries I would pass through were classic empires of an ancient era, and to me they represented a part of my life I would never be able to fully understand. As illogical as it might be, I had fought through two wars in these highly unlikely settings. Now, more than forty years later, I was returning with as little logic for my actions as I had the first time around. At least, no one would be killed this time unless my idiotic smile was fatal.

Today I was not exactly a stranger in this part of the world. The idyllic accounts of my fantasy journey through these fabled lands had preceded me. If that was not enough publicity, O'Riley had inadvertently ensured my immortality when he wrote the book about the battle of Morea. There was also the possibility that his actions were not as inadvertent as they appeared to be.

One other unique feature I had going for me was guaranteed to focus attention on my actions. I was well known to the dominant figure in this part of the world, Chief Council Tyron Jrcy.

As I thought of Jrcy, I realized that he could very well have the same inflated image of me which I had of myself. This could work to my advantage or disadvantage, and I was confident that Jrcy had already taken steps to find out what I was up to. He would be aware of every move I made from the time I stepped aboard ship until I arrived at the capital. I would soon find out if my estimation of the situation was correct; meanwhile, I planned to present a paradoxical front which should keep the name *Richard Mansan* alive. I had waited my entire life for this chance, and had no intentions of blowing it at this late date.

Other thoughts were on my mind as I started my journey north, and they were not all as pleasant as I would have liked them to be.

Since the last disaster, scant news had been coming out of the Northland. This could only mean that the disaster was still having an impact. In O'Riley's country alone, the current count had reached four million deaths, and it was impossible to tell how many other people would eventually die as a result of this latest human blunder. One-half of the people in the world had no permanent records kept of their existence, and as they had no worldly goods to be exploited, their lives and their deaths remained unknown.

There was one person in the world today whose record was well known, and it did not take a genius to guess that he might be battling for his life at this very minute. Tyron Jrcy had alleviated any doubts I had about one person's ability to have a constructive impact on the future of human events. It was too bad the members of the human race could not be a bit more cooperative in our bid for survival, but we seemed bound to a particular lifestyle. We were perfectly content to sit on our butts, backs to the wind, and watch the receding scenery. The rosy picture of the future, as painted for us by our leaders, was all the tonic we needed to salvage what nostalgia we could from years gone by.

Salvaging nostalgia from the past was a luxury I was about to enjoy, and in this respect I hoped to impress everyone who followed my actions that I was, indeed, a living example of how our golden years should be spent. Not only should we watch the receding scene of life throughout our early years, we should, as a culmination of our life's effort, get off the speeding vehicle of time and retrace the past at a much slower pace.

I would be walking back over my old battlegrounds. The battles should never have happened, but they had happened; and on this trek, I was planning to use those same sections of land as an excuse for being in a certain part of the world. No one had ever questioned the inseparable tie between the soldier and his battlegrounds. Whether the cause was just or not, or whether the participant was on location in a voluntary or involuntary sense, made no perceptible difference. Once the battle began, everything else ceased to exist, and the individual's value was exposed for general observation. It was the one time during the life of a man when he had to completely strip his character of personality gimmicks. Yes, the tie between soldier and battleground was very strong, and at least once in later years a return visit should be made.

Of course, any justifications I made for my actions were plainly meant to test the illusionary power those actions would have on others. With all my deception, I understood that I was depending on Jrcy a great deal. My feelings in this respect were very real; and long before the first leg of my journey was over, I would know precisely how favorable, or unfavorable, Jrcy's efforts would be in my behalf.

○

When I requested permission to leave Moran's country, I ensured that the skipper of the Northland ship I would travel on had plenty of time to clear my passage with his superiors. Jrcy would have been alerted to my latest move, and his officers would be watching my actions throughout the countries of my journey. I was depending on this. Now that I was on my way, it was evident to me that Jrcy was, indeed, in the act.

Captain Wades of the Northland did his damnedest to change my mind about leaving his ship at the first port of call. He verged on insisting that I not leave ship until we arrived at Valmy. I had no intentions of returning to Valmy, and I certainly was not about to tell Captain Wades what my true intentions were. To all appearances, I was an aging eccentric on a vacation trip, visiting my old battlegrounds and friends I had not seen in more than forty years.

Jrcy would not buy such a ridiculous story, but I doubted if he could guess exactly what I had in mind. If he could, the man would have to know more about my plans than I did; variables and unknowns could always change my plans around. Jrcy's health was the one unknown which caused me the most concern. The months of exposure to the contaminated rain, wind, and ocean spray could prove fatal to him and the members of his task force. If we lost Jrcy, there was no one else. He was the only person in the world who captured the imagination of all people. This was the secret, the very key to our survival.

During the past year I had begun to have some misgivings about our ability to clean up our pollution. It seemed like a simple job for strong governments to clean up their own mess. I just was not sure we had enough time left. I knew it was crazy, but I actually believed that the world needed a symbolic figure: a veritable hero, someone who could influence all people, a living legend who could take us off our gold

Grabbing the Brass Ring

standards. The person I had in mind could rekindle the last filament of imagination, the thin thread of dignity which still had to exist in each human being. Was there such a person? I thought there were many people who had the necessary qualifications. The one drawback was that these people were not in a position to help even themselves. Jrcy met the requirements, and what was equally as important was the fact that he was in position.

In my own way, I was trying to get a modicum of attention thrown in my direction. Within six months I would be able to see how well any "attention campaign" was paying off.

I lingered in each country until it must have appeared to everyone that I was planning to take out permanent residence. If the truth were known, permanent residence was the least likely thing in the world to occupy my mind. This part of the world was doomed.

The pollution of the world was concentrating at an increasing rate in a belt around the equatorial region. There was every indication of increased air currents, but the most alarming evidence was the migration pattern of several wildlife species. These creatures were in tune with nature's actions. Air and ocean currents were her directional signals, and right now the arrows pointed north. The unfailing instinct of the animals could lead the more dormant human species to safety. I was already heading north, so I felt that the wild creatures and I were not too far apart in the intelligence department.

The final leg of my journey would take me over the vast mountain range which marked the southern boundary of the Northland. This greatest of the world's mountain ranges was a natural weather regulator. It was also a monument to nature's phenomenal landscaping ability.

From the start of my adventure I was reminded of an old story I had read a long time ago. I had forgotten all but a very few of the words: "The traveler's approach to the capital was announced by the ringing of silver bells."

There were no silver bells today, but the present means of communication seemed to be just as efficient. My approach to the capital, however indirect, would be known long before I arrived.

○

Six months had passed since I left a very disturbed Captain Wades, and during that time I had indeed found considerable similarity between actuality and the script I had given to Moran before I left her country.

For the past ten days I had been traveling through the mountains at the

Northland's southern border. My pack train was a trifle larger than I needed, but the only guide I could find had a large family. In keeping with the image I was trying to promote, I had insisted that my guide bring all of his family members along for company.

This was the morning of the eleventh day. We had started to eat breakfast, when I noticed the approach of five horsemen. I had been expecting company for the last several days, and I presumed that my visitors would be the Northland border guard detachment. The silver bells, or whatever communications these people used, seemed to be in good working order. The horsemen were about a mile down the trail from my camp as I trained my binoculars on them. This would be the first time since I began my journey that border guards had showed any degree of energy. Usually, they sat behind desks, or stood listlessly by road barricades.

The first rider was a woman, and for a fleeting instant I recognized an old friend, General Marina Costa. My eyes had to be playing tricks on me. The woman I was looking at was Marina Costa as I remembered her from thirty years earlier.

Lamira Costa?

I had never met either of Marina's daughters, but everything indicated that this woman inarguably was Marina's younger daughter – her looks, her field officer's rank and, finally, my unfailing instinct. If I was right, I might be able to get her a trifle off-balance by upstaging her a little. It was worth a try.

The party dismounted about a hundred feet from my camp, and the woman walked toward us. I rose from my sitting position and waited.

"You are just in time for breakfast, Colonel Costa. Will you and your soldiers please join me?"

The woman smiled slightly and extended her hand. I thought she handled the situation quite well, but then I had to remember that this person was something special. When she spoke, there was a certain flattery in her voice which kind of caught me off-guard.

"Colonel Mansan, you are truly a very unusual person. The patrol and I will be delighted to join you for breakfast."

After asking Colonel Costa if she would stay for breakfast, I was careful not to ask her any more questions. This gave me a small advantage. The choice of conversation was up to her, and I was in a much better position to protect whatever approach I reasoned would serve my purpose best. My direction of travel was north, and there was nothing I could do about that. The previous six months had been spent traveling over an area I could have covered in days if I had been going anywhere in particular.

As it stood, I was not at all certain how Colonel Costa interpreted the meaning of my journey, but I had tried to convey the impression of a rich man enjoying a leisurely vacation, a very well-publicized rich man. The fact that I was traveling north was of no importance; I had to travel in some direction.

I assumed I had gained my first objective, and I could afford to wait for the bits of information which would be dumped into my lap. Colonel Costa was definitely not a border guard, and her presence here was not accidental. I liked her approach. The woman was an expert at putting me on a pedestal, from which I could topple quite easily.

Costa's conversation at breakfast encompassed everything from the last year's food harvests to the changing weather conditions. I could feel the deadly seriousness in the woman's voice. She had been born and raised under the most severe survival conditions. There was no doubt about her ability to analyze the present situation, and her leadership qualities reminded me of her mother.

When breakfast was over, Costa handed me a letter from Chief Council Tyron Jrcy.

By this time my mind was on the past disaster and those negative fringe benefits it was still causing. Reading Jrcy's letter could have signaled another step forward in my own private action plan, but instinct told me that my plans would have to be changed again.

Welcome back home, Richard Mansan. I am looking forward to seeing you upon your arrival in the capital.

Jrcy

The writing had the light touch of a woman's hand, and the content of the letter fell short of what I would have expected from a man of Jrcy's confidence. To confirm what I had already guessed, I turned my attention back to Costa.

"Colonel, what is wrong with the Chief Council?"

Hopefully, she would not play me for a dummy by answering my question with a question. This would be a dead giveaway that the woman lacked leadership, and I had no desire to be wrong in my previous estimation of her qualities.

Costa's voice was just a bit too high when she answered.

"Chief Council Jrcy is in the hospital."

I motioned for the lieutenant of the guard to join us, and Costa requested that he return to the border station and arrange for our transportation to the national capital.

My guide would accompany us as far as the station where a helicopter would be waiting to fly Costa and me to the nearest airport.

For more than six months, I had been waiting for a summons to the capital. Now that it had arrived, I had mixed emotions about the outcome. Jrcy had probably contracted an overdose of radiation during his assault and subsequent cleanup of the contamination. Whatever the outcome of my recent actions would be, I had a feeling that a new twist in future events had been added.

There was another development which was not in keeping with my overall picture of the future. What was Colonel Lamira Costa doing almost a thousand miles from the capital at a time like this? Meeting some old eccentric duffer was not my idea of what a future head of state should be doing. In fact, the appearance of Colonel Costa in my life was the one touch I had with reality. Many years ago I had drawn my own conclusions about the final outcome of human destiny, and today my mind had changed very little. I remained quite a way off-base when I compared my line of thought with the programs followed by the governments of the world. It seemed unreal to me that our leaders could assume such high responsibilities with so little to offer in return.

Our journey to the capital went as planned. Once we arrived, transportation was waiting for us at the airport, and we were driven immediately to the hospital.

○

Jrcy was sitting up in bed as I entered his room. Of course, I knew that the man I was looking at was Tyron Jrcy, and he knew that his visitor was Richard Mansan. I could not help but wonder if Jrcy could recognize me after more than forty years. I was looking at a living skeleton, the remains of a human being who could not possibly have retained the power of remembrance, a mere rack of bones held together by a layer of parched skin. Where the man got the strength to move his body was a mystery, but Jrcy actually stood up and approached me with his arms outstretched. I almost cried for the first time in my life. Here was a human being who, in all probability, had saved the entire world. Now, nothing was left but his skeleton. Even as I held him in my arms, I was afraid he would fall into a pile of bones at my feet.

Jrcy, without a doubt, appeared to be dead. There must have been just enough fighting spirit enduring within the man to keep him from recognizing his true physical condition.

In reality, it was a miracle that Jrcy was still alive. The fact that he was standing was impossible. I did my best to show no outward signs of emotion whatsoever. I was not about to take away the last small thread of his confidence by being overly solicitous.

I talked for the few minutes it took Jrcy to turn and make his way back to the bed. He seemed delighted that I considered him capable of the show of strength he was giving me. I was astonished by his actions, especially when he kind of swaggered. Costa and the doctor could have interpreted Jrcy's slight shifting of the shoulders as a sign of distress, so I shook my head to ward off any action they might have taken. I could easily see that the two women did not think too highly of my actions, but they backed off. He made his return to the bed without incident. The priceless indomitable spirit which all people aspire to was expressed in Jrcy's smile as he sat down on the edge of the bed. He did not have sufficient strength left in his body to talk, but he could smile.

My short visit with Jrcy was most inspirational. I was the one who was supposed to help pick up the pieces, but it turned out to be the other way around. I also gained ground in another direction, a direction in which I did not need any special inducement.

I was furious. The sight of Jrcy had turned me more than ever against the stupidity we used as our guideline for existence. Right at the moment, I did not give a damn whose toes I stepped on.

At the end of the visit, I requested that living quarters at the hospital be furnished both to Costa and to me so we could be near Jrcy. Any idea the Council might have entertained regarding a meeting with me would need to be postponed. I was not leaving the hospital. If the members of the Council did not agree with my actions, they could tell me so face to face.

Today I had reached a milestone in my life, and my emotional outbreak caused me to take a belated second look at the ground I had covered.

For the past months I had been playing a little game with the Northland government, one step forward erased by two steps backward. I wanted no impression made that I was advancing. Stupid? It was very stupid. It was so stupid that I had just stepped back a bit farther to the rear.

Since I had shown reluctance to meet with the Council, I was depending on its members to give my latest actions several different interpretations. Turning my back on them could not exactly be interpreted as a step forward. It could, however, signify that I considered a meeting with the Council to be unethical at this time, or it could mean that I considered a meeting with them to be a wasted effort. There could be no recognition of either side's qualities, so why invest the time? Beyond that, I was not about to insult Jrcy by any discussions with the Council.

I had substantially more on my mind than how the Council would interpret my actions. Our lack of competent health and safety administration was my first worry. Pollution was rampant, a full-time enemy of the people. The sole recourse was good government. All profit, revenge, and status were no longer possible as criteria for leadership. Every nation had to clean up its own mess. If this was impossible, then the international scene was doubly impossible.

Our last disaster had brought our real enemy out into the open, with as yet untold devastation from that error. It might even have been the final particle that caused the saturation point to be reached. Whether the finale would be called the "day of reckoning," the "fulfillment of human destiny," or the "beginning of the long road backward" would have to remain unanswered. It seemed so simple to understand, but like the millions who had already died, my thoughts to date had the same impotent impact.

In each battle I always had a tendency to equate the first dead to myself. The second dead always proved to me that miracles did exist, and that I was one of the chosen few who would make it all the way. Today I was looking for the miracle to come first. Jrcy had to recover; he was the only acknowledged leader in the world who could make the difference. He was a leader who could beat the elements, and would clearly have an impact on world events.

○

I did not, for a second, have any doubts about Jrcy's will to live, and I could honestly see daily improvements in the man.

Our visits usually lasted about ten minutes in the morning, afternoon, and evening. I laughed when I thought of how I had conned Costa into changing her official attire for something less depressing. I had told her that we should be careful not to remind Jrcy of anything connected with the government. Government business, officials' titles, and Army uniforms were strictly taboo. I was taking dead aim at the atrocious baggy uniform Costa wore.

Many weeks passed before I decided to take up residence outside the confines of the hospital. Jrcy was now able to take short walks around the hospital grounds. He began to have the Council in for weekly meetings. This was a healthy sign, but no one other than Jrcy knew if he was ready to assume his duties again.

So far, I had purposely avoided any official contact with the Council for the very simple reason that I had arrived at my destination, and I needed to create a diversion to explain my presence without losing the proximity.

Jrcy was, by no means, out of danger. Radiation was a most unstable and unpredictable affliction. It worked on the human body with the suddenness of a powerful drug. One day the patient would have superhuman faculties, then lapse into a coma the next day. Controlled amounts of radiation could cure or retard several known diseases. Uncontrolled amounts of radiation caused instant to protracted deaths. I was hoping that Jrcy would be lucky enough to survive. If he did not survive, I would need quite a lot of maneuvering room.

My stay at the hospital was gratifying in one respect. Jrcy did make miraculous gains back to normal health. In other respects, my prolonged stay almost drove me out of my skull. I was a firm believer in action. The still-life studies, economic analyses, multiple-use plans, and whatever else the government used to justify its existence were not the vehicles we needed today.

It was an ongoing mystery to me why we had chosen the route we had. I told myself that we were money-crazy, but money only served its purpose when it met our needs. The strongest of human emotions was the will to live a comfortable and happy life. If this was true, then we had lost our sense of real values. The enemy of mankind was just plain everyday man guised as a leader. He did not necessarily have any particular nationality, race, or beliefs. He merely needed one prerequisite to bring havoc to his fellow creatures. The irony of the entire sad affair was that the very prerequisite needed to seal the fate of the human race was created and awarded by the people.

In our rush to reach our Elysium, we had chosen leaders who allowed us to pollute our planet. This covered it all, the air we breathed and the food we ate; even the clothes we wore and our household appliances were contaminated. Again, we, the people, could trace our own guilt back to our choice of leaders. We had lied so much to justify our mistakes that we were blind to the disaster closing in on us.

I sometimes wondered if total destruction was, in reality, the ultimate goal we had set for ourselves. Could this possibly have been true?

It was extremely difficult to believe that the normal human mind would knowingly destroy human life. After more than fifty years of living under those conditions which sharpen the survival instincts, I was probably the one person in the world who saw the very worst in our way of life.

Regardless of the strength or fallacy of my convictions, the predetermined events of the world proceeded in their usual predictable manner. Tyron Jrcy died three days after I left the hospital, and my old friend Lara took over the office of Chief Council.

○

Colonel Costa and I accompanied Jrcy's body to the far Northland where we buried him within a few feet of my old home. This was Jrcy's last wish. It was, more exactly, Jrcy's last order to his people. A man who had consistently led by example was actually setting his final example even after he was dead. The order was to move north, the one area in the world which could resist the spread of contamination. It was difficult for me to realize that the human race was capable of producing such fine leaders as Jrcy, and yet we were failing in our efforts to survive.

Now that I was home again, I appeared to have reached my own Elysium. If I had been expecting my attitude to go unnoticed, I was due for a rude awakening. Colonel Lamira Costa was not taking too kindly to my latest change of pace. When she did voice her objections, the words had a certain remonstrative quality about them which gave me a feeling of immaturity.

"Does the great Richard Mansan think that all he has to do is sit on his butt in this godforsaken shack? That is no way to grab the brass ring."

For one reason or another, I had always imagined myself in the driver's seat. I was a firm believer that the brass ring, as I called my pet fantasy, was mankind's most glittering and elusive bauble. Not even the duly chosen or elected leaders were capable of capturing this valued prize of human aspirations. They did, at the same time, guard it so closely that only a very limited number of men and women throughout our history had come within reaching distance of the free-ride token.

The fact that Costa had guessed my secret was an omen. "Grabbing the brass ring" was just an expression of mine, tantamount to the world tour many people promised themselves. However, I had to admit she had awakened me to the possibilities which still existed. I was more convinced than ever that Costa was a genuine contender, and that somehow her future was tied in closely with my future actions.

During the past two years I had made a complete cycle; I was right back where I started. I found myself sitting in the same overstuffed chair. Nothing had changed, except one very conspicuous addition to the scene. Colonel Costa was standing by the fireplace, and I could easily see that she had no intentions of leaving without me.

"All right, Colonel. If we leave immediately, we can catch the others before they arrive at the settlement."

Ten other people had accompanied us to Jrcy's final resting place, and they had left about an hour earlier. I knew it was silly, but my interest in the future had increased considerably in the last several minutes. I was sincerely looking forward to the trip to the settlement. It seemed like only yesterday when I had first traveled those fifty-five miles, breaking trail for the dogs all the way.

Today there was no need to break trail, and the nine dogs were anxious to get started. They were the same animals I had given the postmaster two years ago, and they seemed determined to capture my undivided attention. Handling a dog team was tricky business; I alone could interfere with their strict social structure. I had learned that any outward show of emotion toward the dogs was no job for an amateur, and that the lead dog must be treated as the undisputed leader. The rest was simple. The other dogs would follow their leader. The human factor entered into the picture solely in the care and welfare of the team, and it was necessary for the lead dog to be present when that care was administered. Because of this, I made sure the harness connecting him allowed for his separate removal and attachment.

The lead dog stayed by my side as I harnessed the rest of the team to the sled, and he watched with interest as I made a big deal about Costa's comfort. After the preliminaries, I connected him to the front of the team, and we were on our way.

Supper was waiting for us at the settlement, and after I returned the dogs to the postmaster, I joined Costa at the inn. She had been quiet the whole day; even my jovial attempt to cheer her up by singing had met with less than moderate success. I would probably have made the situation worse if I questioned her. If she wanted to take me into her confidence, I knew she would. There was a chance that my apparent reluctance to leave my old home had a lasting impact on Costa, and I could not blame her. My actions had been a show of total irresponsibility. If the truth of the matter were known, I had pulled so many ruses during my life that it was hard for me to carry through with any certain play without bringing in a diversion. I figured I could switch back into Costa's confidence much more effectively if I pretended to ignore her preoccupied attitude. At least, it was worth a try.

We had finished supper, when I spoke to Costa about our return trip to the capital.

"Colonel Costa, I realize that you are needed back in the capital, and that you will want to catch the next flight out. I had planned to make the return trip by helicopter. This will permit me to stop over at several points and see some of the country."

I had already guessed that Costa also needed a bit of maneuvering room, and the only way she could possibly get that room was through me. The return to the capital at this time was an excellent way to get lost in the bureaucratic woodwork. An extended tour of the northern part of the country was not the complete answer to Costa's problems, or mine. What it did give me was time to come up with another approach, something which would keep me in the public eye without actually being a threat to Lara and the National Council. I was depending heavily on my estimate of both Lara and the members of the Council. They were not leaders, and they could not recognize a leader. They would, however, notice if anyone made a play for that leadership, and I wanted to be sure my timing was right.

I needed the brass ring at this stage of my life like a hole in my head, but I felt that Costa's chances were tied in closely with mine. Costa was still young, and I recognized her as a true leader, a leader young enough to have a bearing on future events for some time to come.

At the moment, my potential young leader was not too happy with her self-acclaimed benefactor.

"Mansan, what the hell are you trying to pull? First, you gave me that ridiculous pitch about taking up permanent residence back with the wolves. Now, you tell me it was not in your plans at all. If you are thinking about giving me the slip, you can forget it."

Nothing I could say to Costa would have added to or subtracted from the situation, so I stood there smiling like an idiot. I had only one route to follow. Tomorrow morning, Costa and I would fly by helicopter to the next settlement. If all went according to my plans, we should be back at the capital within three months. This would be plenty of time to show Lara and the Council that I had no other designs except to follow the life of a peaceful, non-involved farmer, a decision I had just arrived at minutes earlier. The role of a farmer should put me as far away from the affairs of state as I could possibly get. From such a seemingly inauspicious position, I would be setting my sights on one of mankind's weakest points, the structure of the vital agricultural society.

Chapter Nine

Before Colonel Costa and I left Mansan's outpost, I made arrangements to set up base camps throughout the area we would travel. Food, fuel, and camping equipment, all local products, were purchased and sent ahead. The local dealers even insisted that I accept a discount on supplies. I also hired a cook, a native-born Mansanian. I took a great deal of pride in this. To be exact, I took a great deal of pride in the settlement, the peninsula, and the entire region from the seaport of Valmy to the North Sea. In many ways, the blueprint for our continued survival was right here for everyone to see. If I had to explain it to Costa or to anyone else, I would be wasting my time.

Costa knew the history of the Valmy Peninsula as well as I did, and she knew that the other similar areas in the north were supposed to be developed along the same lines as the peninsula. Now we would see just how well the government had followed through with that plan.

I wanted Costa and the others who accompanied us to enjoy themselves during our tour, and I wanted to see what stage of development the other areas had reached. These were not really my true motives, but they might hide the fact that I needed more time before I met with the National Council. As a fringe benefit, Costa would recognize how totally incompetent the leadership was in the remaining regions. Where would this lead? Well, Costa would be able to see what was holding back our northern development programs, and acting Chief Council Lara would, in all probability, call us back to the capital before our tour was finished. I needed this last possibility to come true. All my life I had connected voluntary action with failure, and I certainly was not entering the Council chambers unless Chief Council, Mr. Lara gave me a special invitation.

Our sight-seeing tour was unquestionably the soundest investment I had ever made. By the time Costa and I had spent three months in the field, Lara requested that we return to the capital. I was as happy as a kid with a new toy. My next move was a command performance, which definitely took it out of the volunteer class.

○

This morning, as I entered the Council chambers for the first time, I had General Lamira Costa preceding me by about ten feet. The members of the National Council were standing and applauding. I attributed this display of enthusiasm to the presence of Costa in her new general's uniform; she was a real eye-catcher, and I could not miss this opportunity to show her off. I could tell by the look she gave me as we entered the chambers that she was well aware of my carnival antics. What Costa possibly did not know were the reasons for my actions.

The lives of most people fell into three main time divisions. The first division included our birth and those early years under our parents' care, which prepared us for the next forty years of life. During those forty years, we passed through the second division of our lives, a time when we peaked out, or established our social standing in the status quo. The final division of our lives covered that period of time when the human body lost its physical and mental faculties at an increasing rate until the life cycle was ended. As mundane as the normal cycle of life appeared to me at this very moment, I could not help but realize that I had never quite made it. My peaking-out time must have happened while I was asleep. This, by itself, did not bother me as much as the realization that the people watching my entrance undoubtedly represented the champions of the status quo, and if they knew nothing else, they would know exactly what phase of the life cycle I was in today. I was depending on Costa to give the members of the Council something more important to occupy their minds than my age. If I had allowed her to walk by my side, this would have been interpreted as an old man's crutch. That was one prop I did not need.

The members of the Council, including my old friend Lara, appeared to be impressed by my entrance. To be frank, I noticed that they were over-conscious of my presence. Only General Lamira Costa's arrogant personality prevented this initial encounter from becoming downright patronizing.

Costa would preside at the meeting, and I was depending on her to keep me as far in the background as possible.

Whether I liked the present setup or not, I was, indeed, at front stage center, quite conspicuous and with no script worthy of my talent. It took a while for me to size up the situation, when something unforeseen came to my attention.

It was critical for a leader to enter the arena exclusively at those times when his or her services were needed. I was fortunate because the Northland system of government accommodated such an entry. I was also fortunate enough not to get carried away with my own ego this morning. By coming up with another diversion later in the day, I could most probably change our first meeting around to fit my own immediate desires. At the present time, I wanted no governing responsibility. True, the development in the far north was not moving the way it should be, but that was a matter the present leadership would have to iron out. I expected that these development projects would give General Costa a challenge she could get her teeth into right away. It was a position tailor-made for advancement. My own tactics no longer included working in the far north; that was a job for a younger person.

All my life I had been on the lookout for the ideal position, that place where I could reach out and grab the brass ring with no effort whatsoever. To a great many people this might sound like the thought of a lunatic. Actually, the rationality of such a thought became feasible among those people whose lives bordered on the survival type of existence. This was unbelievable to the members of the status quo, but it did exist. The odds against a national leader emerging from such surroundings were astronomical. Only in the case of dire national emergency would it be possible. Even the armed services did not look too closely into the lives of their fighters until after the wars were over. Yes, time was equally as important as position was.

I found my thoughts quite amusing. The different versions I had of grabbing the brass ring each embraced position and the elegant props which dressed the stage for my final lunge or coup d'etat. Now, I found myself already in position. One small detail was needed to complete my own version of the changing of the guards. The time factor was totally wrong.

The present lull in human events had again settled into the conventional routine of normalcy, and the merry-go-round of chance had come to a dead stop. This was not my mind's ideal of the way it would happen. There had to be other props on stage, specifically something which stirred the imagination in all people. I called it "timing." Without the right timing, regardless of how favorable the position, my efforts were destined to meet with the same failure which had always plagued governments. Maybe that right time would never come, and maybe this would be the closest I would ever get. At least I could say I had once been in a position where I could have had the whole ball of wax. I honestly could not gain much consolation from my present philosophical thoughts; but who could know...within a few years I might be grasping at straws. "What might have been" might be all that was left. Costa's voice brought my thoughts back down to earth.

"I have with me a land use application from Mr. Richard Mansan, which I submit for the Council's review and approval. The land is located in the Mango Valley, five hundred miles north of the capital. I also have the recent aerial photos of the area, which Mr. Mansan has taken, as well as a copy of the legal description of the property."

Costa had sensed the situation as only a true leader could, and she had made the only diversion pitch that was possible.

Lara barely glanced at the application, then passed it on with his approval.

After my land use application had been approved, Costa gave a long, detailed report on the progress of the development projects in the far north, and I could tell that Lara was embarrassed by the slow progress of the work.

Originally, Lara, the Governor of Valmy, Marina Costa, and I had agreed that the peninsula north of Valmy would be developed first. The entire northern region would then be developed along the same lines. The words meant very little with the political setup as it was so many years ago, but today Lara was running the show, and it was logical to assume he would remember our agreement.

As things stood, the peninsula north of Valmy was fully developed, and most of the rest of the north country was still in the engineering planning stage. I could have made excuses for the lack of resource development if the agricultural groundwork had at least been started.

I could tell by Costa's overbearing attitude that she was highly displeased with what she had seen during our tour. One look from the woman was worth a thousand words. I had remained quiet throughout the meeting, but there was always the possibility that this same Council would one day be listening to a quite different-sounding voice, and I could guarantee them that General Costa's voice sounded much more pleasant.

○

In two days, I planned to leave for my new home. Janus Costa, Lamira's older brother, was setting up our camp in the Mango Valley, and I would bring the engineering personnel with me when I left the capital. Spring was a few weeks away, and I wanted the engineering work finished the first year. This would include land surveys, soil tests, geology studies, groundwater exploration, surface water records, wind velocity measurements for electric power generation, hydroelectric dam site locations, and surface water controls. Provisions would have to be made the first year to control all flood waters caused by excessive rainfall or dam failure. I was not about to allow a faulty dam structure to be built, but I would have to face up to the possibility that nature could destroy any structure. Finally, I would have to prepare the ground for planting, and I would construct the latest in farm buildings and utilities. Mango Valley would be a showplace. Since I had become a very rich man in this country, I would be setting a practical example by reinvesting in it. I was one crackpot who could afford to give something more tangible toward our existence than mere oration or frustration.

The goal I had set for the first year was an ambitious one, but the real issue was not the amount of work I had chosen to accomplish. My biggest problem would be to overcome the possibility of the status quo creeping into my operations. Man's activities tended toward change in respect to quantity. My main job would be to ensure quality changes, not only in the finished products, but also in the actions of the people working for me. After all, there was absolutely no reason for me, or for anyone else, to have more of an interest in the development of the Mango Valley than the most unskilled laborer on the job. We all had to think this same way, or revert to the status quo. The name of the game was survival, and I was trying to use certain people to set up a blueprint everyone could follow. If I were to have trouble with the usual mundane problems within my own ranks, whether they were factual or fictional, I could not expect to accomplish a damn thing.

There were many government and private approaches to our crucial problems, approaches which I did not accept; and each problem dealing with agriculture was crucial. As on the very battlefield itself, human life was in the balance. The difference was that agriculture was necessary and war was not.

In agriculture, we were fighting the obvious and correct approaches with the same atrocious tenacity we used on the battlefield. This seemed to be our hallmark.

Agriculture was mankind's first and foremost show of intelligence; yet, today we overlooked agriculture and built our lives around every nonessential possibility that crossed our minds. It was surprising the number of people whose knowledge of food began and ended with the supermarket, but it was this manner of thinking that made the farmer's transition from serf to free man an unbelievable nightmare. In reality, the transition was still taking place. We either looked down our noses at farmers, or failed to recognize their existence. From the administration of the people involved in farming, through the connected manufacturing, commercial industries, and management of natural resources, we normally took an interest only when it was financially to our advantage.

Jrcy had not lived long enough to have a constructive impact on the life of the farmer. He might have been the one who could have changed it all around. We would never know.

It seemed logical to me to assume that somewhere close to the agricultural picture was the actual position I had searched for throughout my life. I knew I had once even looked in the vicinity of the battle lines for my ideal ambuscade, but now I had to be a realist. Battle lines were becoming rare, and variables were not exactly what I was trying to build my hopes on these days. The ruffles and flourishes for any future stage entrance I made would have a pastoral lilt.

Over the years, we had used education as a supplement for basic intelligence, and in some respects this technique had paid off. As yet, our international relations and the administration of our agriculture remained in limbo. This basically covered it all; but as long as potatoes came in bags and money could be made by someone else's death, our values never quite reached the height they were meant to reach.

Air, water, and food had always made up humanity's first needs. Mankind highly developed education, and had established the fact that ten thousand years ago the human species was using air and water to raise food. The other necessary elements such as iron, sulfur, and magnesium generally came with nature's soil. Whether man was aware of this at that time did not make any difference. What did make a difference was the spark of intelligence which showed when he started to plant and raise food.

In this day and age, we knew significantly more about farming than was known ten thousand years in the past. Not only had we found other natural soil conditioners like calcium, potassium, nitrogen, and phosphorous, but we also had used certain species of other animals to work for us and supply our needs. Yes, there had been undeniable shows of intelligence since the advent of humanity. What I could not understand was how we could have lost our intelligence to a point where we were overlooking our first hope for survival: agriculture.

It had been years since I allowed myself to get emotionally involved in the affairs of state. I remembered the old days with O'Riley and some of the tactical gems the brass used to dream up. Today I could laugh, but at the time my emotions in no way reflected happiness or amusement.

At present, I found myself named to Lara's advisory staff, a position I had not requested, and a position I would only agree to accept without pay. Regardless of many negative aspects involved, I felt as if the appointment had been tailor-made for my immediate needs. We were delinquent in our farming methods. This included our administration of the farm personnel, production of farm equipment, and the use of our natural resources. The way I saw the situation, there was no use improving one fault without improving all three. If the government officers were unsure of their ability to administer to a strong agricultural society, then we were going to "lose the battle on the home front," another of man's time-worn phrases which had a better than even chance of now being fulfilled.

○

Lara and Costa visited with me at Mango Valley on an average of two times a month, and I did my best to make their stays something they could look forward to and enjoy. My selling pitch was not an oral thing; example was the order of the day. If the real live picture could not stir the imagination, the oral offerings were sure to be lost. All I had to do was develop my farm and make my visitors comfortable while they looked at the progress.

I meant to show by example how a farm should be put into operation. There would be drawbacks at first. Nature's water and wind would have to be harnessed for power, and shortages of farming equipment and supplies would need to be overcome. If there had not been some drawbacks, it was doubtful I would have chosen farming as my approach vehicle.

Not all of the obstacles were overcome the first year; however, with the help of Janus Costa, our soil technicians, and a few good heavy-equipment operators, I was able to start a soil-conditioning program. Natural drainageways were reconstructed to harness any excessive runoffs from future flooding. The soil conditioning was done on a contour pattern, and future plowing, planting, and harvesting would follow that same pattern. My policy for the complete development of the area might have confused Lara, so I made sure the man understood my tactics and the thinking behind them. Food was our main need. We already had enough of the nonagricultural goods and efforts. If we kept up the way we had been going, we would soon be the most malnourished rich people in the world.

My spare time during the first year was taken up by meetings with the several engineers I had and with Lara. Lara presented a problem, and the best strategy I knew to handle the situation was to keep him on the farm as long as possible. He was not a leader, and the only way I could qualify my thoughts in this respect was by saying I simply did not recognize him as a leader. Although this served to satisfy me, there was a key to this recognition factor that I trusted with so much faith.

My own special key for leadership recognition worked exclusively under those conditions which warranted a leader – natural and man-made disasters. The remainder of nature's and man's actions required a management type of government, the smaller in size the better.

Currently, I identified a pending natural disaster, and my key to discern leadership qualities in my fellow human beings embraced two simple criteria: Was this pending disaster acknowledged? Were steps being taken to neutralize the resulting impacts? As primary as my recognition factor seemed to be, natural disasters in the history of the world had always caught the people unprepared. Of course, man-made disasters had caught the human species unprepared, as well. Leadership or government, whatever we chose to call it, was not exactly one of man's fortes.

We had known countless rulers and would-be rulers, but I had met only two working leaders in my lifetime, Tyron Jrcy and Nele Moran. I certainly could not class myself with these people, but I did understand the basic characteristic of leadership: "Follow me." I also understood the basic characteristic of the ruler: "Go and do it."

A world of difference separated the two traits.

Right now, I was trying to be a leader by setting an example which would show how our resources in this one area of the country could be used to ensure our survival. It would then be up to the management of Lara and the Council to see that the people got the help they needed. There was no designated recorded procedure to follow. Each region would be different; the land, the climate, the resources, and the people would all be different. There would be problems, and these problems could not be answered by just telling people to go and do it. I had a great many complaints against the ruling type of government which looked upon the people merely as a source of revenue. The government must be first and last the leader of the people.

○

Today I was feeling about twenty years younger, and when Lara arrived at my farm, I decided to say exactly what was on my mind.

I made sure Lara understood that I supported Jrcy's resource development program throughout the Northland, and that I supported the phasing-out of top-heavy government agencies. We were looking for leadership from our officials, and this would not be possible until we had some laws the officials could use as guidelines. I supported government regulation of price control with open ledgers for everyone to see. The welfare of the people was what government was all about, the sole reason for its existence. Unlimited spending was a serious crime against the people. I could have gone on forever, but the more I talked, the more emotional I became. The thought of forcing people to justify their existence by supporting incompetent governments was hard for me to swallow.

Lara was kind of foxy in a primary sort of way. I guess he figured I was a little tightly wound at the moment, so I would have a belligerent attitude toward all government agencies. He knew that I advocated a low-profile type of government during normal times, and that during crucial times I advocated a very high-profile government. As far as I was concerned, the present time was crucial. I did not think we had to be beaten to our knees before we started to take action. The wild animals seemed to avoid such predicaments. Lara was well acquainted with my version of our looming problem, and I talked with him in detail about the possible impacts our polluting habits would have on our country.

There was one topic I had avoided discussing with Lara, or with anyone else for that matter. We were all prone to errors in judgment, but no one wanted to take a chance by reducing our military strength. I was certain I saw our military forces in a completely different light than did any of my fellow citizens. Jrcy had used our military once to save the Northland, and very possibly that one action had saved the entire world. At least it bought us some time. Thousands of our men and women had died as a result of that deployment, and I, for one, considered that our military forces had more than paid their way for all time. To them, we owed a debt which could never be repaid. I was also certain we would need these forces again. There was, however, a question in my mind about how they should be used; in our sophisticated world, the same question could be asked about each of mankind's inventions. What had always started as a basic survival tool soon gathered sophistication in design and use. At the time being, even the word *survival* had a different meaning than it had for our ancestors. If the truth were known, I was a strong advocate of military power, and I was a strong advocate of leadership. Yet, as it stood, I was not in agreement with the general use of either our military or our leadership.

My official duties were to advise Lara and the Council, and I made it clear that our country had already paid me in advance for any services I could render now or in the future. I would do my best not to run out of fuel before I crossed the finish line. Talking was not one of my stronger points, but it was the strongest point with many people. Unlike O'Riley, who had maintained strict silence in the presence of his superiors, I had chosen to push my points just as far as possible.

In a way, my new oral approach seemed better suited for me personally than the action approach I had adopted.

○

There were several features about contour farming which not only efficiently garnered the benefits from the rain and snowfall, but caused the total procedure of farming to become much easier on man, horses, and machinery. Because of that, I had carried the contouring throughout the farm. After the first pattern was surveyed in, plowed, planted, and harvested, the outline would remain visible for years. According to Janus, he had seen fields where this configuration was identifiable after a thousand years.

My second year as a farmer was the most gratifying time of my life. The farm had been primarily planted in clover, with a few hundred acres planted in vegetables and grain. The results were far beyond what I had expected. No other farm in the country could match our production per acre, and we had done the job with old secondhand machinery and a small number of horses.

I had made a big production of the housing I furnished the four families who worked for me, but this was, in fact, my major project. If we did not combine human dignity with our development, we would be in no better shape than we were before we started. I expected a change in quality from the people who worked for me, and it was logical that I had to give a change in quality. Farm help was our most important asset, and the old impoverished living conditions had to go. I was a government official, and I considered that my main job was to administer to a strong agricultural society and to those scientific and industrial components of that society.

To be accurate, I had done nothing new from a farming standpoint. After ten thousand years, it did not seem probable that too many new methods remained unknown. My farm was productive and clean. The buildings and utilities were the latest designs, and the families who worked for me were happy, healthy, and confident. This was what I was selling to the dignitaries who visited me. I had set the stage in such a way that it was our system which was on display, the way it was meant to look.

For some reason, the people had not been getting everything out of life they should have. Was the poor lifestyle of the farmer the result of poor leadership or poor management, or did it make any difference what nomenclature we gave our government? The comfort and happiness which made up our first emotions should have been available for all people to enjoy, with no strings attached. It was the government's only responsibility to see that this was a fact, and whether we called the government "action management" or "leadership" was of no importance. There was really nothing for a government to do during normal times, except to serve the people. We had somehow reversed this process and added another load to the backs of the people. Even during crucial times, a government's only duty was to lead the people in their fight to retain those high standards of living established in normal times. This action definitely fell under the heading of "leadership."

I did not truly believe that the good Lord had laid His hand on my shoulder, or that He had singled me out in any way for special attention. I did have to admit I had been fortunate in my new venture. With the shortage of necessary farm machinery, I was still able to accomplish what I had set out to do the first two years.

Now that I had my feet on the ground more firmly, I had an extensive study made of the groundwater on the farm. Moisture in the preceding two years had been plentiful, and there had been no need for irrigation. Nature, however, had a habit of not always giving us the help we were primed to use. At this stage, I had time to prepare for nature's change of pace.

Ten deep-water wells were drilled, and their operation was set for both electrical and diesel power. My geologists were quite certain I would be able to have a minimum of twelve thousand acres under irrigation. The usual large storage reservoirs would not be necessary, and small storage tanks with purification units would be installed for our homes and for the livestock.

○

When Lara arrived for his scheduled visit, I could tell that the man was worried. As no immediate disaster was facing the country, I assumed that his trouble was of an administrative nature. What I did not expect was Lara's reluctance to continue our development of the far north.

To many people, this development represented a complete rupture of their ties with the status quo, and the thought scared them. There was no doubt in my mind that Lara's latest orientation was influenced by the National Council, and that he could have been looking for some confirmation from me. I viewed the new turn of events as another surfacing of the same problem which had always existed, the ubiquitous difference between the management and the leadership types of government. I was well aware that Lara headed up a strictly managerial government, which could prove adequate only as long as no crucial problems arose.

He might not have foreseen the reaction his newfound hesitation would elicit from me. In all honesty, he had just given me the breakthrough I had been waiting to encounter.

I reminded Lara of the rich natural resources he had in this part of the country. Wealth was dear to the heart of every good manager, and the Valmy Peninsula was an excellent example of what Lara could expect throughout the northern area. Valmy was currently providing a large portion of the nation's economy. The rest of the northern region, with its limitless riches, was a veritable cold storage for all of the world's remaining treasures. I knew that developing the area would do a great deal more than change the status quo, and might very possibly be the one place on Earth where mankind could survive.

Lara also had other things going for him besides the natural resources. Our very capable military forces, who had saved the ball game once, were standing by with absolutely nothing to do. What a shame it was to waste so rich a source of engineering expertise, especially since we could use it to such good advantage.

I could tell by Lara's expression that I had found a "live one." The possibility of selling him my entire line was too good to pass up.

"Mr. Chief Council, if you decide to turn over the northern operation to General Costa, I would like to have your permission to visit with her from time to time. I am not out of the woods here yet, and I will need Costa's engineering advice, particularly on the hydroelectric plants. If these plants are designed to develop maximum horsepower, I am confident I can supply cheap power as far away as the capital. It may even be necessary to construct the main plant north of the Mango Valley, in General Costa's new field of operation."

I had rung the bell three times with Lara, as I mentioned the rich Valmy Peninsula, the fact that our military forces had all the engineering expertise needed to finish the northern development, and the enticing possibility of cheap electric power for the capital. That third one was too much for him to turn down. I thought the whole idea was custom-built to ensure the immortality of both Lara and Costa. No matter what the finale would be, the north was our last frontier. We could only lose by waiting.

Lara was the type of person who gave gold top billing. I was focused on survival; gold, for any reason, played no part whatsoever. I would never be able to sell that pitch to him, and there was a good possibility I would never live to see the day when I could say "I told you so." Maybe it was this philosophy which made me search for gimmicks to dress up the mundane events in my life. Whatever my hang-up was, I was growing stale in my present location.

○

For the first few years in the Mango Valley, I felt sure I had left my vagabond habits behind me. Yet, as the area developed to its full potential, I began to depend more and more on Janus Costa to manage all of our interests.

Lamira Costa must have been watching my actions closely; she and Lara still visited with me quite frequently. Between the two of them they managed to keep my mind occupied with problems which had probably taken quite a bit of their time to dream up. They eventually arranged for an extended inspection tour of the north. I did not need this kind of a diversion, but I went along with it. Anything was better than the absolute tranquility of the Mango Valley.

I had noticed that as we grew older, the answers to all our failing faculties were relentlessly compiled by younger people, who saw each sign of nonconformity as a further deterioration of the physical and mental being. In my case, I was not certain that the word *deterioration* was applicable. I was certain, however, that I needed something to look forward to. Maybe this was only another way of saying I needed something to keep me alive.

CHAPTER TEN

O'Riley, Jrcy, and the Martels

O'RILEY LIVED FOR SIX YEARS after he left his country, and he traveled extensively throughout those years. It was difficult to guess what contributions to the status quo he could have made, but it was doubtful he could have matched Nele Moran or Tyron Jrcy for sheer drive or determination. O'Riley had missed the boat in his move toward the top, and he missed it by approximately twenty years. He should never have written about the battle of Morea. Several other battles which he could have chronicled would have assured his fame as a leader, but instead he wrote about Morea as part of his long-planned meeting with Jrcy. It might have succeeded too, but fate had other plans for O'Riley, and for Jrcy.

Tyron Jrcy, the man who led the first actual assault against worldwide pollution, had himself fallen victim to the exposure he received in the course of that battle. He died two years after his sea and air assault on the polluted atmosphere; and in accord with his revealing final request, Jrcy lay buried in the frozen Northland, on the same section of land Mansan had called home for many years.

The government that Jrcy left had a hard time maintaining the leadership standards he set. Security or insecurity was instilled in the minds of the people by the type of leadership they had. This was not unique. A phenomenon was involved, however, where the people's confidence was reflected back to the leader. Yes, there had been a time right after the disaster when Jrcy's country was riding the highest crest of popularity. It was the first time in the history of mankind that one nation had the influence to show the way, but like O'Riley's bid for power, Jrcy's country had also missed the boat.

Nele Moran's country thrived during those years following her program of western expansion; and when she decided to retire from public life, no other nation in the world could match her country's standard of living. Nele Martel, the small girl with the king-sized temper, became the world's greatest leader of the era. Others could possibly have equaled her record, but they simply did not have the type of people in back of them that Nele had. Although the very important divisions of the Moran system remained strong for a time after she retired from the scene, the government was now a big question mark.

Assuming that the crackpots were right, and that nature's forces were fragile enough to be upset by man's obnoxious bungling, would the planet Earth, at long last, join those other dehydrated masses in our universe? Ridiculous. It was not even within the realm of human comprehension, and the meaning could never be grasped fully until the curtain went up on the final scene of the final act.

There was a certain futility in all human actions, a futility which led to resentment and frustration in the minds of most people. There was resentment to the known fact that man, under the guise of raising his values, had made a mockery of the very qualities which would have ensured his own immortality. There was also frustration, and since the bottom had just about dropped out of the reservoir of human characteristics, only frustration came close to filling the void. Whether frustration was or was not a human characteristic, in truth, made no difference; it was much closer than any of the remaining available traits.

Moran had retired and Jrcy was dead. Both were outstanding leaders. Was there any one person in the world who could effect a positive change in world affairs?

The empires of the past had fallen, and the history books were filled with myths of past heroes who led their people to victory on the battlefields. It did not matter if these stories were true or not. One fact remained: There were no great empires today; and if there ever had been, they must have fallen. Fallen mythical empires left behind very poor precedents to follow.

If such a person did exist in this day and age, a person who could impress all people enough to listen, he or she would have to be recognized. Here again, the members of the human race were a bit out of their element.

John Martel could have been the world's most admirable human being. This did not qualify him for leadership, but his credentials should have caused many people to wonder if indeed this was not the person who had the answers.

Through Martel's efforts, the ocean water could now be economically used to turn the deserts into productive fields, and the oceans could now provide a never-ending supply of food. Humanity could have survived forever. Martel had other accomplishments to his credit, including the wind tunnel to generate electrical power. Nothing was truly original about his basic ideas; only his methods proved more practical.

Martel could have been the one to save it all. His own people recognized him, listened, and profited. On the international front, he did not have a chance. That stage was overcrowded with actors, individuals vying with each other for that one moment of glory which would justify their existence. If Martel had been looking for the perfect perpetual-motion machine, he would have been inspired by the continual and untiring vocal efforts made by the chorus of foreign leaders.

When John and Nele retired, they decided to spend their time managing the Martel fishing fleet. Nele especially loved the fishing business. Since the days her parents had allowed her to sail with Mansan, she had a strong attachment to the sea.

Nele had never been able to separate fact from fiction where Mansan was concerned. The man had a habit of leaving the scene long before anyone really knew him. She remembered how hard Mansan worked almost fifty years ago to make the Martel fishing business a success. That time he left while Nele was visiting relatives. She never forgave him for what she considered a grave slight to their friendship. Years later, during Mansan's last visit, he supervised the work on the first water and power plants. The man overlooked nothing. He was like a small boy. His enthusiasm was contagious; it was a personality all people accepted and shared. Then he left the scene again. That was ten years ago. Both John and Nele assumed that Mansan would return, and they even reserved a room for him at their large home in the western part of the country. The tie with Mansan was unseverable.

○

Richard Mansan

Chief Council Norman Lara, Chief of Military Operations Lamira Costa, and General of the Army Alexander Navaro would be my traveling companions during the upcoming inspection. This whole affair was Costa's idea. I seriously thought the woman was determined to keep me in circulation by sheer proximity with the brass. There was an overbearing streak in Costa's personality, and it manifested itself every time I showed signs of setting up permanent housekeeping. I had to admit that my actions had been slowing down recently, and Costa could have been trying to keep up my interest in current events. To explain my paradoxical lines of thought and action would only add to the already anti-logical aspect which I had created. I was certain that Costa read me quite clearly, and I could expect her to take more of an active part in my affairs from now on.

Today I was headed in the general direction of the Valmy Peninsula and my old home. Could Lara and Costa have possibly guessed that I was still fully capable of jumping ship?

The first stop on our inspection tour was the settlement of Naron, five hundred miles north of the Mango Valley. Costa would be the official master of ceremonies during our tour, and right away she made a big production of her role by showing me in detail what a fine electrical engineer she was. I was impressed by the entire electrical development around Naron. The power plants were the latest designs with generators, transformers, and power lines protected by heavily insulated housing and conduits. The source of water power, which operated the turbine-driven generators, came from a deep mountain lake. A series of eighteen-inch-diameter holes had been drilled through the solid rock bed of the lake to a depth of five hundred feet, where the holes intercepted a ten-foot-diameter tunnel. All holes were plugged before the drills were removed, and heavy-duty well casings with cut-off valves were set and grouted into place. The lower ends of the casings were then connected to a main reinforced service line in the tunnel. Turbine-driven generators operating off the main service line were capable of producing more than two hundred thousand volts; the transformers and power transmission lines could deliver high voltage to any location in the Naron region. As usual, Costa's morale was high, like Jrcy's before her; water used to operate the turbines was purified, and she was working on strategies to recycle the water as efficiently as she could. The hydroelectric plant at Naron was typical of the ten plants which she had designed throughout the far north. The plants operated without the danger of freezing; and as no dams were involved, the danger of dam failure due to earthquakes and floods was also eliminated. Costa stressed this last point.

I had been carried away with Costa's engineering ability, and it had not dawned on me, but I was being harpooned by that same competent individual. When Costa mentioned dams, I recalled I had been instrumental years ago in building a dam for hydroelectric power at the headwaters of the Onque River. That had been a very expensive project. Since I had been kind enough to foot the bill, the government graciously named the structure after me. Costa was well acquainted with the dam on the Onque River, and she knew who was responsible for its existence. The Mansan Dam was, indeed, a monstrosity which I still believed could actually defy the forces of nature and man for all time.

However, I was not about to get into some long-winded discussion with Costa about the relative merits of dams and whatever she called her design. On the contrary, I encouraged her to expound further, not only on the components of the electric plants, but on the progress she had made in farming, food processing, construction of storage buildings, hospital facilities, and waste control. I was an expert at surviving in this harsh land, and I knew that Costa had given us the start we needed.

The one feature lacking in Costa's program was housing development, man's most abused use of nature's land. We had fifty million people in permanent residence throughout the far north, and we could wait until we knew how much of the land would be needed for farming. No longer could we afford to build large cities, and no longer would we build on our choice farming land. As safety factors to prevent a housing shortage, the Air Force could deliver temporary housing within hours, and the people currently in residence could easily accommodate another fifty million.

With the food surplus we had already stored and the good fishing potentials we had off the north coast, it looked as if we could meet our population increase for at least another thirty years.

Natural disasters were something else, and they were also something the majority of our people did not believe possible. If a natural disaster ever struck, we could thank our rapid increase in population for the present development in the north. It was laughable to think what the people's reactions would have been if disaster had been the government's sales pitch.

In a world where listening was not considered a human virtue, the voices of Richard Mansan and my fellow eccentrics were mainly mixtures of polluted nitrogen and oxygen which were all too soon assimilated by the Earth's flora, nature's thin first line of defense against pollution.

We spent two weeks in the vicinity of Naron, and our inspection covered the entire region. The activity was precisely what I needed to snap me out of the lethargy I had fallen into these past months. Costa's programs showed a lot of intelligence...no unnecessary industrial development, just plain survival needs with backup programs using every resource we had. This time we were playing for the highest stakes of all: our lives. We always had been.

Our inspection was not the once-over-lightly type of ceremony we associated with government officials. This time nature would keep everyone honest. Whether we were faced with future overpopulation, pollution, or natural disaster, nature offered no quarter in this part of the world. The time for survival was now, and we knew it. We could not possibly survive at a later date if we overlooked the present elements of nature. In reality, we were the most fortunate people on Earth. In order to live, we had to develop the northern part of our country. We were fortunate to have the vast northern area, and we were more fortunate yet that nature ruled this area with an iron hand. Man and man's polluting habits...yes, including the results of man's pollution in the temperate zones of the Earth...would all have equal chances of failing in this part of the world. Man could make it only if he learned a new set of values, sans gold, pollution, and human debasement.

Our main means of transportation on this tour was the helicopter; however, this comfortable vehicle was usually parked at some residence, and we traveled by horse, automobile, dog sled, or whatever fit the climate and the terrain. Our current housing varied as much as our transportation. Food presented no problem. Since we had nearly a hundred million people engaged in food production nationwide, a few additional VIPs did not exactly cause a major impact.

When we arrived at the far northeastern point of our journey, I figured that this would be the last chance I would have to jump ship. I had been in this same position many times in my life, and I had never varied in my actions. Now, for the first time, I would stay aboard. Not that it would have a hell of a lot of impact at this stage of the game, but for once in my life I would try a different approach. It was not a forward movement, nor was it the usual retroceding feint I had long practiced. If my true thoughts were known, I no longer considered myself a serious threat to Lara, Costa, or anyone else who might have his or her sights set on the brass ring.

What was even more leveling was the condescending attitude I noticed in Lara and Costa as soon as we started on our return trip to the capital. Lara had consistently given me the impression that he expected me at any second to ease him out of his comfortable chair. Costa had that overbearing streak in her which was always most noticeable in my presence. Now the milk of human kindness genuinely seemed to flow in the veins of my two traveling companions. Whatever had changed my status in the eyes of my two admirers must have happened only recently.

○

It was more than ten years ago when I launched my own personality campaign to capture the imagination of all people. At the time, I was riding the crest of a personality wave which could have carried me right to the top, a normal political situation that had nothing to do with my qualifications to handle the job. That I had later turned my back on the opportunity plainly showed both Lara and Costa that I did not consider the job worthy of the qualifications I had to offer. Today there was something else in the wind. Richard Mansan, a naturalized citizen of the Northland, was appointed by the Chief Council to the posts of Assistant to the Chief Council and Secretary of National Agriculture.

In all honesty, I was more amused by the episode than I was surprised. Costa and Lara were making a big production of the affair. Costa even handed me a box wrapped in elegant purple tissue and tied with a gold ribbon. I unwrapped the gift and took a very unique trinket from the box, a small brass ring. The inscription read, "Welcome home, Mr. Secretary."

With the brass ring in the palm of my right hand, I stood there looking at the two people in front of me. The three of us were smiling like cats and, I was sure, for different reasons. I had searched for the hypothetical duplicate of this elusive bauble all my life. I never dreamed that my fantasy would ever assume a tangible form, and then be handed to me by a beautiful woman.

We had taken a long time to get Tyron Jrcy's development program into operation. Now that it was a reality, I meant not only to keep the development alive, but I would also catch up on some of the basic procedures we had overlooked due to our rapid change from still-life study to actual implementation. Schooling, industry, commerce, and government would be oriented toward an agricultural society.

I had completely shaken the lethargy I had fallen into during the last few months of my stay in Mango Valley, but now another matter was bothering me.

To many people, a change from one's old habits or approaches to life might not have a profound impact. Most of us flowed with a certain tide that had a catchall applicability meant for the majority. I was not accustomed to flowing with the tide. In fact, I had become quite famous for my dropping-out tactics. In the past when events settled into the mundane of daily routine, I had always left the scene. It was obvious Lara and Costa had expected me to jump ship, and they had waited until we were on our way back to the capital before informing me that my services were needed. How fragile was the thread of human destiny, or was I again seeing myself in the role of some storybook hero? For once in my life I would adapt to the routine which had, to an extent, already been outlined. If a change in direction was necessary, I hoped I would be able to rise to the occasion.

The job of Assistant to the Chief Council entailed just what it sounded like, nothing. The job of Secretary of Agriculture was the big one, and it touched everything except the smiling Chief of Staff, General Lamira Costa, who was at this very minute standing right beside me. I could only guess what was uppermost in Costa's mind. The smile she gave me said a great deal more than words. She and I could restore the people's confidence in their government. We would, most likely, have the help of a monumental natural disaster. If we could weather that storm, we had it made.

It was difficult to see how either a human or a natural disaster could possibly help us; and yet, due to gold, we had failed miserably in the simple process of shaping our lives. Nothing except a national disaster was capable of giving us a new set of values, and then maybe for just a brief period of time. Whether we subsequently lapsed into the old routine, after the cataclysm had run its course, depended upon the outcome. Surprisingly enough, if we won, we reverted to the old routine. If we lost? Well, the possibilities here were unlimited, from total obscurity to that elysian existence to which we all aspired.

○

I remembered the air-monitoring program Nele Moran had used several years before, and I ensured that our monitoring teams covered every air and sea current known to man. This action was our first line of defense. Of course, I had entertained apprehensions about our atmosphere for quite a while; and if I was right, we needed to know from day to day what our pollution problems were. It seemed inevitable that our next disaster would have a deeper impact on us than the one Tyron Jrcy had washed out of the sky. I had a very pessimistic outlook toward any coming disaster, either man-made or natural. I also had a very antagonistic attitude toward my fellow man. Why man continued to pollute the planet was beyond my comprehension. Undeniably, the very end product of man's achievements was pollution; he could not manage to take care of his own front yard without polluting the air.

No longer were only the fanatics crying wolf. At this stage, the signs of disaster were quite clear for everyone to see. More than ten years ago I had noticed the wildlife migrating north. Now man, the one animal with reasoning power and a soul, was finally looking northward. For some reason, I did not have the compassion necessary to separate the human species into the innocent and the guilty. Nor could I find any consolation in the fact that I had always been a wolf-crying crackpot. If any emotional exhilaration crept into my mind today, it would be that time was running out.

There was a very definite accumulation of pollution within an area of thirty degrees north and south of the equator. Again, I had first noticed this phenomenon when I returned to the Northland. At that time I was too damn busy playing the absurd game I called "imagination." Yes, I had been totally wrapped up in my own scheme to somehow get into a position of leadership. Ridiculous? I would be the first to agree that it was. At least, I was hoping my approach was ridiculous. I would be conspicuously out of place among my peers if it was not.

So many noticeable changes had occurred during the past few years that everyone was becoming a bit edgy. People were even looking toward their leaders for help. This must have scared both the people and their leaders.

My technical advisers kept me well posted on the situation until I fully understood the pattern of this latest disaster. There was a significant increase in air currents throughout the equatorial zone. This phenomenon caused all air currents to be drawn in toward the equator, disrupting the seasonal climatic changes. Our extensive surplus of food and other supplies would save us from immediate danger. To help provide for the future, we started a program of hothouse construction throughout the far north. Our fishing operations were expanded to one hundred times their original size, and large quantities of meat and other food products were processed and stored.

If at all possible, I meant to weather this storm. Maybe this time we would "see the light," "get the calling," or whatever other form our enlightenment took. We needed a new set of values, and as much as it would have pleased me at the moment to cry out my message of wisdom so that everyone could hear, I did not have the time to engage in such a luxury. Buying survival time could be a full-time job, if you were lucky.

As usual, there were both positive and negative fringe benefits derived from all natural and human activities, and these latest events were not proving to be the exception to the rule. Broadly speaking, there was now a great amount of togetherness among the people of the Northland. If we had an internal problem, it came from the mentally disturbed. Sometimes the line between the sane and the insane was difficult to establish, but today a unique situation existed that had popular universal appeal: survival. Those of us who did not possess the emotional urge to survive had to be looked upon as being different, and astoundingly, the Northland had several million people who fit into this dependent category. When the very young, the aged, the sick, and the pregnant were added to the list of our dependents, we could be faced with an impossible responsibility. I was certain we would have to evacuate the southern part of the country, and our hardest job would be caring for the helpless.

If our own internal problems were not enough to keep us occupied, another major impact was developing at our southern border. Millions of people in the southern countries were in the process of moving north. Chief Council Lara asked for my recommendations, and I reminded him that border problems came under the jurisdiction of General Lamira Costa. I also reminded him that he would have to assume more and more power within the coming months. I stressed again that recommendations, still-life studies, multiple-use meetings, and economic surveys were not exactly compatible with the times. We were rapidly entering the front-line zone where all remaining time was reserved for the leaders' actions. Mass participation in administration would no longer be possible.

I might have been a tad rough on Lara, but times were changing, and our people would soon be demanding that he act the part he was being paid to perform. The Northland was currently doing an impossible job through the coordinated efforts of the people. An evacuation to the far north would tax our national resources to the limit, and the additional load caused by millions of foreign refugees would be a precursor to total disaster. Most of us never had to reach this stage in our lives, so it was futile to imagine the hopelessness of such a situation. In wartime the idiots had repeatedly advocated safety in numbers. Jamming extra bodies into the breach and overwhelming the enemy by sheer numbers were the actions of fools, the expressions of fear, and the preludes to calamity. Numbers alone could already defeat any future plans we had for evacuation. Our borders would need to remain closed until our own people were relocated.

After my last talk with Lara, I had a feeling we were running out of tactics to offset the man-caused disasters. This latest one looked like the vehicle we had evidently been wanting: total annihilation of mankind. Our southern border problem defied solution at this time. We would, however, hold a firm line wherever it was necessary to ensure our own survival. *Compassion* could soon become an obsolete word.

○

The natural phenomenon at the equator was gaining momentum at an alarming rate. The days were getting noticeably warmer, and the nights were getting colder. Evidently, the suction caused by the air currents along the equator was thinning the atmosphere. It was nature's way of trying to force the pollution out of our sphere of gravity. In doing this, our blanket of life-giving air was being thinned to a consistency where it could no longer filter the strong rays of the sun during the daytime. At night the reverse was true, and the air could not retain the sun's heat which the Earth had absorbed throughout the day. The world had never been subjected to this kind of treatment before. If it continued for any length of time, all the moisture on and in the Earth would evaporate and be pulled into the air currents at the equator. Nature's next step was unknown. I, personally, figured that nature could destroy mankind without changing her tactics. The air and sea currents were now concentrated and forming a definite centrifugal force at the equator. This could mean complete dehydration of the Earth. Was this the same route to destruction the other planets had followed?

One of a crackpot's main fortes was the absolute necessity to change philosophies and theories to fit the developments. This was only possible with crackpots because they alone were looking into the future and crying wolf. In nature, the wild animal served this same purpose. We called it "being in tune." Inexplicably, man did not generally develop this one unique characteristic, and he spoke of those who did as "being weird." At this point in time, I had changed two of my earlier theories regarding the finale: I was of the opinion that the rat would not survive, and I firmly believed that man did not have enough on the ball to destroy the world. Nature would do it for him.

I was probably the one person who was not surprised at the rapid acceleration of events. We had been around a long time, between four and five hundred thousand years. Our beginning must have been rapid, and it was logical to assume that our ending would be just as rapid. As for myself, I had no other emotions except to wonder why the great reasoning power of the human brain had not retained the survival characteristic it had at the beginning. Somewhere in the interim we had created a medium of exchange which in time surmounted its originator. Now we found ourselves well into the closing chapter of our lives, and everything that was left would be crowded in under the same heading, without the erasure of one single word.

Our eggheaded approach to life had been stripped stark naked of all pervious human input. In reality, it was impossible to tell if there was any human contingency left. On the surface there appeared to be a definite defeatism which prevailed in the minds of the people. I had been exposed to similar catastrophic conditions when I was younger, and the fact that we currently found ourselves on the verge of panic did not surprise me. I did know of one way to combat the present general feeling of defeatism.

To stand and fight this battle, which had already been lost in the minds of the people, would be the action of a fool. To run away would be the action of a panic-stricken coward. We could, however, retreat in an orderly manner and gain better position, time, and confidence. The word *retreat* had become synonymous with man and woman's most crucial hour, and only the highest quality of leadership could restore the confidence the people needed.

The position we presently occupied was untenable, and if the government waited until the people scattered in their own individual flights for safety, we would expedite our final defeat.

There was one escape route for us to take, and I had made up my mind this morning that Chief Council Lara and the members of the Council were going to hear my plan for immediate evacuation.

No longer did I give a damn about the brass ring, or whatever it stood for. I must have been an idiot myself to have harbored such a stupid idea all these years. I had been wrong about many things, and it was probably too damn late to do anything about them now.

I felt very strongly about the people's general panicky reaction to their present problems, problems which were largely their responsibility. Several years ago I had the same feeling when the elected officials got us into war. That time the people also divorced themselves from their responsibility; instead of admitting their error and recalling the officials, the people condemned the returning soldiers by taking away the few concessions the government had granted them.

○

During what must have been a short intermission in my self-evaluation, I took a good look at myself in the bathroom mirror. My face was all lathered up, and the razor was poised for the first stroke. There was also an additional object in my field of vision. Standing not more than ten feet in back of me was General Lamira Costa. I was certain I had been talking to myself while I prepared to shave. A man standing in front of a mirror waving a razor and talking to himself no doubt presented a very unstable picture. If his face was covered with foam, then I would say the picture was ridiculous.

I finished shaving before acknowledging Costa's presence. If she was conscious of my embarrassing position, she did not give her feelings away. Later, as we were having breakfast in the main dining room of my hotel, Costa very methodically gave me the latest information on the disaster approaching our southern border.

There was actually no factual information from south of the 30° north parallel. The increasing winds and ocean currents in the equatorial area made reconnaissance and communication totally impossible. Costa's land forces were presently stationed along a line roughly three thousand miles north of the equator.

What seemed to be an afterthought by Costa was the following statement she made: "Mr. Chief Council, Norman Lara died in his sleep sometime early this morning. The Council is waiting for you at the Capitol."

Of the myriad thoughts that could have come to mind at this very instant, no one would ever have guessed what the new Chief Council was thinking. As hard as I had tried to change my ways over the course of my lifetime, I still remembered one scene from my early life which had influenced so many of my actions in later years. To explain that early episode and give each involved character his due allotment of time would border on the absurd. Besides, I had long ago dismissed all but the bare abstract of the happening from my mind. Today, when I thought of soaking the ashes after the fire was out, I had momentarily forgotten that the fire this time was incalculably larger than my original goal. In fact, the brass ring and the fire were both charter members in the script I had chosen to follow. I could not have one without the other.

Costa had been very quiet on our short walk from my hotel to the Capitol; however, as soon as we entered the building, she came alive. She even opened doors for me and insisted that I proceed ahead of her. The woman was off her rocker.

I remembered my first visit with the Council and the crest of popularity I was riding at that time, but I had a feeling my star had dimmed somewhat during the intervening years. No, popularity and youth were no longer my allies. It was too bad I could not have all the best variables with me at this juncture. Time, location, popularity, and youth were each of equal importance. At least I had two out of four going for me, and that was the most I could reasonably expect to have. The rest was up to me.

The members of the Council stood silently at attention as Costa and I entered the conference room. I needed to break the ice before the meeting started, and this was the time to get them in a relaxed mood. I had crucial business to take up with the Council, and while we chatted about various unimportant subjects, I introduced them to our new Vice-Council, Lamira Costa, and our new Chief of Military Operations, General Alexander Navaro. These were the two people whom we would be depending on, and it was important to me that the Council and the officers visited informally before I started assigning duties.

By the time we had taken our seats for the meeting, I figured that everyone had a clear-enough mind to understand what I was about to say. More important, I wanted everyone to have confidence in our ability to survive. If anyone in the room thought I would continue our waiting game, I wanted to dispel the appearance of any lethargy right from the first.

"Ladies and gentlemen, this morning marks the beginning of our final actions against the unprecedented obstacles which are threatening our existence. From this moment on, we are all leaders and the people will expect us to act out our roles, regardless of any personal shortcomings we might have.

"Some great men and women have been involved in making our survival a possibility. If we fail to do our part, we will all be dead within the coming year. I cannot guarantee that it is possible for us to succeed, but we are sure to lose if we do not try.

"I am now your overall leader, and leading is exactly what I have in mind. Our new home is in the northern section of the country; and if it is possible for us to survive, I mean to see that we survive, with or without me as your Chief Council. It was with this thought that my first official acts were to appoint a new Vice-Council and a new Chief of Military Operations. I advise the Council and the new Vice-Council to follow this same procedure in the future until we can know better times.

"So, if what I have just said is clearly understood, we will spend the rest of the day going over the steps we need to take."

This would be the beginning of a mass exodus without equal in the history of the human race. Unlike other mass migrations, ours was planned to the smallest detail. The resources of the most powerful nation in the world were solidly in back of the people. What had started out unceremoniously several years ago...as one oddball's idea of dropping out from society...later became generally justified by the Northland government as the last frontier for our growing population. Later still, Tyron Jrcy started the development throughout the far north, and Lamira Costa finished it.

During the past ten years, our resources had been predominantly used for the programs in that part of the country. Whatever or whomever we attributed our successful development to was of no substantive importance. The fact was that the Northland remained the one nation in the world which offered a very possible sanctuary for its citizens.

I kept my original orders as simple as possible. Our direction was north, and we would start immediately. The Navy's main job was to transport the very young, the very old, the pregnant, and the infirm to our excellent hospital facilities near the north coastline. Army medical and supply units would be responsible for the patients once they reached their destination. I made a big deal about the transportation and the care of our hospital cases. In all actuality, it would be our most difficult assignment. The morale of our entire operation, now and in the future, hinged upon how well we could care for our weaker citizens.

The foremost duty of the Air Force was to deliver supplies to the people while they were en route to their new homes.

The main Army would stay with the people, and its major responsibility was to ensure that they arrived safely at their destination.

All military units would have communication with each other and with me. I would decide on the next step when we arrived at our new home.

My final instruction to the members of the National Council was that they would join their respective home states and lead their people.

○

It was early summer, and I would leave the capital in two days for the far northern settlement of Naron, where I would set up my headquarters. Costa and Navaro would travel with me. If the truth of the matter were known, I was playing for very large stakes. This time, I could not ambush the enemy, nor could I feint the opposition out of position, nor could I even leave the scene. On the other hand, I only had one route open to me: head north and hope nature's forces spent themselves before they could reach us.

For weeks I watched mass participation at its best. I had not thought it possible anymore for us to combine our efforts and help each other, but I was wrong. As a species, we had fallen so low that we counted heavily on time-consuming studies of all our action, knowing full well that any action we took would merely have a temporary application. As a result, we did nothing, except to get deeply buried in a costly way of life which, in reality, had consumed us. This had changed; we sincerely did want to survive.

Today I was not concerned with the fact that man, with his highly developed brain, was out of tune with nature. The poor devil had made a hell for himself here on Earth, and that he now showed signs of regaining some of his natural instincts was more than gratifying.

I had not overlooked the irony that catastrophes brought out the best and the worst in people, and I thought I had eliminated the worst from happening when I assigned the disciplined military forces to run the show. Tyron Jrcy had used the military years ago to battle disaster, and he had succeeded. At this point, I was depending in large measure on the military; they again carried the lion's share of the responsibility.

In the first few months of our northern migration, there were both natural obstacles and human frailties to overcome. Sometimes these obstacles and frailties were not overcome, and people died. If my reaction to death might have seemed to border upon the hypocritical due to my previous comments on human character, I had a very good reason for my actions. I made certain that each death was a most solemn occasion, and that all burial rituals had to be carried out to satisfy my new demands for human dignity. If we made it this time, human life would have to regain its true value. Gold would no longer purchase even the bare necessities of life.

I had expected the winter months to be warmer this year, and I was not surprised when the daily weather reports showed a twenty-degree increase in temperature. A difference of twenty degrees in this country was not overly noticeable, especially during the winter. What was important was that the temperature was still rising. After the first of March, I realized that there was a definite acceleration in the rising temperature, and I made preparations to evacuate everyone to the North Pole, if necessary. My survival tactics were, indeed, about to assume a ridiculousness about them which stamped all last-minute efforts. Personally, I was getting just a shade on the edgy side, and I was afraid someone would notice my eccentric actions. Spying on the wild animals and measuring sound on a twenty-four-hour-a-day basis were not exactly normal activities.

Well, I had asked for my present job, maybe not in so many words, but I had always tried to be physically in the right spot at the right time. In movie circles, such action was called "being discovered."

Rising temperature was a panic-inducing factor which could only be offset by total exhaustion, and by the end of March I had visited every job site in the far north. Farming of the low-elevation land was progressing at a speed well beyond what I had expected. The construction of new storage and hospital buildings on the higher elevation sites must have given the people the impression that we would be here forever. This time there were no extensive studies. Everyone justified his or her existence by physical labor. Survival was all that mattered; any other functions had suddenly lost their importance.

By the end of my first inspection of our new home, I was pleased with the physical condition and the morale of our people. I had a great deal to be thankful for. Our southernmost units were arriving daily, and our military forces had again saved the country from total disaster. I felt good whenever the military forces came through for us. It was not that I was biased or that I was some kind of a weird military buff. I was well acquainted with our military forces. They had more obstacles to overcome than a salmon going upstream to spawn. The military had to run a gauntlet of foreign and domestic foes, whose identification varied from the formal enemy in battle array to the ultra-deadly enemies from within.

Under Tyron Jrcy, Lamira Costa, and me, the military operated without the usual reviewed action. These were crucial times, and we had a much better chance of surviving if our choice of military commanders was sound. In my own case, if General Navaro was not capable of handling the job, then I was not capable because I was the one who had appointed Navaro. The National Council, in turn, was responsible for me, and the people were responsible for the National Council. In normal times, about the only damage which could happen when government failed to measure up was a depleted pocketbook. In crucial times, a bit more was at stake, and our lives could be added to our losses.

A year ago I would have given odds that the general masses of our people did not have the necessary character to survive. I was wrong, and I was happy to admit my error. I had not focused upon the fact that toughness was an indicator of morale in the human character. The contagiousness of morale could spread like a raging forest fire through the minds of people, igniting the best or the worst in all human beings. Under crucial conditions, we had shown that we were willing and capable of protecting the little bit of human dignity we had left. Even with the exigent problems which faced us, we still thought enough of ourselves to care for our weak, bury our dead with proper respect, and accept our responsibilities for the welfare of nature's wildlife. These were signs of real toughness, which awakened other characteristics like confidence in each other and intelligent reasoning power, an unbeatable combination.

Furthermore, I was thankful for my early wartime experiences, and I avoided developing the same absurd situations.

If there was any remorse in my thoughts, it would be that I missed my old role of "gumbeater." Years before, I could blame the brass for my slightest misfortune. Now the opposition was at its peak, and I did not have a single whipping boy to share my problems. My feelings might only be natural human reactions, but I did believe I was playing against a stacked deck. My feelings were so strong that I began taking inventory of my own talismanic qualities, a sure sign of pending disaster.

○

The date was April 19, and wherever I looked, people were working toward our survival. *Nineteen* had always been a lucky number of mine, but today I did not see how fortune could possibly be on the same time schedule with me. I finally saw myself for what I actually was, a self-alleged leader who had covered our north coastline with every type of ocean-going craft which the human brain could devise. I was a leader who was running out of real estate. I was also guilty of working the people into a state of exhaustion, and for what reason? Could I possibly justify my action? Nature's schedule of coming events would include floods, earthquakes, and total dehydration, and not necessarily in that order.

The daily reports showed that our southern border guards had retreated almost one thousand miles farther north. At this rate, we could plan on another year and a half of survival time, if we could make it to the North Pole. One other bit of information in the reports caught my eye. The temperature had remained constant during the preceding twenty-four hours, not too much to get excited about. When the small fraction that represented the daily change in temperature was considered, there could be many factors accounting for the latest numbers. Errors in instrument reading, errors in arithmetic, and errors in recording were all possibilities.

It seemed I was grasping at straws, and so was everyone else. The people were openly boasting that they were cheating death from day to day. Anytime they spoke of their armada waiting for them on the north shore, they spoke in terms of great expectations. This made me mad...to think we had come so damn far just to take a boat ride into oblivion. And yet, I was determined to salvage every second of life we had coming to us. Yes, I was grasping at straws. Anything that could keep us physically and even mentally away from those boats on the north shoreline was what dominated my mind.

In the past, people of the Northland had been typical of people all over the world; they had never mastered the simple process of government. This weakness had a tendency to propagate the one factor which government could not cope with – the rise to power of special interest groups, a "government-in-being." Meanwhile, the "government-in-residence," or the duly elected government, had been a mere shell of impotency nurtured by the people. In some cases the elected or appointed officials played both parts: one they worked at, and the other for aesthetic value alone.

I was not quite certain what actual crime we had been guilty of committing, any more than I was certain if our government-in-residence truly knew that they alone were supposed to be responsible to the people. Everyone had always drifted with the tide, a tide which demanded and received our support, a tide which gave very little in return except a misleading form of oral and written information. To further complicate matters, we had an in-residence form of life that in no way matched the in-being form of life we were now forced to contend with at any given moment.

By May 1, the temperature was still holding constant. There had been a twenty-degree increase in the temperature prior to April 19, but we could live with that. I had figured we could live with another forty-degree rise in temperature; then we would have to move farther north.

We were currently occupying our northernmost section of land which measured approximately one thousand miles north and south, and five thousand miles east and west. The buffer zone we had established along our southern border extended northward for approximately fifteen hundred miles. The zone was basically the southern half of our country, and it varied from livable in the north to completely desolate in the south. South of the buffer zone would be three thousand miles of probable hell. What was south of the equator, no one knew. How many people we had lost, no one knew. Communications with other countries were down.

By August 1, there was again no change in temperature, and the days and nights were getting longer. All this could mean that the Earth was spinning around its vertical axis at a noticeably decreasing rate of speed.

It could only be assumed that the buildup of water and debris at the equator had finally reached a height where the sub-zero temperature of the upper atmosphere froze the entire mass into a giant ring which completely circled the Earth. This could explain the lack of axial tilt that controlled our four yearly seasons, and it could also slow the Earth's rotation around its axis and make our days and nights longer. Whatever the problem was at the equator, I would have to wait until nature's forces had subsided. Wind, rain, hail, tornadoes, and earthquake tremors were reported as far north as the southern part of our buffer zone.

I made arrangements to inventory the resources we had left. The only visible reduction I could determine was a one-hundred-foot lowering of the ocean level. This undoubtedly had a disastrous impact on Nele Moran and John Martel; they had been depending on the ocean retaining its normal level.

During the summer, autumn, and winter, I stayed close to my headquarters in Naron. The one interest I had these days was in the daily weather reports. We had withdrawn as far north as we could get from the disaster area. All that was left was roughly eight hundred miles of ice and water between us and the North Pole. This was my ace in the hole, my factor of safety, a true crackpot's finale.

I recalled the frame of mind I was in last spring when I was trying to conjure up some supernatural aid. Now I could manage a more rational approach. We had much to be grateful for. We had our Northland with its new developments and its natural barriers; and, of course, we had our people. Everything was tailor-made for our survival.

We were overcrowded, but for the first time in my life I did not notice the people. Everyone had a job to do, and as far as I could tell, groups were working together without the usual dissensions or delinquencies. I found this human attitude in keeping with my original appraisal of our species, and I attributed our display of togetherness to the very primary survival trait that all creatures possess.

For months, I had been expecting something big to happen; as accurately as I could estimate the different possible misfortunes which could befall us, only perpetual nighttime posed an immediate problem. So far, nothing had happened that we could not adjust to, if we put in the effort.

Earthquakes were becoming a daily occurrence in the equatorial zone, especially at those points where the equator crossed the continental coastlines. There was nothing anyone could do to change nature's course of action, and I found no reason to worry about earthquakes or floods. We had the moon, the sun, and our atmosphere. If nature could square away the problem at the equator, we would, in all probability, be given a second chance.

My change of heart toward nature, the elements, and my fellow creatures was nothing new. It was, to be honest, simply my inborn hypocritical approach to justify my very possible future actions. Right now, I was getting a clearer picture of an old familiar scene. The fire was out, and there stood Mansan, hose in hand, justifying his existence by soaking the dead ashes.

Little about nature's actions in the past two years appeared to be sophisticated. In fact, only the beginning of this disaster could be labeled with any degree of sophistication, and yet the existing air currents could have easily been drawn in toward the increasing temperature at the equator. A chain reaction would have developed, creating a giant suction that pulled in the sun's evaporation of the ocean water, the wind currents, dust, vegetation, and anything else which was not anchored down. Regardless of what had happened, or what would still happen, I could not visualize the disaster breaking through the sub-zero temperature layers of our atmosphere. I was confident that we could weather nature's coming attractions, and that we would get another chance. At least, those of us who were left would get another chance.

○

Admittedly, the recent high humidity was having quite an impact on me. Costa had suggested that I leave the far north and join our inspection teams in the southern part of the country. She and General Navaro would accompany me. Costa's idea appealed to me, except I would leave for Valmy and travel south by sea. I also gave Costa and Navaro orders to remain at Naron.

My sole forms of activity these last few months had been listening to weather reports and consulting with my technical advisors. It seemed we were slowly coming back to normal.

The action was currently in the south, and I'll be damned if I did not feel years younger to be heading there. I recalled the time I decided to visit John Martel, and how my body responded to the thought of a new life.

John Martel and his people were probably dead, but I promised myself that I would find out for sure.

Before I left Naron, I called a meeting of the National Council. Lamira Costa was selected Chief Council, and I would be retained in the capacity of an advisor. This did not sit too well with my hot-tempered friend, but I believed she was the best leader the Northland had. If I had been younger, I would have held on to the job of Chief Council; but I was not younger, and I was not content to go through another long period of inaction.

My journey south would take at least six months, and a good portion of that time would be spent at sea. I was afraid my old weakness was coming back. I had this intense dread of being caught up in the backwash of events. Right now, I thought that the worst was over, and that we had weathered the storm. I was convinced of this, and I had never been noted for my ability to tolerate stagnation. I would travel to Valmy by helicopter, and from Valmy I would travel south by one of our special Ice Patrol cutters. Communications would be set up for this operation so Costa could follow our actions on a daily basis. It would be our first step, since the initial stages of the disaster, to contact the rest of the world.

I made as big a deal as possible of my exit from Naron, but my actions did not draw much water with Costa. The face she made at me as my helicopter left the ground did not convey the respect that a mission of this magnitude should have commanded.

The flight to Valmy took ten days. I made several stops, and from what I could see, we had made out quite well. Valmy had been evacuated two years ago, but the people had returned. The fishing industry was picking up, and the first vegetables of the year were being harvested. Most of nature's forces were back to normal. The days and nights were a few hours longer. The sky was overcast, and the mist had a brownish color that the technicians told me was caused by wind erosion. Unprecedented quantities of rain were predicted for the southern region, and we might have general rainfall throughout the entire north. One thing was certain: nature had a lot of moisture to redistribute. Whether we received the major share of rain and snow here in the north was being decided at this very minute on our southern border. Which of nature's air currents would win? All we could do was wait and see. We knew another thing for certain: a great deal depended on the outcome.

The probable buildup of ice and debris at the equator had slowed the Earth's axial rotation, permitting the air currents to regain their normal pattern. Now the battle was between nature's warm moisture-laden air from the south and the cold air coming from the north. We were fortunate to have the massive mountain range along our southern border which allowed for the confrontation of these two opposing forces at that point. The turbulent action caused by the meeting of the two air currents was of such magnitude that our border guards had withdrawn to the approximate 55° north parallel. Tornadoes and hurricanes were sweeping east and west across the land and sea. This time there was no Tyron Jrcy to turn the tide, and it was doubtful if even he could have made a difference in the outcome.

After three days at sea, I decided to return to Valmy. A hurricane at sea was an awesome force which nothing could withstand.

○

Like my previous actions during the last two years, my decision to return to Valmy was made without a board of review. As I thought of my past modus operandi, the action which had drawn the most static from the people was my evacuation of the southern part of the country.

When I ordered the evacuation, I did not have an abundance of factual information as a basis for this decision. To be exact, my only information was a rumor that the disaster had dehydrated all plant and animal life up to a distance of two thousand miles north of the equator. Taking into consideration the time of year, I had figured that the disaster could possibly cover another one thousand miles north before it ran out of steam. This meant that I was expecting complete destruction of plant and animal life within the first three-thousand-mile zone north of the equator. Three thousand miles would put the northern limits of the disaster at the approximate location of our southern boundary and those daunting mountains I had passed through years earlier.

We had never been faced with a disaster like this before. I had split our country into north and south sections and evacuated the people from the south to our newly developed far northern area. The southern half soon became known as Mansan's Buffer Zone to those people who already lived in the far north. To those people who lived in the south, my actions and I were called by other names. At the time I could not afford the luxury of worrying about what the people thought of me, and I did not have the time to let a lot of people get involved in my decision making. I had been charged with the safety of the people, and I saw the far north as the one area which would take a large amount of dehydration before we had to throw in the towel. I actually thought that nature's actions at the equator would level off before the cold atmosphere in the northern part of the country could be overcome. Of course, my main reason for pushing the development of the north years ago was to provide a sanctuary in case of a national or worldwide disaster. I had not wanted to be vindicated.

There were now an estimated one hundred and ninety million people in the far north. And we had other residents in our new home. By land, sea, and air, the wildlife sought sanctuary there, as well. Our extraordinary mass exodus could not be attributed to Richard Mansan; I had followed the animals, and the people followed me.

My feelings toward nature's wildlife had changed significantly over the years. I had always looked upon the wild animals as a source of food. I justified my stand in this matter by knowing that the diner and the "dinee" could very easily change places if I got too saturated with the milk of human kindness. These days I had a different feeling toward the wild animals. I was still not above eating them, but I had purposely left the forest land undeveloped. If we could get by without using that land, it would allow the wild animals to have a home; and as with the military, we owed them a debt we could never repay. If we gave them their chance to survive, I trusted that they would ensure our own longevity. I continued to use the animals as my alarm system, and I had the

Army watching our four-legged friends very closely. If the animals moved, it was best they moved in a hurry, because this time I planned to be breathing down their necks.

As compassionate as I was toward the wildlife, my compassion toward my fellow human beings was not yet as highly developed. I thought the entire human perspective of life was wrong. Most of us had nothing to do with shaping our own destiny. We were drones who drifted with the tide, picking up the scraps of life which were thrown our way. I had considered getting into the mainstream of human events on several occasions in my life, but I sold myself on the idea that leadership should be appointed as needed. Besides, I never had the staying power to occupy a token position. I was always afraid of overstaying my usefulness, and I did not have the patience to administer during the mundane lulls in human affairs. Regardless of my present philosophies, I realized that a totally new set of values had to be adopted. Before nature was through with us this time, we would have to rearrange our priorities and be in tune with our environment.

Months earlier I had come to the conclusion that I could predict what counteractions nature would take to correct man's continual fumbling with our original issue of environment. In this respect, I was never more wrong in my life.

When I left Valmy a few days ago, I was ready for a leisurely southern cruise along our east coastline. When I gave the ship's captain orders to return home, we were approximately one thousand miles south of Valmy, and what I saw was not exactly what I had expected. The ocean was so muddy that our sounding instruments were unable to tell us where the ocean floor was. According to the readings we were getting, our ship was already aground. The rain also presented quite a problem. I had never seen such large drops, and they were half mud. After assessing these unique weather conditions, I had recommended to the ship's captain that we return to Valmy, and I had sent a message to Costa, informing her of the developments. I was on Costa's advisory staff, and my message to her included a recommendation regarding our guard units and weather-monitoring teams now operating in the buffer zone. These units would stay five hundred miles north of the storm front at all times, and their means of transportation would be helicopters.

I had not even come close to the equator, but I had seen enough to tell me that no one else was going to get any closer. Winds exceeding one hundred miles per hour, and land and sea of the same density were nature's main warning signals. And if these were not enough to discourage the most daring, there were indications of earthquake action to the south.

The more I thought of the existing situation, the less I thought of my chances of ever reaching the equator. The situation would get worse the farther south we went. At 3,400 miles north of the equator, we had run into wind and rain which reduced our sight distance to zero. With the huge moraines which were forming offshore along the full length of the coastline, we could easily have run aground and been battered to pieces by the wind within minutes.

I could not imagine what kind of a mess we had at the equator, but there were two facts which were well established. All the water that was missing from the ocean had to be somewhere here on Earth or in our atmosphere, and we were scheduled to get it back. Maybe we would not get our water back in the same places it had been taken from, but we would get it back, every drop of it.

When I arrived back in Valmy, Chief Council Costa and General Navaro were waiting for me. I should have felt like a fool after the elaborate preparations I had made for my voyage south. By comparison, the embarkation of Columbus had been a wake. To make matters worse, Costa made a big deal over my return. Only my imperviousness to the ridiculous saw me through what I considered to be my first major setback.

○

It was late summer when I returned to Naron with Costa and Navaro. The riverbeds had been dredged wide and deep, and they had held up well through the height of the storm. Farm crops were so large that Costa trucked what we could not store to the millions of refugees who were occupying the northern part of our buffer zone. If conditions held steady, we could all weather this last disaster – our people, the refugees, and our wildlife.

I spent the autumn, winter, and spring as Costa's representative in the buffer zone with the refugees. These people currently did not have a lot to work with. Only the strongest had survived, and I was amazed at their will to live. The recent help Costa had given them must have been the spark they needed to rekindle the flame of human dignity.

In early summer, after the crops had been planted, I received orders from Costa to head up an expedition which would travel south from Naron. My orders were to travel as far south as possible. I had great expectations this time. The weather had been ideal for the past month, and the earthquake action along our coastlines nearer the equator had quieted down.

As usual, when a new duty was assigned me, I was suddenly transformed into a young man again. I had worried for months that we would be faced with another trial by fire, and that this time there would be no escape.

During man's relatively short time on Earth, he had, in a negative sort of way, accomplished a staggering number of things. He had accomplished so much, in fact, that the possibility now existed where man could destroy the Earth after he had destroyed himself. I reasoned that the small percentage of human beings who had managed to survive so far were, without doubt, an accidental drop in the bucket. If nature resumed the earthquake phase of her restoration program, we could expect the worst to happen. The union of nature's most powerful force – earthquakes – and man's most negative accomplishment – nuclear substance – would certainly be capable of reducing the number of known planets by one. Such a union could very possibly wipe the entire slate clean.

I spent two weeks at Naron preparing for my trip south. Beginning with the northernmost camp at my farm in the Mango Valley, I would then establish helicopter base camps at two-hundred-mile intervals.

I had a habit of moving quickly once my plans were made. Even Janus Costa, who had recently returned to Mango Valley, could not slow me down. Janus was in the process of caring for about ten thousand foreign refugees, and the farm was a beehive of activity. He tried his best to get me interested in his expanded operations, but I had my sights set on our southern border and the colossal mountains which had broken the backbone of nature's southern forces. It was almost a mania that gripped me. I wanted to see what had happened, and if possible, I wanted to cross the equator and find out if John Martel and Nele Moran were still alive.

My short sea journey south a year ago left quite a bit for the imagination to fill. Today, as I flew over the old capital, there was nothing left for the imagination whatsoever. Tornadoes had hit the outer fringes, and the main part of the city had burned. The capital had been on the northernmost edge of the disaster area. The southern border and mountain range, or what the mountain range would look like, were roughly a thousand miles due south from the capital. If I really wanted to exercise my imagination, I could guess what had happened south of the mountains, in that three-thousand-mile stretch of heavily populated land between the mountain range and the equator. I would be seeing it soon enough, so there was no need for me to imagine a single thing.

When I returned to the Northland years ago, I had crossed the southern border far to the east of where I would cross this time. It was just as well, because I had made many friends on that journey, and I had renewed some older friendships from a long, long time ago.

○

It was noon on the third day after we left the old capital that I had my first glimpse of the southern mountains. They were scrubbed clean of topsoil and vegetation. Even, bare rock glistened in the noonday sun. It was awesome, and yet, it did not surprise

Grabbing the Brass Ring 139

me. For two days I had been able to follow the tempo of the disaster as it had grown larger and larger. Now I was approaching the actual front lines, those endless ramparts of solid granite. The scene meant a great deal to me. I could see it all – the opposing forces, the tactics, the raging battle – and beyond that, I could see what had been won. What I could not see was what had been lost, but tomorrow would answer that question.

I could not take my eyes off this most valuable of the world's real estate, these impregnable mountains where nature had chosen to restore order among her forces. The irony of the battle and the irony of the results were that man, by his fumbling administration and greed, had set nature's forces against each other, and against himself. In the end, there were no winners, but rather, temporary survivors waiting for the outcome of nature's next grasping effort to be rid of the monkey that man had placed on her back.

At night I spent several sleepless hours in our base camp, a short distance north of the border mountains. The heat given off by the bare rocks constantly reminded me that this stalwart range of mountains had been the main battleground for two years.

Where would the destruction end? Nature was no more than a combination of elements which had originally been mixed to perfection by a power far greater than man would ever possess. Since the simple perfection of nature had been disrupted by man's imbecilic pollution of the atmosphere and oceans, we had been experiencing a violent chain reaction of natural forces. And nature's reactions were no more sophisticated than that of a falling stone dropped by man from a passing aircraft. If the stone killed as it hit the ground, who was to blame? Certainly not nature's air or stone.

For the last few days, I could not help noticing what had happened in our buffer zone. The complete devastation of both nature's landscaping and man's construction made me realize the fearsome power that nature's normally gentle forces could generate; and it had all been caused by man, the world's most highly developed creature.

In the past, I had always wondered why mankind was unable to administer so much as the simplest forms of government. At the moment, I was getting an on-the-ground preview of our species' total negative potentials. The fact that man could cause two of nature's beneficial forces, air and ocean currents, to form solid battlefronts was unbelievable. Gentle air and sea currents, with the help of the sun, were the first line of defense against extinction. Could these forces of nature, which had been so helpful, now have caused torrential rains, tornadoes reaching four hundred miles per hour, winds of immeasurable speed, hail that killed all plant and animal life, and bolts of lightning that were estimated to exceed a billion volts? Even these destructive forces were not the end results of humanity's bumbling approach to leadership. Chain reactions in nature's forces would propagate much stronger forces. Volcanoes and earthquakes were already waiting in the wings, along with another force, a force so diabolical in destructiveness that nature and man had to combine their efforts to produce it.

I could not become too excited about the way events were shaping up. I had sung to this tune my whole life; and as all of my early predictions had come true, I saw no grounds to look for a change in the final scene. What would happen would happen. No last-minute heroics were possible. I had thought of every crackpot counter-tactic in the books, including some which were sure to expedite our demise.

To take my mind away from my heroic daydreams, I had the helicopter pilot fly me over the first chain of mountains. There was a full moon, and the reflection of the moonlight off the bare mountainsides lighted up the inverted bowl of the sky. The entire range of mountains that formed our southern border had become a giant solar reflector, two hundred miles north and south by five thousand miles east and west. It was hard for me to look upon nature as an unthinking combination of elements, especially when I considered the perfect reflector I was looking at directly below me.

Normal weather conditions in this part of the world usually meant a slight flurry between the north and south weather fronts in the vicinity of the border mountain range. The southern air currents had never been a match for the cold air which made up the northern front; but, during the past two years, the southern front became warmer than usual and carried with it a continual saturation of moisture. The results had been what I was witnessing. The mountains had been scrubbed clean down to the quartz and feldspar minerals. To ensure the south's continued success, it appeared to me that nature had indeed constructed this giant solar shield to warm the southern air currents as they continued their advance against the northern front. The end of the battle had eventually taken place one thousand miles north of where I was tonight.

To sum up very briefly the explanations for the recent lull in weather hostilities, it looked as though the southern forces had run completely out of fuel. I had gambled on this happening. The years I lived in the far north had given me confidence that the solid cold-air front in the north and the vast mountain range on our border would stop any force the southern air currents could generate. Evacuating all of our people from the southern half of the country gave us a safety factor of approximately fifteen hundred miles. At the same time, it gave me the unenviable reputation, among our people, of being a monster. Now, I would have to admit that I was feeling kind of smug about how events had shaped up. The destruction caused by the meeting of the northern and southern fronts had spread only one thousand miles north of our southern boundary. We still had five hundred miles between us and where the disaster had ended. To be accurate, that five-hundred-mile-wide strip of land through the center of our country was substantially more than just a safety factor. It was the sanctuary for millions of foreign refugees. One question asked these days remained haunting: why had Mansan ordered his fellow citizens to be evacuated so damn far north? The people who asked this question must also have been aware that I stood fully prepared to evacuate everyone clear to the North Pole, if the disaster had not been stopped when it was.

Although I was expecting trouble, at this point I had every reason to feel relatively confident. Our country was not markedly vulnerable to earthquakes. Maybe in the vicinity of our east coast we would prove to be weak, but we could evacuate our people from that area. On the other hand, there was a very powerful enemy which now occupied the far end of the gauntlet we were running. This final enemy did not offer us a lot of maneuvering room – no fancy footwork, no flanking tactics, no overwhelming the enemy by sheer numbers or superior firepower. On top of the many restrictions we would have imposed on us, we would all have to face the last enemy. Age, sex, wealth, religion, race, and political connection could not be considered this time. I had often thought about this, and although I did not consider mankind capable of accomplishing anything of a great positive or negative nature, tonight I realized that I had come face to face with an age-old question. Could man directly destroy the world? Was the last obstacle on the far end of the gauntlet line actually man?

Regardless of who or what would deliver the final coup de grace, throughout the night I was very much in tune with nature. There were seismic waves underfoot, and I was able to tell their direction and magnitude.

By dawn I had made up my mind to withdraw to a base three hundred miles north. I would not try to cross the two-hundred-mile range of mountains on our southern border. The reflection of the sun off those shining surfaces would be blinding, and the heat would become unbearable. I was, however, in an ideal location to set up our instruments and record the magnitude and direction of the seismic waves. Instinct told me that the earth tremors I was feeling came from our east coast and that they traveled in a northeastern direction.

While I was waiting for our seismograph reading to confirm my own suspicions, I radioed my early morning report to Chief Council Costa. Included in my report were recommendations that the people along our east coast be evacuated to higher ground at once, and that all our ships be moved to the far northern coastline.

Our east coastline was particularly vulnerable to earthquakes and tsunami wave action. The people with me were somewhat surprised by my evacuation recommendation, but Richard Mansan had never been noted for his prolonged studies of crucial situations. I also knew, if I was right, that I could eliminate the possibility of reacting too slowly to an imminent threat. If I was wrong, the damage would be of a superficial nature, and a number of chipped teeth and bruised gums in the ranks of our people would be the worst casualties that could happen.

By mid-afternoon, we had finished our seismograph readings, and we were heading north.

I established the temporary base three hundred miles north of the border and settled down to wait for nature's next move.

○

Maybe my imagination was working overtime, or maybe I was closely in tune with nature. I was still classified as a crackpot even by our Chief Council, who was not exactly a member of the status quo herself. Two days ago at our southernmost station, the earth tremors which our instruments had picked up were on a decreasing frequency. Now, as I expected, the magnitude-of-wave reading had decreased, but the frequency was holding constant. I radioed Naron and asked for the latest report from the Valmy area. The answer I received was the same: the magnitude of the tremors had indeed decreased, and the frequency was holding constant.

I could not accept that we were off the hook. Nature's forces had grown to maturity during the past few years. I did not believe that nature's strongest force of all, earthquakes, would turn out to be the weakest, especially since most of the other recently active forces assuredly propagated earthquakes.

Costa must have been suffering from apprehensions of her own about the present lull in nature's activities. When she ordered me to return to Naron, I figured she had another job for me. I had the impression for some time now that Costa knew as well as I did that I was dying. For the last year I had actively taken an interest in life only on those occasions when I thought I was contributing something to further our survival. There were other times when I felt more dead than alive. This was strictly a mental hang-up, and the one way I could get a new lease on life was to keep my mind occupied.

When I had time to think of the past and present, I saw all events as inevitable happenings. Whether or not I had played a part in these happenings had no bearing whatsoever on their ebb and flow. My entire mental outlook this last year was not in keeping with the guidelines which had shaped my life. Today I could only think of what might or might not happen. I was completely without any positive countermoves. Some consolation could be found in knowing that our country was basically impervious to earthquakes, and that the tremors so far were passing along the known fault line off our east coast. What worried me was the fact that the earth tremors appeared to be worldwide; and, sooner or later, the fault lines around the world would give way to nature's most powerful force. The chance of man's forces combining with this would produce a front far more ominous than Chief Councils Jrcy, Mansan, and Costa had ever encountered.

I was not very optimistic about the outcome of nature's latest move. The water and soil had been rearranged during the preceding two years, and pressure points on the Earth's crust had been changed considerably. To compound our problem, the different nations of the world had been engaged in a nuclear race for years, and every ounce of this very unstable nuclear matter remained with us. Whether it was buried at sea, in the earth, or in storage vaults made little or no difference. When I was Chief Council, I had dismantled our nuclear plants, disarmed our nuclear weapons, and neutralized the nuclear material. I realized at the time that neutralizing nuclear material was impossible, and like every other leader, I had finally decided to hide this most cataclysmal product of man's ingenuity. Today, all of our indestructible nuclear matter lay buried throughout the frozen north. Was I right, or wrong? No one knew.

○

Chief Council Costa and General Alexander Navaro met me at the airfield in Naron. I could tell by Costa's formality that we were in trouble.

"Mr. Chief Council, the tremors along the east coast have increased in magnitude and frequency."

I had to smile as I looked at our young Chief Council. She was down to the very last characteristic of a great leader. The smile on her face was quite contagious, and I would have gladly jumped off the moon if I thought it would have helped her.

Costa was no doubt well aware that we were now faced with an unbeatable adversary. At least we were still alive and as ready as we would ever be for the final round.

When I responded, I tried to convey neither recommendations and solutions, nor conversational filler. Out of respect for Costa, I acknowledged the information she had just given me.

"Chief Council Costa, to my knowledge, we are the only people on Earth to have survived so far. We are, indeed, fortunate to live in the most structurally sound country in the world. We are also fortunate to have nature's wild animals with us. If it is possible to survive, they will show us the way."

In reality, I thought we could survive nature's next and final assault. I was not as certain of our chances if the earthquake action struck one of man's nuclear stockpiles or plants.

I had tried to show no emotion at all as I spoke to Costa. The days of Jrcy, O'Riley, and the other great leaders had passed. No longer could one person make the difference between victory and defeat, and I had realized this while I was speaking. Our destiny no longer lay in the hands of a mere human being. It did, however, lie firmly in the very uncompassionate hands of nature, the one true ruler of this material universe.

It was funny how the mind worked. At this very second I was thinking what the basis of our future would be, assuming that we had a future. Historically, we had gone for the gold. At least we now knew that was wrong.

Costa, Navaro, and I checked in at the Capitol shortly after my arrival in Naron. Much had happened during the last hours. The Earth had erupted far to the east of us, and it appeared that all of the Earth's continental plate sections would break loose along the old fault lines. What was even more alarming was the report that new fault lines were opening up.

Our east coast lookout teams had been evacuated, and that area was now the scene of hurricanes and tsunami wave action.

Suddenly, I was very tired, and after saying goodnight to Costa and Navaro, I retired to the sleeping quarters which had been assigned to me.

I took a quilt from the bed and walked out on the balcony where I could get a clear view of the eastern horizon. Dawn was still a few hours away, so I sat down on one of the deck chairs and covered with the quilt.

I must have been a great deal more tired than I realized, because I did not wake up until the strong rays of the sun had actually burned my face. This was all quite unusual, and as I looked at my watch, the time was four o'clock. I had slept fourteen hours?

Costa and Navaro were standing on either side of me, and my attention was drawn to Costa's burning hand on my shoulder. I knew something was wrong when my addled brain concentrated on Costa's wristwatch. It also registered four o'clock on its unique twenty-four-hour dial. I looked up into Costa's face, and she nodded her head slightly and smiled. In utter frustration, I closed my eyes tightly to block out this final scene.

A man's life should not end on a note of failure. Each life had its highs and lows, and we should be entitled to remember that one scene from the past when we had it all.

I faintly remembered a scene from the distant past, but it could have been only an old picture. Nothing seemed to move. From the pale blue sky with its fleecy white clouds to the contrasting green hills which extended down to an azure-colored sea, the scene was that of nature's perfection. I could not pin down the time or the location, but my mind was clear on one point. I had, at one time during my life, found what I had been searching for, and for that I was thankful.

The End

AN EXTRAORDINARY LIFE:

THE BIOGRAPHY OF MICHAEL EARL NOLAN

Compiled and edited by Jean Nolan Krygelski

Michael Earl Nolan, a light forever.

TABLE OF CONTENTS

CHAPTER ONE. 153
    The Early Years
        Finding His Own Way

CHAPTER TWO. 160
    Tucson High School Football
        "Tarzan," the Awakening of an Athlete

CHAPTER THREE. 166
    Tucson High School Track and Field
        Record-Breaking Regional Champion

CHAPTER FOUR. 175
    Tucson High School Legacy
        A Star Remembered

CHAPTER FIVE. 182
    Arizona National Guard
        Service with the 158th

CHAPTER SIX. 185
    University of Arizona Football
        "King Kong of the Gridiron"

CHAPTER SEVEN. 211
    University of Arizona Track and Field – and Beyond
        "Outstanding Athlete" and "High-Point Man"

CHAPTER EIGHT. 219
    University of Arizona and Amateur Boxing
        Donning the Golden Gloves

CHAPTER NINE. 224
    More Amateur Sports
        "Tucson's Ironman"

CHAPTER TEN. 229
      University of Arizona and Amateur Athletics – the Legacy
          "The One and Only Earl Nolan"

CHAPTER ELEVEN. 239
      Professional Football
          Shattering the NFL Barrier

CHAPTER TWELVE. 247
      Professional Boxing
          "Arizona's Heavyweight Sensation"

CHAPTER THIRTEEN. 253
      United States Marine Corps
          "Big Mike," from Guadalcanal to Iwo Jima

CHAPTER FOURTEEN. 296
      Work History and Return to the University of Arizona
          From Hopping Freight Trains to Civil Engineering

CHAPTER FIFTEEN. 306
      United States Forest Service
          "Lasting Monuments"

CHAPTER SIXTEEN. 317
      Family and Personal Life
          A Life Well Lived

CHAPTER ONE

The Early Years
Finding His Own Way

AS BOB ALLISON SAID IN HIS JANUARY 1, 1957 COLUMN, "Along the Way," in the *Phoenix Gazette*, "Around Tucson they tell tales of Earl Nolan like the Minnesotans do about Paul Bunyan; the difference being that most of the Nolan stories are true."

What follows is only a partial life history of an extraordinary man, a hero in every sense of the word, also a man who rarely spoke about himself. This biography is written, in loving tribute, more than twenty years after his passing. The information has been compiled from firsthand experiences, oral accounts, correspondence, newsletters, books, tape recordings, military records, documents preserved throughout the years, as well as newspaper and magazine articles, many of which were found in a yellowing scrapbook started around 1931 by the mother of one of his friends. Over time friends and family added to these clippings; other articles were located through a review of the microfiche files at the local library. Even after the research, we have a feeling that there is still much left to discover. We are most profoundly grateful to everyone who has contributed information. It is a fascinating story.

Nolan never had a birth certificate, which has resulted in some uncertainty regarding the exact date of his birth. He was born Michael Earle Nobles to Harry Bayard Nobles and Flora Elizabeth Hussey Nobles, the family name subsequently changed to Nolan by his father. [Editor's note: The name Nolan is an Irish version of the English name Nobles, deriving from the Gaelic word *nuall* meaning noble, and the subsequent names Nuallan and O'Nuallain.] According to Nolan's earliest elementary school records in Tucson, Arizona, he was born on January 1, 1911, in Vancouver, British Columbia, Canada. His mother told him years later that she had won a prize for him as the first baby of the new year, at one minute after midnight. It has been said that his father, Harry, might have been working in mining in Canada for a while before the time of his son's birth; however, he was a tailor by trade. Nolan was of English descent on his father's side and Irish on his mother's.

After the end of their parents' marriage, Earle and his older brother, Clarence Robert, were left in the care of their paternal grandparents, Charles Noles Nobles and Ella Jane Sprague Nobles, on a farm in the snowy province of New Brunswick, in Kings County, at Hatfield Point near the Belleisle Bay. Nolan used to joke that it was five miles from the nearest school – uphill both ways. In reality, the boys did attend the Hatfield Point school, most likely for only about three months a year due to schedules for planting, tilling, and harvesting on the farm. According to a March 9, 1984 article on the family by Gerry Taylor in the *Telegraph Journal / Evening Times Globe* of Saint John, New Brunswick, the "farm's harvest made them nearly self-sufficient. Only occasionally did they make the 188 mile trip for supplies by raft down the scenic St. John River to its mouth at the port city (Saint John) on the Bay of Fundy."

Through information provided by the neighboring Boyd family, it appeared that Nolan acquired his reputation rather early in life, as an adventuresome and daring young boy. According to Marsha Boyd Mitchell, in *Old Belleisle, Beautiful Still* (Over the Wall Publishing, 1998), "Earle was almost a hero" among the boys at school; he "seemed to laugh in the face of danger." Her grandmother Elsie Boyd, who had gone to school with the brothers, was said to have recalled her somewhat mischievous neighbor with a smile. She told Canadian archivist Elizabeth Drake McDonald in an October 2000 interview that she thought Earle was a favorite of his grandmother; she just knew his grandmother was thinking, "No one like Earle!" She also revealed a sensitive side to the young boy, who was much saddened when the time came for the brothers to leave the farm. In the Taylor article, George Hector, who operated the Gagetown ferry, reportedly met Nolan years later in the mid-1930s, when he came for a visit with his grandparents at his childhood home. Taylor commented from his 1984 interview with Nolan, "In spite of hardships, Earle Nolan recalled his life with his grandparents on the Belleisle near Hatfield's Point with great fondness." The original farmhouse is no longer there, but recent pictures of the site reveal an incredibly beautiful countryside.

Harry was from a large family, one of nine children. After the years his sons spent on the farm, he sent them to live with their aunts Matilda and Florence Nobles, at the family home in Medford, Massachusetts, where the boys resumed their schooling in the Boston area. Although Nolan did not tell many anecdotes from this early period of his life, he had a fondness for lilacs, from the lilac bushes outside the window at his grandparents' farm, as well as a definite taste for blueberries which grew wild there; he would forever love the countryside and always smiled at those rare snowfalls in the Arizona desert. Nolan mentioned that his grandmother taught him how to knit and put up preserves, and that his aunts thought violin lessons would be a good thing for him, but he insisted he never got past learning how to rosin the bow. On one of her visits to

Tucson in the 1960s, his aunt Florence Nobles McCoy would comment about how much she had hoped that young Earle could have stayed with them permanently, concerned that he had been moved around more than enough by then.

His father, Harry Bayard Nolan, enlisted in the United States Army on December 15, 1917, at Phoenix, Arizona, and was promoted to corporal on October 16, 1918. He was designated to 3rd Company, 3rd Battalion, 164th Depot Brigade. Harry received an honorable discharge (by reason of Telegraphic Instruction A.G.O. on November 15, 1918), with the final papers signed on December 20, 1918, at Camp Funston, Kansas. His record noted his character as "Excellent," and his physical condition at discharge as "Good." At this time, Harry was given travel pay back to Phoenix. He moved to Tucson, Arizona, and was working in a tailor shop in 1919. Clarence and subsequently Earle were sent for and joined their father from Massachusetts, Earle arriving in 1923. Harry later married Bertha Lee Foster and had two younger children, Michael Foster "Mickey" Nolan and Mary Deanna Nolan; the four of them would make their home in Santa Monica, California.

When Earle was sixteen, he located and reconnected with his mother, Flora Hayes, who had married Herbert W. Hayes and was living in Portland, Oregon. When she opened the door, he started to identify himself, but she happily recognized him immediately. From then on, Earle would ride the freight trains from Tucson each summer to visit her. He would say that in later years she would attend his boxing matches and was a very enthusiastic, verging on rabid, fan.

As alluded to above, Nolan's records also show that he returned to New Brunswick in 1934 for a summer visit with his grandparents, a year before the passing of his grandfather. Through a February 12, 1940 letter from his Aunt Florence, we know that he remained in touch with his grandmother; at that time both women were sharing an apartment in Malden, Massachusetts.

Clarence Robert "Bob" Nolan, a singer, songwriter, and lyricist, moved to California where he went on to co-found the famous Sons of the Pioneers, writing such classics as "Cool Water," "Tumbling Tumbleweeds," and "Way Out There." Among his many accomplishments, the award-winning musician was selected to the Western Music Association Hall of Fame, the Nashville Songwriters Association International Hall of Fame, and appeared in an estimated 90 Western films from 1935 until 1948.

Michael Earle Nolan took a different path, which led him to many years of phenomenal athletic honors, distinguished service in the United States Marine Corps during World War II, and a professional career as a highly respected civil engineer. Widely known throughout the course of his life as both Earl and Mike, Nolan was an individual of wide-ranging interests…a sensitive and prophetic novelist…a devoted husband, father, and grandfather. He made his home in Tucson, Arizona, where he left us all a rich and varied legacy.

On March 16, 2001, in honor of St. Patrick's Day and Tucson residents of Irish descent, an article, "Color the Old Pueblo green," by Ed Severson, appeared in the *Arizona Daily Star*. The article declared, "Possibly the fightingest Irishman nominated to the list of illustrious Tucsonians is the late Michael Earl Nolan, who died in 1991. A decorated Marine and a member of the Arizona Sports Hall of Fame, he was one of the greatest all-around athletes that Tucson and Arizona – and possibly America – ever produced."

Earle, circa one year of age. Only surviving childhood photo.

Harry Bayard (Nobles) Nolan.

Flora Elizabeth Hussey Nobles Hayes.

Clarence Robert Nolan, 1930.

Bob Nolan, Sons of the Pioneers.

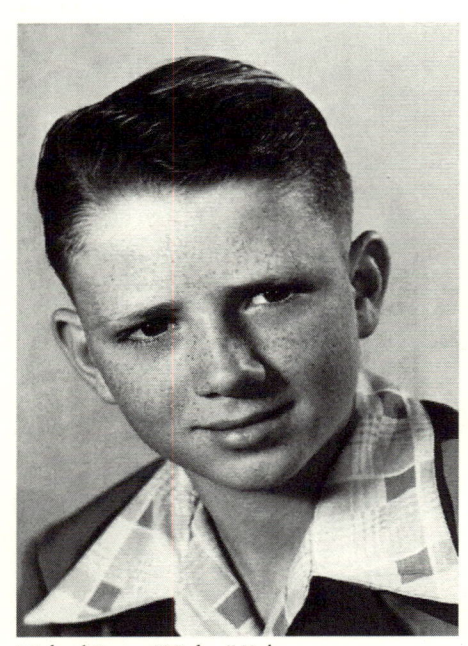

Michael Foster "Mickey" Nolan.

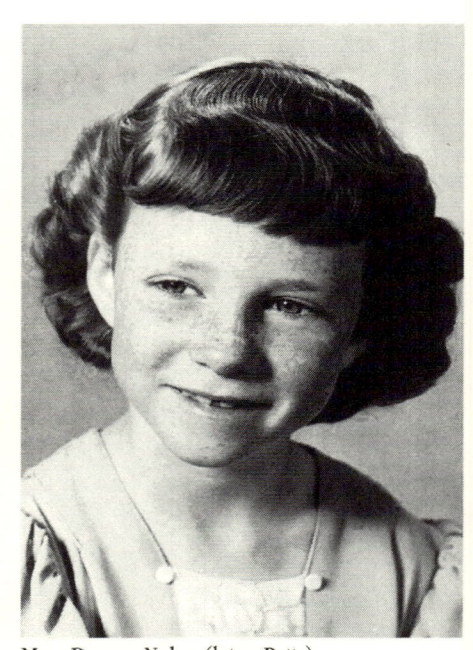

Mary Deanna Nolan (later, Petty).

Nolan with mother, Flora Hayes, in Portland, Oregon, July 1934.

Charles Noles Nobles and Ella Jane Sprague Nobles, New Brunswick, Canada, 1930s.

Nolan with aunt Florence Nobles McCoy, in Tucson, Arizona, 1960.

CHAPTER TWO

Tucson High School Football
"Tarzan," the Awakening of an Athlete

EARL NOLAN ATTENDED SAFFORD SCHOOL and Roskruge Junior High School in Tucson, graduating from Roskruge in 1927. In 1928, he entered Tucson High School, graduating May 27, 1932. Nicknamed "Tarzan" at THS – the first of many nicknames he would be christened with throughout his life – he was a member of the Tucson High "T" Club from 1929 through 1932, and lettered in both football and track. This marked the beginning of a brilliant athletic career that took local sports fans by storm. Young Nolan was big and strong and talented. With dark brown wavy hair and intense blue eyes, he had movie-star good looks, which would take on a rugged maturity over the years. He would quickly be recognized as a living legend in his hometown.

Nolan became a star and one of the most colorful players ever in Tucson High School Badger football, often playing without a helmet and shoulder pads. His high school career would result in being named on five post-season honor rosters.

By his own account, these early football days began inauspiciously. During his freshman year at THS, he was considered too slender to play the game. According to his National Guard records, he was 5 feet 9 inches tall and weighed 135 pounds. He resolutely overcame this objection and was selected in his sophomore year to play on the 1929 second team. Post-season, the 1930 *Tucsonian* yearbook described the now taller, 170-pound Nolan as a tackle who "fought hard – let a man come through but once – he was certainly in for a drubbing from Earl." The young man who had started his high school career as too slender to play developed into a powerhouse.

This 1929 team, coached by Andy Tolson, played the high school teams from nearby towns and had a fine season – won four, lost one, and tied one. The season began with a 6-6 tie with Hayden High School. The next game THS won by default when the Tombstone team did not show up due to the annual Helldorado celebration! The team then defeated Marana, 7-6, and went on to win over Florence, 12-6. As part of the

Armistice Day Classics, THS played Hayden a second time, attempting to defeat the one squad who had matched scores with them thus far in the season. This time Hayden handed the team their only loss of the year, 20-0. In a November 10, 1929 article, "Hayden High School Steamrolls Tucson Seconds By 20 To 0," the *Arizona Daily Star* observed that the Hayden team found it necessary to change tactics this time around: "Failing to do a thing with the Badger line," Hayden resorted to an aerial attack. However, in the final game, a follow-up with Marana, the season did end well, as evident in the title of Chuck Kinter's November 17 article in the *Star*, "Tucson Seconds Smother Marana, 50 to 0...Tucson Linemen Open Big Gaps For Pigskin Carriers...Entire Male Student Body of Neighboring High School Tries to Stem Tide." During the course of the game, every able-bodied male student at Marana took the field against THS, to no avail. By the end of the season, the "seconds" were referred to as "a miniature steamroller" with "a tight defense."

Nolan went on to letter in varsity football in 1930 and 1931. He played tackle and guard, and was a kicker for his team, both on kick-offs and conversions.

The 1930 THS football team won the Southern Arizona Championship, finishing the season with five wins, over the Glendale Cardinals (6-0), Miami Vandals (6-0), Douglas Bulldogs (7-6), Nogales Apaches (22-0), and Bisbee Pumas (34-0); two losses, to the Phoenix High School Coyotes, a team who would make a lasting impression on Nolan, (59-13) and Mesa Jackrabbits (21-14); and one tie, with the University of Arizona Frosh (0-0).

Nolan's name began to emerge regularly in the post-game articles. After the game with Douglas, the October 19, 1930 *Star* reported that he played a steady game at tackle and was responsible for the winning conversion. On October 26, a *Star* article, "Tucson High Badgers Wallop Nogales, 22-0," proclaimed that THS's "Nolan played havoc with their opponents." Throughout the season the *Star* praised THS as "a good defensive team" with "a line capable of holding its own with any secondary school in the state." On November 23, in "Badgers Wallop Bisbee High 34 to 0," the *Star*'s Nathaniel McKelvey referenced Nolan's "trusty toe."

Earl Nolan was selected to two honor rosters in 1930. In the November 30 *Star* article "Badgers Place Two Men on All-Conference Grid Team...Azzi Ratem Has Coaches' Help In Selecting Players...Six Schools Represented by Men Named for Places and Honorable Mention," by Azzi Ratem (W. J. Boand), he was named first-team left tackle on the Conference All-Star Team. Boand explained, "The men selected for first and second team positions were picked for their places by coaches of Southern Arizona high schools. Reasons outlined for first string choices were those given to me by those same coaches....Nolan, of Tucson, was picked for the left tackle position because he has been one of the mainstays on the Badger line all year. He is aggressive, a good defensive player and dependable. He started every Badger game this fall and was seldom relieved. Besides his tackle abilities, he was an accurate place kicker, recording almost every attempt toward the end of the season."

He was also selected tackle of the third All-Arizona Team, as presented by Vic Householder in the *Arizona Republic*.

In a December 3 *Star* article, "15 Badgers to Get Grid Letters," by George Hall, it was reported that Nolan received his end-of-the-season letter at the Annual Football Banquet. He was on his way.

By the start of the 1931 football season, his National Guard records showed him to measure 6 feet 3 inches tall and weigh 190 pounds.

The 1931 THS team also won the Southern Arizona Championship title and proved to be a serious contender for the state crown. The team finished the season with five wins, over Glendale (45-0), Miami (6-0), Douglas (45-0), Mesa (13-12), and Bisbee (48-0); three losses, to the U of A Frosh (7-6), El Paso Tigers (7-0), and Phoenix High School (20-7); and one tie, with Nogales (14-14).

An October 11, 1931 article in the *Star*, "University of Arizona Frosh Defeat Tucson High, 7-6...Badger Eleven Superior for Most of Game...Tucson Line Shows Excellent Ability in Charging; Late Drive Fails," by George Hall, read that the "Badgers out-played and out-fought a heavier and more experienced University of Arizona Frosh eleven.... Never has a Tucson line charged with greater effectiveness than Saturday, nor have its ball carriers been given more assistance. Time and again Co-Capt. Guy McCafferty, husky guard, or Earl Nolan, brawny tackle, put the Frosh to route or stopped plays for no gain."

The October 18 *Star*, in "Crushing Badger Attack Flattens Douglas Eleven, 45-0," declared that "Nolan did fine work on the line."

Before the game with the Phoenix Coyotes, an October 30 article from the *Star*, "Badgers Invade Phoenix Tonight For State Title Game," predicted, "In the line it is the work of McCafferty and Nolan that promises to prove most threatening to the Coyotes...." After the game, an October 31 *Star* recap, "Tucson Badgers Beaten on Capital Gridiron in Hectic Tussle," proclaimed, "Brilliant games for their alma mater were turned in by Earl Nolan, giant Tucson tackle, and Guy McCafferty...."

On November 7, in "Badgers Lose to El Paso, 7-0, in Final Five Minutes of Game," the *Star* commented that "Earl Nolan was a tower of strength in the line."

After the next game, in "Badgers Hard Pressed to Eke Out 13-12 Win Over Mesa," the November 12 *Star* reported, "It was Nolan's well-placed kick for the extra point that gave Tucson its one-point victory."

At the invitation of the Tucson Junior Chamber of Commerce, the Badgers played a post-season charity game with the Brophy Pintos of Phoenix, proceeds going to an orphanage and children's home. Brophy had been undefeated in eight straight games, but the Badgers won the contest, 19-6. The December 2 *Star* article "Tucson High Defeats Brophy, 19-6, in Benefit Football Battle" read that the Pinto forewall lacked power to stop Nolan..."from sifting through to rush passes and kickers....On the fourth play in the opening period Nolan, Badger tackle, broke through the Pinto line and smeared Gallassi's attempted punt and then recovered the ball for his team on the Brophy 15-yard line." There was some déjà vu in the third quarter: "Almost duplicating his feat of the first quarter, Nolan broke through the Brophy line after the kick-off to block a punt and allow Jackson to recover for Tucson on the Brophy 10-yard stripe." The sportswriter concluded that "it was the line wrecking of Nolan, Tucson tackle, that was largely instrumental in the Badger victory." The 1932 *Tucsonian* also recounted that the "Badgers crossed the Pinto goal line when Nolan, tackle, blocked a Brophy punt on two occasions, each being recovered by Tucson men close to the visitor's goal line." By that game, he was referred to as the "crack tackle."

Earl Nolan was again selected to honor rosters at the end of the 1931 football season. The *Star* presented its "All-Southern Arizona High School Teams" on December 6. In "Nogales and Tucson Win Most Places on All-Conference Eleven...Six Badger Players Awarded Positions by Coaches' Vote," it was announced that he had been selected first-team left tackle. Chosen by a vote of conference coaches, "Nolan, Tucson, stood out above opposing tackles...and polled all but one vote for the left side of the line. He has weight and aggressiveness to his credit and has been one of the outstanding linemen in every game the Badgers have played this season."

He was also elected to the All-Arizona High School Football Team as a first-team guard when he received an equal number of votes for both the tackle and guard positions. The *Arizona Republic* article "Here They Are! All-Arizona High School Team of 1931!" read that the team "was selected with a great deal of care by numerous coaches and officials under the direction of Vic H. Householder, who has been given this assignment for the last eight years.... Nolan of Tucson has been shifted from his usual position at tackle, having received an equal number of votes for each position. Nolan is big, aggressive and a fast charger, and has more blocked punts to his credit than any other player in the state. Nolan was on the third All-State in 1930."

In addition, the THS star was selected tackle on the All-State Team chosen by the *Yuma Sentinel*.

This was the beginning of a series of honors which would extend to the professional ranks and establish Earl Nolan as one of the all-time greats in Arizona football history.

Nolan (second row, third from right), Tucson High School Badgers football team, 1930. Southern Arizona Champions.

Varsity letterman Earl Nolan, Tucson High School, 1930. Selected first-team tackle, Conference All-Star Team; tackle, 3rd All-Arizona High School Football Team.

Nolan (first row, fourth from right), Tucson High School football team, 1931. Southern Arizona Champions.

"Tarzan" Nolan, varsity letterman, Tucson High School, 1931. Selected first-team tackle, All-Southern Arizona High School Team; first-team guard, All-Arizona High School Football Team; tackle, *Yuma Sentinel* All-State Team.

CHAPTER THREE

Tucson High School Track and Field
Record-Breaking Regional Champion

EARL NOLAN ALSO COMPETED IN THE SHOT PUT, DISCUS, AND JAVELIN for Tucson High School. He lettered in 1929, 1930, and 1931. During these early years, he regularly won first-place medals; set multiple conference, state, and regional records; attained high-point honors; and often scored more points himself than an entire competing team. As astounding as it might sound, this was the beginning of a field career which would not actually end until 1957.

During the 1929 track season, the THS team participated in several meets, including the March 23 dual meet between Tucson High and the University of Arizona Frosh at Tucson, the April 6 Greenway Track and Field Day at Phoenix, the April 20 Mesa Relay Invitational at Mesa, Arizona, and the May 2-4 Class A Interscholastic "University Week" competition at the University of Arizona. Nolan was entered in the discus and javelin contests in each of these meets, but his first track and field medals were awarded at the Southern Arizona Conference High School Track and Field Meet, Class A, held at St. David, Arizona, on April 27, 1929, when he took a third in the discus and a third in the javelin. Tucson High won that meet with a total of 59 points. It is interesting to note that his entry at the state qualifying Greenway meet would be the first of seven at that event, spanning the years 1929 through 1937.

A March 14, 1930 article from the *Arizona Daily Star*, "Badger Track Schedule Includes Seven Meets," laying out the preliminary schedule for the year, declared that "Nolan has developed into the leading weight man of the squad. He tosses the shot, javelin and discus with ease."

On March 19, a subsequent *Star* article, "H. S. Strong In Field Events, Revealed," by Chuck Kinter, regarding THS prospects for the upcoming season, stated, "One big sophomore, Earl Nolan, seems capable of consistently winning points in the javelin, shot and, to a lesser extent, the discus." In a section titled "Nolan Good Spear Tosser," Kinter remarked that "Nolan's strongest event is the javelin. In practice he has been tossing the spear between 150 and 160 feet, not a bad mark for a prep school athlete early in the season. When the shot is involved, he can secure distance to about 40 feet, and the discus, the poorest bet for him, can be hurled about 105 feet." Kinter's evaluation of Nolan's performance in the javelin and the shot would prove correct, but he had underestimated the young athlete's skill in the discus.

In the first meet of the season, the annual contest between the U of A Frosh and THS, held on March 29, 1930, Nolan won a first in the javelin, second in the shot, and second in the discus. A March 30 *Star* article, "Frosh Eke Out Win In Meet With Prep School," read, "The javelin and pole vault were among the strongest events for the high school athletes, with the Badgers grabbing off eight points in each. Nolan's throw of 150 feet 4 inches in the javelin proved him to be a likely competitor later in the season."

At the Greenway Track and Field Day on April 5, Nolan set a new javelin record for the meet with a first-place throw of 165 feet 10 3/4 inches. His nemesis, the Phoenix Coyotes, won the overall competition, as they would quite often.

An April 7 *Star* article, "Tucson High Athletes To Compete In Mesa Relays," recapped the Greenway event, stating, "Nolan brought home a new meet record when he threw the javelin 165 feet 10 3/4 inches. The spear toss is a favorite event for Nolan, and seems was one of the few sure places for the Badger squad."

The Second Annual Mesa Relays meet was held on April 12, and involved team competitions in the various events. Nolan was entered on both the three-man THS javelin and discus teams. Tucson High was awarded second place in the team javelin competition.

On April 19, THS competed in a dual meet with Douglas High School. Nolan, who by now was referred to as a "star," entered the shot, discus, and javelin competitions. An April 20 *Star* article, "Twelve Firsts Annexed By Tucson Team," singled out his performance: "Best achievements were recorded in the weight events, when Nolan made a nice throw of 160 feet for first in the javelin.... Nolan's winning throw in the discus was 103 feet 11 inches." Along with his firsts in the javelin and discus, he also placed third in the shot with 41 feet 9 1/2 inches.

The Southern Arizona Conference Track and Field Meet, Class A, was held at Benson, Arizona, on April 26. An April 27 article in the *Star*, "Badger Track Team Cleans Up In Meet At Benson," reported that Nolan took a first in the discus at 102 feet 11 inches, a second in the shot put, and a second in the javelin at 156 feet 8 inches.

With the May 2 *Star* referring to him as the "local javelin artist," the final track meet of the season, the First Annual Southwestern Track and Field Meet, was held in Phoenix on May 10, 1930. Nolan finished the year by earning a first in the javelin at 150 feet 10 inches, a second in the shot put, and a third in the discus at the regional meet.

The 1930 *Tucsonian* praised his performance: "Earl Nolan did all that was expected of him and then some" – he put the shot, threw the discus, and "broke the state record in the javelin at the Greenway meet."

Prior to the beginning of the 1931 season, a steady stream of articles appeared in the *Star*. "Badger Coach Again Gloomy...Strength in Sprints and in Weights Only Bright Spots in Team" appeared on March 5. The reporter predicted, "With Nolan back again to do the weight events, the Badgers are certain of a good many points in that department. Nolan is good in the shot, discus and javelin. He holds the Greenway record for the javelin, having tossed the spear 165 feet last year."

On March 15, 1931, in "Preps Stage Meet...Fowler and Nolan Collect Fifteen Points Each in Tucson High Class Meet," the results of the inter-class THS meet were presented: Nolan won first in the javelin at 150 feet, first in the shot put at 44 feet 9 1/2 inches, and first in the discus at 111 feet 2 inches.

On March 16, in "Tucson High Track Team To Meet Frosh Next Saturday...Best Chance in Weights," it was presaged that "Tucson's best chances will be in the weights with Earl Nolan due to annex a few points in all three of these events. Nolan is probably one of the best weightmen in the state in his class."

Then, on March 20, "Schedule Made For Trackmen of Badger Squad" voiced expectations that "Nolan, who tosses the javelin, shot and discus, will furnish plenty of competition for anyone Coach Harold Barron has on his Frosh squad."

Indeed, it would be a good season for him and would later prompt the 1931 *Tucsonian* yearbook to remark, "Nolan, weight man, was very good and could be counted on for at least 10 points in any meet."

The long-awaited meet between THS and the U of A Frosh took place on March 21. On March 22, a *Star* article, "Frosh Trackmen Beat Badger Squad in Fast Dual Contest...Nolan Takes Only First Place for High School in Clash at University of Arizona," by George Hall, commented, "The Badger team was only able to take one first place.... Nolan, Tucson field event ace, accounted for the first place when he tossed the javelin 151 feet 9 inches....Nolan, with a first in the javelin and third in the discus, was high man for the Tucson team."

On April 4, THS met the Mesa Jackrabbits in a dual meet. Nathanial McKelvey of the *Star*, in an April 5 article, "Tucson High Trackmen Beat Mesa, 75 to 44, in Dual Meet Here...Nolan Captures Individual Honors by Taking Three Weight Events," reported that the young weight man won the javelin at 154 feet 8 inches, the shot put at 46 feet, and the discus at 110 feet 6 1/2 inches, and that "Nolan, with a first place in the discus, shot put and javelin, collected 15 points to be high man for the meet."

The Greenway Track and Field Day was held in Tucson on April 11. McKelvey wrote on April 12, in "Tucson High Track Team Takes Second Place in Greenway...Nolan Sets New Shot Put Record," that the shot champion was also high-point man of this meet: "In the weight events Earl Nolan brought glory to himself and the Tucson aggregation by winning first in the shot put with a toss of 45 feet 2 1/2 inches, breaking the old record of 45 feet 1 inch. In an extra put after the close of the event he tossed the brass sphere 45 feet 4 1/2 inches. A heave of 160 feet 1 inch was good for a second place in the javelin, while his mark of 115 feet 6 inches gave him second in the discus. He was high point man with 11 tallies."

An April 18 *Star* article, "Badger Chances In Conference Track Meet Dwindle...Nolan Looks Good," indicated that victory in the meet later the same day might depend on Nolan in the field and Charles Fowler in track, adding, "The husky Tucson weight man tossed the shot out 45 feet 11 inches Thursday afternoon with apparent ease. Last Saturday he set a new record at the Greenway meet with a heave of 45 feet 2 1/2 inches."

After the April 18 Southern Arizona Conference Meet at Benson in which Nolan broke the state javelin record, an April 19 article, titled "Badgers Easily Capture Conference Meet...Javelin Tossed 184 Ft., Two Inches By Nolan," written by McKelvey, stated, "With Earl Nolan, star weight man, heaving the javelin 184 feet 2 inches, bettering the accepted state mark of 174 feet 10 inches, Tucson High School tracksters grabbed a total of 65 points to cop the Southern Arizona cinder track championship for Class A institutions at Benson today....Nolan also distinguished himself by being high-point man of the meet, gathering 15 tallies from a first in the javelin, shot, and discus." He beat his own record in the shot put, set at the Greenway meet.

Four years later, on April 25, 1935, in anticipation of the upcoming 1935 Southern Arizona Conference competition, the *Star* noted, in "Authentic Records Sought by Southern State Coaches," that Nolan's winning 1931 javelin record, as well as his winning shot distance of 46 feet 2 inches, remained the official records for the conference.

On April 25, 1931, at the Arizona State Teachers College at Tempe (later, Arizona State University) Invitational Class A Track and Field Meet, Nolan won first in the javelin at 167 feet 9 inches, first in the shot put at 45 feet 4 1/8 inches, and second in the discus.

Next in line was the nineteenth annual Arizona state meet held May 1-2. In a May 2 article, "Records Fall In State Track Meet...Nolan Breaks Own Mark In Shot Put," after the State Class A University of Arizona Interscholastic "University Week" Meet, McKelvey recounted that Nolan won the shot put with a first-place toss of 47 and 2/10 feet, establishing a new state record, which bettered the old mark of 46 feet 10 inches, set by Verny of Mesa in 1929.

On May 3, McKelvey completed coverage of the meet in "Records Crash in Two Days of Cinder Contest." He wrote, "Nolan, Tucson weight man, by virtue of first places in the shot put and the discus, and a third in the javelin, annexed 11 markers to be high point gainer at the meet. His toss of 120.39 feet in the platter event was by far the best work he has turned in this year. Nolan tossed the 12 pound shot to a new distance mark of 47.2 feet." (The distance was also designated as 47 feet 2 3/8 inches per U of

A meet records.)

In the May 5 *Star*, "15 Badger Tracksters Get Recommendation for Award" cited Nolan's third letter in track, but the season was not quite over. There was still the regional meet, and the newspaper reflected days of local anticipation and nervousness; it was the biggest meet of the year.

On May 6, "Enter Track Meet...Five Tucson Track and Field Men to Participate in Southwestern Meet" announced, "Five Tucson High School athletes will take part in the Southwestern track and field meet at Las Cruces, N. M., Don Van Horne, Badger coach, said Tuesday." Van Horne did not hold out too many hopes of winning the meet, since full teams would be sent by entrants such as Phoenix and Albuquerque.

On May 8, "Badger Squad Leaves Today" read, "Earl Nolan, who has broken the state record in the shot put on two occasions this year, is conceded an even chance for a first in that event and should also place well in the javelin and discus." It was certainly a cautious statement.

However, on May 10, 1931, after the Second Annual Southwestern High School Athletic Conference Track and Field Meet held in Las Cruces, New Mexico, a headline from the *Star* grabbed readers' attention: "Nolan Of Tucson Establishes Two Southwestern Records In Las Cruces Meet." The article reported, "Earl Nolan, giant Tucson, Ariz., high school weight man, established new Southwestern prep school records in the shot and discus as four members of the Southwestern High School Athletic Conference engaged in their annual track and field meet here today. The Badger star tossed the brass ball 46 feet 6 1/2 inches to better the old record of 46 feet 1/2 inch, made at Phoenix last year. He also hurled the discus 120 feet 3 inches to exceed the old record of 111 feet 6 inches." In addition, he took second place in the javelin, and tied at 13 points for the individual honors of the day. It was an incredible ending to an incredible season. The Tucson High newspaper, *Cactus Chronicle*, anticipated that he would enter the Far Western Finals of the Olympic trials for the javelin during the summer after his senior year.

His track coach, J. Don "Doc" Van Horne, was elated and very supportive of Nolan, and wrote in his young star's 1931 yearbook, "I congratulate you on scoring more points in track in one season than any other THS athlete. I also congratulate you on your records. Best wishes and thank you." In 1932, he wrote, "I want to say that I personally appreciated your efforts. More power to you in all things." In a December 31, 1930 article in the *Star*, "26 Report to Badger Coach," Van Horne had commented in particular about Nolan that he hoped "to see him go places and do things on the field this year." He had not been disappointed. The coach loved to tell the story of the first time he had Earl throw the discus; it sailed off the field, over the fence, and onto the next street. In his June 5, 1968 "The Spectator" column in the *Star*, Abe Chanin noted that at the age of 74, with a career which spanned 34 years of coaching, Van Horne still referred to Earl Nolan as "the strongest man I ever had in track and field."

Although he never spoke about his field competitions, Nolan's prowess during high school is silently attested to by the number of medals, ribbons, and certificates which have survived the years. They had been stashed in a storage box.

Letterman Earl Nolan, javelin throw, Tucson High School, 1930. Set Greenway Track and Field Day record in javelin. Won Southern Arizona Conference discus and Southwestern regional javelin championships.

Shot put champion Earl Nolan, Tucson High School, 1931. Set Greenway record in shot; Southern Arizona Conference records for shot and javelin; Arizona state records in shot and javelin; and Southwestern regional records in shot and discus. High-point man in five meets.

Top row—Pritchard, Weinzapfel, Vaughn, Lohse, Piper, Ortega, Nolan, Mathews.
Second row—Patton, Ass't. Coach; Lovett, Mgr.; Mansfield, Smith, Swain, Robertson, Schultheis, Angle, Filbrun, Cotta, Van Horne (coach).
Third row—Lovett, Murphy, Kusianovich, Barbee, Wilson, Captain; Young, Hendricks, Clark Nobles.
Bottom row—Kersh, Asst'. Mgr.; Packard, Caid, Ransom, Hattis, Brinkerhoff, Willeh, Ass't. Mgr.

Nolan (top row, second from right), Tucson High School track and field team, 1930. Competed in javelin, shot, and discus.

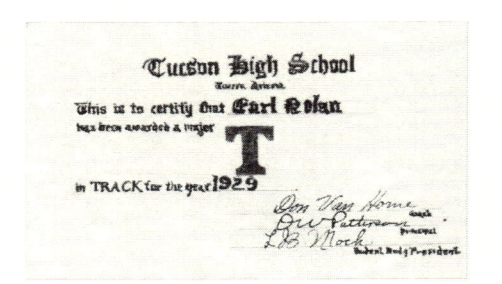

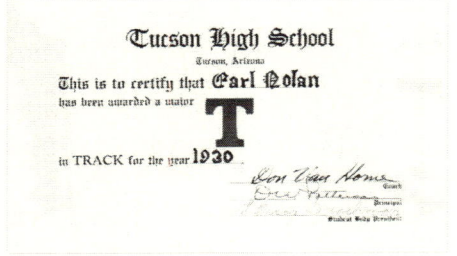

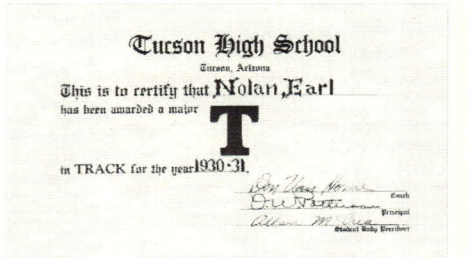

CHAPTER FOUR

Tucson High School Legacy
A Star Remembered

DECADES AFTER HIS GRADUATION, Earl Nolan's varied athletic career at Tucson High School came back into the spotlight once again.

On April 28, 1990, Charles Thornton, one of his oldest friends and an acclaimed local wrestler, as well as a wrestling and track coach at the Arizona State School for the Deaf and Blind, organized a Tucson High School reunion from that earlier era. Several of Nolan's buddies were there, including his good friends THS football player, javelin thrower, and professional boxer Frank "Dutch" Weimer, swimmer and coach John Barringer, and wrestler Andy Tremaine. In his last official interview, conducted by Matt Lemmon at the reunion, Nolan was asked if he remembered who was on the old high school football teams. He showed remarkable recall at the age of 79, naming not only the players but the positions they played, as well as quoting the scores of specific notable games. He mentioned the memorable charity game which was played against Brophy, with THS triumphing. The particular thorn in his side, however, was still Phoenix High School. He never seemed to get over those losses! It was obvious Nolan enjoyed himself that afternoon at the THS reunion, pleased to see his old friends and teammates once again. Time had not dimmed their feelings for one another, even though close to sixty years had passed.

On April 27, 1996, Nolan was elected to the Tucson High School Athletic Hall of Fame. The induction program read, "Earl Nolan – First Team All-State tackle in 1931. Big, fast and tough – 6' 3", 220 lbs. in high school. Probably the most aggressive and agile big man ever in the state. Won state in shot put, discus, javelin. He also high jumped 6' 3"." This height was an astounding feat for the young giant; traditionally, the smaller, lighter jumpers excelled at this event.

Nolan had a soft spot in his heart for his early coaches. Charles L. MacFarland, his Tucson High football coach and friend – who had offered the sophomore his left tackle position on the varsity team by means of signing his 1930 yearbook with "How about the left tackle spot?" – corresponded with him often through the years and visited him each time he came to town. He invited Earl and his wife, Nellie, to come stay with him and Mrs. MacFarland for a vacation in Solano Beach, California, and wrote that he was looking forward to Homecoming time to reconnect with the "old gang." A June 1982 letter, written by Nolan in response to one of the coach's letters, credited the early athletic guidance he had received at THS for his eventual decision to get his college degree. He wrote, "When I think back fifty years, I realize that you, Andy Tolson, Jake Meyers, Don Van Horne, and Rollin Gridley were responsible for any interest I ever showed in athletics. Without that interest in athletics, school and I would have been most incompatible bedfellows. The boredom I felt toward the daily classroom routine was intense." (The reader will recognize this as a sentiment that would be echoed by his Richard Mansan character in *Grabbing the Brass Ring*.)

Nolan believed that a sense of personal responsibility was critical in life and that athletics could teach some valuable lessons. He continued, "Twenty years after I graduated from high school, I registered as a freshman in the college of engineering. That I graduated was incidental. The fact that I was still mentally and physically capable of entering college after twenty years can be largely attributed to the athletic guidance I received during my high school years. I have always thought that the greatest lesson to be learned in athletics is to accept responsibility. I always believed that winning was a responsibility."

He credited the coaches at Tucson High School for much of the success of the University of Arizona football program, with "the development of several football players who went on to the University of Arizona and gave the U of A and Tex Oliver the best football teams." Nolan also believed that having local players on college teams led to a sense of spirit, both in the players and in the town, a spirit which was frequently missing when players were imported from other states. He told MacFarland, "I have often thought that the U of A officials have a short memory regarding the contribution you made to their football program. Today a local high school player on the U of A team is a rarity, so rare that football fans think the state of Arizona and Tucson in particular never developed a college football player."

A touching letter arrived in May of 1996 from Coach Rollin T. Gridley, himself an ex-U of A tackle, relating some of Nolan's achievements, after a lifetime of friendship. The coach added another insight into his athlete's high school career: "I still recall his final wonderful remarks to the student body at Tucson High School at his graduation – very good." This after sixty-four years! We certainly wish we were privy to the contents of those remarks.

Remarks which have survived the years were found in Nolan's copies of the 1930, 1931, and 1932 *Tucsonian* annuals. He had obviously been very well liked and respected at Tucson High School. Reviewing the many extraordinary comments written in his yearbooks revealed only feelings of the deepest admiration for his victories and honors – from National Gavelsman in debate to All-State football – as well as sincere feelings of friendship for the young star. His classmates repeatedly complimented him as "a true friend," "a plenty good man," "a great athlete," "a big he-man," "a great guy," "a mighty strong man," "an all-around fellow," and "a real man." It was also obvious from the remarks that Nolan was not only a friend but an inspiration to many of his fellow students, a role model whose character was highly valued. What follows is just a sampling of these heartfelt tributes. They are certainly not typical yearbook entries.

His fellow students were exuberant in their praise for Nolan's athletic achievements, which were the buzz of the school:

"Tucson High School will never have another athlete like you."

"You are THS's hero."

"It has been an honor to play on the same football team as you."

"I have only one wish, and that is to be as good in football next year as you were this year."

"Here's to the best track man I know of."

"You have been sort of a god to me in athletics."

"When you are in college, remember me, for I'll always try to be as good a football man as you."

"To the best weight man in the state."

"I always admired your good sportsmanship."

"Here's wishing a one-man track team all the luck and happiness possible."

"I've been an admirer of yours for a long time and I hope to be for a long time to come. You are the greatest football and track man that THS has ever known."

All wished him good luck and continued success, hoping to see him play more football and break more records in track:

"What a man – but wait till next year."

"You're a real athlete, and I want to see you do big things for THS in the future."

"Let's see you go thru life as you used to go thru the line."

"I wish you all the success that a splendid athlete deserves."

"I hope you throw the javelin 300 ft. before you're through."

"Make some records that will stand for a few long years."

Many looked forward to seeing Nolan compete at the University, but others also foresaw that he would attain national or even worldwide fame:

"I'm sure you have heard it many times, so I will not take time to say what you are capable of doing next year. But I will look to what you may be doing in the next four or five years."

"Here's hoping you will make All-American."

"You're certainly a record breaker. More power to you. Just keep it up, Earl, and you'll be a national champ some day."

"I hope to see you in the Olympics."

"I expect to see you make good in a big way."

"I know you'll go big in college football."

"You have a big future ahead of you, and I'll be pulling for you. I hope you go to 'A' next year and are a real star."

"You are going into college with the name of being one of the best athletes in the country, and I am expecting you to be the best that there is."

Not only did his classmates praise his athletic abilities, they also praised him as a person:

"You have my highest admiration."

"I wish lots of luck to one of the best and, honest to God, real men in the town."

"You are as swell a guy as an athlete, and that's saying a lot."

"You have the inner stuff to make it."

"I admire you in more ways than one."

"Here's to the best athlete Tucson ever had, and besides that, he's one swell guy."

"I wish you lots of success in future athletics. You can make good 'cause you have sure got it in you."

"You are one of the finest boys and athletes that I know."

"You will always live in my estimation as the greatest student in school today."

And it was obvious they valued his friendship, hoping that he would remember them and that their friendship would continue in the years to come:

"Here's to a friendship I have valued more than any other one."

"I have suddenly realized the importance of trying hard to keep up the name that you have made while you were in 'Ye Olde Institution,' because people throughout the state know that I don't know any more than you alone have taught me. My one and only ambition is to follow in your footsteps. I don't expect to do as much, but I shall try to be honored and respected as Earl Nolan's pal. I won't disappoint you, Earl, because I'll fight like the devil to show them who Nolan's pal is."

"I shall always cherish your friendship."

"Here's to a swell pal and a true friend. I shall never forget the good old times that we have had together."

"I think you are the best friend and athlete I have ever known."

"Just call me when you need a friend."

"If you need a friend, call on me. But if you need protection, I wouldn't be of much help."

Several of his fellow teammates mentioned the good times they had together on track or football trips and how much they had enjoyed being on the same teams as Nolan, and many of his classmates mentioned that they were happy to have shared classes with him throughout high school, whether history, English, debate, Spanish, civics, commercial law, or geometry.

Oftentimes, the yearbook entries were signed with warm words, such as "Your true friend," "Your lifetime pal," or "Remember me as one of your best friends." As time would tell, Nolan did make many lasting friendships early in his life.

There were also messages from the faculty, who expressed their feelings of friendship for their student and predicted good things for him in the future: Lillian Cavett, his public speaking teacher, complimented him on his "splendid voice" and foresaw the possibility of a career for him in public speaking. Anne E. Rogers, his economics teacher, who signed her remarks "Your friend," wrote, "It has been both a pleasure and a privilege to have you in my class. I find you a good thinker – able to form your own opinions." Estella Overpeck, his English teacher, encouraged him to further his education, stating, "I have truly enjoyed having you as a student and friend this year. I hope you go to the University because you really have ability. If I can ever help you in any way, as a teacher or a friend, I shall be most glad to do so. Whenever you come to THS for a visit, come up and say 'Hello.' My best wishes for your success." And Dolores Ochoa, his Spanish teacher, referred to him as one of her "favorites."

No doubt Nolan received these sentiments with humility and grace, a deep sense of personal responsibility, and a self-deprecating sense of humor – all of which would endear him even more.

These comments remained a timeless tribute, as did the comments from Tucson High alumni at the 1996 THS Hall of Fame induction ceremony, both for the fellow student they had known and for the man he later became. Each of them recalled his favorite anecdote about Nolan's athletic and lifetime accomplishments or the fun times they had together at THS, memories which had also lingered in their minds for decades. Not only their words, but the looks on their faces spoke volumes. The legend began early.

Through his independence of spirit, his strength of character, will, and determination, Nolan had begun to forge a life which would only continue to soar upward.

Earl Nolan, junior, Tucson High School, 1931.

Earl Nolan, senior. Graduated May 27, 1932.

Nolan (left), with friends on the athletic field of Tucson High School, 1931.

Back row: J. Runyan, H. Moomaw, F. Curtin, H. Piper, E. Nolan, M. Pesqueira, L. Gardner, R. McGoffin.
Second row: P. Turner, C. Doherty, F. Rasmessen, P. Clarke, G. McCafferty, T. Bland, T. Barthels, G. Bingham
Front row: B. Wyatt, H. Swift, J. Barbee, A. Andrews, B. Wilson, G. Jackson.

Nolan (third row, fourth from right), Tucson High School T-Club, 1931. Two-year varsity letterman in football. Three-year letterman in track and field.

"Tarzan" Nolan (third row, fifth from right), Tucson High School, 1931. Legendary football and track star. Inducted into Tucson High School Athletic Hall of Fame.

CHAPTER FIVE

Arizona National Guard
Service with the 158th

Eager to serve his nation, Earl Nolan joined the Arizona Army National Guard on August 1, 1928, for a three-year enlistment, and re-enlisted August 1, 1931, August 1, 1932, and July 10, 1933, having taken a small amount of time out for business reasons.

He served with the 158th Infantry Regiment Medical Detachment, entering as a private, and becoming a private first class and specialist fourth class. His discharge paperwork also referred to the rank of sergeant, and on the Marine Corps Occupational Qualification Record, dated January 27, 1941, he listed service as a supply sergeant from August of 1930 until August of 1931.

On November 4, 1933, he was honorably discharged, with approximately four years and seven months of active service.

Of note, the National Guard discharge paperwork, signed by Major Frederick P. Perkins, rated Nolan's character as "Excellent."

Among his things, we found the distinctive blue insignia pin of the 158th, with the menacing gila monster and the single-word warning, "Cuidado."

Michael Earl Nolan would remain in the service of his nation for much of his adult life.

Earl Nolan, Arizona Army National Guard, 1928-1933.

First service to nation. Nolan (right), with fellow Arizona National Guardsman.

Nolan (right), 158th Infantry Regiment Medical Detachment, Arizona Army National Guard.

In a lighter moment, Nolan (right) with fellow National Guardsman.

Arizona National Guard camp, 1933. Nolan (center) served as private, private first class, specialist fourth class, and sergeant.

Always working out, Nolan practices an overhead lift.

Nolan, giving a National Guard buddy a lift.

CHAPTER SIX

University of Arizona Football
"King Kong of the Gridiron"

A NOTRE DAME ALUMNUS HAD APPARENTLY lined up Earl Nolan to attend there, but, as Nolan explained in Abe Chanin's 1979 book, *They Fought Like Wildcats* (Midbar Press), "somehow we got mixed up on my high school graduation, and that took care of that." On the advice of some of his fellow National Guardsmen who were also football players in Flagstaff, he then considered attending Arizona State Teachers College at Flagstaff (later, Northern Arizona University). He was about to head out, when he was recruited by Louis Slonaker and Charles T. Tribolet to attend the University of Arizona. He matriculated at the U of A on September 10, 1932.

Nolan's college football career would result in multiple post-season honors, as well as first-ever honors for the state of Arizona and the U of A: the first Associated Press All-America recognition for the state of Arizona, and the first University of Arizona player to join the ranks of professional football. It would prompt the December 21, 1946 *Old Pueblo Sun Dial* to refer to him as "the one and only Earl Nolan...one of the nation's greats in the gridiron world."

Nolan played freshman football in 1932, coached by James Fred "Pop" McKale, who had been the varsity coach at the University for seventeen years until 1930. McKale trained the Frosh team in "Notre Dame shift plays." The team, often inauspiciously nicknamed the "Peagreeners" or the "Kittens," had an undefeated season with no points scored against them during the regular games, playing Phoenix High School (0-0), Tucson High School (25-0), Phoenix Junior College (46-0), and the Arizona State Teachers College at Tempe Frosh (26-0).

On October 28, 1932, an *Arizona Daily Star* article, "Frosh Gridders Play Junior College at Phoenix Tonight," referred to Nolan as one of "the most outstanding former high school tackles in the state." During that game with the Bears, he scored four points after touchdown, resulting from three placements and one pass.

Before the game with the Tempe Bulldogs, a November 3 *Star* article, "Frosh Prepare For Struggle With Tempe Friday," specifically cited Nolan and stated that the team boasted "one of the strongest forward walls in the past several years."

The November 4 *Star*'s "Arizona and Tempe Frosh Teams Battle in Local Stadium Tonight" noted that throughout the season the U of A freshman team got progressively stronger, and that Nolan was placed on the "A" team by Coach McKale. The next day, in "Kittens Thump Tempe Frosh at U.A., 26-0," the *Star* reported that Nolan converted on two placekicks and that he and Ken Adamson "were outstanding in the line."

The final game was the annual game against the varsity team. On November 9, the *Star* article "University of Arizona Varsity Team Slays Freshman Eleven, 18-0" acclaimed Nolan as "starring for the Kittens." In a March 25, 1999 segment of his memoirs, "Drachman History," in the *Tucson Citizen*, Roy Drachman would write that the 1932 freshmen had an outstanding team. They would scrimmage against the varsity once or twice a week, and often outscored them.

At the end of the season, Earl Nolan was awarded his numeral. This proved to be a solid beginning to his amazing career in U of A football.

A June 3, 1967 article from the *Arizona Republic*, "McKale Fast With Quips," by Frank Gianelli, related a humorous story about the veteran coach. Phoenix insurance man John Black, a former U of A football player and freshman football coach years after Nolan's tenure at the school, described the incident: "I remember how Pop lined up us freshman in the first day of practice and declared, 'Anyone who thinks he can whip me – step forward.'" Towering "Earl (King Kong) Nolan...just out of tough duty with the Marines" was visiting campus that day and stepped forward. Black recalled how McKale joked, "Okay – you get off the squad. I won't have anybody on the squad I can't whip."

Nolan, No. 47, made the starting tackle position his first year on varsity, lettering in football in 1933, 1934, and 1936. All three teams had winning seasons: In 1933, they won five, over Occidental College (18-0), New Mexico State (6-0), Arizona State Teachers College at Flagstaff (24-0), Arizona State Teachers College at Tempe (26-7), and Whittier College (26-0); and lost three, to Loyola Marymount University (14-13), Texas Tech (7-0), and University of New Mexico (7-0). Arizona scored 113 points against their opponents, and had 35 points scored against them. The team also defeated Flagstaff in a spring training game, 18-0. In 1934, they won seven, over San Diego State (7-0), Colorado State (7-3), Whittier College (14-7), University of New Mexico (14-6), Oklahoma City University (26-6), Arizona State Teachers College at Tempe (32-6), and College of the Pacific (31-7); lost two, to Loyola Marymount University (6-0) and Texas Tech (13-7); and tied one, with New Mexico State (0-0). Arizona scored 138 points against their opponents, and had 54 points scored against them. In 1936, they won five, over Brigham Young University (32-6), Arizona State

Teachers College at Tempe (18-0), New Mexico State (28-7), University of New Mexico (28-0), and University of Wyoming (58-0); lost two, to University of Utah (14-6) and Michigan State (7-0); and tied three, with Centenary College (13-13), University of Kansas (0-0), and Texas Tech (7-7). Arizona scored 190 points against their opponents, and had 54 points scored against them. The 1936 team became the Border Conference Champions and, to this day, are often fondly remembered by sportswriters and Arizona enthusiasts alike.

This new era of Coach Gerald A. "Tex" Oliver and the famous "Blue Brigade" of the Arizona Wildcats has been referred to by many as the "Golden Years of Arizona Football," with the greatest teams and best-remembered gridders in Arizona history. The teams met several strong opponents, and during Nolan's playing years, no team ever beat them by more than one touchdown. And Nolan himself has been referred to countless times as the best tackle in Arizona grid history. A particularly revealing comment was made on a local television sports program a few years ago. When it was mentioned that the U of A team was rebuilding under a new coach, the response was, "They've been rebuilding since 1936."

Throughout Nolan's years at the U of A, Tucson High School retained pride in its graduate. In a *Cactus Chronicle* article, titled "Former Tucson High Football Players Are Stars at University," he was referred to as "one of the greatest footballers this school has ever and will ever produce."

Seven different post-season Border Conference honor rosters have been located so far for the years Nolan played, including the 1933, 1934, and 1936 official All-Border Conference rosters, and they would agree with that assessment. Nolan made them all. It is interesting to note that at the time, there seemed to be a little bureaucratic vying going on as to which teams were "official" selections.

On December 10, 1933, the *Star* article "U.A., Texas Tech and Flagstaff Win Most Spots on Honor Team...Border Conference Coaches Name Two All-Star Elevens," written by Pat O'Brien, listed Nolan as second-team tackle on the roster of the "All-Border Conference Teams" – the "third annual *Arizona Daily Star* All-Border Conference football team, selected after a poll of the coaches and sports writers in the southwestern district." On January 3, 1934, a *Star* article, "Honor Border Loop Elevens are Selected...Commissioner Reveals Official All-Star Grid Teams," informed that the "conference decided to make official all-star selections at a recent meeting." The official All-Border Conference football team was announced by Dr. Emil Larson, the conference commissioner. Nolan was named second-team tackle. A later article, "Eleven Boasts Great Reserve Power in Line," from the September 28, 1934 *Arizona Wildcat*, stated that he was "rated all-conference in many quarters last fall." This could mean there are more 1933 rosters to find.

Although plagued with injuries much of the season, he was placed on three honor rosters at the end of the year in 1934. Nolan was selected first-team tackle on the All-Border Conference roster. He was named in a December 15, 1934 article from the *Star*, titled "Arizona Places Three Men on Conference Eleven...Robinson, Nolan and Bland Are Given Honors by Border Coaches," as well as a December 14 *Tucson Daily Citizen* article, titled "Arizona Places Three On Border Team...Bland, Robinson And Nolan Named On Conference Eleven," which billed the selection as the "official 1934 All-Border Conference football team," chosen through the votes of all coaches in the conference and compiled by the conference commissioner, Dr. Emil L. Larsen. Nolan was also named first-team left tackle on the December 14, 1934 *Arizona Wildcat*'s "*Wildcat*'s All-Conference" roster. We have one additional newspaper clipping featuring different 1934 selections, the source of which we have yet to identify. "All-Border Conference Choices...Tech, Arizona U. Each Put Three On First String...Coaches' and Officials' Votes Pick Players for Mythical Lineups" listed Nolan as first-team tackle.

Again in 1936, Nolan was named on more than one honor roster. A December 20, 1936 *Star* article, "Four Cats Named on All-Conference Eleven...Warford, Nolan, Preininger and Smilanich Picks," read, "University of Arizona, Border Conference football champions, took the lion's share of places on the all-conference eleven selected by coaches and announced yesterday by the circuit commissioner, Dr. E. L. Larsen." Nolan was named as first-team tackle. The photographs accompanying the article were labeled "These Wildcats Given All-Conference Rating," the caption stressing once more that the players were "named yesterday on the official all-conference honor team."

Another article from the *Phoenix Gazette* of December 15, 1936, "Arizona Lands Five On All-Border Eleven...They're The Best In Border Conference For 1936 Season," by Bob Macon, named Nolan as first-team tackle on the "*Phoenix Gazette*'s All-Border Conference Team of 1936." Macon had high praise for the Tucson star, writing that he could have won a post on "almost any eleven in the country....After a year's lay-off, Nolan returned to the Wildcats' lineup this fall for his last and greatest season. Weighing 210 pounds and unusually tough, the young husky was the defensive bulwark of the conference champions. In addition he kicked off for his team." The December 18 *Wildcat* heralded, "Five Brigadiers Make Border Conference Eleven...Nolan Is Lineman," marking the third year he had gained all-conference recognition.

Nolan played right tackle on offense and left tackle on defense. He used to say that throughout the course of a game, most players would come his way and that when he would go downfield, he would block anyone standing up – including the referee. In addition, he often kicked off for the team and was an excellent conversion kicker. Rumor was that he could kick the ball out of the stadium. According to a May 5, 1936 *Wildcat* article, "Coach Oliver Names Football Medal Winners," Nolan received an honor for placekicking in the March 31 pre-season competition.

No. 47, "Tough as They Make Them"

Articles about the performance of the University of Arizona Blue Brigade were plentiful in the local newspapers. Football fans were very supportive and ready to devour anything written about these powerhouse teams. Earl Nolan seemed to be a favorite topic, and it escalated each year.

In a September 28, 1933 *Star* article, "Arizona Eleven To Be Strong At Tackle Berths," Pat O'Brien predicted that Nolan, who now weighed 205 pounds, "can wreak havoc on defense and is learning the new Arizona offensive system rapidly."

After the game with Occidental, a September 30, 1933 *Star* article, "Cats Score in Last Three Quarters to Beat Oxy, 18-0," pointed out that the "Arizona line stopped dead every running play attempted," and that Nolan "particularly showed up well."

An article appearing in the *Wildcat* on November 3, 1933, "Cats Meet N. M. Lobos," opined that during the game with the Flagstaff Lumberjacks, "Earl (Tarzan) Nolan...looked particularly good in defensive line play."

On September 28, 1934, in "Cats Open Season Tonight...Fast and Powerful Arizona Line to Receive Brunt of Aztec Assault...Eleven Boasts Great Reserve Power In Line," the *Wildcat* predicted that Nolan "is bound to wreck a few Aztecs before the fray ends." On the same date, a second article, "Dark Horse Wildcat Team Enters Fray With Coach Pessimistic...Rated as Dark Horse, Cats Open Season Against Aztecs," noted, "Earl (King Kong) Nolan, all-conference tackle, has been chosen to do the honors at the opening whistle." Even though the initial ratings before the game seemed to go against Arizona, the University came through with a 7-0 victory over San Diego, a great beginning for the 1934 season.

The day of the game with the Colorado State Aggies, the October 5 *Wildcat* disclosed that Nolan had injured his hip during the Aztec game, with a headline over his picture, "Injured Defensive Star May Play."

An October 8 article from the *Citizen*, "Cats Prepare for Whittier," after that game with the Aggies, concluded, "Earl Nolan, the huge 200-pound tackle, was the outstanding lineman on the field. He played most of the game and turned in the most impressive performance of his career." In fact, Tex Oliver himself cited Nolan as the outstanding man on the field. Not bad for a player with an injured hip!

The October 9 *Wildcat*, in "Wildcats Defeat Aggies 7-3...Whittier to Be Met Friday...Wildcat Line Stops Strong Aggie Attack," declared that "Earl Nolan, the 'Muscular Myrmidon' was probably the outstanding lineman on the field, smearing any plays aimed near his left tackle post. This he did despite an injured hip that kept him out of scrimmage the preceding week." As also reported, he made the conversion. In a review of the game, the 1935 U of A *Desert* yearbook would later state that Nolan stood out in defense.

In the October 12 *Wildcat* article "Wildcats To Enter Whittier Contest Underdogs

– F. Enke," it was said, "Earl Nolan, gigantic tackle, will prove an insurmountable obstacle for the Poet ball-carriers, for his hip injury is now okay, and he will be able to smear plays with his old-time gusto." Despite the doom and gloom of that article's headline, Arizona emerged victorious, 14-7.

An October 16 article from the *Wildcat*, "Cats Prepare For Game With Loyola Here Saturday," analyzed the Whittier game: "Earl Nolan, muscular tackle, who was probably the outstanding lineman on the field, place-kicked to convert," not once but twice. Setting the stage for the upcoming Loyola game, the article proclaimed, "No eleven has been able to penetrate the Cat forward wall this year." The paper's "Vittles by Vic" column stressed that "Nolan kept his conversion record intact." He did, however, end up with two badly bruised shins.

To give an example of some of the press hype surrounding Nolan, an October 16 *Citizen* article, "Cats Determined To Defeat Loyola," featured his photograph, titled "Determined To Tame Loyola Lion." The caption was even more telling: "The Loyola Lion is roaring this year, but next Saturday night he will encounter a tamer in Earl Nolan, giant University of Arizona tackle. Nolan has been playing the finest football of his career this season, and great things are expected of him when the Wildcats battle the Lion in the feature of Arizona's Homecoming Day Program." An October 20 *Citizen* article, "Cats Play Loyola Tonight," featured another foreboding picture of him, titled "Ready to Face Loyola's Lions," with a caption stating once again that Nolan, a junior, was playing his best football, and adding that he was "expected to scale new heights against Loyola's powerful aggregation."

Loyola did end up victorious, 6-0, but they had scored 98 points against their other opponents in the first three games of the season. The Arizona defense held the line. Nolan would later say Loyola was one of the toughest teams he had ever seen, and they would do anything on the field to win. He joked to family that they were "pretty ferocious" and would even bite and scratch.

Not only were the teams tough, the one-platoon system could be a little demanding. Quoting an October 26 *Star* article, "Nolan and Beeler Play Most Time," the two men were tied for "more minutes of play in the games played thus far than any of their teammates, a list posted on the varsity bulletin board this week shows." Each man had accrued a total of 3 hours and 32 minutes of action.

Before the game with New Mexico State, an October 26 *Wildcat* article, "Wildcats Enter Aggie Fray Decided Underdogs – Oliver," again mentioned Nolan's injuries: "Nolan has been bruised up since the season started, and constant service against such heavy teams as Loyola and Whittier has improved him not at all." And yet, his excellent playing had still shone through. The *Desert* wrote that "Nolan starred on the Arizona line" during the subsequent game with the University of New Mexico.

In fact, it was altogether not a good year as far as injuries were concerned. A November 12 *Star* article, "Oliver Pleased With Showing of Wildcat

Squad...Henderson, Nolan, Bland and Mullen Injured in Goldbug Tilt," reported that Nolan had been knocked cold in the game with Oklahoma City, and had three stitches in his chin after being kicked while attempting to tackle a Goldbug ball carrier. In "Cats Meet Tempe Tomorrow," the November 16 *Wildcat* commented, "Earl Nolan, giant tackle, is definitely out of the action for the week, having been kicked in the jaw by an Oklahoma back."

However, the November 23 *Wildcat*, in "Wildcats Ready for Texas Tech Matadors," offered some good news: "Earl Nolan, all-conference Arizona tackle, has been able to take part in scrimmages for the first time since the Oklahoma kickfest." He was back on the field for the Tech game.

The U of A team ended the year and surprised the nation with a 31-7 victory in an extra game with Amos Alonzo Stagg's College of the Pacific. Previously, the COP had a scant 39 points scored against them all season. In "1934 Wildcat Swan Song Is Long, Sweet, Happy Melody," Pat O'Brien opined that Nolan "played a great game." The line coach of the COP Tigers, Lawrence Apitz, "was loud in his praise of the Arizonans. 'They've got more than any team we've faced this season,' he said. 'We were really outplayed almost all the way.'"

At the end of the 1934 season, a Phoenix article, "All Star Roles For Cat Trio? Nolan Outstanding," stated, "Nolan, playing in his second year on the varsity, is probably the outstanding defensive lineman in the Conference. Combining his 210 pounds with great strength and a fighting spirit, he is rarely moved out of the play when the opposition attacks his side of the line." The article predicted that the trio of players were "assured of representing the University of Arizona on the mythical all-border athletic conference football team this year, so sparkling have been their performances."

In the words of the 1935 *Desert* yearbook, Nolan "starred" in 1934 and "stood out in line defense."

On February 5, 1935, a *Wildcat* article, "29 Football Men To Receive Awards at Thursday Assembly," announced that Nolan would be receiving the two-year award at the upcoming assembly, a gold football medal. As a returning letterman, he also became a member of the Arizona "A" Club.

A Season Never Forgotten

Having defeated three West Coast teams – San Diego, Whittier, and Pacific – the U of A no doubt foresaw a bright future, and it did come to pass. The 1936 season was the best one for Nolan and for his coach, Tex Oliver, who had many hopes pinned on his veteran tackle. The *Star*'s Bernie Roth, in his June 5, 1949 "Looking Back" column, "UA's First Pro Gridder Now A Fireman," quoted Coach Oliver about Nolan: "He was mean, tough, aggressive and smart. He was by far the best downfield blocker I have ever seen." At other times, Oliver referred to his powerful tackle as a "helluva" football player, who sported a "50-inch chest." [Editor's note: Nolan's 1933 National Guard records indicated that his chest measured 46 inches, 49 expanded. The editor knows for a fact that in the early 1960s, his chest measured 52 inches expanded!] Nolan also spoke highly of Oliver and believed he was an exemplary coach. To skip forward to 1950...when Tex Oliver left to coach in Fullerton, California, Nolan was one of the Blue Brigadiers attending a farewell banquet for him. In his "The Spectator" column, "Tex Oliver Gets High Tribute – And Much Deserved Tribute At That," Abe Chanin reflected the lasting impact these years would have on local football, noting, "There was big Earl Nolan, called by many the best tackle in Arizona grid history...." It would be one of the last gatherings of the legendary Blue Brigade, whose fame was cemented in the 1936 season. The team would never forget their feisty coach. Nolan later credited Tex Oliver as the only coach who could get him to wear his helmet! By the way, that was no insignificant accomplishment.

Nolan was a frequent subject of articles by sportswriters in Phoenix newspapers, who often touted his skills and had obviously missed his presence during the 1935 football season. They seemed to take as much pride in his accomplishments as did his hometown. A 1936 pre-season article from the *Arizona Independent Republic*, "Four Boxing Champs on U. Grid Eleven," spoke about Nolan "who is the university heavyweight champion and holds the 1936 southwestern AAU title in the division. Nolan has been checked for All-American observation this year and will be back in his left tackle position after a season's layoff. Blessed with natural ability, Nolan is a great blocker and a tower of strength on the defense. He is a dependable kick-off man and a reliable placekicker."

Coach Oliver was very pleased with the prospect of having his standout player back on the field in 1936. The reason for Nolan's 1935 hiatus from football is not known at this time. According to a statement made by Tucson sports enthusiast Roy Drachman, freshmen at the U of A were not allowed to join the varsity team. This would indicate that, as with the majority of football conferences at the time, varsity eligibility was limited to three years. Nolan had played varsity football in 1933 and 1934; Abe Chanin, in *They Fought Like Wildcats*, and other sportswriters stated that 1936 marked his last year of eligibility. Could the star tackle have been asked to save his last year of eligibility for the long-awaited 1936 season? Whatever the reason for his absence, he did return to the field in 1936, which was to be a pivotal year for the Arizona football program. His return was much anticipated by the fans and by the local sportswriters. He was, however, very disappointed to see his favored No. 47 unavailable, and would play that season as No. 58.

On January 31, 1936, in "Arizona's 1936 Grid Recruits Asked To Meet," the *Star*'s Vic Thornton looked forward to the expected return of the outstanding giant varsity tackle. Spring practice ran for six weeks, from February 24 through April 4. The "game condition" scrimmages between the Red and Blue teams began on February 28, and Nolan's playing was again deemed outstanding in the press reports. In a May 5 *Star* article, "Oliver Names Spring Grid Medal Winners at Arizona," it was foreseen that "Arizona will seek national recognition in the grid spotlight this fall when they tangle with a galaxy of 'big time' opponents, including Michigan State's Spartans, the Kansas Jayhawks, the Gentlemen of Centenary, Texas Tech's Matadors and the formidable Rocky perennial contenders, the Utes of Utah." A May 24 *Star* article, "Arizona Spring Gridmen Are Presented Medals at Banquet," read, "Outstanding performers on Tex Oliver's spring gridiron squad were honored with a banquet and presentation of medals." Prominent among those eleven best players, one for each position, was Earl Nolan, presented with an intramural gold medal for attendance, improvement, and ability, as well as receiving the aforementioned honor for placekicking. He was ready for the 1936 season. On May 15, Thornton had reflected in his "The Spectator" column that he was looking into his crystal ball to make predictions for the upcoming season and that Nolan was "hailed as an outstanding candidate for All-American tackle."

That summer, Nolan was working for the Arizona Highway Department, measuring traffic usage. Coach Oliver began an August 19, 1936 letter to him by quipping, "Well, how is the car counting business progressing by now? I guess you are one of the very best counters in the whole state of Arizona." The coach advised him about the upcoming scrimmage, and stated, "I know you will be ready for it as you always keep in good shape; I imagine that you are already getting anxious for some action."

Oliver was looking forward to the Blue Brigade's strongest season, and he foresaw a bright future for the team and for Nolan: "Earl, I am counting on you a great deal this year. This should be your greatest year on the football field, and I am counting on you to play a lot of 60-minute football. I feel that you are going to show a lot more science and skill at tackle this year than ever before and that with the experience you have had, you will make practically no mistakes. This should make you one of the best tackles in the entire country.... With the schedule we have this year it should give you a great opportunity to achieve national recognition, and I believe that you will do it. I know that you *can* do it."

The coach was planning out the season, and saw Nolan as a role model for other players: "It looks as though we should have a great outfit this year, probably the best team in the history of the school.... I know you can hold down the left tackle position in championship style.... I am counting on a few of the old-timers, and you especially, to set the pace in the matter of morale and spirit on the practice field as well as the playing field. I know that you will give the other fellows something to shoot at in the matter of morale, spirit and cooperation – as well as efficiency and fire at playing your own position. So, I am expecting a great team spirit this year – not only 'the will to win' but also 'the will to prepare to win.' I feel more confident than ever before that we will have that old hustle and ambition that it takes to master all of the finer points of football, that it takes to come through over the toughest opposition."

It was Coach Oliver's goal to achieve national recognition for the University of Arizona, and he had arranged a tough schedule with prominent opponents: "Speaking of opposition, this year we have the best schedule in the history of Arizona football and the best opportunity the state and the school have ever had to break into national football prominence and to give some of our players the recognition and the credit that they deserve. We are playing some of the best teams in different sections of the country, and if we can come through as I believe we can, we will prove that in Arizona we can play football with the very best in the country."

Nolan certainly did not disappoint Oliver's faith in him.

On September 1, 1936, an article from the *Star*, "Tex Oliver is Back, Anxious to Launch Football Drills at U.," quoted Oliver: "'We will have a better team than last year,' said Tex, when queried as to the Brigadiers' possibility of weathering their 10-game suicide schedule."

The community was anxious to see the 1936 season open and was anxious to see Nolan play once again. In the September 10 *Star*, a picture of him, labeled "'King Kong' of the Gridiron," was captioned "Earl Nolan looks like a mighty tough hombre when he shifts into high gear on the gridiron, and Coach Tex Oliver is counting on him for 'big things this fall.'" An accompanying article, "Arizona Holds First Football Practice Today," read, "Tackle berths should be well handled by a rugged gang of iron-thewed huskies, including Earl Nolan...." On the same day and on the same page, an article by Joe Ahee, "Pick and Shovel Jobs Appeal To Gridders During Summer," stated, "Earl Nolan, giant tackle local experts have begun to boom for All-American consideration, has spent the summer swinging a pick and shovel for the Arizona Highway Department."

The hype surrounding his return to the field continued on September 12 in the *Star* article, "Brigadiers To Hold Public Workout Tonight." In a section titled "Nolan Returns," in premature anticipation of his appearance, the article predicted that "Earl Nolan, hailed as an outstanding tackle prospect...will be in uniform tonight."

On September 21, a precursor to sports celebrity endorsements appeared in the sports pages of the *Star*. A local bakery featured a picture of Nolan, captioned "209 Pounds of What It Takes. That's 'King Kong' Nolan – 1933 and 1934 letterman who will register today. He is 22 years old and stands six feet two in his dress socks. He is a great blocker and a constant source of pain to defensive backs...a dependable kick-off man and a reliable place-kicker in tight spots. On defense...Ouch!" The second paragraph read tellingly, "We don't know what kind of bread Earl Nolan prefers. We haven't asked him. But if he shows the same rare judgment in getting around his meals as he does in getting around the gridiron, we'll lay a bet that his choice is

Stonecypher's."

When Nolan appeared for drill, a September 22 *Star* article, "Joe Sachen and Earl Nolan Are Out For Drills," determined that he looked "as good as ever."

A September 22 *Citizen* "From The Press Box" column by Hank Squire, "Nolan Should Have Best Year," indicated that the sportswriter was also happy to see his return: "A stronger and huskier Earl Nolan has returned to the University of Arizona's football squad after a season's absence, and this, his final year of eligibility, should be his best with the Blue Brigadiers. The return of the giant Nolan, who towers six feet two and tips the weights at 225 pounds, 15 more than he weighed during the 1934 season, brightens Coach Tex Oliver's hopes for a powerful wall.

"Nolan has all the requirements to become the greatest tackle in the west and one of the best in the nation. Provided he consistently plays the football of which he is capable, he has a fine opportunity to be named on some of the All-America teams for 1936." Squire ended his column by saying that "there is no one who would rather see him on an All-American eleven than this writer."

The season was viewed as a challenging one, and momentum was building. On September 25, in "Arizona Opens Grid Season Against Cougars," *Star* sportswriter Rick Richards predicted that 1936 would be "the toughest season in the history of the school," and Vic Thornton would later point out that the season included the first game with "Big Six" competition in the Kansas Jayhawks.

A September 25 *Wildcat* article, "Blue Brigade Opens Season Tonight Against Brigham Young; Cats Are Favored," observed, "The return of Earl 'King Kong' Nolan plugs up the dangerous gap in the Arizona line." On September 26, in "Arizona Thumps B.Y.U. In Grid Opener," the *Star* acclaimed him as "a power on the defense."

An October 2 article, "Blue Brigade Invades Utah: En Route to Salt Lake City with the Arizona Wildcats," which appeared in the *Arizona Independent Republic* before a game scheduled the following Saturday with the Utah Utes, focused on Nolan's kicking prowess: "An intensive dummy drill on the high school field at Colton, Calif., this morning drew a crowd of approximately 300 fans. Attention was directed by Oliver toward offensive and defensive kick-off formations, and Earl Nolan and Hoss Nielsen brought the fans to their feet with several boots that sailed over the end lines." Although his other skills got most of the coverage, Nolan's kicking skills were quite extraordinary – referred to as "first-class," "accurate," "trusty," "dependable," and "reliable."

After the game with Utah, an October 4 *Star* article, "Brigadiers Bow To Utah Utes, 14-6...Nolan Is Standout," by W. R. Mathews (William R. Mathews, publisher and editor of the *Star*), read that the "line of the Blue Brigade played a magnificent game. The Redskins were able to gain only a little ground through the line. Earl (King Kong) Nolan was everywhere, and Rasmussen, the famous Ute line plunger, throughout the game butted his head against a stone wall." On October 8, in "Bulldogs Hope To Keep

Intact Victory String," Richards wrote that Tex Oliver had also praised Nolan for his work in the Utah game.

The October 6 *Wildcat* featured a formidable-looking photo of Nolan, titled "Eveready Earl." The caption touted him as the "man mountain on the defense and a tower of strength on the offense. The ground gained over Earl's position during an entire season would not amount to a first down. Nolan is big and tough, and no matter where the play is when it is stopped, generally the man who has the ball carrier on the bottom of the pile is old King Kong."

On October 11, in a *Star* article, "Arizona Gridders Crush Tempe, 18-0," Vic Thornton declared that "Earl (King Kong) Nolan, Arizona left tackle, was the outstanding lineman on the field for the Brigade."

A picture, titled "Brawny Brigadier Tackle," appearing in the October 13 *Star*, was captioned "Earl (King Kong) Nolan, Arizona's titanic 215-pound left tackle, will be primed to give Centenary's famed Southern Gentlemen a rousing reception when the grid rivals battle under the arc lights of Varsity stadium here Saturday evening."

After the Centenary game, an October 18 *Star* article, "Arizona, Centenary Tie 13-13," called Nolan "a standout for Arizona in the line." The account also detailed his opening 55-yard kick-off, as well as two others which sailed over the goal line.

On October 25, after the game with the New Mexico Aggies, the *Star* article "Arizona Downs Aggies In Conference Tussle...Brigadiers Overpower New Mexico Aggies As 7,000 Watch In Stadium," by Vic Thornton, cited Nolan as a defensive star for Arizona. On that same date, the *Arizona Independent Republic* mentioned that in the October 24 win over the Aggies (28-7), he also made his three conversions.

Regrettably, injuries occurred once more in the 1936 season. On November 1, in "Arizona Gridders Battle Kansas Jayhawks To Scoreless Tie in Intersectional Game...Arizona - Kansas Game Ends in 0-0 Deadlock," Thornton reported that Nolan "was removed mid-way through the second half with an injured leg." He was still named as outstanding for Arizona on the defense. A November 6 *Wildcat* article, "Border Patrol Faces Tough Foe in Lobos in Homecoming Fray...Nolan Is Injured," lamented, "Nolan, the big Cat All-American prospect, suffered a knee injury in the Aggie and Kansas games and will be on the bench at the start of the game."

Another photo of Nolan appeared in the November 20 *Wildcat*, this picture titled "Tackle Meets Test." The caption read, "Earl Nolan, gigantic Arizona tackle who has been suggested by Alan Gould, sports editor of the Associated Press, as a prospective All-American tackle, will have his chance to make the grade tomorrow when he leads Tex Oliver's Blue Brigade into action against the Spartans of Michigan State."

A November 21 article, "Arizona Faces Michigan State Eleven Today," by Leon Gray for the *Star*, relayed some of the comments on the minds of the Arizona players as they headed to this long-anticipated game. His friend Earl made a low-key remark: "It'll be a long trip home if we don't win, and we want to spend an enjoyable trip home." Unfortunately, this win would not be the case. On November 22, in "Wildcats Lose By One Touchdown," Mathews, while reviewing the contest, stated that "Nolan played his usual good game."

On November 23, after that big game with Michigan State, an account appeared in the *Star* which no doubt pleased Tex Oliver. In "Detroit Scribes Laud Cats," Mathews quoted the *Detroit News* as stating that the "game developed into one of the hardest fought battles here in recent years," and the *Detroit Free Press* singled out Earl Nolan for his excellent work.

An article on the same day from the *Citizen*, "Wildcats Praised For Showing At Michigan," mentioned that Detroit and Lansing sportswriters acclaimed the U of A for being the "most underestimated team to appear in the middle west.... 'Tex' Oliver's fighting Wildcats earned a reputation for themselves in this part of the country that established Arizona as a football competitor of national ranking.... With the exception of the first five minutes, the Wildcats outplayed the mighty Spartans."

A picture, which was titled "Clear the Road, Cowpunchers," appeared in the November 28 *Star*. The caption read, "Here is Earl (King Kong) Nolan, Arizona's 210-pound tackle who will swing into high gear against the Wyoming Waddies when they clash with the University of Arizona Wildcats in Phoenix tonight." This time the Brigadiers won, 58-0.

"Titanic Tackle Gains National Grid Spotlight"

As had been foreseen at the beginning of the season, Arizona was in for some good news in the fall of 1936.

On October 15, a photograph of Nolan, which posed the question above it, "Is He Headed for All-American Rank?" and an article, "Nolan, Arizona Tackle, In All-American Possibilities," by Alan Gould, appeared on the front page of the *Star*. A bold headline on the sports page announced, "Nolan Nominated as Potential All-American." Accompanying headlines indicated the buzz which was created in his hometown: "Only Southwestern Name in All-Star Selections Made Through Sports Scouts of Associated Press for Alan Gould Is That of Veteran U.A. Tackle," and "Titanic Tackle Gains National Grid Spotlight...Is Only Border Circuit Player Named on Honor List."

Phoenix fans seemed equally enthusiastic about their rival's nomination, as evidenced by two articles from the *Arizona Independent Republic*. The headlines in the October 15 issue read, "Arizona Wildcat Tackle Is Prospect For All-American...Nolan Rated With Best in College Game...Enters National Limelight." Nolan, the article said, "blessed with a lot of natural ability, has won renown as a great blocker. He also is a first-class man at kicking off and a dependable place kicker." On November 11, the second notice about his candidacy appeared: "University of Arizona football followers have searched earnestly for an All-American candidate...for a number of years." In the fall of 1936 they had their man. "Nolan has consistently opened the way for long gains by Arizona backs and has proved an impregnable wall of offense against opposition advancers."

In December of 1936, Earl Nolan was indeed named All-America Honorable Mention, the first time in history that a University of Arizona player received such an honor. This time the captions under the newspaper photographs of the local star proclaimed to sports fans, "All-America Recognition." The selection marked the achievement of another of Coach Oliver's goals for the 1936 season, and the achievement of another milestone for Tucson and the state of Arizona.

On December 5, a front-page article in the *Star*, "Arizona Player Recognized for All-America," declared that Nolan "received a signal honor by being given honorable mention on the 1936 All-America team yesterday.... The selection of Nolan marks the first time in history that an Arizona player has received such recognition."

A December 4 *Citizen* article, titled "Earl Nolan Is Ranked with All-America Football Stars... Giant Tackle Placed Among Nation's Best... University of Arizona Is Given National Grid Recognition," offered some insights into how his hometown viewed this honor and its star tackle: "Earl Nolan was rewarded today for three seasons of brilliant performances with the Arizona Wildcats when he was given honorable mention on the All-America football team chosen for 1936 by the Associated Press. The giant tackle's name was added to the roll of stars that includes the greatest players from coast to coast.... Alan Gould, general sports editor of the Associated Press, selected the gridiron stars for the honor roll.... The choices were made on merit alone as seen through the human eye and the records."

A section of the article, subtitled "First Recognition," discussed the groundbreaking nature of the honor for both the University and the state of Arizona: "This is the first time that an Arizona player has been ranked with the cream of the nation's gridiron crop, and Nolan's place among the stars is a new honor for the University of Arizona team that is advancing rapidly up the football ladder."

The honor came to King Kong during his final year of Arizona football; no doubt the local fans would miss him. There was just one more game left: "Nolan is playing his last season with the Wildcats. He will bring his colorful career to an end tomorrow afternoon when the Felines tangle with the Red Raiders from Texas Tech."

Coach Oliver was quoted, pleased with the national recognition given to his star player: "Informed of Nolan's selection, Head Coach 'Tex' Oliver praised the husky lineman for his splendid playing. 'He is the best tackle I have seen this year, and I might add we have played against some good ones during the season,' the coach stated. 'He is by far the best I have ever seen in this section of the country. I am glad and extremely proud that Earl Nolan has been given this recognition. I am confident that it won't be long before other boys will receive similar honors.'"

Not only was the coach happy, but the community was looking forward to the future of Arizona football, as well: "Elated over Nolan's selection, a number of Towncats, a businessmen's organization interested in Arizona athletics, expressed the opinion that it is another step forward for the Wildcats and that future years should bring further recognition to Arizona players."

More national recognition was in store, in a publication with a circulation of approximately three million: Nolan was also chosen honorable-mention tackle on the 1936 *Liberty* magazine's All-Players All-America Team. As Norman L. Sper titled his article, this was "A Unique and Authoritative Selection...The Gridiron Greats of 1936, Chosen by Vote of the 1,498 Leading Candidates Themselves," a chance for players to rate those they personally played against throughout the season. Resulting from votes carried out at "ninety-four major universities and colleges," the selection was referred to by Sper as the "finest mythical aggregation that could be assembled." Tackles were judged in terms of "speed, charging ability, ability to diagnose opponents' plays, aggressiveness, running interference if their team's system required it, and blocking." Sper believed that the firsthand knowledge definitely distinguished this selection: "Their judgment came from actual bodily contact with the players they have chosen."

Yes, Earl Nolan was tough. An example of his toughness occurred in the final game of the 1936 season against the Red Raiders (Matadors) of Texas Tech, in which his nose was broken. It was ironic that this happened at the last game of his college career.

The episode inspired several articles at the time and over the years, adding to the legend. A December 6 *Star* article, "Wildcats Battle to 7-7 Tie With Matadors," related, "Earl Nolan, his face clotted with blood, was taken from the game in the final stanza. The stands rose and applauded as the graduating 212-pound tackle – an All-American honorable mention – strode off to the showers." A similar account appeared in the *Citizen* on December 7, "Controversy Rages as Wildcats and Matadors Fight To Tie," which read, "In the final quarter, Earl Nolan, great Wildcat tackle, came off the field with a broken nose. He was injured in the first quarter but remained in the game until only minutes were left to play. He trotted to the showers with the applause of the crowd ringing in his ears." Years later, a December 10, 1945 *Citizen* "From The Press Box" column, written by Hank Squire, recalled that Nolan "stood against Texas Tech for three quarters with his nose smashed all over his face and challenged 'em to come on."

Even with the injury, this last performance was stellar. Recapping the final game on December 8, 1936, Mathews affirmed in his "The Spectator" column, "Of course Earl Nolan did his usual good job. He could make any football team in the country."

Squire's December 9 "From The Press Box" column, "Nolan Deserves To Play," began, "Bruised and battered, Earl Nolan made his final appearance on the Arizona gridiron something that always will be remembered.... Give the giant tackle credit for the great performance he turned in under the handicap. His nose was broken in the first period, but he stayed in the game until the middle of the fourth quarter. He played his best, fought his hardest despite the painful injury."

Squire quoted Nolan about the injury: "It hurt a little when it was first struck, but after that it didn't bother much because it was hit so often." He continued to make light of his injury and joked, "I was going to have it broken and re-set after the game, so it doesn't matter. It saves me the trouble of having it done."

The columnist was definitely a supporter and was hoping for more accolades for the Arizona star: "Earl Nolan, a fine player and a gentleman, deserves a chance to play in the East-West game at San Francisco on New Year's Day. It is certain there will be no better tackles on the field than the Arizona husky. His coach, 'Tex' Oliver, who has seen quite a few pretty fair lineman during his coaching career and as a player, says Nolan ranks with the best."

When Squire asked him whether he could play with his damaged nose, Nolan replied, "Just give me a chance. I don't care about the nose. I want to get into that game. It would be worth having it smashed up again."

The injury was severe, however. On December 8, in "Arizona Gridsters Select Gents as Toughest Club Met This Year," the *Star* noted that at the post-season meeting when the Brigadiers were assessing their all-opposition contenders, "Earl Nolan, the All-American tackle honorable mention, strutted into the meeting with his nose swollen up as big as a tomato. It was broken in the torrid engagement with Tech Saturday."

After the season, Nolan did have his nose reset. He later said he could not tolerate the packing material and ripped it out. His nose remained semi-flattened, a memento of his final college game, and his sense of smell remained slightly affected.

On December 11, the "If and When" columnist of the *Wildcat* remarked, "We just received notice from the *Michigan State News* that Joe Sachen and Earl Nolan made the all-opposition of the Michigan State team.... Sachen and Nolan both completed their careers in the Tech game, but their fame as linemen will remain as long as Arizona lines have the power and superiority they exhibited this year.... Both boys were injured in the Tech game, but while they were in there, the Tech gains through their sides of the line were negligible." The columnist summed it up by saying that "old All-American honorable mention Nolan was good all year."

The Towncats honored the Brigadiers at a banquet on December 16, when the year's lettermen, including Earl Nolan, were introduced to the group. It was the end to the amazing 1936 season.

One amusing afterthought occurred in the Christmas edition of the column "The Spectator," by Vic Thornton: Asking Santa Claus for the perfect gift for Nolan, Thornton suggested a Texas Tech guard, no doubt the one who broke his nose.

Nolan would later sum up the 1936 season, citing Centenary (13-13 tie) as the toughest opponent they faced, followed by Michigan State (7-0 Spartans) and Texas Tech (7-7 tie). It had definitely been the season that Coach Oliver had envisioned, and it did propel the Arizona team into national prominence, as well as its star tackle.

A Mythical Athlete

Throughout his years of U of A football, Nolan was often named in newspaper articles as outstanding lineman or player on the field, e.g., in games against the Colorado Aggies, Loyola Lions, Centenary Southern Gentlemen, Kansas Jayhawks, Whittier Poets, Michigan State Spartans, New Mexico Aggies, and Tempe Bulldogs. Articles referred to his "great strength" and "fighting spirit," and declared him to be the "outstanding defensive lineman in the entire conference." As mentioned earlier, he also often came out on top when measuring most time spent in the game, a remarkable feat when considering his injuries, but ever indicative of his spirit.

As well as playing with injuries, another mark of his dedication to the game and to his community occurred on April 14, 1934, during track and field season. Nolan, a field star, not only volunteered for but repeatedly requested permission to play in a spring football game against the Flagstaff Lumberjacks, a game to be held for the benefit of the Tucson underprivileged children's fund. Coach Oliver eventually granted permission and released him for a week from his track and field activities to concentrate on football duties. Arizona won the game, 18-0. And, of course, later that year the previously cited blockbuster post-season game, for the benefit of the underprivileged children's fund of the Phoenix Kiwanis club, was played in Phoenix against the College of the Pacific. Nolan was then – and remained – eager and willing to give back to the community in whatever way he could.

Earl Nolan was usually surrounded by a group of admirers; in later years he would lightheartedly refer to this as a kind of "entourage." The attention always baffled him. However, many of his football fans remained fans for life, following his sports, military, and professional careers. His enduring popularity was evident at the U of A Homecoming events when he would be introduced on the field, decades after he left the game. His daughter accompanied him in 1959, for the 25th anniversary of the 1934 team. They sat in the end zone to watch the game. At halftime, he went down to the field for the ceremony. His daughter, having been raised by the modest hero, had no idea what to expect, and was thrilled as the loud applause and outpouring of affection erupted from the thousands of people when Nolan's name was called. Time had not dampened their memories of him; the fans still loved their star. He returned quietly to the stands and gave her his golden "A" pin, a remembrance she treasures to this day, along with other commemorative awards given to her father, including team plaques, an "A" blanket, and a trophy from the 1936 Border Conference Championship.

Accustomed to giving his "all" during a game, Nolan did not care for the two-platoon system which was instituted in college football after his playing days. He was interviewed in a January 14, 1953 article, "Strong, Varied Reaction Locally Over Death of Platoons," by the *Star*'s Abe Chanin, debating the pros and cons of the change back from the two-platoon system. Chanin reported, "Earl Nolan, former line great for Arizona in the '30s, said, 'It's a very good change. I kind of lost interest in the game since they put in the two-platoon system. You just didn't get to know the players – they were on and off the field so much. I think if I had played under the two-platoon system, I would have quit football.'" Opposing viewpoints centered mostly on the belief that it was too much exertion to play an entire game, as well as worries that the one-platoon system would slow the game.

The press remained enamored with the colorful local hero, and retrospective articles on his career became the norm. In his June 5, 1949 article, Bernie Roth introduced the first of his "Where are they now?" series on athletic stars. His premier column was on Earl Nolan. Describing the football luminary, then a fireman "behind the wheel of the Menlo Park wagon," Roth wrote that "you'll remember him for that square jaw and determined look.... He still looks every bit the athlete that made him one of Tucson's all-time greats. Back in the early 1930s, The Earl was a great tackle for Tucson High School and then the University of Arizona. His ferocious line play made him a feared opponent throughout the Border Conference. He was on the All-State high school team for three [two] consecutive years and then three more as All-Border Conference."

Roth stated that King Kong "has one story he likes to tell that sums up his type of charging play," and quoted Nolan: "We were playing a hot College of the Pacific team in 1934 in Phoenix. They had the ball on our five-yard line, and Oliver put me and Ken Adamson into the game as tackle replacements. COP thought they had an easy touch in the new replacements, and they went right to work on us. It was first down and goal to go when we went into the game. Five downs later – I say five downs because Ken and I were called for unnecessary roughness – the COP team lost the ball on our twenty-yard line. We had pushed them back fifteen yards in the series."

Regarding the tackle's tough reputation, Roth commented that "Nolan often was tagged as a mean, rough player. However, he can easily explain why he was so." He again quoted Nolan: "In those days I believe the Border Conference was a bit tougher. Two years ago Texas Tech was knocking off everything in the Southwest Conference, but the teams we played against in those days would take on any of today's Border Conference teams. We played football without too much fancy stuff. We charged hard and tackled hard. Today the boys seem to depend upon the coach much more, and instead of the team captain calling the next move, it always comes from the coach. Whenever we played teams such as Tech, Loyola and Centenary, you could always look for a rough and tough battle. Those were the kinds of teams and games we enjoyed in those days, and if you were going to get anywhere, you had to be rough."

"And," according to Roth, "Nolan got places. Nolan's coach tagged him as one of the greatest in Arizona football.... To look at him you would think he could still perform as he did fifteen years ago. Well, you're right – he can." And it was true; ever the athlete albeit a tad heavier, he kept in good shape – tossing the shot, lifting weights, and doing a little boxing for conditioning.

In 1949, Earl Nolan was named tackle on the All-Time Arizona Honor Grid Team, selected by a cross-section of Tucson sports fans, in honor of the 50th year of U of A football. He was referred to in a November 4, 1949 article in the *Star*, "All-Time 11 Chosen by Grid Fans," by Abe Chanin, as "an almost mythical athlete.... Nolan, a 210-pounder who stood off offensive blockers with great shows of power, starred on the 1936 team."

A June 22, 1969 article in the *Star*, "All-Time Grid Greats Chosen in Centennial," by Bill Waters, and a June 23 article in the *Citizen*, "All-Time Grid Team," announced that Earl Nolan was chosen Honorable Mention on the All-Time Rocky Mountain-Southwest Football Team, selected by area sports editors and sponsored by the Football Writers Association of America and the Western Athletic Conference, to commemorate the 100th year of college football.

In his June 26, 1969 column, "The Spectator," Chanin presented eleven players as "one man's selection of the all-time University of Arizona All-Star football team." His choice for tackle was Earl Nolan.

In October of 1969, in honor of the 70th year of football at the University of Arizona, Chanin and the *Arizona Daily Star*, with the aid of veteran football observers, named Earl Nolan tackle on the Modern All-Stars U of A Football Team (1936-68). In his October 8, 1969 article, "UA Grid History Yields Many Stars... Greatest Wildcat Gridders Receive All-Time Honors," Chanin called him "a star of the 1930s who was feared for his great strength."

The November 9, 1985 article "Bear Down boys among top 11 Wildcat players," by Greg Hansen, sportswriter for the *Star*, presented the "all-time University of Arizona 11 best football players" – regardless of position – selected by the *Star*'s 20-man Centennial Panel of UA Football History, in honor of the University of Arizona's 100th Homecoming. Earl Nolan was selected as one of the eleven best players ever to perform for the U of A. Hansen remarked, "Outlined against a blue-gray Centennial sky, the Bear Down Boys ride again." Even with the passage of so much time since their playing days, "decades later, on a crisp autumn afternoon near Arizona Stadium, you can surely hear the echoes of their greatness."

Hansen went on to quote what panel members had to say about their honoree: Clarence "Stub" Ashcraft, U of A letterman in 1938 and '41 – "Earl Nolan was fabulous. Man, was he tough! Tough as anybody I ever saw. One of the best linemen ever." Coach Tex Oliver – "No one had more courage than Earl. He was his own man, did things his own way, but when it came to football, he was a terrific charge."

As an insight into Nolan's character, he was asked in a September 25, 1985 letter from Hansen to contribute information on U of A football history, including his recommendations for the best players. A copy of his list was found with the letter; needless to say, one player was notably absent. He did, however, name three tackles, all of whom were at one time his teammates. Those of us who knew Nolan can say in total honesty that we never once heard him promote himself; it was simply not his nature.

Abe Chanin, the longtime sportswriter and editor, believed that the stories about Nolan were some of the most colorful in U of A sports history, referring to him as a legendary "superhero," and many times stating that he was the greatest at his position at the U of A. Later, Chanin would feature Nolan both in his 1979 book, *They Fought Like Wildcats*, and on his KPOL television series, *Eyewitness to History*, December 20, 1987, a program which was promoted by Corky Simpson of the *Tucson Citizen* as interviews with "three great Wildcat football heroes from the era of Coach Tex Oliver." Chanin quoted sports editor Vic Thornton as saying that Nolan was a legend in his own time, who had exhibited an unusual method of blocking a punt. A favorite story in Tucson was that in one game he "charged across the line, grabbed the blocker, and threw him right into the punter." Thornton was quoted as saying that Nolan was "enormously strong and tremendously talented. He wasn't only a great football player, he also was outstanding in track and field." There were also the often-told local stories about one town game in which Nolan accrued 180 yards of penalties for unnecessary roughness, and another time when he was standing with a blocker on each leg but still made his tackle.

The estimations of Nolan's height varied from article to article, as did his weight and age! As noted earlier, his National Guard records listed him as 6 feet 3 inches tall. Nolan himself said he was about 6 feet 2 inches; however, as his wife once explained, the bearing and presence of the man made him seem even taller. In a December 28, 1945 article, "Tucsonians Seen At The Towncat Banquet," Nolan was described as "one of Arizona's immortal gridiron stars." The following statement was made about him: "When he stood up, everyone gasped at that 6 foot 4 inch figure that now weighs 240 pounds. Any coach in America could use Earl, and that includes the West Point coach," a reference to the 1945 National Champions.

On April 5, 1989, the title of an article in the *Citizen* raised the question, "If they did retire numbers at the University of Arizona, what athletes should be so honored?" Earl Nolan was one of the small number of football players suggested by the *Citizen* – fifty-three years after his last game for the U of A.

An article by Jeff Dimond of the UA Sports Information Office, "Early Wildcats Established Arizona's Place in Major College Football," addressed the nickname "King Kong," a nickname, by the way, Nolan did not like. He was quoted by Dimond as saying, "I don't know how I got that name. I was always a gentleman on the field. I think the guys on the team used to give me a new nickname every time a horror movie came out."

"King Kong" and "Tarzan" were certainly not the only nicknames Nolan's athletic performance inspired – to name just a few, "Whataman," "Twice-A-Man," "muscular Myrmidon," "Heez-all Man" – all summed up in one phrase by Robert E. Wilson in his January 1935 *Arizona Alumnus* column, "With the Wildcat Athletes"..."tough as they make them." Others referred to him as the "legendary superstar," a "legend in his time," the "best tackle in Arizona grid history," an "unmoveable blockade on defense," a "path clearer when the Arizona backs go into action," a "great blocker," a "tower of strength," a "gladiator who took no prisoners," an "insurmountable obstacle for ball carriers," the "defensive bulwark," a "one-man wrecking crew," a "vicious charger," a "terror to opposing ball carriers," a "feared opponent," the "toughest man on the team," a "man mountain on the defense," a "superhero," as well as a "pathfinder" and "trailblazer," for the new territories he opened for the University in the All-America ranks and in professional football. His playing was referred to as "ferocious line play" and "slashing viciousness," as he would "maim opposing linemen with impartial savagery" or "mow down everything in his path" or "smear plays with gusto."

Nolan was described as "enormously strong," "tremendously talented," "fast," and the "giant / rugged / tough / huge / powerful / gigantic / elephantine / titanic / great / outstanding / colorful / stellar / fearless / standout / rough / excellent / barrel-chested / husky / towering / brawny / star" tackle with a "million-dollar physique." As writer Jerry Eaton phrased it, no adjectives were spared to describe "his strength and unswerving will to win." At the same time, Nolan was referred to as an "agile," "nimble," "well-coordinated," and "graceful" athlete, who served as an "inspiration to others." He was characterized as "independent," with a "mind of his own" and a "great sense of humor."

The man himself, however, never "bought his own press." He was consistently described by his family and friends, as well as people who had met or interviewed him at any stage of his life, as a very "shy / quiet / unassuming / modest / humble / gentlemanly / tight-lipped / self-effacing / polite" man. The fascinating thing, and a large part of the mystique surrounding the man, was that all the myriad descriptions were true! Nolan was a quiet, unassuming, and yet awesome force.

Earl Nolan was a large man for his day, but the most astounding fact was his strength. When it was coupled with his spirit, he seemed unbeatable, and a legend continued to grow.

On July 13, 1989, Bonnie Henry of the *Star* wrote a nearly full-page feature story, recapping some of the anecdotes and legends about Nolan; "For bruisers only...Tucson High, UA football star recalls battles of old" appeared in her "Another Tucson" column. She included one of his typical wry remarks: "It was unusual to think about going out and playing a gentlemanly game of football. There had to be a fight in there somewhere. I never remember saying, 'How do you do?' before a game."

Many features on Nolan also appeared in U of A football programs over the years, as well as in the *Arizona Alumnus* magazine and the *Bear Down Bulletin*. The press always seemed to enjoy writing about the colorful hero; the interest in his life did not fade.

The Fight of Wildcats, a 1996 promotional video for the University of Arizona football season, featured a quote they attributed to Nolan: "I used to think that everyone playing in front of me was my deadly enemy. I thought I was the better man, and I worked myself into a frenzy in every game." The narrator, Tedy Bruschi, All-American tackle and now New England Patriots Hall of Famer, commented that the words summed up the feelings of the U of A defensive players, who "have always made their opponents pay the price since the days of King Kong Nolan."

On September 10, 1996, Fox 11 KMSB, a local Tucson television station, aired *Glimpses of Glory*, a documentary written, produced, and directed by Dana Cooper and narrated by Dave Sitton. The tribute recalled some of the great players in U of A football history, referring to Nolan as one of the most colorful players in Tex Oliver's Blue Brigade. His friend and teammate A. V. Grossetta remembered him as "big, strong, and tough." As a blocking back scrimmaging against Nolan when he was playing defensive tackle, Grossetta remembered that Earl would just pick him up and throw him to the side "like a sack of wheat." The documentary went on to highlight Nolan's professional football career and his service in the United States Marine Corps. More often than not, mention of Earl Nolan included details that went beyond the particular matter at hand; the totality of his life was fascinating.

In later years, Nolan would always maintain that he was "not much of a football fan," but he was talked into attending one Parents' Day game at the U of A. The October 3, 1970 game against the Iowa Hawkeyes of the Big Ten Conference was an exciting one for the Wildcats. Arizona took the day, 17-10. When the Wildcats scored the winning touchdown, he stood, clapped heartily for the team, and had a big smile spread across his face. Of course, for a non-fan, he always seemed to know the stats and histories of current players, and was particularly intrigued when George Blanda was called in during the last minutes of the game for the Oakland Raiders in the 1970s. Blanda had a talent that Nolan deemed almost mystical, a term he had not applied to an athlete since Clarence Sample in the early 1930s.

Although Nolan's football history at the University of Arizona was a major component of the legend and legacy of the star, his performance in other sports would definitely contribute to many later tributes.

Nolan (third row, fifth from right), right tackle on offense, left tackle on defense, and kicker, University of Arizona freshman football team, 1932. Awarded numeral. Team was undefeated in regular season play, with no points scored against them.

Nolan (third row, fourth from left), University of Arizona Wildcats "Blue Brigade" varsity football team, 1933. Team had winning season. Scored 113 points against their opponents, with 35 points scored against them.

Varsity letterman Earl Nolan, No. 47, University of Arizona football, 1933.

"King Kong" Nolan, University of Arizona, 1933. Selected second-team tackle, All-Border Conference Team and *Arizona Daily Star* All-Border Conference Team.

Nolan (fourth row, left), University of Arizona football team, 1934. Team had winning season. Scored 138 points against their opponents, with 54 points scored against them.

Formidable lineman Earl Nolan, 1934. Often named outstanding player on the field. Selected first-team tackle on three honor rosters, including All-Border Conference Team and *Arizona Wildcat* All-Conference Team.

Varsity letterman Earl Nolan, University of Arizona football, 1934.

Nolan (second row, left), University of Arizona football team, 1936. Border Conference Champions. Team scored 190 points against their opponents, with 54 points scored against them.

Earl Nolan, No. 58, varsity letterman, University of Arizona football, 1936. Mythical athlete, described as a great blocker and a tower of strength on defense. Selected first-team tackle, All-Border Conference Team and *Phoenix Gazette* All-Border Conference Team. Named Honorable Mention, Associated Press All-America Team and *Liberty* magazine All-Players All-America Team.

CHAPTER SEVEN

University of Arizona Track and Field – and Beyond
"Outstanding Athlete" and "High-Point Man"

EARL NOLAN COMPETED IN TRACK AND FIELD at the University of Arizona for the Varsity Inn intramural track team in 1933, and for Alpha Tau Omega fraternity in 1934. He was also a member of the U of A squad, winning his numeral in 1933 and his letter in 1934. Nolan specialized in the discus, shot put, javelin, and high jump. During his college career, he participated in Border Conference, Greenway, and Long Beach meets, as well as dual meets with Arizona State Teachers College at Tempe and San Diego State, again setting records and attaining high-point honors. A March 9, 1934 "Inside Dope" column in the *Arizona Wildcat* called Nolan the "outstanding weight man on the squad," and declared that "great things are expected of him." In 1935, he set a meet record in the javelin, which lasted for 32 years.

The annual intramural track meet was held March 13-17, 1933, with Varsity Inn tying with Phi Gamma Delta for first place. Articles covering the meet in the *Arizona Daily Star* followed Nolan's progress in the competition: March 14, "Varsity Inn Leads U.A. Track Meet" – he earned first place in the shot put, with 36 feet 2 inches [corrected to 41 feet 5 3/4 inches]; March 16, "Varsity Inn Leads Intramural Meet" – he won the javelin, with 177 feet 7 inches; March 18, "Nolan Sets New Record In Discus" – he set a new intramural discus record of 128 feet 8 3/4 inches, beating the old record held by Jack O'Dowd by almost 10 feet. As indicated, the distance reported in the *Star* for the shot put proved to be inaccurate; on March 17, an article from the *Wildcat*, "Intramural Track Meet," affirmed that Nolan had won the shot put at 41 feet 5 3/4 inches.

The 1933 track and field season was slow getting started at the University; it was Coach Tex Oliver's first year as track coach, and there also appeared to be some funding shortages which curtailed the activities of the squad. For the March 3 Long Beach Relays, Coach Oliver transported only two senior team members by car to take part in the event. We do know that Nolan participated in the annual handicap meet between the Tucson High School Badgers and the University of Arizona Freshman. This year, when he was classed as "Frosh" (second semester) and found himself competing against his old school, he placed first in the discus with 128 feet, first in the shot put with 51 feet, and third in the javelin. A subsequent, rather complexly handicapped meet was conducted between THS and the entire U of A squad. On March 22, in "University and High School To Hold Meet," the *Star* previewed the upcoming event, later reporting that Nolan won the javelin competition, with a throw of 186 feet 4 inches.

On April 2, in "U.A. Tracksters Hold Squad Meet," the *Star* covered an intrasquad competition, in which Nolan, of the "Red" team, won second place in both the discus and shot put. He placed second (as he would throughout the rest of the season) to teammate Clarence "Bud" Sample, a senior whose athletic prowess he would always hold in the highest esteem. To skip forward in time...in the 1960s, Nolan made a side trip to Calexico on a family vacation in an attempt to touch base with Sample, an indication of the regard he had for him. Regrettably, Sample no longer lived there. The family was quite disappointed, looking forward to meeting this legendary athlete and putting a face to the interesting tales they had heard; not the least of which was the story told by Nolan that Sample's eyes were so intense, looking at them made your own eyes start to water. How much this vignette had to do with placing second to him all season we will never know!

Finally, on April 20, in "Wildcat Tracksters To Get First Competition of Season Saturday," the *Star* advised that the team's first outside event of the track season would be held on April 22, with the athletes traveling by train to the annual Greenway competition. On April 23, it was reported that Nolan had won second in the javelin and third in the discus.

An April 25 *Star* article, "Cat Trackmen In Dual Meet Here Friday," before the competition with Arizona State Teachers College at Tempe, expressed regrets that the season had been so limited: "The Cat team has shown itself to be one of the strongest in the history of the school, being especially strong in middle distances and field events." This evaluation proved to be correct, as reflected in the April 28 article, "Cat Tracksters Crush Tempe In Meet, 97-33." Nolan won a second place in the shot put at 40 feet 6 inches, and a second in the javelin at 184 feet 2 inches.

Earl Nolan was chosen by Oliver to compete in the annual Border Conference meet. A May 14 article from the *Star*, "Arizona Runs Away With Conference Meet by Scoring 89 Points," summarized that at the 1933 Border Conference meet held in Albuquerque at the University of New Mexico on May 13, he again won second-place medals in both the javelin and shot put.

A May 16, 1933 *Star* article, "Track And Net Awards Made By Arizona Board," announced that Nolan had won his numeral in track and field for his freshman year of competition.

On March 2, 1934, looking ahead to the Long Beach Relays, the *Wildcat*, in

"Trackmen Leave For Coast Meet," referred to Nolan as the team's "heavy field threat" in the weights. The following day at Long Beach, the Wildcats faced some rather stiff competition in the meet, including Southern California, Stanford, U.C.L.A., Loyola, and Whittier. Nolan began the season at the hotly contested event by placing third in the shot put and fourth in the javelin at 182 feet 3 inches, which caused the paper's "Inside Dope" columnist to look forward with anticipation to his future performances.

Next on the schedule was the final 1934 intramural track and field meet, held March 7-10. The *Star* covered the meet over the course of the three days: Nolan, competing for Alpha Tau Omega, won the shot put at 42 feet 11 inches, the discus at 117 feet 6.5 inches (against that day's strong winds which, according to the sportswriter, prevented "record feats"), and the javelin at 189 feet 4 inches.

At the 9th Annual AAU Greenway Track and Field Day on April 28, 1934, the powerful weight man won four medals, high-point honors, and was named the outstanding athlete of the meet. His performance created quite a stir at the University. In "Cat Tracksters Set New Marks," from the May 6 *Wildcat*, he was referred to as a "sophomore phenom." The article proclaimed that "Earl (Whataman) Nolan covered himself with glory at Greenway." In a section headed "Track," the *Arizona Alumnus* summarized the Greenway meet: "Earl Nolan, gigantic Wildcat weight man, was proclaimed the outstanding athlete of the meet and high-point man, winning two firsts, a second, and a third." The final tally, without a doubt, lived up to the expectations of him expressed early in the season. With a total of 14 points, he won the javelin with a throw of 192 feet, and the discus with 134 feet, placed second in the shot put, and recorded a third-place high jump, once more a noteworthy feat for such a large man.

At the conclusion of the Greenway meet, Nolan was presented with both the "Outstanding Athlete" and the "High-Point A.A.U. Athlete" trophies.

What was even more astounding about this victory on April 28, 1934, in Phoenix was that two days earlier on April 26, Nolan had won the heavyweight title at the Southwestern Amateur Boxing Tournament in Tucson. This was an astonishing example of the incredible versatility, and both mental and physical endurance of this extraordinary athlete.

Of course, the athlete himself would normally only relate the amusing or self-deprecating aspects of his career. For example, years after the Greenway meet, when interviewer Jeff Dimond asked about the high jump, Nolan joked about his technique and admitted that he injured himself quite regularly: "I'm not sure how I did it. I think it was the way I carried my feet. I jumped with one foot pulled up, and when I landed, I used to spike hell out of myself."

After the 3rd Annual Border Intercollegiate Athletic Conference Track and Field Meet held in Tucson on May 12, 1934, a May 13 *Star* article, "Five Records Topple as Wildcats Annex Conference Track Crown...Nolan High Scorer," written by Pat O'Brien, stated that "Earl Nolan of Arizona copped high-scoring honors in the meet with first places in the javelin and discus and a second to Clarence 'Swede' Carlson in the shot put." Additionally, he again placed third in the high jump.

Nolan threw the javelin 200 feet 9 inches (nearest competitor – 167 feet) and the discus 136 feet 1 1/2 inches (nearest competitor – 124 feet 4 1/2 inches). He put the shot 42 feet 3 inches. In a May 19 *Wildcat* article, titled "Five Marks Fall in Border Meet...Cats Retain Track Crown," he was acclaimed as the "all-around star of the meet."

At the end of this amazing season, the sophomore field ace was awarded his letter in track and field.

It appeared that Nolan participated in only one meet in 1935 (which might have been due to a recurring problem with an injured arm), but that competition turned out to be quite memorable. On March 15, 1935, he set a meet record in the javelin at the dual meet with San Diego State, the Southern California Conference Champions, which was not broken until 1967. The March 17 *Star* chronicled, in "Wildcat Track Team Beats San Diego," that he won first in the javelin, with a throw of 191 feet 7 inches, and first in the discus with 131 feet 4 1/2 inches; he also placed second in the shot with 44 feet 8 3/4 inches.

An excerpt, titled "The Legendary Earl (King Kong) Nolan," from a question-and-answer column, "The Spectator – From the Mailbag," by Abe Chanin, in the May 11, 1967 *Star*, summed up this achievement. A letter from Ernest Lacy, Arizona '36, stated, "As an old track and field enthusiast, U of A alumnus and reader of the *Arizona Daily Star* newspaper, I read a recent issue which carried the results of the U of A / San Diego State track and field meet. Is it true that M. E. Nolan's javelin record lasted 32 years, or was this a misprint?"

Lacy commented, "I knew Nolan as well as anyone did. He was a very quiet man. It was years later when we were both with the Marine Raiders during WW2 that I became a real Nolan fan."

Chanin replied, "Michael Earl Nolan was one of the legendary figures in all of Arizona athletics. He was unmoveable as a tackle in football, and he did letter in track, too (1934). Because he was such a phenomenal athlete, he did in one season of competition throw the javelin 191 feet 7 inches. The distance set in a meet with San Diego State stood as a record until this year when Jim Garner threw 206-8 in a dual meet with the Aztecs....Nolan also was a decorated hero during World War II for his bravery in action in the Pacific."

In fact, a 1970 U of A *Arizona Spring Sports* booklet still listed Nolan under the "Arizona Top Ten Track Performers – Javelin."

The 1936 Greenway meet was highly touted in the newspapers. On April 24, 1936, in "Famed Track Stars Enter A.A.U. Greenway Meet," the *Star* described the event as featuring "a dazzling array of Pacific Coast track and field athletes," following up on April 25 with the articles "Competition Is Expected To Be Unusually Keen," and

"Arizona Cinder Stars Enter Greenway Meet." The latter article remarked that in the trials, Nolan threw the javelin around the 200-foot mark and tossed the shot around 44 feet. At the April 25 11th Annual Greenway Track and Field Day in Phoenix, Nolan, competing as unattached, placed first in the javelin with a throw of 200 feet, second in the shot put, third in the high jump, and fourth in the discus.

An April 25, 1937 article from the *Star*, "Earl Nolan Registers 11 Points for Individual High Honors," recapping the previous day's 12th Annual Greenway Track and Field Day in Phoenix, stated, "Earl Nolan, former Arizona star competing unattached, captured the individual scoring trophy with 11 points," winning the javelin at 195 feet 8 inches, and the shot put at 45 feet 5 1/8 inches, and placing fourth in the discus. Found among his possessions was the impressive 1937 Greenway "A.A.U. High Point" trophy, a beautiful tribute. Fortunately, he saved countless medals, ribbons, trophies, and certificates from this phase of his track and field career.

Twenty years later, in July 1957, at the age of 46, Nolan competed in a Peruvian national track and field meet in Tacna while he was working as an engineer for an open-pit copper mine in the Andes Mountains of Peru. He was awarded first place in the 16-pound shot put on July 7, and second place in the discus on July 14, by the Liga Provincial de Atletismo, his last events in an amazing twenty-eight-year span of field competition.

Nolan (third from left), University of Arizona track and field team, 1933. Competed in javelin, shot put, discus, and high jump.

Nolan, Varsity Inn intramural track and field team, 1933; Alpha Tau Omega team, 1934. Two-year javelin, shot, and discus champion.

Record-setting intramural discus champion. Nolan, University of Arizona, 1933.

Track and field star Earl Nolan. Awarded numeral at University of Arizona in 1933, letter in 1934. Awarded four medals, Outstanding Athlete and High-Point A.A.U. Athlete trophies, 1934 Greenway Track and Field Day; four medals and high-point man honor, 1934 Border Conference Track and Field Meet. In 1935, won three medals and set 32-year javelin record at Arizona / San Diego Dual Meet. Competing unattached, he won four medals at Greenway, 1936; three medals and A.A.U. High Point trophy at Greenway, 1937.

Nolan (left) chats with Peruvian discus champion. Tacna, Peru, 1957.

Peruvian national track and field meet. Nolan, second in discus, July 14, 1957.

After a 20-year hiatus from competition, Nolan became the shot put champion at a Peruvian national track and field meet, on July 7, 1957, at the age of 46. Awarded a Diploma de Honor from the Liga Provincial de Atletismo, he capped a track and field career which spanned 28 years.

CHAPTER EIGHT

University of Arizona and Amateur Boxing
Donning the Golden Gloves

ANOTHER SPORT EARL NOLAN LOVED WAS BOXING, and he was a multi-titled amateur heavyweight champion – Southwestern AAU (1934 and 1936), University of Arizona intramural (1935-36), and Arizona Golden Gloves (1937). He fought on the University of Arizona boxing squad from 1933 until 1935, and at other times was designated as competing for Varsity Inn, Co-Op Book Store, or Tucson YMCA, or as competing unattached. Accurately tracking down boxing records from the 1930s proved more difficult than football or track records, complicated by the fact that some sportswriters later confused the different amateur venues of the day, e.g., the Amateur Athletic Union and Border Conference tournaments.

Pictured with the 1933 University squad in a photograph which was labeled "University Amateur Boxing Team," appended to the *Tucson Daily Citizen*'s "From the Press Box" column, Nolan was called a "brilliant and sensational amateur heavyweight" with a "murderous" right-hand punch. He was nicknamed "Twice-A-Man," the "University bone-crusher," and the "University bad man" by *Arizona Daily Star* sportswriter Ade Abbott. Abbott predicted that if Nolan "fights as rough as he plays football, some of the fighters will be bouncing out of the ring."

In the January 8, 1933 *Star* article, "Amateurs Hold Public Drill at Temple Today," it was announced that he had entered the AAU tournament as a heavyweight at 205 pounds. In the course of the three-day event which was held on January 17-19, Nolan, fighting for the U of A, won a first-round decision against Mike Simmonds, but was decisioned himself in the semi-final round.

What was billed as the First Annual Southwestern Amateur Boxing Tournament was held in Tucson on April 24-26, 1934. The AAU tournament was sponsored by the YMCA. On April 26, Nolan, alternately mentioned as representing Varsity Inn and the University of Arizona, knocked out Norman Johnson of the Phoenix Indians in 1:58 of the first round in the heavyweight bout of the tournament. In an April 27 *Star* article,

"Redskins Annex Three Titles In Fistic Meet," Abbott wrote, "Earl Nolan, ponderous University of Arizona athlete, required only one minute and 58 seconds to plaster Norman Johnson, Phoenix Indian, to the mat. Johnson was completely out and remained draped over the lower strand of ropes after the fatal toll until the seconds rushed into the ring and carried the stricken Indian to his corner." Subsequently, Abbott stated, "We sort of insulted Nolan when we called him only 'Twice-A-Man.'" The Phoenix Indian heavyweight "said that it wasn't fair to make him fight against a quartette. Nolan packs an awful sock, and we feel sorry for the opposing football teams next year."

With the victory over Johnson, Nolan won the AAU tournament and was presented with the "1934 Winner SW Amateur Heavyweight" gold medal.

Shortly afterward, he received a May 5 letter from E. T. Cusick, YMCA chairman of the event, written "to express our sincere appreciation of your excellent cooperation and assistance.... Your appearance added much to the success of the tournament, and we trust you will again appear next year."

It was at this time that boxing took its place as one of the major sports at the University, albeit for a brief period. In a December 14, 1934 *Arizona Wildcat* article, "Boxing Will Be Recognized As Major Sport in Border Loop," Joseph L. Picard, boxing coach and assistant professor of physical education, released plans for the school's upcoming participation in Border Conference tournaments, as well as the Amateur Athletic Union fisticuffs. Referring to the progress of the preliminary training, the article read, "Now that the football men have hung up their cleats for the year, the list of boxing candidates has considerably increased. Earle Nolan, last year's southwest amateur heavyweight champion, is shaking out his football kinks...."

In a January 15, 1935 *Wildcat* article referring to the upcoming AAU event, "Arizona Tourney Chances Are Good Says J. Picard," it was noted that "the heavyweight duties will fall on the massive frame of Earl 'King Kong' Nolan, football and track star." However, on February 19, 1935, an article from the *Star*, "University To Enter 15 Men In Boxing Meet," cautioned that Nolan, who was the 1934 heavyweight champ, and who would be representing the U of A, had an injured arm and would not enter the 1935 AAU contest unless his arm had healed sufficiently. During the event, it was reported that he had not entered due to this injury. It appeared that his injured arm kept him out of the spring schedule, including the first Border Conference tournament.

In 1936, he won the AAU title for the Tucson YMCA. A February 13, 1936 article in the *Star*, "Southwestern Boxing Tourney Gets Under Way Tonight," referred to the "local 'Y' team, headed by Earl Nolan, bruising 200-pound heavy." That night, in the opening round of the tournament, he was scheduled to meet Edwin Best of Phoenix. The final article on February 15, "Indians Win Four Titles in Fight Tourney," listed Nolan, Tucson Y, as the uncontested heavyweight titleholder. He was presented with a particularly unique medal, a small gold boxing glove with the engraving "First Hvy. Wt.

SWA '36."

An April 7, 1936 *Citizen* article, "Intramural Boxing Meet Begins Today," promoting the 4th Annual U of A Intramural Boxing Tournament, stated that "Nolan, well-known local heavy, is the undisputed champion of his division." The *Star* announced, in "Boxing Finals Scheduled at U This Afternoon," that he was competing in the heavyweight class for the Co-Op team. After completion of the event, an April 8 *Star* article, "Co-Op Captures Boxing Tourney at Arizona Gym," reported that the U of A Co-Op Book Store team captured the tournament, with Nolan winning the heavyweight honors when no opponent could be found to take him on in the finals. With his memorabilia was the gold medal for the 1935-36 intramural heavyweight boxing championship, his first and only season in this competition. The versatile athlete's schedule was certainly a tight one; he had gone directly from the spring football drills to the intramural boxing event.

In 1936-37, he was also registered with the Southern Pacific Amateur Athletic Association as a boxer. Currently, we have no records on this endeavor; however, Nevada sportswriter Ray Germain wrote that Nolan won several bouts on the Coast.

An April 16, 1937 article from the *Star*, "Golden Gloves Finals Slated For Labor Temple Tonight...Nine Events On Final Card of AAU Meet Here...Capacity Crowd Expected To See Best Fights of Tourney," featured a section titled "Nolan to Fight." It heralded, "The main attraction will be the clash between Earl Nolan, towering native Tucsonan whom fans remember as a former Arizona grid star, and J. McIntyre, St. David, in the heavy class."

Earl Nolan, fighting as unattached, won the 1937 Arizona Golden Gloves tournament heavyweight finals by defeating Jim McIntyre. An April 17 account from the *Star*, "Nolan Scores First Round Kayo In Heavy Finals Of Fistic Meet," referred to him as "a formidable opponent." The article described the contest: "Poker-faced Earl Nolan, after stalking his opponent around the ring for nearly a minute, connected with a swinging right to send Jim McIntyre into oblivion and put an end to Arizona's Golden Gloves tournament at the Labor Temple arena last night. The broad-shouldered All-America tackle never got out of a slow shuffle as he followed his lighter opponent over the canvas, waiting for a chance to land one of his pile-driver blows. He smacked McIntyre once or twice with a haymaker left as the bout opened slowly, and they clinched and fell to the floor when McIntyre tried to get in close to the towering ex-gridder. A slow but hard right full to the face slapped McIntyre's head to the floor so hard that it could be heard all over the hall."

Although we do not have details of all of Nolan's amateur fights, some of which apparently occurred elsewhere, most notably California, it has often been reported that of his wins, first-round knockouts were the norm. In fact, he was famous for them. Predictably, interest in him grew in professional boxing circles.

In his June 11, 1937 "Hot Off The Grill" column in the *Phoenix Gazette*, Larry

Grill quoted boxing promoter Freddy Cohen as saying about Nolan that "in the recent Golden Gloves Championships held here he scored one of the most sensational knockouts ever seen in Tucson to win that title." Regarding Nolan's future in boxing, Cohen informed that he had "received offers from all parts of the state for his services," had made arrangements for him to headline a fight card in Tucson, and was trying to line up a bout in Phoenix.

Earl Nolan (first row, left), University of Arizona boxing squad, 1933. Won 1934 and 1936 Southwestern Amateur Athletic Union, 1935-36 U of A intramural, and 1937 Arizona Golden Gloves heavyweight championships. Famed for scoring first-round knockouts.

After knocking out Jim McIntyre in "one of the most sensational knockouts ever seen in Tucson," Nolan (right) wins Arizona Golden Gloves heavyweight championship, April 16, 1937.

CHAPTER NINE

More Amateur Sports
"Tucson's Ironman"

University of Arizona Wrestling

IT WILL COME AS NO SURPRISE that Earl Nolan also had an interest in wrestling; and, in his only year of intramural competition, he made his mark on this sport at the University of Arizona.

A May 5, 1936 *Arizona Daily Star* article, "U. Mat Matches Are Held Today," stated, "Highlight of the program finds Earl (Tarzan) Nolan of Co-Op trading grips with Clyde (Tank) Watkins of Sigma Alpha Epsilon for the unlimited championship." A May 6 follow-up article, "Co-Op Matmen Win Team Title...Final Bouts Are Held in Arizona University Wrestling Meet," announced that Nolan had won the bout over Watkins, with a 47-second time advantage.

Among his souvenirs was the gold medal for the 1935-36 U of A intramural heavyweight wrestling championship.

University of Arizona Baseball

As a pledge in 1934, Nolan pitched for Alpha Tau Omega in U of A intramural baseball. To quote an article, "Earl Nolan Hurls Team to Victory," from the local newspaper, "Earl Nolan, the young University of Arizona athletic giant who can toss the javelin around the 200-foot mark, turned his talents to other channels yesterday afternoon as he chucked the horsehide down the alley for Alpha Tau Omega in an intramural baseball game. Needless to say, the A.T.O. nine shellacked the Phi Gamma Delta delegation, 8 to 2."

As a side note, Nolan did maintain a later interest in both wrestling and baseball; this time, his involvement was limited to watching the matches or games on television!

Reportedly, he also tried his hand fleetingly at a few other sports, including the rodeo and ski jumping, neither of which appeared to have kept his attention. The only comment he made about either was that finding himself in the air shortly after takeoff on a ski jump, he re-evaluated the wisdom of the whole undertaking.

Weightlifting

Throughout his varied high school and university athletic careers, Earl Nolan had a sustained interest in weightlifting and acquired a widespread reputation for his astounding strength. Mention of his weightlifting prowess often appeared in discussions and articles about him over the years.

According to Johnny Gibson, Tucson weightlifter and trainer, Nolan was a "powerhouse weightlifter and did repetitious overhead presses with 200 lbs. as a warm-up. I witnessed this in the later '40s at the Congress Street YMCA."

The legendary lifter was remembered for having poured his own enormous concrete weights in the 1930s. Several photographs show him hoisting fellow weightlifters, friends, or the huge weights above his head with one hand. When the subject of the homemade weights was broached by Matt Lemmon in the 1990 Tucson High interview, Nolan recounted how he and his friends would pour concrete into a five-gallon can and insert a pole in it to dry, then fill another can for the other end. It would result in weights of about 205 pounds. He joked that when they started out, they would need to shave off some of the concrete, and as they improved, they would pour them all over again.

A January 22, 1949 article, "Weightlift Team Has Good Workout," from the *Tucson Daily Citizen*, named Nolan as a state judge for the YMCA at meets.

Gibson related an incident from the 1950s when Nolan was head judge at one of those meets, and a "lifter lost control of a heavy overhead lift and ran forward toward Earl and the crowd. Earl leaped from his chair, grabbed the weight and replaced it to the platform. The gym floor was saved, and possibly the front-row crowd."

Gibson wrote in 1996 that he proudly displayed photographs of his friend Earl at his barbershop, and in the "Hall of Fame Department" at his gym store.

Through the years, Nolan kept a set of weights on his back porch, professionally made this time, and worked out periodically. The amount of weight he could lift, seemingly effortlessly, would astonish everyone who came out on the porch and lifted even one of his dumbbells.

Powerhouse weightlifter Earl Nolan (right, pictured with spotter), hoists 205-pound homemade concrete barbell.

Nolan (left) with fellow weightlifters, including his future brother-in law George Ahee (right), circa 1936.

Nolan (second from right), weightlifting workout with professionally made weights.

One-arm lift by Nolan.

One-arm overhead lift by Nolan.

Arizona Highway Department, 1936. Nolan keeps in practice.

The legendary strength of Earl Nolan.

CHAPTER TEN

University of Arizona and Amateur Athletics – the Legacy
"The One and Only Earl Nolan"

TRIBUTES TO EARL NOLAN CONTINUED WELL into the late 1990s and beyond, with retrospectives mentioning both his University of Arizona and other amateur performances, as well as his professional forays. He also received new honors along the way.

On October 9, 1969, Coach Rollin Gridley, who was a member of the selection committee for the Arizona Sports Hall of Fame, sent his Tucson High School gridiron protégé a letter, stating that he wanted to nominate him for charter membership on the statewide honor roster, and asked him to fill out a form furnishing information on his career. Nolan, who never spoke about his achievements or promoted himself, predictably let the deadline lapse.

On September 13, 1996, five years after his passing, Earl Nolan was elected to the University of Arizona Sports Hall of Fame. The response to his nomination was overwhelming. Among the individuals sending letters wholeheartedly supporting his induction were several prominent Tucson residents, many of them his friends for life.

Justice of the Peace Manuel Avalos called Nolan "a lifelong friend and one of the finest athletes that I have ever known. His friends affectionately nicknamed him 'King Kong.' Earl's past athletic accomplishments and honors truly justify his being selected to reign once again among those who are to be listed in the University Hall of Fame." Avalos praised him as "one of the most worthy athletes of all time!"

University of Arizona Professor Emeritus, sports editor, and author Abe Chanin of Midbar Press summarized some of his memories about Nolan: "As a youngster I watched him play football and track for the UA. I can recall Earl – he was a big man for his day – standing off two blockers as he played the tackle position for Coach Tex Oliver. He lettered in football in 1933, '34 and '36, and also lettered in track in 1934. He was the first Wildcat named All-American (honorable mention) and also the first to enter the pros, playing for the Chicago Cardinals. At the time of the UA's Centennial celebration he was named to the all-time UA football team. In addition to his celebrated athletic career, Earl Nolan was a great hero in the South Pacific during World War II. Highly decorated, Earl won battlefield promotion in the Solomon Islands to lieutenant. It is also to his credit that he returned to the University to earn an engineering degree in 1955 and went to work for the U.S. Forest Service."

Chanin also corresponded with Nolan's daughter in 1996, referring to Earl as an "all-time great and a personal friend," and stating, "I believe you know that I hold very high regard for your father. Your dad was more than a great athlete; he was a fine man." Chanin believed that "Michael Earl Nolan was a most unusual man, certainly worthy of a good book," and he kindly offered copies of his pertinent interviews and tapes.

Roy P. Drachman, Tucson civic leader and founder of Roy Drachman Realty Company, wrote that he strongly endorsed Nolan's selection to the Hall of Fame: "Earl was an outstanding athlete in football, track, and boxing. He was known as 'King Kong' Nolan because of his size and his antics on the football field. He was the first University of Arizona football player to play in the National Football League. He played for the Chicago Cardinals before that team moved to St. Louis (and most recently to Phoenix). After his career as a football player, he returned to the U of A, got his degree in engineering and practiced in the Tucson area for many years. During World War II, he enlisted in the Marines and had an outstanding career in that organization." Drachman stated that Nolan was known by many "because of his bravery in action."

In an April 8, 1991 article in the *Tucson Citizen*, "UA football figure dies," by Corky Simpson, Drachman was quoted as saying that Nolan was "one of the biggest, strongest and best football players this school ever had, and a heck of a nice guy, too." When he was 92 years old, Drachman would reminisce about treating his friend Earl to T-bone steaks at the Grand Café in the 1930s. As an aside, he believed that because of the physique on the famous World War II Marine recruiting poster, the Marine depicted must have been Nolan. [Editor's note: It was not, but the sentiment is appreciated.]

High school principal Henry E. Egbert spoke highly of his childhood idol: "As a youngster attending Roskruge Junior High School, I walked to the fence outside the Tucson High School football stadium to watch Earl play football and engage in track. He became an inspiration to me, and I followed his career at the University of Arizona, then into professional football with the NFL Chicago Cardinals. I attended the University of Arizona, participated in sports, and after serving six years in the military, I returned to education, becoming a teacher and principal of two Tucson high schools. Most youngsters have an idol, and mine was Earl Nolan. We named our son after him. Earl Nolan was a motivating factor in my life and the lives of others."

Weightlifter and gym owner Johnny Gibson emphasized that he could not think of anyone more deserving to be in the Hall of Fame, referring to Nolan's "illustrious career," and recalling that King Kong "was a super sturdy football player, track man and boxer. He preferred to play football minus a helmet. Earl lettered in football at the U of A in 1933, 1934 and 1936. He also lettered in track & field. As near as I can remember, he was the first U of A football player to play pro football. His record in the javelin lasted for 30 years. Earl Nolan was my personal friend and a customer at my barbershop for 35 years. We had great visits. He was one great athlete and truly a role model to remember."

Educator and Tucson High School football coach Rollin T. Gridley remembered Nolan as "a very capable student and athlete," mentioning his football and track performance, the distinction of being the first U of A player in the National Football League, and his graduation from the College of Engineering. The coach was proud of the fact that his former student "served with distinction in the U.S. Marine Corps during WWII in the Pacific area," and added, "I personally vouch for his good character." In a letter to Nolan's daughter, the coach expressed his sorrow that his friend could not be present to receive the honor.

Former U of A teammate and Air Force Colonel A. V. Grossetta wrote, "I have known Earl since we were in Tucson High School together from 1929 to 1932. He was always a quiet, unassuming, determined young man, and a sincere, loyal friend. He was a fierce, confident competitor in all his athletic endeavors. The largest man on our football team at 205 pounds, he was agile, quick, very strong and well coordinated. He lettered in football and track, boxed and even played some basketball. In college I again played football with Earl, and he improved with every year. I can vouch for his toughness and strength, since as a blocking back, I often scrimmaged against him and usually found myself flat on my back or tossed bodily to one side." (Sentiments he echoed in *Glimpses of Glory*!)

"Earl was All-Border Conference tackle, and he received All-American honorable mention. In track he participated in all the weight events – javelin, discus, and shot put – and held the school javelin record for many, many years. Earl was fast for his size, high jumped over six feet, and I'm sure could have been an outstanding decathlete."

Colonel Grossetta went on to laud Nolan's reputation as a Marine: "Earl left school after his senior year to try his hand in professional football with the old Chicago Cardinals, but when WWII came along, he volunteered for and enlisted in the Marine Corps. In the island-hopping action of the Pacific operations, he was highly decorated for bravery in action and received a battlefield commission as a 2nd Lieutenant. I've been told by persons who knew him or knew of him that he was as tough, mean and fearless as any Marine out there. I can surely believe it.

"As evidence of his mental ability and determination, witness the fact that he returned to Tucson after the war, worked his way through college, and graduated from the U of A with a degree in civil engineering. Earl married into an old-time Tucson family, the Ahee family, and became a devoted husband and father."

It is noteworthy that the letters of recommendation, just like so many of the articles and documentaries about him, not only covered Nolan's outstanding athletic achievements but addressed the totality of the man's life and character.

Jim Livengood, University of Arizona Director of Intercollegiate Athletics, wrote the family on August 13, 1996, regarding the upcoming induction into the Hall of Fame. The letter read, "We obviously selected a very special person. Michael Earl Nolan certainly accomplished some incredible feats during his intercollegiate career as well as setting records and high standards for those who followed, and we are proud to honor him this fall. You have every reason to be very proud of your father's extraordinary accomplishments throughout his lifetime."

On August 20, 1996, the family received a letter from David W. Murray, U of A Director of Track & Field. Murray wrote that Nolan "was, and is, a true 'Wildcat,' and an outstanding inspiration to past, present, and future Wildcats. As an Arizona alumnus myself, class of 1965, and as a former student-athlete, I can appreciate his legacy, not only what he contributed to Arizona athletes, but also his contribution to his city, his country, and his family. I am so pleased that he is to be inducted in the University of Arizona Sports Hall of Fame."

On September 24, 1996, Thomas S. Sanders, U of A Associate Director of Athletics for Development, wrote to the family that everyone was extremely happy to induct Earl Nolan into the Hall of Fame, stating that "he clearly was an amazing man." In February at the time of the selection, he had written, "It is quite clear that Mr. Nolan was not only an extraordinary athlete but an extremely colorful character as well. He'll be a welcome addition to our Hall of Fame."

The 1996 U of A Sports Hall of Fame printed program began with Nolan's early athletic achievements: "Legendary, powerful football lineman, track and field performer and boxer who was Arizona's first player in the NFL (with the Chicago Cardinals in 1937), he was an early proponent of weightlifting to enhance athletic performance. He was twice [three times] All-Border Conference in football and in 1936 was All-America honorable mention, the first UA player so honored. In track and field, he set a UA dual-meet record in the javelin that lasted for 32 years and high jumped 6' 2½"." Bringing the tribute more current, it continued, "A much-decorated Marine during World War II, he was named to the *Arizona Daily Star* 'All-Time Arizona Honor Grid Team' in 1949. In 1969, he was named to the *Star*'s 'Modern All-Stars UA Football Team' and the 'All-Time Rocky Mountain-Southwest Football Team,' selected by regional sports editors."

The Hall of Fame induction ceremony featured an inspiring taped tribute to Nolan, recapping his accomplishments and firsts, and stating that the honor was "long past due." Narrator Brian Jeffries noted that over time some of the stories might have faded, "but even today, no Arizona sports legend matches his. During his years at Arizona, Earl distinguished himself in football, track and field, and boxing, dominating opponents, setting records, and amazing everyone with his feats of strength and endurance." Referring to him as "an incredible physical specimen for his day," Jeffries remarked, "Off the field, friends knew him as quiet and modest, but between the goal posts, he was a holy terror." Nolan "rarely talked about his triumphs, and if he told a story at all about himself, it was usually a humorous tale about one of his defeats." During the war, "his feats of strength and bravery were renowned throughout the South Pacific."

In the November 1996 issue of *Tucson Lifestyle*, the magazine featured a special editorial section, "100 Years of University of Arizona Athletics," in honor of the 1897-1997 athletic centennial. Under "The Border Conference," the article stated, "Alumni and Tucsonans who saw any of the games during the Tex Oliver years love to recount stories about watching his star players in action. One such gridder was Earle 'King Kong' Nolan, who at six-feet-two and 230 pounds was a giant in his day.... Nolan went on to play football with the Chicago Cardinals and then served with the Marines in the South Pacific." Under "Tagged Cats: Enduring (and Endearing) Wildcat Nicknames," the article identified King Kong Nolan as a "legendary strongman and early proponent of weightlifting for athletic conditioning" and "the first Wildcat to play in the National Football League." Under "Top Cats," he was mentioned once again: "Excelling at football and track in the early '30s, he earned his nickname not only because of his six-feet-two-inch height and 50-inch chest, but because of his unstoppable power on the field."

On July 25, 1998, Nolan was further honored by selection to the Pima County Sports Hall of Fame. The day before the induction Dave Silver, sports editor for KGUN TV-Channel 9 in Tucson and a fellow inductee to the Hall, featured a stirring tribute to him on his television sportscast. Silver began the program by stating, "The man they called 'King Kong' was one of the great athletes of his day," describing him not only as a "huge man" and a "star athlete" at Tucson High School and the University of Arizona, who participated in all sports, but as a "war hero," and in many cases, "larger than life." Silver commented that "Nolan's friends remember him as a big, fun-loving guy, a talent on the field with the strength of two men."

Nolan was touted on the program by his old teammates and friends. According to A. V. Grossetta, Earl "was one of the best all-around athletes I've ever seen." He noted that his teammate "didn't talk a lot. When he said something, it was meaningful. He was very polite, but he could also be real rough when he wanted to be." John M. "Pat" Turner remarked that he had been in Arizona since 1929, and that Nolan was "one of the most outstanding athletes in University history." Turner recalled that he himself weighed around 135-140 pounds and, on U of A football trips, was used as a "dumbbell" by the weightlifters on the team. He joked that he never got to sit down because he was "always up in the air." To quote Abe Chanin's book, "Pat Turner, one of Nolan's teammates, still worships him." Turner told Chanin that Earl "was so strong that he could stand straight up in the line, take a blocker on each leg and still make the tackle. And he was fearless.... He was a big, shy guy, but he was awfully damn rough on the football field." When Dave Silver asked gym owner Johnny Gibson if Nolan was a "king of the gym" type, Gibson responded, "No, he was kind of a shy guy. He never threw himself at anybody. But he had everything to back it up. He was just an all-around great guy. He was truly a legend, for sure, and a great man in his day." Gibson went on to cite his friend's wartime service: "He got a battlefield commission, became a captain. He was a fearless soldier beyond any doubt."

The Pima County induction program referred to Nolan as a "legendary athlete whose career spanned several sports. He excelled in sports at Tucson High School. At the University of Arizona, as a football player, track & field competitor, boxer, and wrestler, he set records of high standards for those who followed. He was named by the *Arizona Daily Star* as tackle for the All-Time University of Arizona 11 Best Football Players. He was also the first U of A player to play professional football (Chicago Cardinals, 1937-38). Earl also lettered in track at the U of A in 1934, setting records and attaining high-point honors. In 1934 [1935], he set a meet record in the javelin at the dual meet with San Diego State that was not broken until 1967." As a boxer, he "won the Southwestern Heavyweight Amateur Championship" [1934 and 1936], "won the Arizona Golden Gloves tournament, and boxed professionally. Additionally, Earl won honors at the U of A as an intramural heavyweight wrestling champion in 1935-36, pitched baseball, and was a weightlifter."

In his June 16, 1998 *Citizen* "Along the Way" column, "Local Sports Hall of Fame additions truly a worthy bunch," sports columnist Corky Simpson referred to Earl Nolan as "a Tucson superstar." Later, in his July 27 column after the ceremony, Simpson echoed the sentiment: "Nolan was a truly remarkable athlete, excelling at Tucson High and UA in football, track and field, boxing, wrestling and weightlifting."

A July 8, 1999 article in the *Citizen*, "Portraits from a century of UA football – 'King Kong' Nolan," by Dave Petruska, recapped the myriad ground-breaking accomplishments and colorful legends surrounding Michael Earl Nolan – sixty-three years after the renowned tackle's last game for the University. He added that not only had Nolan been a standout in football and weight events, but he had been athletic and nimble enough to high jump 6 feet 4 inches. Petruska concluded by commenting that "Nolan certainly was someone you wanted alongside you in the trenches, especially in battle. He was a highly decorated Marine in World War II."

The *Citizen* presented a retrospective of the "UA's First Century" on August 26, 1999. The results of a reader survey were presented, and Earl Nolan was among the top ten vote-getters for the U of A's "best football player ever." He was the only player named from the pre-1950s era, and one of only two before the 1980s. Under a section titled "Wildcat moments, great and small," he was memorialized once again as the first U of A player in the National Football League.

An October 16, 1999 supplement to both the *Star* and *Citizen*, "Gridiron Heroes 1899-1999," by Thomas S. Sanders of the University of Arizona Athletic Heritage Center, cited Nolan's All-America selection, professional football career, and Hall of Fame recognition, referring to him as an "incredibly powerful, intimidating lineman" and "an early proponent of weightlifting who became a much-decorated member of the U.S. Marine Corps in the Pacific during the war."

On August 11, 2013, Nolan was named to "The Top 50 UA Football Players of All Time," in an article by Anthony Gimono on *TucsonCitizen.com*. Seventy-seven years after his final game for the U of A, he was named No. 22 on the list of top players. Gimono acknowledged that it was "most difficult to rank players from long-ago eras, as the comparisons to modern players break down, but Michael Earle Nolan rates here because of his mythical place in school lore." Citing many of Nolan's honors and accomplishments as well as several of the widely told, colorful anecdotes about his life, Gimono referred to him as a "fearsome force on the football field," and a "legendary UA athlete in track and field (discus, shot put, javelin and the high jump) and boxing." Although almost eight decades have passed...although subsequent generations of sportswriters and fans are far removed from seeing him on the field, it is no surprise that Nolan's star still shines brightly to this day.

A particularly notable tribute appeared in the "Arizona Legends" section of the February 1999 issue of the magazine *Harnett's Sports Arizona*. Jerry Eaton declared in his three-page article, "King Kong Nolan," that "Tucson's ironman may have been the state's greatest athlete." Referring to him as an "athlete who could seemingly master any sport he chose," Eaton described Nolan as a "muscular but graceful athlete," who was "built along the lines of a Mr. America," and used "these physical gifts brilliantly." He also described him as a "one-man wrecking crew who destroyed opponents," but noted that he not only "manhandled linemen unfortunate enough to face him across the line of scrimmage, he also set records in track and field in the shot put, discus, and javelin, and won boxing championships." As a boxer, he presented what Eaton called "an awesome appearance in the ring" – no doubt enhanced by an astounding 77 1/2-inch reach. In summary, Eaton wrote, "Awards and honors followed Nolan throughout his life." He speculated that sportswriters and spectators alike took "Nolan's heroics in stride. It's what they had come to expect from him....King Kong Nolan played football as he lived his life: with gusto and class. He knew no other way." Earl Nolan truly "became a legend in his own time."

Earl Nolan, senior, University of Arizona, 1936.

"Tarzan" Nolan (center), University of Arizona *Desert* yearbook, 1935.

Nolan (third row, second from left), Alpha Tau Omega fraternity, 1934.

Described as "Tucson's ironman" who could master any sport he chose, Nolan was renowned for his strength and agility. He made his mark in football, track and field, boxing, wrestling, weightlifting, and baseball.

A larger-than-life athlete, Nolan was often called the state's greatest.

Nolan (second row, second from left), shown with the University of Arizona track and field team, 1933. A versatile and record-breaking field competitor, he won medals in the javelin, shot, discus, and high jump.

The immortal gridiron great "King Kong" Nolan, University of Arizona football, 1936. Three-year varsity letterman. Three-year All-Border Conference tackle. First player from the state of Arizona to be named Associated Press All-American (Honorable Mention, 1936), and first University of Arizona player to enter professional football. Selected to six all-time honor rosters between 1949 and 2013. Inducted into University of Arizona Sports Hall of Fame and Pima County Sports Hall of Fame.

CHAPTER ELEVEN

Professional Football
Shattering the NFL Barrier

As MENTIONED, EARL NOLAN WAS THE FIRST University of Arizona player to join the ranks in professional football. In 1937, he was offered positions with three clubs – the Pittsburgh Pirates, the Chicago Cardinals, and the Cleveland Rams. A March 17, 1937 letter from Edward Bernhard of the Pirates offered a "special concession" agreed to by President Arthur Rooney, in an attempt to entice Nolan to sign the contract they had sent – bus fare from Tucson to Pittsburgh. The monetary standards in the industry were a trifle different from today's. A March 29 letter from Cardinals Coach Milan Creighton enclosed a contract, and a March 30 letter from Damon "Buzz" Wetzel, general manager of the Rams, also enclosed a contract.

Nolan accepted the top offer and salary from the National Football League's Chicago Cardinals, and would play with the team during both the 1937 and 1938 seasons. On July 31, 1937, Coach Creighton sent him a letter to report for practice on August 16 at Mills Stadium, and to bring his own shoes, pads, and practice uniform. While in Chicago, Nolan stayed at the Midwest Athletic Club, described by the coach as a "very exclusive club."

As the first professional football player coming out of the University of Arizona, Nolan still had some barriers to break. He would often say that in those days it was not widely believed a player from that part of the county could make the grade in the pros. Sources reported that he scrimmaged all day against the entire Cardinals team, until even the coach suited up against him. Bernie Roth quoted Nolan as saying, "I finally got to play for the club after I convinced them that we played the same kind of football in Arizona." With his success on the team, the door was opened to other University of Arizona alumni to play in the pros.

A pre-season article from a Chicago paper advised its readers, "Keep an eagle eye peeled on Tarzan Nolan, Cardinal tackle. He'll be one of the best in the big league this season. Turk Edwards, Washington tackle, recommends him highly."

Nolan, No. 17, again played right tackle on offense and left tackle on defense. On November 30, 1937, the *Chicago Daily News* described Earl "Tarzan" Nolan as the "young tackle from Arizona who has proved one of the best first-year men on the roster of the Cardinals."

The 1937 Cardinals had an improved 5-5-1 season (win/loss percentage .500), bettering their previous 1936 season record of 3-8-1 (win/loss percentage .250). The Cardinals scored five wins, over the Green Bay Packers (14-7), Washington Redskins (21-14), Cleveland Rams (6-0, an "All-Time Cardinal Shutout," and 13-7), and Pittsburgh Pirates (13-7); five losses, to the Detroit Lions (16-7 and 16-7), Green Bay Packers (34-13), and Chicago Bears (16-7 and 42-28); and one tie, with the Philadelphia Eagles (6-6). One site also showed a win over the Chicago Gunners (19-3).

After his first season with the Cardinals, Nolan was named All-Pro Honorable Mention, chosen by a poll of the league's coaches.

In a December 10, 1937 *Tucson Daily Citizen* "From the Press Box" column, after Nolan's return from his first season of play with the Cardinals, Hank Squire wrote, "Husky, towering Earl Nolan, Arizona's contribution to professional football, lost no time returning to Tucson after his team, the Chicago Cardinals, completed its 11-game league schedule last Sunday against the powerful Chicago Bears. Nolan, who was in the lineup 57 minutes in the final tilt, hopped a train the next day for the Old Pueblo." To quote a November 30 article from Chicago, that game with the Bears would be the "second game in their civic pro football strife" for the season, and no doubt the December 5 game was rather intense as always.

Squire continued, "He's still the modest, unassuming Earl Arizona grid fans took to their hearts during the three years he was a pillar of strength in the Wildcat forward wall. Tucson still is, and always will be, his home....Arizona fans undoubtedly will be glad to learn Earl's first season in the professional ranks was marked with success, because there never was a more popular player at the University. He deserves all the good fortune that may come his way."

Nolan was indeed happy to be back in his hometown. He commented in the interview, "It's great to be back. I never knew how much I would miss the climate and the people here." He might not have cared for the Chicago climate, but he did say he was treated very well and "got along fine with the players and the other friends I made." He said he even played a "lot of golf" while he was there and did enjoy his stay, but "there isn't any place like Tucson." Nolan retained his attachment to the "Old Pueblo" throughout his life. He always returned, and he always said that it was the only place he could ever imagine living.

Nolan did tell Squire that he went to one college game while he was gone – Northwestern and Michigan. He was not impressed, said the teams did not "hit hard at all," found the game dull, and left after the first quarter. Ever loyal, he added, "I can tell you this much – Arizona has a lot better team."

An October 7, 1937 letter from Nolan to Philip "Soapy" Clarke, in which he was encouraging Clarke to re-enroll in school and engage in sports there, demonstrated the type of self-deprecating humor which marked Earl Nolan's interaction with others. Although the press extolled his virtues as a football player, he told his friend, "You're a good football player, so why not play it before you die of old age. I'm still playing a great game as left guard. I am guarding the water bucket from the left."

Nolan received a letter from Coach Creighton on June 23, 1938, enclosing a contract for the 1938 season with the Cardinals, asking him to report for practice on August 15 at the Morgan Park Military Academy, and advising that the first game of the season would be on September 11 against the Chicago Bears at Soldier Field. Again, he was requested to bring his own hip pads and shoulder pads; however, the club would be paying for all expenses during practice.

In 1938, Creighton brought back only eighteen of the veterans from the previous year, relying on Nolan "to take care of that right tackle position." He wrote, "Everything points to a whale of a year. We are going to field a spirited, winning ball club with veterans like yourself to mix with the new blood. I believe we will be plenty hard to stop."

As alluded to earlier, salaries in the 1930s differed substantially from those received by today's football stars, although they were still high compared to other salaries of that era. On May 3, 1937, a photo of Nolan appeared in the *Arizona Daily Star*. In "Gridder Signs Pro Contract," it was said that the former Wildcat was "given material recognition of his ability last week when he was signed by the Chicago Cardinals, one of the leading members of the national professional football league, at a salary of $135 per game." During his tenure, he received from $135 ($120 beginning offer) to $150 per game, amounts referred to as "breathtaking for the day." He was reportedly the highest-paid lineman on the team. He also received, as a bonus, railroad fare in 1937 and airline fare of $96.45 in 1938. In addition, the Cardinals covered travel expenses throughout the season, including $2 per day for meals. [Editor's note: We found an interesting Internet site, *Restaurant-ing through history: Exploring American restaurants over the centuries*, which noted that in 1937, a hamburger meal, complete with dessert and a beverage, at Toffenetti's Triangle Restaurant in the Chicago Loop cost 30¢.] In a July 14, 1938 letter, Coach Creighton sweetened the pot a little: "As you no doubt are aware, your present salary is a very fine one – but to show that we like your fighting spirit and your ball playing, Mr. Bidwill has agreed to pay you ten dollars per game bonus, providing we meet the winner of the eastern division for the National Professional Championship."

However, Nolan only played four games in the 1938 season. The reason he left the Cardinals was never discussed with family. He did laugh about it once and said he took a swing at the coach, but the background of the "disagreement" remained a mystery. After his departure, the Cardinals returned to a less successful record of 2-9 (win/loss percentage .182) for the 1938 season.

All things considered, Nolan seemed to enjoy his stint with the Cardinals, but later would maintain that there was more spirit involved in college playing. During the 1990 interview with Matt Lemmon, he was asked about the differences between his amateur and professional football days. Nolan recounted that he had no trouble adjusting to the playing; it was the city life he did not care for. When he first arrived in Chicago, he grabbed a taxi to look for a small cottage in the country. He joked that he had no idea that the city extended to South Bend! One of the few mementos Nolan brought back from his Chicago experience was a souvenir Pullman menu, a special steak luncheon for the Chicago Cardinals football team on the October 2, 1937 train trip to Cleveland. He also brought back a ticket to the September 11 game with the Bears. In 1949, he did mention to Bernie Roth that the first touchdown of his career occurred during his play with the Cardinals, when he blocked a punt and fell on it in the end zone for a touchdown.

Nolan received a telegram from Coach John "Blood" McNally of the Pittsburgh Pirates on October 6, 1938, again offering him a contract, and subsequently received another offer from McNally on June 7, 1939 and a contract in July of 1939. He also received offers on August 28 and September 9, 1939 from Choppy Rhodes to play with the St. Louis Gunners. Rhodes stated, "Bill Wilson, who is with us, recommended you." The next year, Nolan received a May 2, 1940 contract from Arch Wolfe, business manager for the Cardinals.

Though he was offered contracts from the various teams through May of 1940, he did not sign up again after 1938, preferring to pursue other interests.

Nolan's professional football career might have ended, but it had been lucrative and it had resulted in some memorable experiences and friendships. One anecdote that he loved to tell involved an All-Pro great, Bronco Nagurski of the Chicago Bears. In 1937, Nolan found himself across the line from Nagurski and had really charged hard. About halfway through the game, Nagurski asked him, "What's the matter, kid? Are you trying to earn your letter in the first game?" A friendship developed between the two men, who often ate together and swapped stories. Nolan would later say that it was Nagurski who introduced him to the benefits of garlic, the beginning of a lifelong favorite.

Another friendship developed with Ross Carter, a Cardinals teammate; the two men stayed in touch over the years and stopped by to visit each other during family vacations. Carter wrote the family on January 9, 1992, after Nolan's passing, reminiscing about his friend Earl: "He was a tremendous athlete. When he showed up at training camp for the old Chicago Cardinals, he was nicknamed 'Tarzan' because of his outstanding physique. He had an upper torso that would rival any of the weightlifters. I recall I bought a new suit that year and Earl was attracted to the suit coat, so I let him wear it occasionally. His size expanded the coat so that I had to have it remodeled when I returned home.

"I know his passing is a great loss to you. I just want you to know I will miss him, too. He was not only a great athlete but a wonderful person."

Nolan ended his football career with a volunteer appearance in the Goulash Bowl in Phoenix on December 29, 1956, three days before his 46th birthday, as a favor to his brother-in-law George Ahee, the coach of the Tucson team. The first annual charity game, featuring former Arizona collegiate players, drew a crowd of 7,000, and raised $8,000 for the Hungarian relief effort. It was one more in a series of Tucson / Phoenix contests, with the Phoenix Pests victorious over the Tucson Budas, 19-0.

This final performance did not go unnoticed. On January 1, 1957, the *Phoenix Gazette*'s Bob Allison commented after the bowl game that "one of Arizona's truly fabulous sports characters was in the spotlight for perhaps the last time.... There are a lot of college players hereabouts who still bear scars left by the way he used to maim opposing linemen with impartial savagery. The old slashing viciousness of Earl Nolan might not have been seen in the Goulash Bowl. But the spirit was there. And old King Kong was still a tough man to move around." Allison believed that Nolan, "one of the state's greatest," handled himself pretty well on the field, especially since he had not worked out for a single day before the game, "left his job at Silver Bell mine near Tucson at about 11:00 a.m. Saturday and drove to Phoenix just in time to suit up. He didn't even know most of his teammates." No doubt Nolan had other ideas about the situation when he tried to get out of his sitting position from his car on the return to Tucson!

As had been the case with his college playing, a March 2, 1982 letter from Don Wojcik, unofficial Cardinals team historian, demonstrated that Nolan's brief career in Chicago had made a continuing impression. Wojcik was attempting to assemble a current directory of the former Cardinal players, and wrote, "I have been a rabid Cardinal fan for many years, and also a fan of yours, who enjoyed seeing you play many times in your great career at Arizona and with the 1937, 1938 Cards.... Thank you for years of exciting football. Great players like you deserve to be remembered."

Nolan is included in *The Official Encyclopedia of Football*, by Roger Treat (A. S. Barnes and Co., Inc., 1972), as well as on several Internet sites dealing with professional football. He succeeded at opening the door to professional football for University of Arizona players. It is one of the interesting ironies of his life that his former Chicago team has since moved to Arizona.

Nolan, No. 17 (second row, sixth from right), Chicago Cardinals football team, 1937. First professional football player from the University of Arizona.

Earl ("Tarzan") Nolan, young tackle from Arizona, who has proved one of the best first-year men on the roster of the Cardinals, and who will face the Bears Sunday at Wrigley Field in the second game of their civic pro football strife.

"Tarzan" Nolan. (Printed in the *Chicago Daily News*, November 30, 1937.)

Nolan (left), Chicago. Called "one of the best first-year men on the roster of the Cardinals." Named All-Pro Honorable Mention, 1937.

Back in the snowy country. Nolan (left), Chicago, 1937.

Earl Nolan, giant tackle, in Chicago Cardinals jacket, 1937.

CHAPTER TWELVE

Professional Boxing
"Arizona's Heavyweight Sensation"

ALL IN ALL, LITTLE INFORMATION IS CURRENTLY AVAILABLE regarding Earl Nolan's professional boxing days. According to some yellowed clippings, he frequently boxed in Tonopah, Nevada (a town known for its silver mining), at times residing in Manhattan, Nevada, as the guest of Mr. and Mrs. Harry Weimer, friends from Tucson. In the column "Ray's Sport Gossip" of the *Tonopah Daily Times-Bonanza*, Ray Germain informed the local fans that "Harry Weimer, brother of light heavyweight boxer 'Dutch' Weimer, has under his wing two young giants, who are claimed to be above the ordinary in ability with regards to the squared ring." The article stated that Nolan was one of two fighters Weimer brought "to spend several months with him and to further condition these boys for the ring. Nolan, who weighs close to 220, and looks nearly as big as Primo Carnera, was at one time amateur champion and holds wins over many of the coast's most promising boxers. He played on the University of Arizona's football team this past season, and if his size is any indication as to the rest of the squad, the old school had a mighty powerful line. Weimer is said to have his eye on a fighter to match with Nolan, and if arrangements can be worked out, the fight may be staged either in Tonopah or Manhattan within the next couple of months."

Nolan fought in the 4th of July "Silver Jubilee" event, which was promoted as "Tonopah's Greatest Show!" Opponents mentioned in Nevada included Jerry Delanoy and Tommy Jordan of Las Vegas. Another clipping from Tonopah, "Popular Fighters Scheduled for 'Jubilee' Card," read, "Promising one of the greatest fight cards ever to be presented in the state, Freck Lydon, chairman of the boxing committee of the 'Silver Jubilee' celebration, last night announced a few highlights of the proposed card.... The second main event fight of ten rounds will bring two of the most popular heavyweight fighters in the state together.... Angelo Ricci, the pride of the Hawthorne Marines, and Battling Nolan, popular Manhattan fighter. A great deal of interest will be centered around this fight, with Manhattan and Mineral county backing their fighters to the limit. Both of these boys are exceptionally popular in their respective communities." The outcomes of these various fights are not known to us.

Nolan also spent some time in Livermore, California, as a sparring partner for Max Baer, one-time Heavyweight Champion of the World.

After signing with the Chicago Cardinals, he boxed professionally during the pro football off-season. In 1938, the muscular fighter was dubbed "Arizona's Heavyweight Sensation – 47," under the personal direction of Frank Paccassi of Phoenix, Arizona. He carried with him his favored number from University of Arizona football.

Several letters from Paccassi were found among Nolan's papers, encouraging him to pursue a career in professional boxing. On April 16, 1938, Paccassi wrote, "You definitely have what it takes to be a successful boxer. I know you can do it." He mentioned that there was current interest in Nolan from both the Salt Lake City and Los Angeles areas, and enclosed some contracts he hoped to have signed. On April 20, 1938, Paccassi wrote again, telling him, "There was a nice piece out of New York on you yesterday, and *The Ring* magazine will have a story on you next month. We are a cinch to go places. I know we can't miss." It seemed that Nolan had not made up his mind about the pursuit, and later comments would indicate that it certainly was not his first choice.

A 1938 article from the *Arizona Independent Republic*, "Pugilistic Hopes Flare...Paccassi-Nolan Ring Team...No. 47 Steps Into Picture," written by George Moore in the column "Moore About Sports," announced hopes that "from the cactus will come a 199-pounder" who would start a "revolution among the promoters and heavyweights in the pugilistic business."

By the time of the article, Paccassi had apparently been successful in getting the written commitment he wanted: "Paccassi, who once directed the fortunes of three world heavyweight champions, returned from Tucson late yesterday afternoon – his face wreathed in smiles. Shortly after his arrival, he airmailed to the New York State Athletic Commission for registration of a managerial contract which he had signed along with Nolan earlier in the day."

Moore definitely thought the Arizona heavyweight had all the necessary qualifications. He asserted that "Nolan won't be a stranger to the leathertossing business," having held the championship of the Southwestern Amateur Athletic Union, as well as doing his share for the Wildcat boxing squad. Nolan, he declared, had "become probably one of the best ring prospects ever developed in the circuit."

Paccassi also believed that his boxer's long-term potential was stellar: "Nolan, according to Paccassi, has the face and spirit of a fighter....Paccassi has managed Dempsey, Primo Carnera and Max Baer, and in comparing Nolan with the latter at the same stage of their experience, Nolan has 'em both topped, he claims."

In the article, Paccassi described Nolan as having a 77 1/2-inch reach, a 34-inch waist, an 18-inch neck, and a chest measuring 46 inches normal and 48 expanded.

Moore concluded by writing, "Nolan has had some 15 amateur fights, all of which Paccassi says failed to go more than a round.... A pair of shoulders that have helped both on the gridiron and in the amateur ring have given him a punch, while he has plenty of speed afoot, as evidenced by his ability to do the 100 in a fraction under 11 seconds.... Here's luck to him... and if he comes up to the expectations that a lot of people have for him, don't say you weren't warned."

It appeared that his career did live up to expectations. Bob Allison referred to Nolan's professional boxing as 6 feet 3 inches of "destruction-bent ferocity... just a single intent to destroy the opposition."

In his pre-season letter of June 23, 1938, Cardinals coach Milan Creighton wrote to his returning tackle, "I hear you are bowling them over in the fight racket," and recommended that playing football would be the best way for him to keep his name before the sporting public should he want to fight in Chicago.

In Phoenix, Nolan knocked out Moose Irwin in the fourth round on March 25, 1938, a fight that netted a winning prize of $50. Included in an April 16, 1938 accounting from Paccassi, in three fights – Irwin, Davis (Tucson), and Sperland – after expenses and fees, Nolan's take was a total of $100. On April 3, 1939, fighting at a weight of 185 pounds, he knocked out "Battling Blackjack" in the first round. This last bout was cited in the June 1939 issue of *The Ring* magazine, in the column, "A Corner in the Fistic Market," under the category of "Heavyweight fights of importance." An article appearing in Phoenix after the fight, "Nolan Wins Bout In First Round," referred to his "fistic prowess" and stated that he "appeared much improved since he made his professional boxing debut a year ago, although he knocked out two opponents at that time." In a less successful fight on April 17, 1939, he was disqualified for holding Danny Alberts against the ropes while punching.

"Ex-Wildcat Gridder's Ring Prospects," from the April 30, 1939 *Arizona Independent Republic* "Rounding Up State Sports" column, written by Les Hegele, asserted about Nolan, "He came back here and really displayed a booming right. When he hit 'em, they stayed down. And when a boxer can bop them like that, he should go places in the fight game." Hegele described him as "packing an awful wallop" and being "the best prospect in the state heavyweight ranks."

Earl Nolan boxed professionally until 1940, including bouts in Arizona, California, Nevada, Texas, Oregon, and perhaps Illinois and Washington; presumably, there were others. He challenged the reigning champion Babe Ritchie for the state heavyweight title in El Paso, Texas, on June 21, 1940. Nolan is currently mentioned on Internet boxing sites, although the coverage is incomplete, as was the record keeping back in the day. Since he fought in multiple states and likely used pseudonyms or nicknames as appeared to have been the custom of the time among many boxers, uncovering this information would be a daunting task.

In 1949, Bernie Roth wrote about this foray into professional boxing: "When he got out of college, there was talk of making a professional heavyweight boxer out of the big guy. But Nolan would rather forget about his pro boxing experiences – football was and still is his first love." Roth stated that when asked about his professional boxing years, "well, Nolan shrugs that off," and quoted him as laughing and saying, "We won't talk about that. By the time I got into boxing, my shoulders were so broken up from football that I couldn't raise my arms above my head." Many of his professional opponents would no doubt have disputed his humility.

Nolan obviously decided not to pursue his professional ring career. He eventually decided to take up fighting on a different level, with the U.S. Marine Corps. On May 21, 1944, Vic Thornton would write that Nolan "took a whirl at professional boxing, but dropped that in favor of the more rugged and exacting fighting chores of the Marines." While in the Corps, however, he did box as a sideline. His drill instructor at boot camp entered him into the camp boxing tournament, where he was said to have won five bouts in one day, becoming the heavyweight champion. In all, he was reputed to have chalked up twenty victories in twenty fights.

In the 1970s, Nolan pursued his interest by judging professional boxing matches at the Tucson Community Center Arena, as a favor to his friend Mike Quihuis.

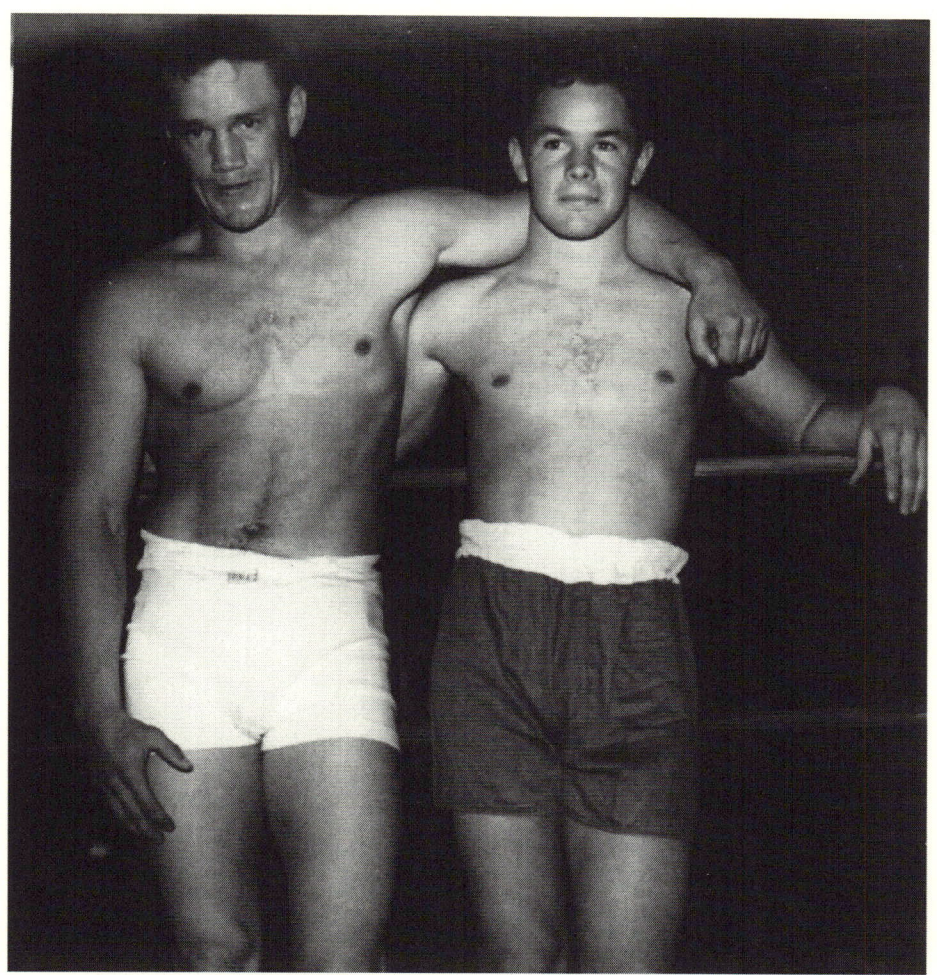

Pictured with another fighter from the evening's events, circa 1938, Nolan (left) boxed under the management of Frank Paccassi. With a "booming right," he fought professionally through 1940, including bouts in Arizona, California, Nevada, Oregon, and Texas.

Earl Nolan, "Arizona's Heavyweight Sensation – 47." Publicity photo, circa 1938.

CHAPTER THIRTEEN

United States Marine Corps
"Big Mike," from Guadalcanal to Iwo Jima

IN HIS JANUARY 13, 1948 "TUCSON SPORTSFOLIO" FEATURE in the *Arizona Daily Star*, artist Gee Tee Maxwell presented a portrait of Michael Earl Nolan and illustrations of his life, captioning one of them – "Many fabulous tales are told of his bravery in the last war. He was commissioned in the U.S. Marines on the field of battle at Guadalcanal."

Nolan fought from Guadalcanal to Iwo Jima, often in hand-to-hand combat. It was in the Marine Corps that he became known exclusively by his first name, and was nicknamed "Big Mike," "Iron Mike," and "Saddle Up Mike." He was promoted from private to captain during World War II, and retired a major.

We are most grateful for the prompt, courteous, and expert assistance of United States Senator John McCain from the state of Arizona in obtaining for us the existing file of Nolan's military records currently available from the National Personnel Records Center (NPRC). We had only received a much smaller, incomplete package on our previous request, complicated by the fact that Nolan had both an enlisted and a commissioned serial number. These documents have provided us with a general overview of his years in the Corps. [Editor's note: Anyone who has researched these records no doubt knows that they are not a complete event-by-event chronicle; there are time gaps in coverage, occasional omissions, contradictions, and misfilings. (We received a few pages of someone else's file mixed in with ours; digits in his serial number apparently had been transposed as the papers were filed.) Mostly administrative in nature, the files contain no specific details about the battle or service assignments. There also was an allusion to confidential files to which we were not given access. However, on the whole, the information is extremely valuable. We are definitely appreciative that these records were kept, and the noted problems are more than understandable given the scope of the material and the conditions under which it was assembled.]

In addition to including information from the available official sources, we have also included details and comments from various unofficial sources, both written and oral, as they have been presented to us over the years. Many accounts of Nolan's service and bravery in action, as well as numerous anecdotes from those years, have come through the press and newsletters; others have come through phone calls, visits, letters, and emails from the men who served with him, the men whose lives depended on Nolan's leadership, returning veterans, and friends who kept track of him over the years. When the myriad details are pieced together, they make a compelling and fascinating story.

Michael E. Nolan enlisted in the USMC on January 16, 1941, for four years of service; he often joked that the line was shorter for the Marine recruiting than it was for the Navy, so he decided to save time and join the Marines. He entered boot camp, and served in the 3rd Platoon, 3rd Recruit Battalion, Marine Corps Base, San Diego, California.

After his induction into the Marines, the January 25, 1941 *Arizona Independent Republic* printed a release from San Diego, "Earl Nolan Signs With Devil Dogs." After being asked if he planned to play football in the Marines, Nolan replied, "I joined to be a Marine. I don't care whether I actively compete in athletics again or not.... I'm in the Marines now, and I'm ready to take orders. That might be hard to do for a time, because ever since I was in grade school, I've done pretty much as I wanted. I was my own boss, and if I wanted to go someplace, I just packed up and went. That's all different now, I guess."

The article read, "Nolan's decision to join the Marines was as sudden as many of his other decisions. The afternoon of January 15 he was working for a construction company in Tucson. 'Along about 3 o'clock that afternoon,' he recounts, 'I decided I'd join the Marines. I figured I'd have to do my bit for Uncle Sam some time or another, so I just packed a bag with an extra shirt, grabbed the train to Los Angeles after I finished work, and applied for enlistment the next morning. They ran me through in one day, couldn't find anything wrong with me physically, and sent me down here that night.'"

Despite the light tone of the article, Nolan had taken his decision quite seriously, and as early as September of 1940 had begun making inquiries. Although the timing of his enlistment date might have been spontaneous, his commitment to service in the Marine Corps was anything but.

Years later, when comparing his Marine years to football, he would tell Jeff Dimond, "I used to think that Tex ran some tough workouts, but compared to the war, football was a Sunday afternoon picnic."

Stories have been told about Nolan's boot camp days. Vic Thornton of the *Star* would write on May 21, 1944, "His friends say that during 'boot training' at San Diego, Nolan applied himself so ardently to bayonet and rifle drill that he snapped his bayonet on the first lunge, broke the stock on the second thrust and was left standing with only the bolt in his hands." In 1989, Nolan himself would tell Bonny Henry of the *Star* that he initially flunked the bayonet course: "They had one of those dummies with a hinge at the hand that was supposed to give way. But instead of me poking the dummy, the dummy poked me. By the final drill, I was so mad that I ran over it. They disqualified me." Another story from boot camp related that he did not care at all for the treatment of the young recruits by the drill instructor, and stood up for them – in "no uncertain terms."

Nolan's archived Infantry Weapons Record indicated that despite any initial problems, he did indeed pass his bayonet qualification course on February 13, 1941; his pistol qualification on February 24; his rifle qualification on March 7; and his M-1 qualification on June 4.

From March 15 through June 20, 1941, Nolan served with Base Service Company, Base Service Battalion, Marine Corps Base, San Diego. He became a private first class on May 14, 1941. Two days later he was diagnosed with German measles. On June 20, he joined Battery H, Machine Gun Group, 2nd Defense Battalion, Fleet Marine Force; and on June 30, he transferred to Parris Island, South Carolina, through November 30. As an interesting sidelight given that cooking had always been a talent of his, Nolan was detailed special duty as a messman in the month of December, upon his return to San Diego. His performance was rated as "Outstanding." Subsequently, as a member of Battery H, Machine Gun Group, 2nd Defense Battalion, 2nd Marine Brigade, FMF, at San Diego, he was assigned to duty in the field in January of 1942, shortly after the attack on Pearl Harbor.

The 2nd Marine Brigade was said to have been the first wartime expeditionary force, and was deployed to American Samoa. A certificate was found among Nolan's papers – "Domain of Neptunus Rex, Ruler of the Raging Main" – initiating him into the "Solemn Mysteries of the Ancient Order of the Deep," a traditional seagoing ceremony for those crossing the equator for the first time. The certificate read that on January 14, 1942, at 0° Latitude and 152° Longitude, P.F.C. Michael Nolan-U.S.M.C. was aboard the *SS Monterey*, a fast troop carrier. The 2nd Defense Battalion, 2nd Marine Brigade arrived in American Samoa on January 21. Defense Battalions served to anchor bases and airfields in the South Pacific theater, protecting pivotal sea routes to Australia and New Zealand, as the Japanese advanced.

On February 4, 1942, Nolan was promoted to the rank of corporal, and served as a rifle squad leader.

A Lieutenant on the Battlefield

As of April 1, 1942, Corporal Nolan joined the Special Weapons Group, 8th Defense Battalion, 2nd Marine Brigade, Reinforced, FMF. The designation was changed on April

29, 1942, to 8th Defense Battalion, 8th Defense Battalion, Reinforced, FMF, Tutuila, American Samoa, by order of the Group Force Commander, dated April 28. On May 27, the 8th Defense Battalion moved southwest from Samoa for the landing and occupation at Wallis Island (actually a common reference for Uvea in the Wallis Islands), and was later designated as the Defense Force. It is believed that Nolan remained there until he was transferred temporarily to the 1st Marine Division, Reinforced, Solomon Islands invasion. The Division had been fortifying its ranks since late June or early July. He would later say that the time he spent on the Solomons during the course of the war "seemed like forever."

The first landings of the Guadalcanal campaign at Guadalcanal and nearby Tulagi (located twenty miles away), British Solomon Islands, took place on August 7, 1942. The major objective in Guadalcanal was a nearly completed Japanese airstrip, which would later be known as Henderson Field. The June 11, 1946 *Tucson Daily Citizen* reported that Nolan "was with the first Marines who landed at Guadalcanal, and received his commission in the field." On August 12, 1942, he was commissioned as a second lieutenant, USMCR, on the battlefield, with rank from May 1, 1942. The procedure utilized during the war was to issue the enlisted man an Honorable Discharge from the USMC and award an appointment to the newly commissioned officer in the United States Marine Corps Reserve, involving the issuance of a new serial number.

Nolan had been vetted for commission as early as April of 1942. In a May 10 recommendation from Captain H. B. Atkins, the commanding officer of Special Weapons Group, 8th Defense Battalion, it was said that "Nolan has demonstrated outstanding qualities of leadership, initiative and endurance. He has proved himself an excellent instructor of automatic weapons and basic military subjects. It is the opinion of the undersigned that Corporal Nolan is well qualified in all respects for this appointment and that his services as a second lieutenant would be extremely valuable to this organization." He was also recommended by Lieutenant Colonel Augustus W. Cockrell, the commanding officer of 8th Defense Battalion, in the Field, on May 12; and by Colonel Raphael Griffin, the commanding officer of 8th Defense Battalion, aboard the *USS Harris*, on May 20. A memorandum from the Marine Corps Reserve Examining Board, dated July 31, 1942, concluded, "We hereby certify that Corporal Michael E. Nolan, United States Marine Corps, is mentally, morally, and professionally qualified for appointment in the U.S. Marine Corps Reserve as a second lieutenant, and recommend him for appointment." One of the signers of this recommendation was Brigadier General Walter Newell Hill. Already recommended for promotion, Nolan was advanced on the battlefield during the Guadalcanal campaign.

Captain Atkins, in closing out the enlisted record, specified Nolan's character as "Excellent" and added, "Recommended for Good Conduct Medal." It is of note that the "Professional and Conduct Record" for Mike Nolan's entire enlisted service showed almost unanimous ratings of "Excellent" in all the specified categories of military efficiency, neatness and military bearing, intelligence, obedience, and sobriety.

[Editor's note: An anomaly was found while reviewing the NPRC records themselves... on two separate record-of-service forms in his file, Nolan was designated as serving with the 7th Marines for the entirety of his enlisted service. This reference contradicted the other information presented in the same file, and as of yet, we have found no corroboration. However, we do know that he definitely crossed paths with this unit. The 7th Marines were training on Parris Island from April 8 through the latter part of September 1941, and their 3rd Battalion landed in Samoa on April 28, 1942. The 3rd Battalion, 7th Marines, Reinforced, then went on to Wallis Island on May 27, 1942, to garrison and defend the Samoan Islands, and would later fight with the 1st Division on Guadalcanal in September 1942. A third, notarized record-of-service form, which was signed by Nolan, was also found in the NPRC file; it listed his service as proceeding from the Base Troops in San Diego to the 2nd Defense Battalion, 8th Defense Battalion, 1st Division, 3rd Raiders, 4th Regiment, 5th Division, and finally to the Corps Troops. This form accurately represents information we have located.]

Nolan was honorably discharged from the enlisted ranks in a "Special Order Discharge" as of August 19, 1942; his enlisted service record booklet was stamped as received by the Adjutant and Inspector's Department on October 5, 1942. It should be noted that he received a bullet wound in his left leg between the time of his enlistment physical and the final physical information included with that enlistment paperwork, as well as a physical form received by the A & I Department on October 12, 1942.

On November 2, 1942, the "Service Dept." section of the *Citizen* announced, "Michael (King Kong) Nolan, an almost legendary figure in Arizona football because of the way he played tackle a half dozen years ago," was among a group of Marines selected from the enlisted ranks to become officers "because they had demonstrated qualities of leadership."

An article with an enigmatic heading had appeared in the *Citizen* on October 22, 1942. "Marine Missing In Action Promoted to Rank of Lieutenant" read, "An outstanding record of service, while in the ranks of the Marine Corps for the past one and one-half years, rewarded Michael E. Nolan with his promotion from corporal to the commissioned rank of a second lieutenant, it was learned today. Lieutenant Nolan was one of 29 men selected from the ranks of enlisted men and non-commissioned officers for commissioned ratings. The promotions were made in the field upon the recommendations of their commanding officers. Advancements such as these conform to a Marine Corps policy of advancing capable and deserving men from the ranks to positions of leadership and more responsibility." (A Marcorps memorandum in the NPRC file listed Nolan among 22 men promoted in the field to second lieutenant.)

The last line of the article offered no explanation, simply stating, "Nolan had been reported missing in action shortly after the outbreak of war." No further information has been available on the origin of the initial missing-in-action report. When asked years later if the report had been accurate, Nolan shook his head in a firm *no*, and his wife related how devastated she and her family had been at the news, and how relieved they were when they learned of his safety.

Hitting the Beaches with the Raiders

Mike Nolan volunteered for and served with the hand-picked and specially trained assault force – the Marine Raiders – from September 20, 1942, until January 31, 1944. In 1987, when asked in a letter from author Ken Haney why he had volunteered for the Raiders, Nolan joked, "Wallis Island was truly in the backwash of WWII, and anyone in his right mind would try to get the hell out of the place."

The Raiders were described in *The Marine Raiders Historical Handbook* (American Historical Foundation, 1983), by Colonel Martin J. "Stormy" Sexton, USMC Retired: "The Marine Raiders were activated for the same reason as the British Commandos – to provide fast, hard-hitting assault units that could inflict surprise strikes by landing from submarines, destroyers, air transports, or regular Navy transports. Lightly equipped amphibious hit-and-run raids, rather than sustained operations, were the intent." In the introduction to the *Handbook*, Robert A. Buerlin, the President of the American Historical Foundation of Richmond, Virginia, stated, "The men of the Raiders not only stepped forward to defend their country in wartime military service, but they also volunteered for duty that promised dangerous missions behind enemy lines. They were the first force of this type to be established by the United States in World War II." Sexton wrote, "Although the Marine Raiders existed just two years as a special United States Marine Corps organization, their contributions were tremendously significant when the War in the Pacific is viewed in retrospect." Histories, such as *History of the Marine Raiders: More Than A Few Good Men* (Turner Publishing Company, 1999), have noted that the Raiders, famed for their "fighting prowess," would leave in their wake a "legacy of courage."

Lieutenant Colonel Jon T. Hoffman, USMCR, Marine historian, kindly provided us with some details on the formation of the 3rd Raider Battalion. The formation was ordered on September 13, 1942, with an ending date of September 19 for selection of personnel. The already established 1st and 2nd Raider Battalions were to each provide 2 officers and 25 enlisted men. The 8th Defense Battalion was tasked with providing manpower for a rifle company (D), consisting of 5 officers and 130 men.

On September 20, 1942, Nolan joined the 3rd Marine Raider Battalion, FMF, in the Field, as rifle platoon leader of 2nd Platoon, Company D, which was organized on Wallis Island, code-named Strawboard. On December 19, Company D embarked on board the *USS Chestnut*, arriving at Pago Pago, Tutuila, American Samoa on December 21. On December 24, 1942, the designation was changed to 3rd Marine Raider

Battalion, in the Field.

Nolan was promoted to first lieutenant, USMCR, on December 31, 1942, becoming company officer in Company D.

As a member of the 3rd Raider Battalion, Lieutenant Nolan was then alternately designated to the 1st Marine Raider Regiment, in the Field, Company D (April 1, 1943), company officer; Company M (May 1, 1943), company officer; and Company K (July 15, 1943), company officer. As of September 1, 1943, he was designated to the 2nd Marine Raider Regiment, Provisional, in the Field, Company K, company officer; and as of January 26, 1944, the designation was changed to the 1st Marine Raider Regiment, in the Field, Company K, where he would become commanding officer.

During his tenure with the Raiders, Nolan was deployed in Tutuila, American Samoa, sailing aboard the *USS American Legion* on January 17, 1943, and disembarking in Espiritu Santo, New Hebrides, on January 25. On February 15, he sailed on board the *USS Stringham*, arriving at Guadalcanal on February 17, embarking once more on February 20. He participated in the landing and occupation on Pavuvu, Russell Group, British Solomon Islands, from February 21 through March 21, 1943. The Russells had been a staging location for Japanese barges during the Guadalcanal campaign, and were seen as a strategic stationing area for American fighter planes for the New Georgia campaign. The extreme tropical weather on the island caused quite a few health problems for the Marines; it is believed that this was where Nolan became ill. He embarked aboard the *USS Sands* at Pavuvu on March 21, disembarking at Guadalcanal, and embarking that same day aboard the *USS President Polk*, where he was diagnosed with malaria on March 24, and began approximately two months of treatment.

After a period of training in Noumea, New Caledonia, Lt. Nolan sailed aboard the *USS President Adams* on October 7, 1943, reaching Guadalcanal on October 11, and embarking once more aboard the *USS Fuller* on October 19. He arrived at Efate, New Hebrides, where pre-invasion landing rehearsals were conducted from October 21-25, for the upcoming Bougainville campaign. On October 27, he departed Efate for Espiritu Santo Harbor, New Hebrides, arriving at Guadalcanal on October 30, and sailing that same day. He landed at the Empress Augusta Bay area and participated in the successful assault on Puruata Island on November 1, 1943, where heavy enemy resistance was encountered. The objective was to take out the artillery and automatic weapons to allow for safer passage to the nearby main island.

Nolan then participated in the seizure and occupation of Bougainville, British Solomon Islands. Bougainville was a heavily fortified Japanese-held island, with pivotally located airfields. His service began at the front-line perimeter between the Laruma and Torokina Rivers. He took part in the victorious Battle for Piva Trail, as well as reconnaissance patrols behind enemy lines, and remained on the island until January 12, 1944.

Over the years, two sources indicated that Nolan had also seen action on New Georgia, British Solomon Islands; however, we have no further information or the exact time frame. [Editor's note: Raider participation in the ground operations during the Battle of New Georgia spanned late June through late August of 1943. As one of the possibilities we are researching, we do know that there was a Marine presence in that area over the course of the months prior to the battle, in the form of several special amphibious reconnaissance patrols from the 1st Marine Raider Regiment, which included voluntary personnel from the battalions. Although the first few of these are well-chronicled, we have as yet discovered little regarding personnel in subsequent patrols. To complicate matters, there was no consistent or detailed information about Nolan's deployment in the late-spring and summer months of 1943, during the time of both the recon missions and the battle itself. After a two- to three-month gap in specifying his location, his archived records indicated only that he was with Company K on Noumea sometime in August; no inclusive days were listed. At this point in our research, it appears that he was likely available during this time period for a special assignment in New Georgia.]

A May 23, 1943 article in the *Star*, "Arizona Alumni Are Fighting On World-Wide Battlefronts," by Victor Thornton, reported that "Lt. Earl (King Kong) Nolan, a giant of a man whose football feats at the University are legendary, is with the Leathernecks on some South Pacific island battlefront. Nolan won his commission under fire. For valor in action he was promoted from corporal to second lieutenant."

In the September 30, 1943 *Star*, an official U.S. Marine Corps photograph, titled "Tucson Marine Corps Hero," pictured Nolan pulling the pin on a smoke grenade. The picture was captioned with a brief history from his "King Kong" days through his battlefield commission. An accompanying article, "With the Armed Services," read that First Lieutenant Nolan "is stationed with one of the U.S. Marine Corps' hardest-hitting units somewhere in the South Pacific, according to information received here yesterday." The article stated that he "was commissioned a second lieutenant for heroic action on the battlefield," and added, "According to a Marine Corps release from the South Pacific, 'the men of Lieutenant Nolan's command are looking forward with delight to the day he wades into the Japs again, declaring it should be wonderful to watch.'"

Nolan was reputed to have often participated in recon patrols, and we offer the following information which we have found thus far from the Raider years. After the landing on Pavuvu on February 21, 1943, his 2nd Platoon was deployed to patrol the nearby islands of Baisen, Money, and Leru, to check for Japanese occupation. Then, according to Dan Marsh's *Marine Raider Page*, on November 10, 1943, Company K was deployed to reconnoiter the Numa Numa Trail as far as Piva Village during the battle of Bougainville.

Regarding a third patrol, Nolan received a June 14, 1987 postcard from author, historian, and Marine veteran Corporal Ken Haney, discussing the campaign on the island of Bougainville in November of 1943, and referring to Nolan's participation in "a recon patrol in that area a few days prior to the actual battle." We subsequently were able to contact Cpl. Haney and discovered that, in response to enemy artillery fire, members of the 3rd Raiders, Company K patrolled the suspect area a week before the November 29 battle of Koiari, with no contact. Haney, who wrote to Nolan concerning his involvement in the patrol and would later quote him in his definitive book *Hold the Line!* (Eagle, Globe & Anchor Pub., 1993), kindly sent us copies of their correspondence. They provided one of the very few firsthand accounts given by Mike Nolan of wartime events. In the letters, we were not surprised to read his comments in praise of both the Seabees, who had "constructed coral paved roads and the best airfield I have ever seen, mahogany log base with 2' of solid coral surface" in the swampy conditions of Bougainville; and the actions of the Navy and Marine artillery, which he termed "excellent, the very best in the annals of warfare." A U.S. Marine Raider Association & Foundation chronology identified the date of the patrol as November 22-25, stating that the reconnaissance was conducted "in the vicinity of the Reini-Tehessi River areas, about nine miles east of Cape Torokina, in Empress Augusta Bay." Nolan drolly wrote to Haney that the "only enjoyable feature on Bougainville was the climate. It was perfect, and I made up my mind to enjoy my stay on this tropical paradise." Of course, the Japanese "had other ideas, and it was not long before I found myself aboard a landing boat with 30 other poor souls. We were headed for some native village down the coast.... The Marines don't exactly like to be the recipients of artillery fire, so they sent K Company and one Australian coconut plantation owner" to Koiari, which was thought to be the source of the shelling. According to Nolan's letter, it was later found to have actually been coming from a submarine off the coast.

After the battle at Bougainville, Nolan embarked aboard the *USS President Adams* on January 12, 1944, and disembarked at Guadalcanal on January 14. He was promoted to captain, USMCR, with rank from January 31, 1944.

On February 1, the Raiders were reorganized and renamed the 4th Marines. Captain Nolan was assigned to the 4th Marine Regiment, 3rd Battalion, Company K, as commanding officer. (One piece of paper he saved was an officer's mess assessment for the month of February, $5.00.) The designation was changed to 4th Marine Regiment, Reinforced, on March 16. He served with the 1st Marine Amphibious Corps, FMF, in the Field, from February 1; and the 3rd Marine Amphibious Corps, FMF, in the Field, from April 19.

On March 17, 1944, he embarked aboard the *USS Callaway* at Guadalcanal. From March 20 through April 11, 1944, he participated in the occupation and defense of Emirau Island, St. Matthias Group, Australian Mandate, an island that was considered prime for an air base. The natives of Emirau informed the Marines that the Japanese had fled, and that a contingent was located on nearby Mussau Island. This area, which included a seaplane base, was shelled by destroyers after a night recon patrol. On April 11, Nolan embarked aboard the *USS Crescent City* at Emirau, disembarking at Guadalcanal on April 14.

"Don't You Know There's a War On?"

Mike Nolan returned to the States in May of 1944, on his first leave after twenty-eight months overseas. On April 24, he embarked aboard the *USAT Sea Corporal*, arriving in San Francisco, California, on May 10. This period from May 16 through June 15 would also be his only leave during his combat service. Both local newspapers covered his homecoming. On May 22, 1944, the *Citizen* announced, "Captain Nolan Has First Leave in 28 Months" from duty in the South Pacific.

On May 21, 1944, an article from the *Star*, "Earl Nolan Is Home On Leave...Marine Raider Captain Is Reticent About War Experience," by Vic Thornton, gave some insights about Nolan's experiences to date: "Today Capt. Michael Earl Nolan of a Marine Raider company is home on leave – his first in 28 months. He's a strapping six-foot-two, 220-pounder, looks much the same as he did eight years ago when known as 'King Kong,' an All-Border Conference left tackle on the University of Arizona football eleven. His prowess on the gridiron became legend, but his feats on the field of battle, when told, promise to be more spectacular. Diffident and naturally reserved, Captain Nolan is tight-lipped about his experiences. Even his best friends don't know how many campaign ribbons or decorations he's entitled to wear. His Marine Corps insignia and captain's bars are the only extras on his khaki uniform. He came up the hard way with the rugged 'devil dogs.' A terse Corps press release over a year ago told of his battle promotion in the steamy jungles of Guadalcanal from a corporal to a second lieutenant. Since then his friends say he hasn't spent more than four months on one particular island or atoll."

Thornton quoted Nolan on progress that had been made since he was shipped out: "On December 25, less than three weeks after Pearl Harbor he was headed for the Southwest Pacific. 'We knew we had a lot to learn about jungle fighting when our convoy headed out,' said Captain Nolan, 'and the men were determined to learn. Our first operation (Guadalcanal in the Solomons, although Nolan wouldn't be pinned down on it) was rough, but there was no griping. Air protection was erratic, and supplies had to wait upon the shipping to get through. Smokes were a luxury. Chow wasn't fancy or abundant. We had to make the best of it, get along on bare necessities. It wasn't until Christmas of 1942 that cigarets and mail were rolling in regularly. We had chicken that day. It was a treat. Since then conditions have changed greatly. We've got everything on our side now; supplies roll in on time-table schedule to each new beachhead – we're on the winning side... but it's still going to be rough.' Captain Nolan said that supplies and air protection had improved so much that on Christmas of 1943 he enjoyed three turkey dinners only 200 yards behind the main lines." [Editor's note: The cryptic nature of the words within Thornton's parentheses regarding Nolan's first operation left room for speculation that he might have been referring to an action which preceded Guadalcanal, the May 1942 landing and occupation at Uvea Island, Wallis Island Group. Either way, it appeared that Nolan was following military protocol; for example, a 1945 memorandum from the 5th Division to Marines returning to the States addressed statements made to the press, and directed, "On returning from combat areas, remember the necessity for exercising caution in the discussion of naval and military matters."]

Additionally, "Nolan had high praise for the jungle fighting tactics evolved by the Americans. 'It's a new type of warfare that has been developed to grim efficiency through highly co-ordinated teamwork and training,' he said."

The interview ended on a lighter note: "Is Captain Nolan anxious to return to the Southwest Pacific? 'Yes,' he replies with a grin, 'the sooner the better. I like to doze in those foxholes, and I'm kind of attached to that Marine chow.'" The article, by the way, featured a photograph of a more gaunt man than the robust one who had left in 1941, the rigors of war now showing on his face. Nolan was, however, smiling. In May of 1944, he was no doubt happy to be home for a while.

One anecdote he told years later did reflect the fact that the Marines were often lacking in supplies, and he was quite inventive in providing food for his men. One of his favorite tricks involved laying primacord in a bay. The concussion ensured that his men had an abundant supply of fresh fish. Combined with coconuts and pineapples, this did the trick.

Another story he would tell with a smile occurred when he arrived in San Francisco to begin his leave. Nolan was looking forward to his first stateside meal, went into a restaurant, and ordered a steak. The waitress promptly chided him: "Don't you know there's a war on?"

A Phoenix article appearing in the *Arizona Independent Republic* of September 3, 1944, "Nolan Gets Combat Duty," stated that he had been home on leave, "but immediately requested his transfer back to the combat zone....His demonstrated leadership abilities on Guadalcanal brought him a field promotion to second lieutenant, and soon thereafter he joined a unit of the famed Marine Raiders. With the Raiders, he fought in the vicious 60-hour battle of Puruata Island, off Bougainville, and took part in the occupation of Emirau Island, south of New Britain....Conspicuously 'rugged' even among the hard-hitting Leathernecks, he commands the complete respect and admiration of his men."

To Japan: On the Crest of a Tsunami

Captain Nolan attached to the 3rd Battalion, 27th Marine Regiment, 5th Marine

Division, FMF, San Diego Area, on June 16, 1944, as the commanding officer of Company G. On August 11, he embarked aboard the *USS Arthur Middleton* and arrived at Hilo, Hawaii, Territory of Hawaii, on August 18, where extensive training would take place for the next landing. As of that date, the designation was modified to Fleet Marine Force, Pacific. On September 14, he was detached to the Headquarters and Service Company, Weapons Company, 27th Marines, 5th Marine Division, as commanding officer; and on October 25, 1944, he became the commanding officer of the 5th Amphibian Truck Company (battalion-sized), 5th Motor Transport Battalion, 5th Marine Division. He sailed from Hilo, Hawaii, on January 10, 1945, on board LST 795.

From February 19 through March 22, 1945, Nolan participated in the assault and capture of Iwo Jima, Volcano Islands. This heavily fortified Japanese island measured only approximately 4.5 miles long by 2.5 miles wide, at its greatest expanse. Approximately 22,000 Japanese troops were garrisoned there long before the battle began, with a complex network of bunkers, underground tunnels, and concealed artillery emplacements. The island was considered pivotal as an air base for fighter escorts to support the bombing of the Japanese mainland. Iwo Jima would be remembered as one of the fiercest battles in American history.

After the battle, Nolan's NPRC records show him sailing from Iwo Jima on March 27. With his personal papers was his initiation card for the "Imperial Domain of Golden Dragon," presented in a U.S. Navy ceremony which marked the crossing of the 180th Meridian, the International Date Line, in Latitude "Censored," duly inducting him into the "Silent Mysteries of the Far East." This placed him on the *USS Cape Johnson* (AP-172), a USN troop transport, at 0846 on April 7, 1945. He arrived back in Hilo, Hawaii, on April 14.

During the occupation of Japan, Nolan, as commanding officer of the 5th Amphibian Truck Company, participated in the 5th Division's amphibious tank landing at Sasebo, Kyushu, which secured the area. This operation occurred around the time of a fierce typhoon with tsunami-like waves, and was a feat the native people of the area were astounded and awed by, comparing it to the Khan invasion which had been attempted in the thirteenth century and was thwarted by a similar storm. Nolan embarked aboard LST 1074 on August 23, 1945, at Hilo, Hawaii, and landed in Japan on September 23. With his papers was an October 2, 1945 memorandum under the heading of the Fifth Amphibian Truck Co., which stated, "Capt. Nolan is on authorized duty with U.S.M.C. Vehicle Number 111077 and seventeen (17) amphibian trucks with operators." He left Japan on October 25, 1945, via the *USS Tazewell*.

Mike Nolan arrived in San Francisco, California, on November 9, 1945, with a total of forty-four months of foreign and sea service credited. (And, if that were not enough, he had spent much of his pay on war bonds!) He was assigned to Headquarters Company, Headquarters Battalion, Department of Pacific, in San Francisco, California. On November 15, he received the Honorable Service Lapel

Button and the Marine Corps Reserve Button. With 66 days of accumulated leave plus travel time, he would finally be headed back home.

On January 22, 1946, Nolan was honorably relieved from active duty, with the rank of captain. He received a United States Marine Corps Certificate of Honorable and Satisfactory Service in World War II, which read, "Michael E. Nolan, USMCR, has satisfactorily completed active service and is this date relieved from active duty." He was assigned to the General Service Unit, 11th Marine Corps Reserve District. His military specialties were designated as "Amphibian Truck Officer" (0668) and "Infantry Officer" (1542).

Captain Nolan, "Legendary in Pacific"

A November 25, 1945 *Star* article, "Home From Japan...Capt. Earl Nolan Honorably Discharged," appeared upon his return to his hometown. In part, it read that "Captain Nolan enlisted in the Marines early in 1941, and he was headed for the Pacific less than three weeks after the Japs struck at Pearl Harbor. He was commissioned on the field during the sanguine Solomon Islands campaign, the battle for Guadalcanal. As a Marine Raider he hit the beaches at Bougainville, the Russell Islands, and Emirau and Mussau Islands. He took part in six actions before being returned to the States on his first leave after 28 months overseas. Then he returned and attached to the Fifth Marine Division and participated in the bloody battle for Iwo Jima."

It is noteworthy that the wartime Officer Fitness Reports filled out on Nolan reflected a preponderance of "Excellent" ratings from his commanding officers, who included Lieutenant Colonel H. B. "Harry the Horse" Liversedge (later, Brigadier General). Comments handwritten on the reports stated that Nolan "was an excellent non-commissioned officer, and it is believed he will be an excellent officer," and that he was "very thorough, capable, and efficient," a "capable young officer." "Outstanding" ratings were also given in the categories of judgment and common sense, loyalty, handling enlisted men, handling officers, physical fitness, and military bearing.

One of Nolan's strong points during the war was his extensive training of the men who served under him, training specifically designed for survival, as well as effectiveness, in the South Pacific. Among his things, we discovered various island area maps which often had his writing on them, including detailed terrain diagrams. His mathematics and engineering talent and expertise manifested themselves in the complexity of the training he provided. On one map we found the notes for a test he had prepared for his men. The topics included the explanation and usage of the mil formula, including problems using glasses and measuring stick; explanation of methods to estimate direction, including the sun, moon, Southern Cross, planet Venus (Evening Star, Morning Star), watch, and compass; explanation of the back azimuth and its uses, including resection and back-trailing; phases of the moon, including causes, and hours of moonlight; tides, including frequency, times, extremes, and what governs the tide; direction of the rising and setting of the sun and moon; taking a grid azimuth reading and transferring it to a compass reading; taking a compass reading and transferring it to a grid map; grid declination; the dial of the compass and how it measures; longitude and latitude, e.g., values of one degree; grids and meridians; and semaphore.

On another map we found his complex mathematical computations, tables, and diagrams designed to maximize the effectiveness of machine gun and mortar fire, including positioning and trajectory, headed "Deflection and elevation tables for mortar and machine gun" – mil ratio in deflection for the different yardages for either mortar or machine gun, mil ratio for machine gun in elevation, and degree table for mortars. The problem he had set for the lesson was, "For any number of mortars or machine guns, from any position and at any even or uneven distance from each other – to bring them to bear on one point." He had written the step-by-step solution and sketched out an accompanying diagram. It is little wonder that both his commanding officers and his men frequently touted Nolan's superior ability to teach and train.

Toward the end of the war and for years afterward, numerous accounts appeared in Arizona newspapers and publications regarding Mike Nolan's legendary status in the South Pacific. A few days after his marriage, a June 15, 1946 article in the *Citizen*, "Strictly Chatter," reflected a sentiment that would be heard countless times, stating that he "made a brilliant record throughout the Pacific theatre with the Marines as a captain."

Colonel A. V. Grossetta and Ernest Lacy, who were quoted earlier, were not the only 1930s Arizona football alumni to comment on their teammate's exceptional reputation as a Marine. John M. "Pat" Turner, Air Force Colonel Leon Gray, and Navy Lieutenant (JG) Charles Fowler also publicly mentioned hearing about Nolan's legendary bravery from others serving in the Pacific during the war. In Abe Chanin's book, *They Fought Like Wildcats*, Turner was quoted as saying about Nolan that "in World War II in the South Pacific he was a legend. They called him 'Iron Mike,' and he was one of the most decorated Marines in the war." Gray, who received the Silver Star and the Distinguished Service Cross among other awards, was quoted by Chanin as saying, "I remember they used to call him 'Big Mike,' and whenever you talked to someone who served in the Pacific, he would rave about Nolan's feats of bravery."

In a *Citizen* "Press Box" column from January 4, 1946, Hank Squire quoted Fowler, former captain of the U of A track and football teams and head of the lettermen's "A" Club, who was on Navy leave in Tucson: "Charley put in a tour of duty in the Pacific and is now stationed in California. He said that wherever he went in the Pacific he heard stories of the bravery of Earl Nolan, known to the Marines as 'Big Mike.' Nolan, he added, 'really is a legendary figure.'"

A particularly notable tribute appeared in the *Star* on August 13, 1945, titled "'Big Mike' Nolan, Legendary In Pacific, Is Modest Hero," by Tech Sergeant Allen Sommers, Marine Corps Combat Correspondent. The title above Nolan's photograph read, "Tough Marine," and the dateline read, "Somewhere In the Pacific, Aug. 12." Sommers stated that "Marine Captain Michael E. (Big Mike) Nolan...veteran of Iwo Jima and other Pacific campaigns, modestly denies any major role in the war.

"'The men do the job,' the 240-pound ex-Raider from Tucson, Ariz., declares. 'All I'm doing is satisfying my urge for adventure.'

"Big Mike became almost a legend to Marine fighting men in the Pacific after his action with the First Marine Division on Guadalcanal and with the former Third Raider Battalion on Bougainville. And, after listening to enlisted men serving under Big Mike, it's not hard to understand why the deep-voiced captain gets the almost-impossible out of the men he commands."

Tech Sgt. Sommers related an often-told story about the landing on Iwo Jima: "One Marine recalled the landing on Iwo. Nolan was leading an amphibian tank company of the Fifth Marine Division, and it was his job to get field artillery on the island. 'He stood up on the beach, directing the Ducks,' the Marine said. 'Every time the Japanese sent us a welcome card in the form of mortar shells, the captain's voice boomed orders to dive into foxholes. He saw to it we found shelter. We dived for the first one we saw, sure. But Big Mike didn't care. When the barrage was over, there he was, standing upright as if nothing had happened.'"

Sommers wrote about the devotion shown by the captain's men. "Devotion to Big Mike by his men is typified by the following incident, which he tells on himself: 'The second night on Iwo was hell, and I decided to take all my Ducks off the beach. We collected wounded, plowed through the rough surf to the nearest ship and then began circling for the night. I was on a vehicle with two of my men. We planned night-long watches, alternating hourly. I left orders to be awakened for the second watch. When I awoke, it was daylight. My man allowed me to sleep the night through. That isn't easy to forget.'"

The article concluded with a summary of Nolan's service thus far: "On January 16, 1941, he enlisted in the Marine Corps as a private and went to the Pacific the following year with a defense battalion. Later he was transferred to the First Marine Division for the Solomons invasion. Before the year was gone, Nolan found himself in a hospital with malaria. It was on Guadalcanal in September, 1942 that he received his field commission. [Commission was dated August 12, 1942.] Later he joined the Third Raiders and when the Raider battalions were disbanded, the Fifth Division."

As a point of information, Tech Sgt. Sommers was quite familiar with Iwo Jima. Having witnessed the battle himself, he would later co-author the book *Iwo – Hell's Half-Acre* (1945).

Nolan's dedication to his men was another hallmark of his Marine career. It has been said that he took his responsibility as a commander to be a sacred trust. To quote Hank Squire from the December 10, 1945 "Press Box" column in the *Citizen*, "Nolan went up from the ranks, but he never for a moment forgot the men in the ranks. He realized that the success of all operations depended upon the spirit of the enlisted men. 'They were,' he says, 'my best friends.'"

References to medals won by Nolan were found in archived articles from three Arizona newspapers, including the previously cited November 25, 1945 *Star* article "Home from Japan," the December 10, 1945 *Citizen* column by Squire, and the January 1, 1957 *Phoenix Gazette* "Along the Way" column by Bob Allison, as well as articles written at the time of Nolan's engagement and marriage (including the December 28, 1945 *Star* article, "Nellie Ahee, Nolan To Wed," the December 29, 1945 *Citizen* article, "Miss Ahee Will Wed Earl Nolan," and the June 11, 1946 *Citizen* article, "Miss Nellie Ahee, Earl Nolan To Marry Tomorrow Morning"), which variously mentioned the Bronze Star, the Silver Star, a Presidential Unit Citation, which was most likely the award given to the 1st Marine Division, Reinforced, for service in Guadalcanal (August 7-December 9, 1942 campaign), as well as the Asiatic-Pacific Campaign Medal, reported in some accounts as being accompanied by seven stars. [Editor's note: Researching the criteria for the stars, we discovered that individual engagements were consolidated into campaigns. In whatever manner Nolan's multiple deployments would subsequently be officially grouped, we are thus far aware of landings and service at Wallis Island, Guadalcanal, Pavuvu, Puruata, Bougainville, Emirau, Iwo Jima, and Sasebo (and the probability at New Georgia).]

Squire wrote that Nolan did not believe in medals and declined to wear them. It was the captain's judgment that heroism was widespread, and often went either under- or unrecognized officially. According to Squire, he explained, "I've seen fellows who did enough, in my opinion, to win the Medal of Honor, and who wound up with the Bronze Star. I've seen men who should have won the Bronze Star and who received nothing at all. You see, in war so many men do so much that it is difficult to single out a few individuals for high honors."

Mike Nolan did indeed believe that his men were the backbone of the operation. Over the years, one of the highest compliments he could give was "He was a good Marine."

To further quote the Squire article, "The big fellow made football history at the university, and made more as a private, and then as a captain in the Marine Corps. He came out of the Marines the other day the modest fellow you knew when he went away to do his stuff for Uncle Sam....Nolan enlisted in the Marines going on five years ago. He went overseas as a private, won a field commission on Guadalcanal. Eventually, he became a captain and company commander. Don't ask what he did. He won't tell you. On Bougainville, he was awarded the Silver Star. Again he refuses to say for what act of heroism this high honor came his way. He never wore the ribbon nor did he wear the Asiatic-Pacific medal with seven battle stars, nor the Presidential citation, nor anything else denoting service across the seas."

Nolan himself rarely spoke about his wartime years. On those infrequent occasions when he did, it was most often either a philosophical remark or an amusing anecdote. He was truly modest and self-deprecating. In 1989, the 78-year-old hero had partially filled out an application which had been sent to him by a fellow Raider for membership in the Marine Corps Mustang Association; Nolan still had his service dates left to fill in. That application was later found with his papers; in typical fashion, he had not mailed it. There, under the section "Brief Statement of How Commission Was Obtained," he had written, "In Solomons – running out of officers. I happened to be nearby when promotions were passed out. I got a commission – the last one they had."

Even if he preferred to neither acknowledge nor accept acknowledgment for his acts of valor, many others acknowledged them for him. Stories of Nolan's bravery, whether under fire or in hand-to-hand combat, reached from the South Pacific to his hometown. Eyewitness accounts of these events found their way via word-of-mouth to Tucson servicemen, including Lieutenant (JG) Charles Fowler and Lieutenant (JG) George Ahee, who both served with the Navy during the war, and Colonel A. V. Grossetta and Colonel Leon Gray, both of the Air Force; to Arizona newspaper writers and sports editors, including Sergeant Henry Squire, who served with the Army in the Pacific theater, Army Corporal Abraham S. Chanin, Victor Thornton, and Robert Allison, all of whom alluded in their columns to his bravery; and to longtime Tucson residents, such as his former classmates, teammates, and coaches, and well-known civic leader Roy Drachman, who preserved much of the local history through interviews and in writing. Two of the most intense and widely told stories described incidents of hand-to-hand combat: one incident involved Nolan singlehandedly charging Japanese who had shot one of his men; another involved a situation when the Marines found themselves outnumbered and, once the ammunition had been exhausted, engaged the enemy in hand-to-hand combat – after which the remaining Japanese were taken prisoner. If these accounts are any indication, this would be a circumstance where the legend most likely could not live up to the reality of the man. We are fortunate that these narratives have been preserved. One thing is certain: Nolan's actions were prompted by an abiding dedication to the courageous men fighting by his side and by his enduring personal responsibility for their safety and well-being.

In this light, he did not believe in risking the lives of his men and was remembered for courageously taking dangerous patrols himself behind enemy lines, and mining the approach to his front line for hundreds of feet to protect his men as they slept in foxholes. The Bob Allison article reported, "Then came the war and next thing you know there was a press dispatch out of Guadalcanal about a Marine lieutenant named Michael Earl Nolan who spent his spare time volunteering for patrols

– or singlehanded forays – into the jungles." As alluded to earlier, the above comment, and others made throughout the years, led us to research recon patrols which took place in areas where he was stationed, when he was stationed there. It was often said that Nolan was an exceptional leader, and that he did not hesitate to put himself in harm's way to protect the men who had been entrusted to his care. Nor did he send them off to do something he preferred not to do himself.

Squire concluded his 1945 post-war column: "Nolan went through the hell that was Iwo Jima. He saw an awful lot of men die; he saw thousands wounded. Miraculously, he escaped. He doesn't know how. Maybe, he figures, he was just lucky.... He couldn't forget, either, the poor guys who aren't coming home anymore.

"Earl Nolan went into the Marines with the idea he owed America a debt, a bill for the privilege of living in this country. He set out to square the account. He did his job. He did all, and more than, he was asked to do. If war came again, though, he would go back into the Marines. 'You can't beat them,' he insists. 'They're a great outfit. I don't like war, but if need be I'd volunteer again.'

"As for fear in combat – well, Nolan says it isn't so. 'I've seen a lot of men who actually weren't afraid. I've seen little mild, meek sort of fellows go into some awfully tough spots, and they had no fear at all. No kidding, these guys were ready for any kind of mission.'"

In retrospect, we owe a definite debt of gratitude to Tech Sgt. Allen Sommers, Victor Thornton, Henry Squire, and the other fine columnists and reporters of the World War II era for chronicling details of Nolan's history which otherwise might not have been available to us.

The Scars of War

One insight into Mike Nolan's war experience came from one of the very rare times he spoke to his family about those years, and it is no doubt a moment shared by so many who have been in this situation. He remembered the first shot fired at him, the stark moment of realization that for the first time in his life someone was trying to kill him; he was in a battle for survival.

Nolan was wounded several times, including a gunshot wound in the lower left leg, shrapnel in the left shoulder, hearing problems due to a nearby exploding mortar, injuries to his hands, as well as a training injury to his back. He also became deathly ill with malaria, and it is believed that he might have contracted dengue fever. Each time he was injured, he returned to combat.

Nolan's medical records stated that he was diagnosed with malaria aboard the *USS President Polk* on March 24, 1943, and was treated at U.S. Naval Base Hospital No. 3 in Mapusaga, American Samoa, on March 30; transported on the hospital ship *USS Rixey* on April 3; and transferred to U.S. Naval Mobile Base Hospital No. 4 on New

Zealand's North Island on April 8, being "discharged to duty" from that facility on May 14. A May 27, 1943 memorandum to Nolan from the Commanding Officer of the U.S. Naval Operating Base, Navy 132, R. B. Phillips, advised him, "Upon receipt of these orders and when directed by the proper authority, and having completed medical treatment at the U.S. Naval Mobile Hospital Number Four, you will proceed via the first available government transportation to such port as the Regulating Station, First Marine Amphibious Corps may be. Upon arrival report to the Commanding Officer, Regulating Station for further assignment to the Third Raider Battalion." Less detailed information in his general records showed that his medical treatment at the above facility might have continued until June 1-4. Exactly when and how he left New Zealand is not known, nor is his destination. Nolan did speak of the incredibly high fevers from this illness, and how packing himself in wet sand on the beach aided in reducing them. He also spoke of the rigors of the Atabrine treatment, which itself turned skin yellow and caused nausea and weight loss. He thought very highly of the people he met in New Zealand, and spoke of the many kindnesses they had shown during his recuperation.

Although included with the archived material, medical records were incomplete, most likely due to the fact that Nolan received treatment in the field. However, among his papers we discovered original 1943-45 physical examination records which showed the location of the circular scar on his left leg, along with two urgent medical tags bearing his name, one designating his rank as second lieutenant, Company D, 3rd Marine Raider Battalion (which would have been between September 20 and December 30, 1942), and one designating him as first lieutenant (which would have placed it between December 31, 1942 and January 30, 1944). We have also located documentation for a few of his injuries, which continued to bother him after the war.

A May 16, 1949 affidavit from Captain W. K. Moody, who had been 2nd Platoon leader, Company K, 3rd Marine Raider Battalion, detailed an injury Nolan received during the 1943 Bougainville campaign, an account which also gave some insight into the conditions on Puruata Island. Moody wrote, "K Company was committed to the initial assault on Puruata Island. This was a very strategic point, as I recall, and afforded the Japanese an unexcelled observation point of the entire roadstead for the fleet and beachhead for the ground troops. Artillery emplacements and heavy anti-aircraft batteries were indicated by intelligence reports.

"Upon landing, we were met with withering small arms fire. The Japanese were heavily emplaced, with bunkers made of several thicknesses of palm logs, and we were three days in driving to death all of the defenders. The Island was 300 by 500 yards in size, and very thickly covered with jungle vegetation.

"First Lieutenant Nolan became acting K Company Commander, and while directing one of our assaults, came into my Platoon Sector, checking up on his front-line positions. I noticed a burst of smoke and a large explosion near Lt. Nolan during the fire fight. I do not know whether it was from a large mortar shell or an artillery shell. Lt. Nolan was thrown violently to the ground and remained there in a stunned and shocked condition for what seemed like a great period of time but in reality was probably only a few minutes. As soon as we got to him, I noticed that one of his hands was swollen and lacerated. Pharmacist Mate First Class Eugene Ward, of Roanoke, Texas, my corpsman, rendered Lt. Nolan cursory first aid. Being the conscientious soldier that he was, Lt. Nolan did not leave his command until Captain Page, our regular Company Commander, reassumed command two days later.

"When we had wiped out all the resistance on Puruata Island and had gone over to Bougainville proper, I would see Lt. Nolan every day." Moody stated that the wounded hand "had become infected and was sore and inflamed for the rest of the campaign." When Nolan left on leave in 1944, he had begun to lose weight and was suffering from an intestinal ailment, as well as "a considerable amount of trouble" with his hand. "From the time of the blast I noticed that he was in a sickly condition for the remainder of the time we were together overseas."

A June 11, 1949 affidavit from Captain James C. Brennan, who had served as commanding officer of Company G, 27th Regiment, 5th Marine Division, relayed an incident which occurred in the autumn of 1944: "We were stationed on the Island of Hawaii, and at that time we were engaged in some very rigorous training exercises, preparing for the assault on Iwo Jima, in the Bonin Island group. It was during one of these drills, which took place on a beach about 15 miles from the Marine camp, that I noticed that Captain M. E. Nolan, of the Fifth Marine Amphibious Truck Company, fell from one of his vehicles. It was near my station and I was very well acquainted with Captain Nolan. He fell in such a position that he injured his back. He had to be helped back to his quarters. He was confined to bed for about a month. During this period he was given chiropractic and heat lamp treatments by the Army Medical Department near the Marine camp." This did not stop Nolan from fighting on Iwo Jima, although Brennan noted that "he was much weakened physically as a result of his accident."

A May 15, 1950 affidavit from First Lieutenant Frank H. O'Reilly, who had been platoon leader in Company G, 3rd Battalion, 27th Regiment, 5th Marine Division, stated that on the night of February 19 or 20, 1945, during the attack on Iwo Jima, he saw "Captain Michael Nolan, Commanding Officer of the 5th Marine Amphibian Truck Company, knocked to the ground by enemy shell fire. Captain Nolan was hit on the hand and had his breath knocked out of him for several seconds. Captain Nolan continued with his work of unloading artillery pieces and ammunition."

An April 19, 1949 affidavit from First Lieutenant Alfred A. Paulson, who had served as platoon leader and company executive officer for the 5th Amphibian Truck Company, 5th Motor Transport Battalion, 5th Marine Division, recalled the same two incidents. Paulson described the fall from the DUKW (amphibian truck): "Captain Nolan was troubled with the results of this injury until the end of the war. At the time of the accident, the Navy did not have facilities to treat this type of injury. Captain Nolan received some care at a nearby Army hospital. He was bed ridden for several weeks." Paulson also related that "Captain Nolan led his Company in the assault and capture of Iwo Jima, where he was rendered unconscious by concussion from an enemy artillery shell and was also wounded in the hand. He was treated by a Navy Medic, but refused to be evacuated and stayed with his Company."

Years later, Nolan still bore the obvious scar from the bullet wound on his lower left leg, in addition to remaining shrapnel in his shoulder. Information located in his medical records indicated that the bullet scar was not present at the time of his enlistment physical. In a section which called for identification of "indelible or permanent marks upon his person," other scars were detailed, from a small vaccination scar to a 6" scar on his anterior left thigh, most likely from his athletic endeavors. This enlistment physical was conducted in Los Angeles, California, and signed by Z. A. Barker, Lt. (MC) U.S.N., Ret. However, as mentioned previously, the final diagram in Nolan's enlisted service record and separate physical examination papers did indeed show the circular scar on his left leg for the first time. The scar was described as located on the "left leg, anterior surface, medial third."A new 4" scar on his anterior left knee was also present. The Termination of Health Record and the physical were both signed by L. D. Bibler, Lieut. Comdr., MC-V, (G) USNR. As of now, we have no details regarding how this injury was incurred. The presence of the scar was again documented in all subsequent physical examinations, including a physical conducted for the USMC Reserve in Tucson on September 25, 1958, by S. V. Hilts, Lt., MC, USNR-R, who described it as located on the left upper tibia; and a November 11, 1962 Reserve physical, by Tucson physician Delbert L. Secrist. Doctor Secrist identified the scar as a "bullet wound antero-lateral aspect of left calf." (As an aside, Secrist also summarized the former football star, at age 51, as being "unusually well developed" and in "excellent physical condition.") The multiple pieces of the metal shrapnel embedded in Nolan's left shoulder were also easily detectable decades after the war.

After this brief synopsis of his service, there is little doubt why Nolan's hometown selected him upon his return to be marshal of a local parade. In typical fashion, there is an amusing anecdote attached to this honor. His wife explained that he had never had a set of dress blues and had to find one, actually a composite from other Marines, for the parade. She said he looked magnificent on the dais in the impressive uniform and had even located a sword to carry. However, Nolan had a prejudice against socks, and as the program progressed, it became obvious that he had not worn any that day.

Major Nolan of the Ready Reserve

A few months after he arrived in Tucson, Nolan received a March 4, 1946 letter from Commandant of the Marine Corps Alexander Archer Vandegrift: "My dear Captain Nolan: Your readjustment to the life of a civilian has, I hope, been fully accomplished, and with as little difficulty as you experienced in adapting yourself to military life when you came on active duty. No one is more familiar than I with the essential role which you of the Reserve assumed in the War. Together we accomplished our missions, however difficult they may have been. Together we developed the Marine Corps into the finest of all fighting forces. It could not have been done without you. Your patriotism and fine devotion to duty have been an inspiration to the officers and men who shared the responsibilities for final and complete victory.... Please accept my personal and official thanks and my best wishes for your continued success."

On March 14, 1946, Colonel Randolph McCall Pate, the director of the USMC Division of Reserve, wrote to him, as well: "My dear Captain Nolan: This is to hope that you are comfortably located in your post-war activities and that civilian life is all that you expected.... During the first World War, and even more during the second, I have had the privilege of observing the magnificent performance of 'civilians in uniform.' Those who had prepared themselves for war in time of peace made a particular impression on me and convinced me of the soundness of our policy of Reserve training. It is my firm conviction that our hope for lasting peace lies principally in the strength and instant readiness of our civilian soldiers. Our plans are still in their early stages, and the enclosed circular contains all the information available at the present time. However, we do want you to know that your war-time training and experience, plus your civilian background, can be of great value to us, and we would like to be free to call upon you for advice and assistance as the needs arise."

As mentioned previously, Nolan became part of the 11th Marine Corps Reserve District upon relief from active duty; later he was designated to the 12th Marine Corps Reserve & Recruitment District. He officially accepted the permanent appointment to captain as of October 4, 1946 (with rank from January 31, 1944), and began his post-war Reserve career.

Nolan requested a change of status into the organized Reserve on June 24, 1952, and continued his service to his nation as a member of the U.S. Marine Corps Ready Reserve. The commanding officer of the 3rd Supply Company in Tucson, Major Morse Holladay, fully endorsed this transfer: "Captain Nolan is considered mentally, morally, physically, and professionally qualified for transfer to this organization."

Mike Nolan attained the rank of major, USMCR, as of June 28, 1952, receiving an official appointment on July 9, 1953.

Two articles appeared in the local papers on August 8, 1952, announcing his Reserve service: "Marine Unit Assigned New Executive," from the *Star*, and "Nolan Takes Reserve Job," from the *Citizen*. He became the executive officer of the 3rd Supply Company in the Tucson Reserve and, in the course of his attachment, also served as a platoon commander of the General Supply Platoon, and was a member of the Volunteer Training Unit (Guided Missile).

During his tenure in the Reserve, which included regularly scheduled drills,

Nolan remained as active as possible, given his escalating career responsibilities. In an article titled "Marine Reserve Unit Trudges Over Desert," it was reported that "Tucson Marine reservists trudged through sagebrush and cactus Thursday night to run through a scout patrolling problem in the Sahuaro National Monument here. At least 26 men stalked over hundreds of yards of desert terrain to concealed checkpoints with only compasses and directional bearing instructions to guide them. The problem, a compass march and infantry scout patrol trial, was led by Capt. Michael E. Nolan, of the Third Supply Company, Marine Reserve." On December 9, 1952, the *Citizen* article "Local Marines Rifle Shoot" read that Tucson's 3rd Supply Company had won a district rifle shoot; Captain Nolan came in fourth. He also served as Athletic Officer and Senior Member of the Recreation Council.

Nolan's records show the following course work taken through the Marine Corps Institute while he served in the Reserve: General Ammunition, Basic Electricity, Interior Electric Wiring, Military Geology, Basic Machine Shop, Communist Guerilla Warfare, Protection from Nuclear Explosion, General Military History, Principles of Surveying, Water Supply, Basic Engineer Equipment Operator, Shop Mathematics, and History of Strategy. A 1959 memorandum to Major Nolan from Randolph McCall Pate, who was then Commandant of the Marine Corps, stated, "Your enrollment and active participation in the Marine Corps Institute Correspondence Course Program is evidence of your desire to improve your military proficiency and increase your professional qualifications. Please accept my congratulations."

Additionally, Nolan requested and was selected for a voluntary period of active duty. As a member of HQ Company, HQ Battalion, he participated in Cold Weather Training from January 11 to January 23, 1957, at Pickle Meadows, Marine Corps Base, Camp Pendleton, California. The exercise was described in a USMC memorandum as providing "an excellent opportunity for a limited number of reservists to participate and receive valuable instruction in the latest concepts employed by the Marine Corps in tactics, logistics, and administration." Nolan was granted "Secret" security clearance, and his performance was rated as "Excellent."

The Officer Fitness Reports from his commanding officers in the Reserve continued to reflect his active-duty "Excellent" and "Outstanding" ratings. Nolan was given the highest possible ratings in categories of handling officers, handling enlisted personnel, training personnel, attention to duty, cooperation, initiative, and personal relations, as well as in the performance of additional duties. His skills and experience were also consistently highly rated:

"The resoluteness of purpose, military proficiency and bearing of this officer make him an outstanding leader."

"This officer has displayed outstanding capabilities as an instructor and his professional character is well rounded."

"This officer is particularly well qualified as an instructor in any of the general military subjects. He has a great deal of engineering background."

"This individual is an excellent officer with a varied background. His experience and abilities are a real asset to the Marine Corps."

"Major Nolan is a vigorous and capable officer, and I feel sure his experience in construction would be valuable to the Corps should his services be required."

At this time, his military occupational specialty was listed as "Engineer Officer."

After attaining twenty years of satisfactory federal service and five years, seven days of actual active duty in the Corps, Major Nolan joined the Retired Reserve on July 1, 1963, a transition in Selective Service status that he did not approve and protested; he much preferred to remain at ready-status to defend his nation. On August 21, 1963, he received a letter from General David M. Shoup, Commandant of the Marine Corps, stating, "Upon your transfer to the Retired Reserve, I wish to express my personal appreciation for your service to our Corps and to our Country. It has been my privilege to observe the performance of our Reservists on many occasions, in both peace and war. I fully realize that their sacrifices have been great; however, these were required and accepted in the best interests of our nation." Regarding Nolan's assessment of retiring, Shoup wrote, "Your personal feelings in the matter are appreciated and respected. Even though you are retired, it is hoped you will continue to support the objectives of the Marine Corps in the future. Your many friends in the Corps join me in extending every good wish for the future."

On October 23, 1963, he received the following Certificate of Retirement: "This is to certify that Major Michael E. Nolan, having been transferred to the Retired Reserve after honorable service in the United States Marine Corps Reserve, is awarded this testimonial as an acknowledgment of duty faithfully performed." The certificate was signed by Shoup, who, in the accompanying communication, again wished Nolan well, and noted his appreciation for "the many contributions you have made to the Marine Corps."

On January 1, 1971, Nolan retired from the United States Marine Corps. After he retired, he received a Certificate of Retirement from the Armed Forces of the United States of America, which stated, "This is to certify that Major Michael E. Nolan, having served faithfully and honorably, was retired from the United States Marine Corps on the first day of January, one thousand nine hundred and seventy-one." The certificate was signed by General R. E. Cushman, Jr., Commandant of the Marine Corps. Forever loyal, Nolan remained involved as a lifetime member of the United States Marine Raider Association. His contact with his fellow Marines continued throughout his life.

Tributes to a "Man's Man"

We are eternally grateful for all of the ensuing information, and for the men who have provided it. Out of respect for their service to our nation, we have included current ranks for the following Marines, as they have been available; and, in some other instances, we have provided 1943 ranks from a Bougainville roster which was found among Nolan's papers. The following comments fill in many details from the World War II years, and offer insights into the character and personality of the man.

The issues of *The Raider Patch* newsletter brought us a few telling glimpses into Mike Nolan. In the September 1987 issue and in a subsequent letter to the family, Colonel Archibald B. Rackerby, who had served with him in Company K, relayed the following Nolan story: "He was a USMC corporal. He was commissioned and then the ExO of K Co. on Bougainville. In January 1944, he took over as CO of K Co. and was then rotated back to the U.S. after Emirau. He went to Iwo Jima as the CO of a DUKW Company charged with running supplies from ship to beach, a chore that was not Mike's way to fight a war. He intimidated a Lt. of artillery out of a 75mm Pack Howitzer, got some of his guys to help him, dismantled the Howitzer, manhandled it to where the fighting was raging, reassembled it, and fired point-blank into Japanese caves." Indeed, Nolan had turned over the operation of hauling artillery and supplies to a lieutenant, and joined the front-line action. Rackerby ended the account by mentioning his friend's very familiar and lifelong trait: "Mike could tell much more if you can get him to talk."

In the January 1990 issue, Rackerby wrote, "And who can forget big Mike Nolan, mustanged from corporal, to become CO of 3K after Bougainville. I admired Mike's Bougainville foxholes. A 6X6 truck could be garaged in one."

Under the "Salty Sea Stories" section of the July 1988 issue, John Newberry of 3K (Corporal, 1943) sent in details of a frequently told tale: "Capt. Nolan was then a Lt. with K Co. when we were in New Caledonia for R&R. He is the man who was refused custody of those from the 3rd Bn., who, on spending one of two nights of liberty in Noumea, were being detained in the Army brig for such sins as not buttoning their sleeves or collars, speaking suggestively to chaste French ladies or complaining about the quality of the kerosene in the butterfly brandy. I was not on guard detail at the time, but I was told that Lt. Nolan, a large man, reached across the M.P. counter, grasped the O.D. by the blouse and drew him up. Nolan then communicated, saying, 'I said, let those Marines go!' The Army released the Marines."

Nolan's comments in the July 1983 issue, complimenting the *Patch*, reflected the viewpoint of *Grabbing the Brass Ring*'s Richard Mansan: "Even the most incommunicative of us get around to writing. Your many years of tireless efforts in keeping our old Raider units together are unequaled in the annals of Marine Corps activity. My old Drill Instructor, Pete Kosovich, told us that we would remain Marines all of our lives. It was a chance to start all over. Kosovich was right. Even in today's greed-dominated world I am certain that we still have the option of starting all over."

A second comment published in the May 1974 edition of the *Patch* revealed the humility of the man and his dedication to the Corps. It read simply, "I consider it a great honor to be a member of the Marine Raider Association." He did, and he enjoyed the issues of the *Patch*, reading them from cover to cover as soon as they arrived, and leaving them out for the family to read, as well. In the November 1980 edition, Nolan was quoted in "The Bullsheet" (Raider comments section) once more. He sent in a donation "to express my appreciation for the fine *Raider Patch*."

Ever considerate, Col. Rackerby was kind enough to send us copies of letters Nolan had written to him in the 1980s. In a June 23, 1987 letter, which referred to the Raider reunion in Reno, he had commented, "The last time I was in Reno I was working in the mines in Manhattan, Nevada, and I took a job as bouncer at the old Four Star Casino in Las Vegas for $8.00 a day, a small fortune in those days."

Nolan then spoke about his time spent after retiring from the Forest Service: "I have done nothing since, so I guess you could say I started riding freight trains and wound up even farther away from the production field. I must have read too many of Jack London's books."

Apparently, they had been discussing weaponry. Nolan's July 7, 1987 letter read in part, "The best weapon on Iwo was the bazooka, but it took a while to realize this, and by that time most of the weapons had been discarded. I still think this is a great weapon, but like the 60mm mortar, carrying amo is a problem. Just maybe the whole idea of war is obsolete. We now have weapons that should make war a thing of the past. I was in Japan after WWII, and it was a mess."

Another couple of letters referred to Puruata, a subject which seemed to have been initiated by Rackerby. Nolan wrote, "My recall of Puruata is not very good.... I was in command of the CB working party, but when we landed, the front lines were still on the beach, so we played front-line soldiers. The battle was of short duration. We got a half-track knocked out of the action, along with [Captain Robert N.] Page, who was shot in the shoulder. When [Lieutenant Colonel Fred D.] Beans saw me come ashore with my blue-and-white clad Seabees, he put me in command of the battle. I did the only thing possible at the time. We began spraying all the trees with rifle and machine gun fire, as the Japanese seemed to always take refuge in trees. By then night had fallen, and we 'dug in' and secured for the night. In the morning the Japanese were gone. Evidently, they tried to swim over to the mainland. That swimming act was a maneuver I would have passed up. They have a fish in that part of the world called the great white shark, and they don't look too kindly on the human species. The next morning our patrols covered Puruata with no contact."

On June 1, 1983, Rackerby requested that Nolan send in a brief history of his Marine Corps tour for the Raider archives being compiled by then-historian Lowell V. Bulger. In a draft of his response, Nolan had crossed out an incomplete passage which is of interest in light of his fictional Richard Mansan character: "Today I am a firm believer that humanity will have an ever-increasing difficulty surviving in the future, and my guess is that inflated economy, high taxes, and wars will expedite our...." As a side note, the typically modest Nolan did submit his history; it consisted of seven lines, including his enlistment and discharge. His active duty was confined to five lines, which only mentioned year, unit designation, and rank.

One anecdote that Nolan related directly to his family involved "hitching a ride on a submarine." Although the circumstances of the venture are not known, he detailed the conditions on the sub, which he described as not very accommodating to his size or to his dislike of being confined. He said that whenever the submarine would surface, he would grab a blanket and sleep on the deck, and that it would take about an hour for him to straighten out. The food, however, was great.

Over the years, Nolan received countless calls, visits, cards, and letters from men who had served with him, reminding him of incidents that occurred during the war, or just checking in to see how he was doing. The telephone calls often came around the holidays, including one group of his men who placed a conference call to him for many years on Christmas Eve. He was always extremely pleased to hear from these men; in fact, the whole family looked forward to the calls asking for Captain Nolan. After returning from South America, the family was treated to a luncheon visit from Major General Alan Shapley (later, Lieutenant General), a delightful gentleman who had been Nolan's commanding officer in the 2nd Provisional Raider Regiment at Bougainville in 1943, and later in the 4th Marine Regiment in 1944. It was obvious that the two men held each other in very high regard.

A June 1, 1955 letter from Corporal Henry Gilkes, who served with Nolan on Iwo Jima, stated, "Memorial Day has just passed and I can't think of a better man to write to than yourself. I think back ten years ago when we hit Iwo Jima. I know that every man in our outfit respected your bravery. I think it's the officers who must show the way, and I and many others felt better under your command....I hope that this letter finds you in the best of health, which you so justly deserve. It is my hope that some day I can visit you. Until then, I remain a former Corporal in the 5th Amp. Batt. of which I was very proud."

Nolan's dedication to and protection of his men did not fade with the years. In 1973, he was informed that one of his men (for the purposes of this biography, referred to below as "Mr. X") had been given a Bad Conduct Discharge in 1945 due to conduct while at a hospital in the States. On April 4, 1973, Nolan forwarded a letter on his behalf:

"I will state my protest and recommendations in outline form. This will have a dampening effect on any emotions that I feel....As one of his commanding officers, I assure you that Mr. X lacked none of the high character traits so necessary in the makeup of the American fighting man. I can only assume at this time that the military decision to discharge Mr. X was reached without the understanding that the human mind can stand just so much of the killing, maiming and destruction so necessary in war. We must remember that he was in the hospital as a result of the expenditures of his physical and mental resources as demanded by me and other battlefield commanders.

"The life of the American fighting man is never a pleasant one. Battle itself is against our natural way of American life. The rewards are only in the self-satisfaction that our characters were strong enough. The participant must also adjust to a point where all his physical actions and mental emotions reflect the rules as set down by the military branch of our government. This must be accepted by the American fighting man; but when the final human resources are drained from the human body, we must not compound the damage by penalizing the man, his wife and family for the rest of their lives. The B.C.D. is a permanent stigma and tends to propagate more during the lives of our more productive citizens.

"If we do find it necessary to give the B.C.D., we must be very sure that the man is represented by every living commanding officer he ever served.

"I firmly believe that Mr. X's rights as an American fighting man and citizen were not protected. His character as a fighting man was excellent and warranted my support and the support of other commanding officers he served. This support should have been available and considered by the military court before the B.C.D. was given. I recommend that Mr. X's case be reopened and that this time he be represented by former Marine officers who drew on this man's character resources to defeat an enemy that was fighting to inflict mortal injury to our country. I have a very reverent image of the United States Marine Corps, and I find a very incompatible comparison between that image and the military decision rendered to Mr. X.

"Please understand, I advocate only military action. Mr. X was a military man of excellent character. The B.C.D. was given by the military, the same military of which I was a representative. I firmly believe that an error in judgment was made, and this error should be corrected by the military."

It should be noted that the nature of the discharge was overturned.

At times Nolan would receive first-time correspondence decades after the war had ended. On April 16, 1986, a letter arrived from Navy Corpsman Manuel M. Maya (PhM3c, 1943), who had served with him on Bougainville. Maya wrote, "When I was a young man, I was proud to have served under you and Captain Page. You were both courageous in action.... I grew to love the U.S. Marine Corps." This came from a man who had himself won the Silver Star.

Nolan often doubted the wisdom of returning to the part of the world he had seen during World War II; he would state that he had seen enough of it. However, at one time he revealed a conflicting thought in a September 9, 1974 response to a letter from Lieutenant Colonel Marvin D. Perskie, a fellow Raider and currently a lawyer, who had written to him for the first time. Perskie explained that "as you get older, your mind goes back to the old days and the associations you have had in the past."

Speaking of his impending retirement from the Forest Service, Nolan described himself as "not the retiring type," and remarked that he was pondering the possibility of more foreign construction work. He stated, "In some respects, the clock has been set back thirty years, and some old memories have been brought back into focus. I attended my first U.S. Marine Raider get-together in Long Beach [August 1, 1974]....It should have been held in the Solomon Islands. I think we could all stand at least one such meeting....Give my Solomon Islands meeting idea a little thought. It would give us all a better chance to get reacquainted and evaluate the potentials of those South Sea Islands. I know it sounds ridiculous, but it is possible that law and engineering, as practiced by a couple of ex-Camp Fire Girls, are in demand at our old picnic areas." Whether he was serious at the time or not, Nolan's words did sound a bit "Mansanesque." In any case, he never did return.

Years after his passing, his fellow Marines were kind enough to forward letters to the family, detailing some of their anecdotes about Nolan, for inclusion in this biography. One January 27, 1997 letter from Thaddeus Wietecha (Corporal, 1943) relayed the following comments: "I knew your dad and never will forget him. Mike Nolan was a newly commissioned 1st Lt. of the 2nd Platoon, D Company, 3rd Raider Battalion when I joined the Raiders and his Platoon in January of 1943 in Samoa.

"Mike was big, tough, strong, and as very brave a Marine as you could ever find. He also was a quiet, serious, and no-nonsense kind of a guy. Mike indeed was fearless and like a bull in a china shop. He always insisted on leading the way. His 'follow me' really meant *follow me*. As I write, his image is clear in my mind, and I can almost hear his voice."

Wietecha went on to describe a revealing story about Nolan's bravery: "One of the reasons why I'll never forget Mike Nolan is because of an episode that happened in the Russells. We landed on Pavuvu, the main island, in rubber boats. The landing was unopposed, and our Platoon was ordered to reconnoiter the outlying small islands of Baisen, Money and Leru to see if they were occupied. They were not and we stayed on one of the islands for several days. The Japanese left a lot of supplies in small squad-type landing barges. There was food and fuel.

"It rained, and since there was no cover, we stayed soaked and wet. We soon came up with an idea. There wasn't anything that we could burn, so we picked up fallen, wet coconut palm fronds and put them into piles. We found naphtha (benzene) in 55-gallon drums, and using our steel helmets which held nearly a gallon of liquid, we sloshed the naphtha on the palm fronds and set them on fire, hoping to warm ourselves and get our clothes dry. Being wet after sundown, we were cold.

"One of the men next to me and around the fire decided to throw more naphtha on the fire. As he attempted to slosh half of the full helmet contents, the fumes backlashed and ignited his helmet that was still half full with naphtha. He instinctively threw the helmet away from himself and directly on me, hitting me in the chest. I lit up like a torch with the burning naphtha on me."

Apparently, Nolan was not around during this procedure, but did appear as help was needed: "I don't know where Mike was when this happened, but the next thing I knew he took a flying leap on me, and with my rolling around on the wet coral sand and Mike beating on me, the flames were extinguished.

"I had most of my hair burned off, my face and chest area singed, but fortunately and thanks to Mike Nolan, I was not seriously burned.

"Mike Nolan was quite a man's man."

A letter dated May 17, 1988, and found among Nolan's papers, detailed the same wartime memory directly to him. At the close of the letter, Wietecha stated, "In several seconds, you had the presence of mind, and also the guts I am grateful to add, to dive on me and extinguish the flames. Most of my hair was burned away. The wet dungaree jacket was burned through, and to this day I carry the scars. Mike, I am sure that my fate would be much worse if it were not for you. I also remember Mike Nolan as a most competent and brave Platoon leader whom I had a great deal of confidence in."

Wietecha ended his 1997 letter with a humorous statement which would be echoed in many communications: "Please remember that we all are in our 70+ years, and going back 50 or more years is difficult – especially as some of us don't even remember what we had for lunch."

On June 9, 1996, Master Sergeant Fred W. Raber wrote that Nolan "was my Commanding Officer of K Co. and I was the 1st Sgt. I found him to be a very good CO. He told the company what he wanted and how he wanted it done. With this kind of request he had very little trouble. He insisted that all the company be properly trained. With me he was like a brother. We shared problems and how best to solve them.

"We were together on only one occasion, Emirau Island. When the Marines arrived, the Japanese had already left. Could understand why. It was a leper colony. We stayed about two weeks, waiting for the Navy to come and take us back to our base camp, Guadalcanal. We shared the same foxhole at Emirau, and with nothing to do he tried to teach me how to play chess. After about two hours he gave up and we played checkers."

Nolan's men were always foremost in his mind, as shown in a brief vignette written by Raber: "The Officers had a clubhouse on Guadalcanal. Each week all the Officers received a quart of whiskey. I guess he didn't drink as he brought his bottle to me. I invited all the Battalion 1st Sgts. and we shared. The Colonel found out and would not let the Officers take their bottles out of the clubhouse.

"This is about all I can remember. After fifty years the memory starts to go. But I shall always remember Big Mike Nolan."

A June 13, 1996 letter from Bill Jordan (Private, 1945), who was quite young at the time he served under Nolan on Iwo Jima, and who subsequently maintained a lifelong friendship with his commanding officer, gave an insight into the man's presence, unequivocally stating, "My Captain could get all the respect he wanted, just by standing in front of you."

The Marine units, it seemed, had a long history of not receiving the supplies they needed – whether it was food, ammunition, or clothing. They apparently made quite a few "midnight requisitions" (to use Col. Rackerby's term) to obtain supplies. Jordan related a story that happened when they were in Japan: "The Captain called the Company to formation one day, and informed us that he had received a complaint from the Army. We, with our DUKWs, would unload the ships' supplies. They said there were lined vests (sheepskin) missing, so the Captain opened up his shirt, showed his vest, and said that the first man he saw wearing his vest outside, and not as he was wearing his, he personally would court-martial him. When it came to supplies for our Company, we were always last to receive them, if any."

On several occasions, Jordan traveled from Maine to visit his captain in Tucson. He brought him authentic maple syrup, called him every Christmas Eve, and kindly visited the family after Nolan's passing to share stories and reminisce.

In 1996, Jordan forwarded a copy of a speech made by Boatswain's Mate 2nd Class William Broderick of the U.S. Coast Guard, a member of the U.S. LST Association, at a 1995 commemoration for the 50th anniversary of the battle for Iwo Jima. Broderick and Jack Atherton were crew members on LST 795, which "beached on Iwo Jima and disembarked part of the 5th Marine Division amphibious force as well as equipment and supplies." He told an amazing story about the two of them being accidentally left behind on Iwo Jima by their unit. Luckily for them, they were "adopted" by the Marines. Broderick wrote, "We stayed with the Marines, who, by the way, took good care of their two swabbies" – among other things, advising them not to sleep by tanks at night (a definite target) and instructing them on the proper digging of foxholes. On March 14, the two men were finally dispatched to a Coast Guard LST to return to their duty. When returning to LST 795, still in "our Marine clothes with helmets and rifles...we soon found out we were listed as AWOL and perhaps subject to a summary court-martial. Thanks to a letter of explanation in our defense written by Marine Captain Michael E. Nolan, the AWOL charges were dropped and we were once again happy hooligans back home on the 795. Let me now say 'thank you' to the Marines for taking such good care of Jack and me." Jordan wrote that Broderick had wanted to look up the captain after the war to express his gratitude.

On June 14, 1996, Colonel Arthur Haake took the time to relate a couple of humorous incidents he recalled about Nolan: "During the 3rd Raider Battalion training period on New Caledonia before Bougainville, the Island Command had taken over a hotel in Noumea as an officer's club. The club was patronized by officers stationed on Caledonia but also served many transients. The club had a bar and threw an occasional dance on Saturday nights. The rule was that no single male was allowed into the dance hall. I suppose that having M.P.s keep order on dance nights would have been inappropriate since the primary problem was drunken officers attempting to crash the dance. Island Command's solution was to commandeer different units stationed on Caledonia to take turns policing the dance as unobtrusively as possible.

"Bad luck for the Raiders, they got the duty. Worse luck for me. I was Battalion XO and got the detail. Mike was an obvious choice for this kind of situation, so he, I and two others were ordered to be watchdogs at the dance. We quasi-M.P.s shut one-half of the double door into the dance hall and took turns at the entrance. A few drunks (from the bar) tried to get in but were turned back without incident.

"However, when I had the station at the door, an Army Air Force Brigadier General and his buddy demanded entry. I explained that the rule against single males was without exception. When pulling rank didn't work, they became belligerent and threatened to go 'through you.' Mike was close at hand and I called him over. I then told the BG and his friend that they could go through me after they went through him. With Mike filling up the doorway, they elected to go back to the bar." The power of Nolan's physical presence had once more become obvious.

A second incident Haake related occurred when "the 3rd Raiders were on the line in Bougainville and an alert went out after midnight. Mike was asleep, and two young Marines argued about who had to wake him. I suspect that this diffidence resulted from the awe these really young kids felt for some of their leaders, but the joke went around that the troops were more afraid of Mike than of the Japanese."

On June 15, 1996, Col. Rackerby also shared some humorous stories: "There are so many fond memories that I and others in K Company have of Mike. In the jungles of Bougainville, we were required to dig-in every night and sleep underground to avoid being hit with shrapnel from Japanese 'daisy cutter' bombs during nighttime bombing. We all had jungle hammocks for slinging between trees, but none of us used them, except Mike. He wanted to be comfortable AND secure, so he dug a foxhole large enough to hide a jeep and slung his hammock down in the hole.

"During the first week of December 1943, on Bougainville, a young, blond second lieutenant fresh from officer's school was assigned to K Company as an extra officer. Capt. Page, the K Company Commander, had no troop assignment for him, so he told Mike to let this young officer share his foxhole. Mike definitely did not like that, as he had gone to a lot of trouble digging his monstrous hole and slinging his hammock therein. Mike let 'Golden Boy,' as he called him, sleep on the ground under his hammock. If the hammock broke, Mike would have squashed him. It frustrated Mike terribly to have 'Golden Boy' sit on the bottom of the foxhole and eat from his candy and cookie boxes without sharing with Mike."

Rackerby gave us insights into Nolan's relationship with the enlisted men: "But Mike was very compassionate with the enlisted men who, incidentally, shared their 'goodies' from home with everyone, including Mike and me. On long, hard marches, particularly in the jungles and in steamy hot weather, some of the smaller enlisted men struggled under the weight of their normal pack gear plus weapons and extra ammunition. Good officers and NCOs often kept the little guys from falling out as stragglers by carrying their machine guns, mortars and heavy ammo for them. Mike was good about this and often carried a couple of extra weapons plus his own BAR (Browning Automatic Rifle). In fact, I wouldn't doubt but what Mike may have picked up some struggling 125-pound Marine and carried him for a while."

Nolan was always fastidious, and believed that one way to keep morale up was to maintain regular hygiene habits, even in extreme conditions. Rackerby provided a few details of this policy: "On New Caledonia, Mike and I lived in adjoining 4-man tents and were good friends. Every morning, Mike and I would each fill our little canvas pans with cold water for our daily face-wash and shave. Mike located a French-speaking native in a quaint village a couple of miles from our camp who would wash and IRON (with old flat irons) our khakis and other soiled clothing. About once a week, he and I would check out a jeep to run our clothing over to the old Tonkinese lady, and it was hilarious to see and hear Mike talking to her in Spanish, telling her what to do when she couldn't understand a word he said. This was really a lesson in communications. The main problem was to keep her from starching the underwear."

Of course, sometimes things did not run smoothly: "After we got back from Bougainville and Mike became K Company Commander in January of 1944, we also got a new battalion commander. He was making an inspection of the tent quarters of all the men in his battalion with the company commanders in tow. After they had inspected the quarters of the men in my Weapons Platoon, Mike left the inspecting party and came back to me, saying, 'Arch, your tent area smells like a #88@!#*!! distillery. Move those cans of fermenting raisinjack out of your tents. The Major didn't say anything, but he had to have smelled it.'" Rackerby then had his men hide the "stills" in the jungle behind the "heads."

On a more serious note, Rackerby mentioned that in February 1944, he and Nolan "designed a system for firing the 60mm mortars with just the mortar tube...not using the baseplate, bipod, aiming stake, or complicated sight. Although neither Mike nor I was with K Co. on Guam in July 1944, Mortarmen Merton Graham and Gerald Fitzpatrick of K Co. told me after the war that they helped break up a major Japanese banzai night attack using the tube-alone method of mortar firing and that they fired so many rounds so fast that the hot tube blistered their hands."

We are most grateful for all of Col. Rackerby's stories. One of his comments rang particularly true: "It's sad how the memory declines...too bad we didn't have tape recorders and camcorders in those days to record history. To be very honest, at our ages we don't recall a lot." We are just happy he remembered what he did.

A July 18, 1996 letter from Private First Class Eddie Youhas, K Company runner when Nolan was K Company executive officer, was forwarded by Col. Rackerby. Youhas wrote, "'Big Mike' Nolan was one of my idols. I vividly recall going on a ten-mile hike with full pack and gear. Near the end of the hike one of the guys collapsed – heat exhaustion. Mike came along, picked up the fallen grunt with one arm, and transferred the pack and rifle to his other arm. The fallen guy eventually continued on and completed the hike." Youhas added, "There was also talk that Mike had boxed with Max Baer and had knocked Baer off his feet!"

Another runner, who was briefly attached to K Company, might have been the source of a few boxing stories. Corporal Michael "Kayo" Janic, himself a featherweight boxing champion, had also been at Baer's camp. In one of his letters to Rackerby, Nolan stated, "As I recall, we were attached to the 3rd Division for the Bougainville operation, and Janic was assigned to us. The assignment lasted only while we were camped in the 3rd Division area." Regarding the old days at the Baer camp, he said, "Baer used him as a sparring partner. If Janic thought Baer roughed him up, he would chase Baer with a club. The camp was always in an uproar."

A photograph, sent through the Inter-Island Mail from Janic to Nolan during the war, showed Janic instructing Marine boxers. He inscribed on the face of the photo, "To my good friend and sparring partner, Captain Mike Nolan. Always the best, Kayo Janic, Trainer of Marine Champs." On the back, Janic had written a poem: "To Captain Michael Nolan. For 'tis Captain Mike Nolan that's leading the band / Yes, 'tis Captain Michael that's in full command / A one-man Raider some will say / but he's one of the many from the U.S.A." Janic quipped, "Not bad for a Corporal."

From First Lieutenant Frank H. O'Reilly, a Bronze Star recipient who served with Nolan in the 5th Marine Division, came the following remarks from 1996 letters: "Mike was my company commander while we trained on the island of Hawaii. Before we left for Iwo Jima, he was transferred to the 'Duck' battalion.... One day about halfway through the Iwo campaign, he came up to visit me and gave me a handful of cigars, which we both enjoyed later while playing chess back in Hawaii. He received the cigars from a U.S. Survey Team that requested the use of his 'Ducks' to make depth soundings around the island.... Mike was a real man's man, an outstanding Marine and a great leader of men. He was a great inspiration to all Marines under his command and to those he associated with." O'Reilly was another of Nolan's lifelong friends who regularly kept in touch with him after the war and visited him in Tucson. As so many had said over the years, he added that Mike "didn't talk about himself."

On March 25, 2012, the family was surprised and pleased to receive an email communication from Ken Meyer: "I am the son of a Marine who served under the command of Mike Nolan on Iwo Jima. My father's name was Harvey Meyer, Corporal. My dad told me two stories that related to your father that you may not have heard. To start, my dad was 6' 5", 250 lbs., and one of the biggest men in the outfit along with your dad. As my dad told me, your father said, 'Meyer, you and I are going to put the gloves on.' (This was said in front of the unit.) My dad replied, 'No, sir,' and your dad said, 'That's an order.' In the ensuing bout your dad tore some skin off my dad's nose, at which point my dad let out an expletive and threw down his gloves. To that your dad replied, 'That's *******, *Sir*!'

"Secondly, in the battle on Iwo, my dad drew number 'two,' so was co-pilot, and Charles Erne number 'one,' so was pilot of the amphibious truck. As they were approaching the beach on the fourth wave, the Japanese opened fire. The vehicle became stuck at water's edge, and my father yelled, 'Erne, get out!' He then jumped out and into a crater with Erne soon following. (Later Erne told my dad that two bullets hit his seat.) At this point another Marine, named Addison, dove into the crater, and my dad looked up and saw your dad waving the landed soldiers and vehicles on, while firing his .45 at the Japanese with bullets hitting all around him! My father then said, 'I would follow him into battle anywhere.'"

Ken Meyer subsequently sent a link to an interview with his father at the June 1, 2004 National World War II Memorial Dedication, and noted that Corporal Meyer had "a deep respect" for Nolan. In part, Cpl. Meyer was quoted as saying, "I was on the fourth wave...I was an amphibious truck crewman, and I had to take the supplies, ammunition, lumber, whatever, back up to the troops. I had my baptism of fire...I had to circle around before I came in, because the beachmaster said they were still shelling the beach. But there were destroyers over here, firing rockets." Cpl. Meyer was between the destroyers and the target, Mt. Suribachi. A hero himself, he said, "I'm not gonna stay out here. I'm going in anyway!" His account continued, "There was no footing on the beach, and (farther inland) the first wave slowed up, and they were caught...in like, a killing field. You had Suribachi and the cliffs, where the Fourth Marine Division was held down. It's called enfilade and plunging fire; that's why it took a toll the first day. I got ashore and I reported to my CO, Mikey Nolan. He used to play football for the Chicago Bears. He was my CO, and I tell you, I'd follow that guy anywhere. He walked like...as if he was as big as Suribachi. He'd just walk around there (under fire), .45 in the back pocket, captain bars on his head. I wish I could see him today; I'd shake his hand." It was obvious that Nolan was not trying to hide his officer's rank under fire.

On February 24, 2013, the family received an email from Chuck H. Meacham (Private First Class, 1943), "an M1 and then a BAR man," with the Raiders, who currently serves on the Board of Directors of the U.S. Marine Raider Association. Meacham wrote that "1st Lt. Mike Nolan, affectionately known as 'Saddle Up Mike,' was our executive officer in Co. 'K' 3rd Raiders....I landed with 1st Lt. Mike Nolan 1 November 1943, on Puruata Island...adjacent to the big island of Bougainville. We secured the small island in 2 days; day 3 we were off to Bougainville itself. Our 'Skipper' Capt. Page was severely wounded, basically on the landing. Capt. Page refused to be evacuated and continued through the fight. His fever, from the wound, became serious and he was evacuated. 'Saddle Up Mike' then commanded Co. 'K.' We were on Bougainville for 72 days. I estimate your father was in command of 'K' Co. during the Bougainville campaign, all except the first week. He took us back to Guadalcanal and remained as EX officer." Meacham added some insights into the training provided by Nolan: "Whenever you went in the field training under 'Saddle Up Mike,' you were sure to have a lot of 60mm mortar and machine gun exercises." He described Nolan as "a fearless charger," and "a great Marine and warrior."

Emmitt Hayes (Private First Class, 1943) of the 3rd Raiders, Company K, and currently also a member of the USMRA Board of Directors, contacted the family on June 5, 2013, with the following words: "I remember Capt. Nolan well. I was a 17-year-old kid on Bougainville, and he is one of the very few things I remember well enough to write a few thoughts about. Capt. Nolan was a very big man, tall and muscular, a born leader. He carried a Browning Automatic Rifle in combat. That was a very heavy rifle, and he used it as a pointer in one hand when giving directions to the Platoon leaders."

The following communications have been saved for last; they further showed the steadfastness and loyalty of the Marines, men who, through the strength of their character and the depth of their compassion, did not turn their backs; they themselves also appeared just when they were needed most. Directly after Nolan's passing in 1991, the family heard from several of his fellow Raiders. Needless to say, these heartfelt words were profoundly valued.

In an April 17, 1991 letter, Major Robert Popelka recounted that he "first met Mike on Wallis Island out between Samoa and Fiji in 1942. We volunteered and were accepted into D Co. of the Third Raider Bn. He led the 2nd Platoon, and I had the 1st. From then until I joined the Fourth Raider Bn., we shared the same tents, foxholes, etc. We were in Samoa, the New Hebrides, Guadalcanal and the Russell Islands together. Mike Nolan was a great Marine officer and loved by all. He always took care of the men under him. I last saw Mike overseas in New Caledonia in about September or October of 1943. He was getting ready to go to Bougainville. I have heard many good things about his Marine Corps service from then to the end of the war."

Popelka was successful in getting Nolan to his first reunion: "About 15-20 years ago when the Marine Raider Assn. had its first big reunion on the Queen Mary in Long Beach, I talked Mike into meeting me there and sharing a stateroom. What a celebrity he turned out to be! Thereafter, we stayed in touch and I visited him in Tucson three or four times. Mike was a wonderful person. War is all 'hurry up and wait.' During the many hours of 'wait' we had some very interesting conversations – what experiences he had to relate.... I have some very fond memories of my friendship with Mike and am going to miss him." Popelka later came to visit the family in Tucson, a visit which was both enjoyed and deeply appreciated.

Brigadier General William L. Flake expressed his sympathy at Nolan's passing, and wrote, "Mike and I go back a long way together. I came to the U of A in 1939 from junior college, so I never actually played football with him. But he was around and often came over to the campus.

"The last time I saw Mike was in January on Guadalcanal [1944]. We were sitting under a palm tree, discussing Arizona and his aspiration to sometime go back and finish his schooling, which he of course did after some years with the fire department. His accomplishment at that late date, both of going back to school and not only completing his education but doing so in engineering, was amazing, and I have used it since to encourage others to exert the effort that he did." (April 15, 1991)

Russell D. Calvo (Corporal, 1943) stated, "This is a shock as Major Mike Nolan was a 'mountain' to us Raiders and Marines. Following Capt. Robert Page, he became my K Company CO. I was not only his runner and bugler, but also one of his boxers in the Third Raiders. He will never be forgotten by me. The memory of 'Big Mike' will be held in affection by all of us who knew him and served under him." (April 15, 1991)

Alfred Grimes (Sergeant, 1943) wrote, "So sorry to hear about your father passing on. You can be proud of him – he was a 'helluva' Marine and Raider. I served in K Co. with him although not in his platoon. Last time I recall seeing him was when we had a Raider Reunion on the Queen Mary at Long Beach. He sat at the same table as I....Be PROUD of him – all of us Raiders are." (April 15, 1991)

Sergeant Frederick W. Matter expressed his sympathy, adding, "I knew Mike and recall some amusing incidents during the time we were in 3K. Mike was well liked and respected, especially with his boxing background. Rest assured that he will be missed by all of us who knew him." (April 13, 1991)

Dean Allen (Corporal, 1943) wrote that Nolan was "*a mighty fine man.* I wanted so much to come and see him, and I never did. He was one of my lieutenants during the war in the 3rd Marine Raiders. I did some boxing in the Raiders, and he refereed some of my fights. He was always a real happy-go-lucky sorta guy, and I will always remember him that way. I know for a fact that he was real proud of the Marine Corps, too!" (April 12, 1991)

Raider historian Major Jerome Beau, referring to Nolan as "my old friend," recalled that they had served together in K Company, 3rd Raider Battalion, "through the Bougainville campaign, 1Nov43 - 12Jan44, to 26Jan44, when I was rotated back to the US," and stated that Nolan "was a great guy and a fine Marine, and will always be remembered." (April 12, 1991)

On April 9, 1991, Colonel Rackerby, Nolan's longtime letter-writing buddy, somberly wrote, "It was certainly a sad feeling to hear of your father's expiring on this Earth to join his many friends on our Raider Honor Roll. Mike was a very special friend to me during the ten months I was in the islands during WWII. We shared many interesting experiences and swapped tales on New Caledonia, in the New Hebrides, and on Guadalcanal, Puruata, and Bougainville....He will be honored during our Memorial Service in Scottsdale.

"Your father was one of the most interesting men...and he was certainly ALL MAN...whom I've had the privilege of knowing."

On October 3, 2007, Rackerby would write, "Of all the Raiders I ever served with, your dad was one of my closest friends. I cherish the memory of our visits in Tucson."

The words of these loyal, kind, and gentle men brought much comfort to the family at a time of almost unbearable sadness.

After his death, Nolan's family received a number of medals awarded to but never received by him (under his commissioned service number only): the Navy Unit Commendation Ribbon, the Asiatic-Pacific Campaign Medal with four Bronze Stars, the Navy Occupation Service Medal – Asia, the American Defense Service Medal, and the World War II Victory Medal.

[Editor's note: The Navy Unit Commendation Ribbon was likely awarded to two units in which Nolan served. According to the May 1978 issue of *The Raider Patch*, the 3rd Raiders, attached to and serving with the 3rd Marines, were entitled to wear this ribbon for the Bougainville campaign (November 1 - December 22, 1943). The ribbon was also awarded to the 5th Division for the Iwo Jima campaign (February 19-28, 1945).]

In June of 1991, a certificate signed by President George H. W. Bush was sent to Nolan's family. It read, "The United States of America honors the memory of Michael E. Nolan. This certificate is awarded by a grateful nation in recognition of devoted and selfless consecration to the service of our country in the Armed Forces of the United States."

On November 20, 1998, Michael Earl Nolan was inducted into membership in the Marine Corps Mustang Association, after his application was completed by his family and mailed in. The certificate read, "In recognition of superior leadership and professional skills, the above named Marine Officer has risen from the enlisted ranks and has therefore earned the title 'Mustang.'"

A summary of his service and pictures of Nolan are featured in *History of the Marine Raiders: More Than a Few Good Men*.

An engraved brick honoring his service with the 3rd Raider Battalion can be found at Raider Hall, on the Marine base at Quantico, Virginia. In 2001, his photograph and biography were submitted to the National World War II Memorial Registry of Remembrances.

One of our great regrets is that we waited so long to assemble this biography. We are left with some ongoing mysteries which we have as yet been unable to solve without Nolan as our guide. At this late date, with official records thus far serving only as an outline, and with the ruthlessness of time and fading memory, we are still searching for more information to fill in the blanks. We continue to make inquiries, in an effort to find relevant official records, and we are hoping that additional firsthand reports might surface which have somehow been preserved over the years. The repeated references to Nolan's bravery and legendary status – such as the 1945 article by Marine Corps Combat Correspondent, Tech Sergeant Allen Sommers, "'Big Mike' Nolan, Legendary in Pacific, Is Modest Hero," which referred to Nolan's heroism and his actions on Guadalcanal, Bougainville, and Iwo Jima – certainly indicate to us that there is obviously much more to learn.

The end of the war marked a change in the direction of the events in Nolan's life. After he returned, he embraced the traditional "American Dream," which he had fought so hard to protect. He married, built a home, started a family, returned to the University of Arizona, studied seriously, and pursued a successful career as a civil engineer. In these ways, the next phase of his life would prove equally fascinating. In his quiet and understated way, he symbolized the intelligence, creativity, and love found deep within the human soul.

Private Nolan (top row, sixth from left), United States Marine Corps, 3rd Recruit Battalion, San Diego, California, February 1941.

Nolan, somewhere in the South Pacific jungle, World War II.

Officers of Company K, 3rd Marine Raider Battalion. First Lieutenant "Big Mike" Nolan (seated, right), executive officer. New Caledonia, September 1943. Prior to battles of Puruata and Bougainville. Second Lieutenant Archibald B. Rackerby (standing, left) would become a lifelong friend.

Tucson Marine Corps Hero

First Lt. Michael Earl Nolan, 230-pound former football star at the University of Arizona where his gridiron exploits gained him the nickname of "King Kong," pulls the pin on a smoke grenade somewhere in the South Pacific. Lt. Nolan is attached to one of the U. S. Marine Corps hardest-hitting units. He enlisted in the marines in January, 1941, and was commissioned a second lieutenant on the battlefield last September.—(Official U. S. Marine Corps photo.)

First Lieutenant Nolan of the 3rd Marine Raider Battalion, pictured pulling the pin on a smoke grenade. Official U.S. Marine Corps photo. (Printed in *Arizona Daily Star*, September 30, 1943.)

Captain Nolan (left), on only leave during World War II, May 1944. Credited in 1945 with 44 months of foreign and sea service.

Captain Michael E. Nolan, commanding officer, 5th Amphibian Truck Company, 5th Motor Transport Battalion, 5th Marine Division, November 1, 1944.

Hilo, Hawaii, November 1, 1944. Captain Mike Nolan (standing, left), commanding officer, 5th Amphibian Truck Company, with company officers. Prior to battle of Iwo Jima.

Captain Nolan (left), with captured Japanese Rising Sun flag.

'Big Mike' Nolan, Legendary In Pacific, is Modest Hero

By Tech Sgt. ALLEN SOMMERS
Marine Corps Combat Correspondent

SOMEWHERE IN THE PACIFIC, Aug. 12.—Marine Captain Michael E. (Big Mike) Nolan, 34, former professional football player, boxer, mining engineer, iron foundry foreman, traveler and veteran of Iwo Jima and other Pacific campaigns, modestly denies any major role in this war.

"The men do the job," the 240-pound ex-Raider from Tucson, Ariz., declares. "All I'm doing is satisfying my urge for adventure."

"Big Mike" became almost a legend to Marine fighting men in the Pacific after his action with the First Marine Division on Guadalcanal and with the former Third Raider Battalion on Bougainville.

And, after listening to enlisted men serving under "Big Mike," it's not hard to understand why the deep-voiced captain gets the almost-impossible out of the men he commands.

On Iwo Jima

One marine recalled the landing on Iwo. Nolan was leading an amphibian tank company of the Fifth Marine Division, and it was his job to get field artillery on the island.

"He stood up on the beach directing the 'Ducks'," the marine said. "Everytime the Japs sent us a welcome card in the form of mortar shells, the captain's voice boomed orders to dive into foxholes. He saw to it that we found shelter."

"We dived for the first one we saw, sure. But 'Big Mike' didn't care. When the barrage was over, there he was standing upright as if nothing had happened."

Devotion to "Big Mike" by his men is typified by the following incident, which he tells on himself:

Devoted Men

"The second night on Iwo was hell, and I decided to take all my 'Ducks' off the beach. We collected wounded, plowed through rough surf to the nearest ship and then began circling for the night.

"I was on a vehicle with two of my men. We planned night-long watches, alternating hourly. I left orders to be awakened for the second watch. When I awoke it was daylight. My man had allowed me to sleep the night through. That isn't easy to forget."

A native of Canada, the captain is a former student of the University of Arizona, where he studied mining engineering. He also played varsity football, and after that joined the professional Chicago Cardinals for whom he played first string tackle for two years.

Unable to control his lust for adventure, "Big Mike" quit his football job and began traveling throughout North America, stopping to work only when he needed funds.

On January 16, 1941, he enlisted in the Marine Corps as a private and went to the Pacific the following year with a defense battalion. Later he was transferred to the First Marine Division for the Solomons invasion. Before the year was gone, Nolan found himself in a hospital with malaria.

It was on Guadalcanal in September, 1942 that he received a field commission. Later he joined the Third Raiders and when the Raider battalions were disbanded, the Fifth Division.

TOUGH MARINE
CAPT. M. E. NOLAN

Article on Captain Nolan, by Technical Sergeant Allen Sommers, Marine Corps Combat Correspondent. (Printed in *Arizona Daily Star*, August 13, 1945.)

Major Nolan (second from left), with friends from Company K, at Marine Raider reunion aboard the *Queen Mary* in Long Beach, California, August 1974.

CHAPTER FOURTEEN

Work History and Return to the University of Arizona
From Hopping Freight Trains to Civil Engineering

THROUGHOUT THE YEARS, THERE HAD BEEN MANY INTERESTS that Michael Earl Nolan pursued. He always found a way to support himself and to give to others, even in the toughest economic times of the Depression. In addition to professional football and boxing, he was a sparring partner for Max Baer at his Livermore training camp, labored on the docks in San Francisco, and worked one summer for Jack London's widow on a farm in Sonoma, California, which he described as "beautiful country." He later wrote that she was a "wonderful person to work for. She had apple and pear orchards, and in those days mules were still used on the farm. I had lived in the wilds of British Columbia, so farm work with mules was well known to me." At other times, Nolan took jobs as a bouncer, served as "chief assistant maintenance man for the athletic department" at the University of Arizona, went "up to the northwest to pick fruits and vegetables," or worked in the mines in Nevada. In fact, on his first application for the National Guard, he listed a position as a mine trammer. We believe he even was employed for a time as a roustabout in a carnival. He was certainly no stranger to hard work and had a definite sense of adventure, oftentimes hopping a freight train to the next destination.

Before becoming a professional civil engineer in 1955, Nolan had extensive experience in many facets of construction, and also chalked up duty with the Tucson Police Department and the Tucson Fire Department.

From May of 1929 through January of 1941, he gained firsthand building knowledge as he worked his way from laborer to foreman with contractor Carl Larmour, Carl G. Larmour & Son, both on residential and commercial construction projects. Nolan developed his skills as a carpenter, bricklayer, plasterer, cement finisher, and plumber before becoming a foreman in 1938, eventually supervising all work on up to ten homes under construction at one time. He was again employed by Larmour in the 1940s and 1950s, with increasing responsibilities in overall job management and site engineering, including building, roadway, and residential area design; layout of building sites, subdivision roadways, water lines, and septic/sewer systems; grading; timber, steel, reinforced concrete, and foundations; checking of plans and specifications; estimating of work and materials; and supervision of the construction on up to twenty homes at one time, and as many as thirty to fifty men. Carl Larmour remained his friend for life. There were several times throughout the years when people would proudly come up to the family and say that Nolan had worked on their homes.

It is true that Nolan loved construction and took much care in all of his projects, large or small – whether he was working for others, building an adobe addition for his father's home in the Tanque Verde area during the 1930s, constructing the first family home after his marriage in 1946, helping a friend with a concrete patio for his backyard, putting in a back porch for relatives, or personally remodeling the new family home upon returning from Peru. He enjoyed it all – except for plumbing and painting, which he wholeheartedly disliked!

During the 1930s, Earl Nolan was employed part-time in construction for the Pima County Highway Department, operating heavy equipment, and with the Arizona State Highway Department. He also held a commission as a "Special member of the Tucson Police Department with the rank of Patrolman." A civil service commission examination card from 1938 for Patrolman, Second Class, and his TPD identification card from 1940 were with his things. In the latter part of 1940, he was recommended via telegram to the Marine Corps by Acting Chief of Police Ben West of the City of Tucson

[Editor's note: We would like to put a bit of misinformation to rest. An interesting but tangential addition to the stories surrounding Nolan took place on January 21, 1934, when the Tucson Police Department captured the John Dillinger gang. A patrolman named Earl Nolan played a pivotal role in the arrest of Harry Pierpont, the "triggerman" of the Dillinger mob. When the stories reached the local papers, it seemed that a few Tucson residents assumed that the patrolman was none other than "our" Earl Nolan. Even though Nolan himself had never even vaguely alluded to the event, we had heard about it once or twice and decided to do some research. The current TPD historian informed us that they did not have the personnel records from that time period. However, with the help of Stan Benjamin, local law enforcement historian, expert on the Dillinger episode, and author of *Without A Shot Fired: The 1934 Capture of the Dillinger Gang in Tucson*, we uncovered some amazing coincidences. We had found that Tucson was still a relatively small town in the 1930s, the Chamber of Commerce estimating around 32,000 residents in 1930; and a blurry newspaper photo of the TPD force from February of 1934 pictured only 37 men. According to Mr. Benjamin, the number of personnel varied depending on what services were needed, and at times there were substantially fewer on the force. The young patrolman involved in the capture was indeed named Earl Nolan, and in a startling coincidence, he was often called "Mickey," the nickname for Michael. However, his middle initial turned out to be "C." Mr. Benjamin produced two photographs from his files, both labeled "Earl Nolan," and they were definitely not our man. At least now the reasons for the confusion were obvious: two young men in the same small town on the same small police force in the same era, both with the name Earl Nolan, coupled with the Mickey/Michael connection! Another truly strange coincidence was that before he joined TPD, Earl C. Nolan had worked for the U.S. Forest Service in the 1920s, the same organization Michael Earl Nolan would retire from in the 1970s.]

Prior to his military service and from January of 1946 through 1955, Nolan was employed full- or part-time with Austad Steel Construction Company as a welder (both electric arc and oxyacetylene), an equipment operator, a superintendent, and a steel structural designer, e.g., frames, trusses, and tanks. He worked the summer months while attending the College of Engineering. Detailed in a June 26, 1953 article from the *Arizona Daily Star*, "'Papago Statler' is Plush Hotel," the largest job he supervised was the construction of forty-two large steel-shell water tanks with reinforced Gunite interiors for use by Papago cattlemen on the Sells Papago Indian Reservation (currently, Tohono O'odham). On the rambling 400-mile course of the project, from the border with Mexico to the desert and the mountain foothills near Casa Grande, the tanks were often miles apart, sometimes thirty to forty miles deep in the desert. The project took place in the hottest part of the summer, and included the supervision of between twenty and twenty-five men. Nolan was, by the way, quite complimentary of the quality of the camp cooking. According to the article, a project trailer, "a converted aircraft moving van with the dimensions of a boxcar and the luxuries of a model home," was provided for sleeping accommodations. An interesting anecdote is that Nolan himself slept outside. He always did say that the perfect bedroom would have a ceiling which could open to the night sky.

On April 9, 1946, Nolan obtained his contractor's license in cast stone, ornamental plaster, cement, and concrete. His work was flawless. His daughter remembers an incident when he was laying concrete for a patio at John Austad's house. It was on a weekend and he took her along to watch. After the patio was completed and still wet, she inadvertently walked across it, leaving a six-year-old's trail of footprints. Her father was not annoyed with her, chuckled, and got his tools out again.

The December 21, 1946 edition of the weekly Tucson publication, the *Old Pueblo Sun Dial*, referring to Nolan as one of the "Old Pueblo's greats in the football and boxing world" and citing his "field promotion under fire on Guadalcanal," announced, "'The King' is now a member of the Old Pueblo's Fire Fighters." Six months earlier, the June 28, 1946 *Tucson Daily Citizen* reported that he had been successful in his examination for the Tucson Fire Department; he became a firefighter and driver with

TFD, where he worked until May 4, 1951, resigning to enter the University. During his firefighting days, he was a member of the Arizona State Firemen's Association. According to Bob Allison, the man's bravery was once more very apparent in the fire department; he stated in his January 1, 1957 column that Nolan "made at least one dramatic rescue of a trapped person, seriously endangering his own life and suffering severe burns in the process." On another occasion, Nolan's wife mentioned injuries to his eyes which he had suffered in a fire.

Nolan returned to the University of Arizona in 1951 and earned a Bachelor of Science Degree in Civil Engineering on May 25, 1955, while working summers as a superintendent not only for Austad Steel but also for Carl Larmour. Allison referred to Nolan's decision to return to the University as making "a decision that was brave in a more quiet way." Indeed, his decision would serve as an inspiration and an example to others over the years. He had become a strong proponent of getting a college degree, and felt that it could open many doors which otherwise might remain closed. His area of interest in the 1930s had been mining engineering, and he regretted spending too much time on athletics and not enough time on his studies during that first go-round at the U of A. His focus on athletics, coupled with the fact that he had been his own sole means of support from an early age and often had to work several hours a day when school was in session, had taken a great amount of his time. He now had to apply himself doubly hard to neutralize that first batch of grades! This he did. And his second course of study was a rigorous one; in addition to his civil engineering classes, he also studied electrical and mechanical engineering, physics, chemistry, mathematics, geology, economics, and anthropology. Nolan's belief in education, as well as his legacy at the University, would live on; not only his daughter, but his three grandchildren all earned their degrees at his alma mater.

On March 17, 1955, Nolan received a certificate from the Guard of Saint Patrick, a tradition on engineering campuses since 1903, naming him a Knight of Saint Patrick. According to our research, the award was given for leadership, excellence in character, and exceptional contributions to the college and students. In their farewell song, to the tune of "So Long, It's Been Good to Know You," the class of 1955 commemorated him as "our 'Congressman,' with 'a bit' of a drawl." He was as well liked by his classmates during the 1950s, as he had been in the 1930s.

During his second tenure at the University, the new freshman made several younger-generation friends, whose devotion lasted a lifetime. One of them, John Higgins, sat quite somberly at Nolan's service almost forty years later. Another of his classmates, Hobart Bauhan, sent a letter to the family on December 28, 1991, after learning of his friend's passing. It read in part, "What a man! Such a kind and gentle person for such a giant of a man, a fighting Marine who led a battalion into Iwo Jima and our first All-American football player at the University. All of you can be so proud of Mike. He and I first met in a Statics class at the UA in '51. We sat in back of the class and tried to figure out what the instructor was talking about, and we used to study together for exams." Bauhan also fondly remembered the "best Mexican food in the world" that Mrs. Nolan would fix after the study sessions. It was obvious from the letter that Bauhan treasured Nolan's friendship even after he moved away from Tucson: "Mike and I seldom met after college, but we always sent cards. He is the godfather to my son. My flag is at half-mast for a week."

In the period of time when Mike Nolan received his degree, civil engineering was an extremely complex and encompassing discipline that incorporated numerous fields of engineering which have since been splintered off into separate professions. This was exemplified by the incredible diversity of his notes, designs, and calculations. It was also in the era before personal computers, so all of the extensive computations, tables, and sketches were generated by hand. Nolan held in his head a comprehensive knowledge of the design and construction of the structures required in a civilized society – and how to ensure the safety and durability of those structures. His notes and calculations revealed an astonishing expertise in the field. He took his studies to heart, and every project received his intense concentration.

Fortunately, many of his U of A notebooks and projects have been preserved. The surviving civil engineering course notebooks covered bridge design, truss design, reinforced concrete design, steel mill design, indeterminates (e.g., beams, trusses, girders, loads, spans, stress, deflection, and moment), electricity, hydraulics, sewage treatment, and water purification. A sampling of the sketches contained in the well-organized notebooks revealed more of the scope of his education, covering designs as varied as basement walls, pile foundations, beams reinforced for compression, reinforced concrete stairs, overhanging beams, gravity and cantilever retaining walls, girders, water purification and sedimentation tanks, sewage treatment facilities, footings, steel beams, and connections, both riveted and welded. Numbered among the large, hand-drawn assignments were a detailed sewer project (design and operation), with pump, flow, wet well, and mass diagram data; a neighborhood sewer project, from the plant through individual houses, with pipe diameters and slopes; a road and sidewalk design, noting grades and sub-grades, pavement, finish surface, expansion joints, curbs, and an intersection; a road diagram accident analysis, showing point of accident, degrees of curves, sight distances, and gradient; a mass diagram of a mine railroad in the Tucson Mountains; a plan and profile of a mine railroad, showing elevations and bearings. Of particular note were beautiful and intricate renderings of bridge and truss design, which the family had framed and now display proudly.

Along with the seemingly endless pages of in-depth mathematical calculations, we also found special reports, which gave some insight into his inquiring mind. One fascinating paper combined Nolan's love of anthropology, archaeology, and history with his love of engineering, as he presented a detailed analysis of ancient mound-building techniques and compared them to modern engineering standards. He examined the Etowah Mound in Georgia and the Spiro Mound in Oklahoma, detailing the methods of construction and the possible uses of the structures.

Nolan evaluated the Etowah site for stability of soil for earth construction, with a graphic analysis of slope stability, and compared it against modern approved construction methods, finding the construction "competent." He did make an amusing circumspect remark: "Of course theory is not needed on structures as old as Etowah; however, it provides an interesting pastime to check the old against the new." He computed the volume of the gigantic structure and the amount of earth used, and speculated that "it is possible that the great structure was once an ancient Gibraltar." Regarding his calculations of the labor involved, Nolan estimated that using current-day hand standards based upon a seven-day work week, eight hours a day, "1,000 men with wheelbarrows would take more than one year to build this structure. Without wheelbarrows, 1,000 men would take three years." He determined the use of clay on Mound C to be an excellent choice and stated, "Only clay of all the soils has the cohesive properties suitable to form and retain this design." He diagramed a cross-section of the construction by the type of soil used, and commented, "The fact that clay was used in Section 4, Plate IV, instead of the less cohesive soils, shows sound engineering reasoning." Nolan did disagree with the relative placement of the sand, stating that it was one place the ancient engineer failed; water did not drain properly. He concluded that if Mound C was originally used as a burial site as had been proposed, "a change such as suggested above would have resulted in finding human remains instead of richly fertilized soil in Section 1 of Mound C."

Spiro Mound was chosen due to its unusual architectural design; the great mound of Spiro was conical. It was much destroyed but similar to the Hughes Mound in Arkansas. No evidence seemed to exist of its reputed inner chamber. Nolan noted that the structure extended five feet below ground level and that six inches of settlement was the norm. Using the old description, in conjunction with information on the Hughes Mound, to draw a replica of the Spiro cone, he concluded that "the slope angles of the cone are well within reason....Again we have the problem of burying the dead in clay soil and the badly decomposed remains that were found." Appended to the report were beautifully hand-drawn maps, diagrams, and elevations.

It was obvious that he both thoroughly enjoyed the subject matter and dedicated himself wholeheartedly to his engineering curriculum.

Nolan continued his education throughout his life, including several correspondence venues, e.g., the International Correspondence School, the American School, and La Salle Extension University, in addition to the U.S. Marine Corps Institute mentioned earlier. He took courses in civil, structural, and mechanical engineering, surveying, electricity, blue prints, shop layout, machine shop, American history, physics, speed-reading, Spanish, and one course in French. He was, by the way, fluent in Spanish and found ample occasion to use it at many times over the years. (Colonel

Rackerby's comments notwithstanding!)

After receiving his degree at age 44, Mike Nolan worked as a pit engineer, and was also responsible for drilling and blasting at the open-pit mining operation in Silverbell, Arizona, for Isbell Construction Company, from July of 1955 through May of 1957. He was in charge of all engineering, surveying, and heavy equipment. In his words, "This work consisted of laying out triangulation stations and traverse lines in order to compute all ore, leach, and waste hauled from the two open pits at Silverbell; design, layout, and supervision of the construction of more than eight miles of haul roads, as well as ramp roads, and slope and toe lines for the operational crews." Additionally, he "figured all the surfacing materials for roadways, all water pipeline network, and sewers for the town of Silverbell (1957 construction)."

As engineer for drilling and blasting, he laid out and "supervised all drilling patterns and hole loading in order that the maximum quantity of muck could be realized per pound of powder," and was responsible for the critical quarterly ore and waste yardage computations. "New types of blasting primes and agents were tried with success, raising production from 4 cubic yards of rock per pound of powder to 6.5 cubic yards per pound of powder. Cost was also reduced due to the use of ammonium nitrate agents instead of the compounds generally used. Slope and toe lines were laid out and checked. Holes had to be drilled in patterns and depths so as to ensure maximum breakage without disturbing the walls of the pit. Holes then had to be loaded and delayed in such a way as to break the burden to the front, but leave a clean, hard wall in the rear."

Nolan supervised fifteen to twenty men, twelve Chury and rotary drills, and four electric shovels; was in charge of all blasting; and moved between 60,000 and 104,000 cubic yards of waste and copper ore per 24-hour period, amounting to a $36,400+ daily operation.

From May 26, 1957, through March 1, 1958, he was employed as an engineer for Utah Construction Company (C.I.A. Utah Pacific, Ltd.), and held a supervisory position in charge of engineering and excavation for the mill site area on the Toquepala Project open-pit copper mine in Peru (near Incapuquio, Tacna), at approximately 11,000 feet in altitude. This encompassed all pioneering work and layout of engineering work, grading, supervision of all drilling and blasting for the excavation, hauling, and dumping. In Nolan's words, "The first phase of this job entailed the estimating of men and machinery necessary to complete the excavation of more than 5,000,000 cubic yards of rock. The second phase of the job was the checking and revising of primary plans for making the various cuts through the mountains and out of the mountainsides. The actual operational phase of the job consisted of laying out the work for three engineering crews; heavy-equipment operators – thirty tractors, six 4" to 12" rotary drills, six 2 1/2-cubic-yard shovels, thirty-five 14- to 16-cubic-yard Euclid trucks; and maintenance and mechanical crews, a combined total of from fifty to five hundred men.

"This job was all engineering. For example, some of the mountainside cuts of 500,000 cubic yards were as high as 300 feet. This necessitated constant engineering supervision to establish slope and toe lines for the drilling and blasting crews. Blasting holes had to be spaced and loaded correctly so as to not destroy the stability of the slope. In this type of work, 30-foot benches were established with 20-foot-wide safety benches every 60 feet. Constant engineering was needed in laying of road and railroad slope and toe lines, and road alignments."

Other engineering positions held by Nolan were in 1955 with Luepke and Marum Associates, and 1958 with Maddock and Associates Engineers. Beginning in July of 1958 until his employment with the U.S. Forest Service, he was also employed as a survey party chief, for the Stevens, Pafford Associates civil engineering firm in Tucson, engaged in land surveying for subdivisions and improvement districts, lot surveys, and mineral surveys, as well as inspection of street and subdivision construction. He found the perfect position in early 1959.

Arizona Highway Department road crew. Nolan (second from left), 1936.

Nolan, taking a break.

Earl Nolan, measuring traffic usage for the Arizona Highway Department, 1936.

Nolan, firefighter and driver, Tucson Fire Department, 1946-1951.

Tucson Fire Department, 1951. Nolan in front of Menlo Park Fire Station.

Andes Mountains, Peru, 1957. Nolan (right), engineer, Toquepala open-pit copper mine project.

CHAPTER FIFTEEN

United States Forest Service
"Lasting Monuments"

MIKE NOLAN BECAME THE FIRST FOREST ENGINEER for the Coronado National Forest on February 9, 1959, a career from which he retired on January 1, 1975. The 1,875,000-acre forest, with its seven ranger districts and high volume of yearly visitors, provided him with a perfect opportunity to use his diverse engineering skills. The job description specified, "Sound and mature judgment, initiative, originality, creative thinking and a thorough understanding of engineering concepts and practices are required to properly perform the duties of the position." This endeavor was not an easy one: "The nature of the forest's topography, diversity of conditions, geographical dispersion, and range of assigned functions make engineering activities broad and complex. Rough mountainous terrain over much of the forest lands, varied weather conditions, freezing and thawing temperatures, elevation differences, unstable soil conditions, limited operating funds to complete projects, shortage of trained assistants, and complex ownership of land are problems frequently encountered." The responsibilities of the forest engineer were, in one way or another, crucial to all major functions and operations in the Coronado. They found the right person in Nolan.

In 1964, Bob Thomas of the *Arizona Daily Star* stated, "The burly chief engineer for the Coronado National Forest has tackled a lot of big jobs in his Forest Service career. He has supervised construction of bridges, cabins, roads, picnic and camping areas, ranger stations, dams, watershed improvements, erosion controls and wells." In a way the position was that of "Renaissance engineer," an all-encompassing and challenging assignment. A U.S. Forest Service report stated that Nolan "donated a yearly average of 120 man-days of work performed before and after daily duty hours and on holidays and weekends." The scope of his responsibilities would seem daunting, at best.

Nolan was in charge of all engineering: development and implementation of overall engineering and construction long- and short-range plans, consisting of new construction schedules, the Forest Transportation Plan (which became critical in areas as diverse as timber management, fire control, and recreation), fiscal-year work programs, environmental plans and upgrades, and anticipated needs; budgeting and administration of Forest Roads and Trails funds; preparation of designs and specifications, estimating, surveying, layout, and construction, including roads, trails, bridges, dams, and buildings; inventory; all structural, mechanical, operational, and safety inspection, maintenance, and repair. He took the safety of existing structures quite seriously and set up regular schedules for routine maintenance and repair. He was particularly sensitive to any possible electrical hazards, considering them a high priority. His old firefighting days were no doubt still fresh in his mind.

The vast Coronado Forest — and its attendant engineering responsibilities for design, construction, and maintenance — encompassed 40 administrative sites, which ranged in size from single buildings to small communities with necessary utilities, and included guard stations, lookouts, ranger stations, residences, warehouses, work centers, and the visitors center; 1,781 total miles of roadways; 882 miles of trails; 420 cattle guards; 50 bridges; 12 large masonry canyon crossings; watershed improvements; 11 Class A and B dams, measuring from 25 to 125 feet high, plus approximately 1,500 range dams; wells, water systems, and sanitation, with the necessary bacterial testing and chemical analysis; sewage projects; erosion control and erosion docks; 75,000 feet of 18"- to 72"-diameter metal culverts; solid waste programs and 11 open pits; electric plants and installations; heating and ventilation systems; picnic, camping, and recreation areas, with all necessary utilities; permittee constructions, such as summer homes, the ski lift, Smithsonian installations, and University of Arizona installations; television, radio, and telephone towers; and cooperative construction with Arizona counties and the state. Nolan was also responsible for the forest radio and telephone communications systems, and for improvements in the fire-communication network; all boundary and right-of-way surveys, cadastral and aerial; mapping and corrections, e.g., transportation plan maps, locations of proposed roads, trails, and dams; complete historical records of all roads; and signage. Signage alone consisted of installation, repair, and maintenance of 3,681 road directional signs, 862 trail signs, and 4,500 traffic regulatory signs. The vandalizing of these signs always confounded him; he sometimes even came upon the act of vandalism as it was actually wantonly occurring. Wanton destruction was not part of his makeup.

There was more to the job description. Nolan was in charge of engineering personnel; heavy-equipment operators; maintenance men; construction equipment and compressors; and a large fleet of up to 100 vehicles, valued at approximately $700,000 and ranging from 1/2-ton to 15-ton capacity, in addition to tractors, end loaders, road graders, and other heavy equipment. His responsibilities covered the efficient operation of all the vehicles, cost and use records, repair, inspections, assignment of use, and the determination of replacement and additional needs. He was in charge of engineering recruitment, which entailed meeting with U of A professors, interviewing interested senior students prior to graduation, and hiring engineering students to work on summer programs each year. Plus, he reviewed and evaluated the results of the monthly field-safety meetings, promoted a safe working environment, and developed safety consciousness in engineering personnel.

Of major importance were critical emergency situations, involving forest fires, landslides, and flooding. Many times Nolan was called in the middle of the night to deploy to the location of a fire and was sometimes on site for days. He went so far as to have a second phone line installed at his home, dedicated only to these emergency calls, so that he could be reached at any time. His bag and survival kit were always packed and ready to go at a moment's notice. The family had it down to a routine to get him out the door quickly, but then the long hours would begin, waiting for his safe return.

The number of personnel supervised by Nolan ranged from 16 to 30. It is of interest to note that his dedication to these individuals was evident, as well. In an August 17, 1964 article in the *Star*, "Two Forest Service Veterans Honored," it was Mike Nolan who was praising the two longtime employees, Rudolph Kambitsch and Lloyd Harris, for their depth of knowledge and skill in the field. Both of these men became his friends, friendships which lasted long after retirement from the Forest Service.

Along with his myriad "hands-on" responsibilities, the USFS chief engineer performed many administrative functions: staff advisor to the forest supervisor, regarding engineering plans, policy, programs, and objectives; representative of the forest supervisor in discussions with federal, state, and county agencies, including the Department of Commerce, National Park Service, Bureau of Public Roads, Arizona Game and Fish Department, Arizona Highway Department, and county engineers, as well as with engineering companies, utility companies, water users associations, contractors, and private landowners; representative of the contracting officer; acting forest supervisor, as designated; member of the Forest Board of Survey; accident investigating officer; supervisor of training activities; and member of the Forest Fire Control Organization. He was also charged with reviewing special-use permits and applications for power lines, water power, and road rights-of-way; checking plans and construction work performed on the forest by other agencies; overseeing road cooperative agreements; and preparing numerous periodic or special reports and analyses.

Nolan was prolific in his written communications; documents which were located among his papers provided an insight into the breadth of some of his concerns, responsibilities, and interests, together with his priorities for the allocation of the funds he was budgeted. One of his primary concerns, implicit in the job, was always financial. He prepared meticulous cost estimates and analyses for road and building construction, maintenance, and restoration. A 1970 road construction cost analysis consisted of 127 factors from 1969, plus a unit cost comparison with 1962. Another analysis of estimates per one mile of roadway broke down construction costs in terms of width of road and percentage of side slope involved. A 1970 building cost analysis contained 33 factors, and provided a compound-interest formula for subsequent years.

As an example of the particular and varied nature of his duties, a review of a September 16, 1971 engineering report for the Nogales Ranger District showed that in addition to long-range plans, Nolan prepared inspection and immediate-recommendation/solution reports. The issues covered for just this limited area included new building and road construction, as well as repair or replacement due to outdated or dangerous conditions – such as termite infestation of adobe construction from the 1930s, and improper drainage in road construction from that same era, causing problems with road width and tread, and failing to meet current traffic standards; correction of the erosion of creek and canyon banks, the washout of a road, and the deposit of silt into a lake, entailing construction of a reinforced channel lining, installation of culverts, and provision of a silting basin; safe drinking water and the addition of a horizontal well; sanitation and sewage improvements, involving the installation of vault-type toilets; collection and hauling of solid waste; correction of various safety hazards, e.g., his design of an engineered roofing structure to rectify a problem with a permittee's storage tank; and reports on fleet maintenance, fuel orders, and estimates for the fire-suppression season.

As would be expected, the engineering reports for the entire forest were vastly more varied and comprehensive.

Citizen safety and environmental protection were among his foremost concerns. Nolan deeply appreciated the exceptional beauty of the forest area and knew that it attracted many visitors. He was a strong proponent for road and trail safety and proper maintenance, believing that the transportation system was the most critical; and he took very seriously the "great responsibility we have to the American public by ensuring safe road travel." The basic transportation system was constructed during the 1930s by Civilian Conservation Corps (CCC) and Works Progress Administration (WPA) crews, and was upgraded in large part by Nolan, who rigorously inspected to safeguard the user. To quote the introductory remarks in a paper he wrote on September 10, 1973, referencing guidelines for the transportation system, and outlining his priorities and recommendations, "As administrator of the Coronado's transportation system for the past fifteen years, I recognize that those roads used by our Forest visitors are our greatest responsibility." In order to best use the available roadway funds, he explained, "I concentrate more on runoff-control structures in the forms of correct road crowning, road superelevations, crown ditches, side road ditches, culverts, and placement of stable material on road treads.

"The Coronado's roads are used by people for a number of diversified reasons, and the people expect to use them on a yearlong basis. Some roads have excellent recreation areas; some have scenery not equaled anywhere else in the world; some pass through the habitats of exotic birds and animals; some are shortcuts for general traffic; some have famous names; and some pass through famous areas. Regardless of the drawing power, people by the hundreds of thousands travel through our trust lands each year. All of the people expect and receive safe passage over our transportation system roads. It is my responsibility that a prudent effort has been made to ensure this trust." It was of critical importance to Nolan that all roads and trails, available to the public in any way, were properly maintained at all times. As he had throughout his life, he took his responsibilities to heart.

Nolan's lifelong interest in history surfaced as he penned an extensive history of the activities of the explorer Francisco Vasquez de Coronado in the area, as well as the history of the Santa Catalina Ranger District, detailing the roads, trails, administrative buildings, water systems and testing, solid waste disposal, sewage, dams, recreation sites, and land surveys. And as the first engineer for the Coronado, he also prepared future administrative guidelines, establishing the task breakdowns and work hours involved for the position.

At this phase of his life, Mike Nolan was often mentioned in the newspapers with respect to local Forest Service projects and issues, including the construction of a three-foot-wide, eight-mile-long trail connecting Sabino and Bear Canyons, plus additional main trails in each of the ranger districts, to be used by "hikers, nature lovers and packers, forest rangers to haul supplies to fire lookout stations, and firefighters to reach blazes" – *Arizona Daily Star*, July 18, 1964, "Sabino-Bear Canyon Trail Set," by Bob Thomas; the improved and more scenic road to Parker Canyon Lake, which would solve washout problems – *Arizona Daily Star*, February 1, 1970, "Rod and Gun" column, by Tom Foust; the rebuilding of unsafe portions of Ruby Road – *Arizona Daily Star*, August 6, 1972, "Rebuilding Ruby Road – Good or Bad," co-written by Mike Nolan and Pete Cowgill; Nolan's environmental concerns, and his advocacy of reseeding the slopes of the new Mt. Graham highway – *Arizona Daily Star*, July 12, 1973, "On The Trail" column, "An Endless Road," by Pete Cowgill; the new sewer systems in Sabino Canyon and Rucker Canyon, addressing both pollution abatement in the canyon streams and improvement of aesthetics, e.g., revegetation, landscaping, and fertilizing the area at natural pH values – *Tucson Daily Citizen*, December 4, 1973, "Sabino's image coming clean," by Edward G. Stiles.

Naturally, always his own man and holding strong convictions regarding the safety of his fellow human beings, Nolan was sometimes involved in controversy. One of these events was chronicled in a *Star* article, "County Crews Battling Deep Catalina Snows...Too Much Weight For New Structure," of December 20, 1961. He had strongly protested the engineering of a new Palisades Ranger Station to be built at an altitude of 7,945 feet in the Santa Catalina Mountains; the structure had been designed by a New Mexico architect and approved by the regional Forest Service office in Albuquerque. Nolan maintained that the roof was in no way strong enough to withstand the weight of a heavy snowfall, but he was overruled by others who argued that the area would not get heavy snow. Shortly after the construction of the $18,000 building (approximately $140,000 by today's standards), three and one-half feet of snow piled up on top, collapsed the roof, and the building was a complete loss. Luckily, no one was inside!

Not only did Nolan have to contend with perennial budgetary constraints relating to improvements he considered critical, as the job description foretold that he would, but he also had to contend with public differences of opinion. At times, he found himself with a perspective different from that of *Star* Outdoor Editor Pete Cowgill. In the above-mentioned article "Rebuilding Ruby Road – Good or Bad," one such difference surfaced over whether a particular stretch of road should have been improved or left as it was, and Cowgill invited him to co-write an article on the issue. Nolan enumerated his reasons why the substandard and dangerous stretch of roadway had definitely needed to be modified, a roadway originally built in the 1930s and currently showing a growth in traffic volume, reaching 15,000 vehicles a year with a yearly increase of 15 percent. The road had been improved at his behest, a concern shared by its main users; most notably, a quarter-mile section had deteriorated into what he characterized as a potential "death trap." The condition of the road had been completely unacceptable to him, and improving it was a priority. Cowgill's position was that the road was a "scenic route," and there "was nothing wrong with the old Ruby Road if you accepted it for what is was – a narrow, winding, at times one-lane road that had to be driven at a slow pace." All users contacted after the improvements were happy with both the engineering and the aesthetics, and, as always, Nolan had accepted personal responsibility for their safety. The increase in allowable speed was actually minimal, but the increase in safety was immeasurable. Even with their difference in perspective over the project, Cowgill expressed his ongoing confidence in Mike Nolan's "honesty, integrity, dedication" and "engineering competence," stating, "He's a good man and I'm really glad he is the Coronado National Forest Engineer."

The tributes written to Nolan at the end of his engineering tenure would reflect the many varied challenges the position presented.

Upon his retirement, he received many letters and cards from those he had worked with in the USFS, all reflecting the extraordinary and lasting impact he had on the Coronado Forest, and wishing him well in the coming years. Although his longtime supervisor, Clyde Doran, had left the Coronado by then, recently arrived Forest Supervisor K. R. Weissenborn, characterizing Nolan as "very conscientious and cooperative," thanked him for a job well done, and expressed sentiments that would appear over and over again: "Your accomplishments while Forest Engineer will benefit all of us for many years to come."

Recreation and Lands Staff Officer James L. Perry stated, "The Coronado National Forest has shown much improvement in roads and trails and other structures during your tenure as Forest Engineer. Although many projects required considerable effort to be brought into final form, I believe they are a testament to the fine engineering skills that you displayed on the Forest. I am certain that the many personnel who have passed through the Coronado during their Forest Service careers have benefited greatly from your counsel and service."

Range and Wildlife Staff Officer Charles R. Ames wrote that "the whole Coronado will miss your expertise and ability. Your knack for getting things done in spite of seemingly insurmountable obstacles stands out as a personal monument to you. Your early Marine training clearly shows in the axiom 'The difficult we do immediately; the impossible takes just a little longer.' As the first full-fledged engineer on the Coronado, you have left many lasting monuments during your sixteen-year tenure. This is a record not likely to be duplicated."

From Forest Engineer John P. Haynes, Tonto National Forest in Phoenix, came the following remarks: "My Forest Service career has been greatly enriched by knowing and working with you. Your high character added to the stature of the whole outfit. You generously shared the color and excitement of your personality and experiences with those who visited with you. As an R.O. [Regional Office] specialist, my visits to the Coronado were something special. Your dedication and hard work helped me and others to do our jobs and contributed more than your share to achieving regional goals. Now that I am on the Tonto, I rely upon your example. I guess what I am saying is 'thank you.'"

On July 4, 2001, after his own retirement from the USFS, Haynes sent the family a letter: "I met your father when I was a young engineer with the Forest Service. My older brother had attended the U of A in the 1930s. When he came to visit, I asked him if he knew Mike Nolan when he was in school. He thought for a while and said he had not known a Mike Nolan, but he knew Earl Nolan. He said they called him 'King Kong' Nolan, and your father was the strongest man he ever knew. He told of the time his knee went out while throwing the discus. Earl came over, and with one hand threw him on his shoulder and carried him the quarter of a mile to Bear Down Gym without stopping; then he added, 'I weighed 200 pounds.'

"Some of my most memorable times were the times spent with your father." Haynes described an evening in Douglas, Arizona, spent with Nolan and a gentleman from the Washington office, who had also been a Marine officer and served on Iwo Jima. "They swapped stories all evening while I sat in amazement."

After Nolan retired, Haynes visited him and invited him along for a final inspection on a contract in the Coronado. "That was another enjoyable day for me," he wrote. At the end of the trip, Nolan laughed and said, "Just wait until Riley hears I went out and made an inspection." His good friend Santa Rita District Ranger Randolph Riley was also retired.

No doubt Nolan did enjoy that day.

Mike Nolan, forest engineer, United States Forest Service, 1959-1975.

Nolan (right), USFS civil engineer in charge of design, construction, and maintenance for the massive Coronado Forest.

Responsible for citizen safety and the protection of the environment, Nolan walks a section of the 882-mile trail system, used by hikers, forest rangers, and firefighters in the 1.875 million-acre Coronado National Forest, 1964.

At his desk, Nolan balances budgetary concerns with the broad and complex engineering projects on the Coronado.

Nolan (third row, second from right), Continental Divide Training Center, New Mexico, September 1965.

CHAPTER SIXTEEN

Family and Personal Life
A Life Well Lived

EARL NOLAN MARRIED HIS TRUE LOVE, the former Nellie Ahee, in a Catholic Nuptial Mass at All Saints Church in Tucson on June 12, 1946. He had shared a long history with the Ahee family, and was a frequent visitor at their home over the years. He and Nellie's brother Joe were teammates in track and field at Tucson High School; and during Nolan's University of Arizona years, he formed a friendship with her brother George, who became his weightlifting and football buddy. No doubt their petite and vivacious sister Nellie caught his attention early on. In 1944, while on his only leave from the Marine Corps, Nolan asked her to marry him. She accepted, and they were married after he returned from the war.

Nellie was beautiful, intelligent, and an exceptional individual in her own right. The third of ten children, she was born on November 26, 1909, in the tiny borough of Scalp Level, Pennsylvania, to Solomon and Sara Haddad Ahee. The family moved to Arizona, first to Superior and eventually to Tucson, where Nellie attended Safford School and Tucson High School. By the many comments written in her *Tucsonian* yearbooks, it was obvious that she was a popular young woman, with a ready smile and kind words for her fellow classmates. An energetic student, she had many interests and participated in several extracurricular activities while at THS. She was a subscription manager for the *Tucsonian*; a sports editor for the award-winning *El Sahuaro* newspaper, "the only Spanish paper printed in any high school in the United States"; and a member of the Cervantes Club, Allegro Club girls' chorus, Dramatic Owls, Tennis Club, and Tuc-Hi Club (the local branch of the YWCA Girl Reserves). In her senior year, she performed in the operetta *Pickles*, "the quaint musical comedy of old Austria."

Although she had decided during high school that she wanted to become a teacher and had begun her studies at the University, Nellie's college years were put on hold for a while when she went to work full-time to support the family following the passing of her father. She graduated from the University of Arizona in May 1938, earning a Bachelor of Arts Degree in Education with a major in Spanish and a minor in English. As the years passed, she would continue her education through the U of A Graduate College and in professional workshops, focusing on speech pathology and language development, child development and psychology, educational philosophy and methodology of mathematics and reading, and English. After securing her teaching certificate on July 18, 1938, Nellie taught briefly in Prescott, Arizona; then returned home to Tucson, where she taught first grade, as well as English to non-English-speaking students, in Tucson School District No. 1, until her retirement in December 1974. She taught at El Rio, Davis, Tully, Howell, and Van Buskirk Elementary Schools, with a brief foray out of the country during the Nolans' move to Peru when she taught at the company school.

Nellie loved her students and she was dedicated to teaching first grade; she believed that it was of crucial importance to start children off with good basic skills and a love of learning which would serve them throughout their lives. During the course of her 36-year career, she gave all of her lessons, from reading and science projects to music and art, her greatest creativity and effort. Widely respected by both her professional peers and the community itself, she was frequently asked to evaluate new programs or teaching methods, such as Addison-Wesley Math. She served on the science resource team, and was an enthusiastic and active cooperating teacher in the University of Arizona student teacher program. Nellie Nolan was an outstanding educator; she was referred to by her friends and associates as a "wonderful woman," and a "superb" teacher. A June 1971 Evaluation Report referred to her as a "master teacher in all areas," whose students showed the "effects of expert instruction." Mrs. Nolan had excellent relationships with the parents and family members of her students; as the years progressed, she often found herself teaching the children of her early students, with younger brothers and sisters looking forward to the time when they could be in her class. In fact, according to the evaluation, she was highly regarded by all concerned: Not only did parents enjoy helping her as volunteer aides in the classroom, but Mrs. Nolan was also "a reliable friend and assistant to each of the staff" and "cooperative and helpful with colleagues." To quote the concluding words, there was "no teacher more dedicated or loyal than she." Upon her retirement, Tucson Public School Superintendent Thomas L. Lee wrote, "I have known Mrs. Nolan for years. She is a truly exceptional person, one who exemplifies the best in education." Over the years, she received many cards, letters, phone calls, and visits from her former students and their parents – many crediting her with her students' later successes in life by getting them started on the right foot.

Shortly after their 1946 marriage, Nolan himself designed and built their first family home in the foothills of "A" Mountain near the Santa Cruz River, even pouring concrete furniture since money was tight. He very much enjoyed working with wood and hand-made several other pieces of furniture, crafting bookcases and a beautiful round tamarack table with tooled legs, all of which the family still has. In every way, it was a lovely home with the proverbial white-picket fence, a large picture window, french doors, a volcanic rock fireplace, built-in bookcases, an oversized tiled bathtub, a thirty-foot kitchen, and a huge tree-filled backyard with a masonry barbeque pit. The family lived there until their trip to Peru in the late 1950s. Nolan did build to last, and that first home still appears to be in great shape today. One thing is certain: it housed a lot of happy memories.

Nolan had a true talent for creating warm and inviting living environments. When they returned from Peru, the Nolans purchased a new home which he remodeled, adding "a few personal touches." He again did all of the work himself, complete with perfectly matched brickwork – a dining-room addition with a wood-paneled ceiling, a patio wall and curved retaining wall, tree wells, and planter boxes; a new carport with decorative block walls and wrought-iron columns; a new concrete driveway and walkways; a picturesque back porch with heavy wooden beams; landscaping from scratch, with olive, mimosa, pepper, and mulberry trees, rose and cactus gardens, hibiscus and bougainvillea, a mint patch (for summertime iced tea), and several flower beds which often did double duty growing chiles; and, of course, floor-to-ceiling shelves to house his ever-growing book collection. Found among his papers were copies of the hand-diagramed plans of the remodel specs he submitted to the City of Tucson.

With his many projects, coupled with his wife's "green thumb" and classic taste, the result was a much cherished family home. Nellie Nolan was a meticulous homemaker, with talents that rivaled those of her professional career. Not only was she a world-class cook, she also sewed beautifully, a skill which was no doubt a necessity during the Depression but continued as a hobby. Nellie often made clothing for herself, as well as elaborate costumes for her daughter's dance recitals. She delighted in adding creations of her own to the home: intricate crocheted tablecloths, embroidered linens, and artistic accessories she lovingly made by hand. Memories abound once more of comfortable, light-filled rooms accented with healthy green houseplants, vases of homegrown flowers, and family photographs; rooms decked colorfully for the Christmas season; the sounds of music and laughter; and visions of the Nolan family gathered around the dinner table each night, sharing their stories from the day.

Michael Earl Nolan was a devoted husband, father, and grandfather, who knew the importance of family life. He was sentimental, caring, and a steadfast source of strength and comfort. Throughout their almost forty-year marriage, Earl and Nellie closely shared life's highs and lows. Their marriage was for life, the bond only becoming stronger over the years. Nolan's constancy and commitment to his wife were obvious. He had seen her work to support the large Ahee family when her father passed away in 1931, at the height of the Depression. After the family lost its breadwinner, Nellie had taken it upon herself to assume her father's position at their business, The Fair, a clothing and dry goods store on Congress Street in downtown Tucson. Due to the ill health of her mother, she also took a primary role in raising the younger children, as well as sharing the day-to-day cooking responsibilities. Earl valued her tireless spirit and courage, her strength of character, intelligence, discipline, and determination. Against the odds, she had accomplished the almost impossible, and she had won his unending admiration. In the years that followed, he highly respected his wife's commitment and exceptional skills as a teacher; he was very supportive, helped with setting up her classroom, and never missed one of the holiday shows starring her first-graders! He lovingly commemorated the years of their marriage with romantic gold charms for her bracelet, and never missed her birthday or Valentine's Day. In their years together, he always strove to make her life easier and more enjoyable. She, in turn, provided for him the stable and comforting home life which had eluded him as a child. As mentioned earlier, it did not hurt that she was one of the best cooks on the planet! Family vacations were the highpoint of Nolan's year, and each trip he managed to drive by way of the Grand Canyon, where he and his wife had honeymooned.

 A year into their marriage, the Nolans' daughter, Nellie Jean, was born. She followed in her parents' footsteps, and obtained a Master of Arts Degree in Government with a minor in Counseling and Guidance from the University of Arizona. Married to author John David Krygelski, Jean is currently a book editor, focusing on both her father's and her husband's novels. After their retirements, the Nolans were overjoyed at the births of their grandson and twin granddaughters. All of the Nolans' grandchildren maintained the family tradition at the University. Michael John Nolan earned a Master of Fine Arts Degree in Studio Art. Michael is a professor of art and nationally acclaimed artist, whose works have been featured in multiple professional journals and annuals, and are shown in exhibitions across the United States. Dr. Karin Krygelski Nolan, married to computer engineer David Andrew Willard, received her Doctor of Philosophy Degree in Music Education with a minor in Educational Psychology. Karin is a highly accomplished music professor, conductor, researcher, and author. Sara Nolan McCallum, married to software engineer Jeffrey Richard McCallum, earned a Bachelor of Arts Degree in Journalism with a minor in Classics. Sara is the devoted and loving mother of the Nolans' two great-grandchildren, and relates with a smile that the youngest generation family members have already made some plans of their own for the future. Five-year-old Jean Belle Nolan McCallum wants to be a rock star when she grows up; and three-year-old Mally Paige Nolan McCallum would like to run as fast as a cheetah! One thing is certain: as time progresses, the family will remain forever grateful for the solid foundations provided for them many years earlier.

Whether it was the unpredictable nature of his early upbringing, the sum of his extraordinary life experiences, or a matter of his innate character, Nolan always did his utmost to provide a constant and secure haven for his family. A psychological assessment test which had come with a book he ordered, and which he took for fun, was found in his library. Of note was the question that asked what he rated as most important in life; Nolan checked "family." In an interesting aside, there was a fill-in question that asked for his biggest fears; he wrote "snakes" and "speeding drivers." When he took the engineering position in Peru, family housing was delayed a few months. During that time, he sent two letters nearly every day, one to his wife and one to his daughter. He vowed to never be separated again – and he kept his word.

Family life with Michael Earl Nolan was an incredible experience. He was quirky and playful, laughed easily, and always had time for his family. Nolan loved to play board and card games, and performed some rather spooky card tricks. In one of them, he would ask the other person to draw a card at random from the deck, and he would invariably guess the correct card on the first try. An astounding variation on the game involved rapidly flipping through the deck face-up, and asking the other person to select a card mentally. Nolan guessed the correct card every single time. On one occasion, his college-aged daughter inadvertently selected two cards in her mind. Her father looked up at her and said, "No. You picked two this time. We'll try it again." Whether he was just incredibly dexterous – both mentally and physically – or whether he was doing a little bit of mind reading, we will never know. Either way, it was great fun.

Nolan created a fantasy play world for his child, adding real-life magic for her. She loved the story of Peter Pan, so her father gave her a container of "pixie dust" – an Edgeworth tobacco tin full of powdered strawberry Jell-O – and provided her with exact instructions about the proper conditions that must be met to use the powder. She loved getting "supermarket samples" at the grocery store, so she would wake up to a breakfast with sausages cut into sample-sized pieces on a plate, toothpicks inserted exactly the way they did at the store, and each piece marked with a "5¢" sign. He took her on regular rock-hunting excursions, showed her how to "dowse" for water, built a replica of their house as a dollhouse for the backyard, and constructed four-foot-high Tinker Toy structures with all sorts of moving levers and spinning wheels.

Years later, he would take her to see his Forest Service projects on the weekends, and they would sing the entire way there and back, taking turns to pick a favorite song. On a more serious note, weeks before she was ready to enter as a freshman at the University of Arizona, he took her on a walking tour of the large campus so that it would feel familiar on her first day; needless to say, there were a lot of anecdotes and much laughter along the way. The excursion did eliminate her fear of the unknown, and provided a comfortable continuity between her experience and that of her father decades before.

There were many other activities to share, several of them involving nature. Nolan was interested in bird-watching, hoping to sight a yellow-bellied sapsucker or a copper-throated trogon, a bird which he maintained was so rare that it had never been seen! He enjoyed sitting on the porch and watching the awesome Arizona monsoon thunderstorms, loved it when it snowed in Tucson, made six-foot-tall snowmen complete with floppy hats and old-fashioned pipes, and could point out every constellation and planet in the night sky. And there were yearly traditions, like hanging the hundreds of Christmas lights around the house, putting up the flag on all the patriotic holidays (never forgetting the birthday of the Marine Corps), and making a $1 bet with his daughter before each U of A football game. Nolan, by the way, was rarely wrong on those bets; he would even get the point spread. He enjoyed entering the *Arizona Daily Star*'s weekly college football contest to pick the winners, and won 27 games of bowling, which he gave to his daughter. He also taught her how to mix mortar and be a hod carrier on his home projects, not to mention how to correctly perform the important tasks of tool-handing and iced tea-bringing.

When Nolan's grandchildren were babies, he stretched out his favorite blue satin quilt in the living room for them to lie on, and rigged up a colorful Yipes Stripes stuffed toy on the end of a pole. From his favorite chair, he would dangle the orange-and-white striped mouse over their heads like a mobile, much to their delight. Later, he invented creative and funny little games to play with them, like "puffball" games of catch and a chalkboard drawing game where they would all add their own personal touches to the pictures. He would play together with his grandchildren for hours on end, and enjoyed it as much as they did.

Nolan was an amazingly patient individual, often taking hours to explain algebra problems to his daughter or to painstakingly glue together a beloved object she had broken. She never heard him raise his voice. He took seriously every question that was asked of him and did his best to gently teach the lessons he had learned from life. All the while, he instilled values which would last a lifetime. Through the years, he always shared the responsibilities of child-rearing with his wife, even alternating days off work to care for his daughter when she was home sick. And he was an extraordinarily compassionate caregiver – never once failing to take her temperature or bring the scheduled dose of medicine, a glass of orange juice, a bowl of hot soup, or the daily "funnies" from the newspaper.

Earl Nolan loved the holidays and took the extra steps to make them memorable and fun for his family. On Valentine's Day, there were always beautiful heart-shaped boxes of chocolates. On Easter, he sat with the family and decorated eggs with really unique designs, notably Marines, and every member of the family would get a special chocolate Easter Rabbit from him. On Halloween, he would place a lighted skeleton mask on his teenaged daughter's bed to add a scary note to the day, and he would stock up on Whoppers and Mounds to pass out to the neighborhood trick-or-treaters.

On Christmas, he loved to sing carols with the family and truly relished sitting in the darkened living room with only the Christmas tree lights on. His favorite ornament was an old "Santy" with kindly eyes (which is still the first ornament to be put on the family Christmas tree each year). He loved holiday fruitcake, and his wife would make it from scratch for him every December. She also remembered to fill a bowl with the ribbon candy he had loved in his childhood. A good portion of Christmas day was spent playing together with the new toy his family would give him – usually something like a ring-toss or suction-cup dart game. He liked guessing what was in his presents, and focused on finding the bag of pistachios that his wife would try to disguise each year. She was very good at it; they never even rattled. And he played a perennial game with his daughter – "At the count of three, we both yell out what is in one of each other's presents." There was no surprise how that game turned out every time! Nolan's birthday was January 1 at 12:01 a.m., so the family would wake him up, sing to him, and give him his presents. He seemed to enjoy the tradition, but would immediately go back to bed after the festivities!

As noted before, Nolan looked forward to family vacations each year, and it was great fun to be with him. California was a favorite haunt of his. He rode the rides at Disneyland with his wife and daughter, and had a good time walking around Knott's Berry Farm and taking the boat trip out to Catalina Island – although he was puzzled about the passengers constantly circling the deck of the boat to the tune of "When the Saints Go Marching In." Most particularly, he loved the bridges – the Golden Gate, Oakland Bay, and Richmond-San Rafael – and must have "inadvertently" repeated driving that circle of bridges around the bay, until his wife finally picked up the map and led him into downtown San Francisco. One of the things he looked forward to on these trips was getting some fresh seafood, something he missed from his youth.

He also was interested in visiting the national parks – the Grand Canyon, Yosemite, Yellowstone, the Petrified Forest and Painted Desert, the Redwood Forest, and Grand Teton, staying in picturesque Jackson Hole, Wyoming. He was quite impressed by the beauty of Lake Coeur d'Alene in Idaho, and was especially interested in Hoover Dam, a project he had worked on briefly in the 1930s. One year he took the family up the West Coast to British Columbia, Canada, and thoroughly enjoyed his stay there, absorbed by outings to the Stanley Park Zoo and the Cleveland Dam. He did pass, however, on riding the Grouse Mountain Chair Lift. While in Vancouver, Nolan appreciated the architecture as he walked around the capital city, but as usual preferred to spend the nights in scenic small towns like Princeton. For a person who had seen so much of the world, he was always the most comfortable in the countryside. Nolan had a definite zest for life, and adventures were decidedly more pleasant when he was along to share them.

Having lived on his own much of his life, Nolan had definitely perfected his cooking skills. He was an excellent cook who fixed special Sunday breakfasts for the family. They were elaborate spreads that everyone looked forward to, whether he chose from all-time family favorites like chorizo, refried beans, thin-sliced potatoes, fried eggs, bacon, or ham, accompanied by cornbread, orange juice, fresh-sliced tomatoes, cucumbers, onions, chiles and, of course, Nolan's special "fried cheese" – or whether he chose a special treat like blueberry pancakes. After his wife became disabled with arthritis in the late 1970s, he took over cooking all the daily meals and traditional Sunday family dinners, as well as birthday and holiday dinners. He had countless cookbooks and had spent years developing his own recipes for cured olives, which he grew himself; outrageous baked beans; beef jerky, which he spiced and hung to dry inside the house; hot salsas that would make the top of your head sweat; old-fashioned pot roast and beef stew; barbecued spareribs; carne seca and red chile con carne, better than any restaurant's; and the Irish favorite corned beef and cabbage. His steaks on the grill were two inches thick and have never been equaled, nor has his signature coconut layer cake with strawberry filling. Of course, he maintained an array of blenders and juicers, never forgetting his athletic days and the benefits of carrot juice! He was great at creating new vegetable or fruit concoctions, guaranteed to give you any vitamin you could think of. On the other hand, he also had an ice cream maker; his specialties were homemade vanilla and peach. He was a gracious host and often invited members of Nellie's family and out-of-town visitors to share a meal. Whatever the fare, it was always obvious that everyone was quite pleased to be asked to the house.

Nolan was a gentle-hearted man who always offered to lend a hand. He was a constant and loyal friend, kind and giving of his time. This was a side of him that his lifelong friend Charles Thornton most wanted people to know about. He once said that although Nolan's accomplishments were outstanding, what set the man apart was his character. He provided us with a photo of his friend Earl from an article, titled "Businessmen Contribute Time, Money," heralding the construction of a new gymnasium for blind youths, a project spearheaded by Thornton himself. Earl was pictured laying block for the building: "Nolan trues up first corner on new gymnasium." Thornton deeply admired his friend's selflessness, charity, and community-mindedness. On June 14, 1992, he wrote the family, "I sure miss my visits with your dad, and am proud that I had him for a friend."

Closer to home, Nolan was also ready to lend a hand in his own neighborhood, whether it was teaching teenaged boys how to box, or assisting students with their school projects and science fair exhibits. He helped many young people get summer jobs and even helped some decide on careers and find permanent positions.

He was indeed a generous man who never forgot his leaner days and was ever willing to donate to good causes and help out financially. The house was always supplied with address labels, calendars, greeting cards, and pens from various veterans groups. And he could never refuse anyone who came to his door selling something. Whether it was peanut brittle or teddy-bear ornaments, he bought it all. Why? Not because he needed it, but because he tried to help out. He also bought a full cabinet of Girl Scout cookies each year when the daughters of the Forest Service employees took part in the annual cookie drive.

Nolan could never pass by a person in need. He bought meals for those who were hungry, and found "odd jobs" for people to do when they needed work; whether it was mowing the grass or painting the eaves, he would always find a project. He was forever thinking of others, and he never turned away from a problem. Nor could he pass by an animal in need. He always had a moment to scoop up a fallen baby bird and replace it safely in the nest or put out a bowl of food for a stray cat. In the early 1950s, Nolan noticed that the local alley cat, who frequented the yard, was ready to give birth. He built her a wooden house in one of the tree wells, complete with an access ramp, a home she readily inhabited. One of her kittens, Christopher, was adopted as a well-loved Nolan family pet. In the 1960s, Nolan arrived home after work with a horse. He had been riding the horse on the trails and had not finished work in time to return him to the stable, so the enormous horse spent the night in the utility room. Yes, the horse had a peaceful night and was returned the next morning.

Of course, Nolan was also extremely giving to his wife and daughter, not only with major things but with the small gestures that meant so much. If he had to go out of town, he never failed to call and to return with presents for both of them – chocolate-covered toffee, crystal jewelry, and delicate figurines for his daughter's collection. If they had a project, he put their needs before his own. If either of them had a problem or a dilemma, he was always there to listen and help in any way he could. In later years, he adapted easily to the role of grandfather, which he embraced with a full heart, giving the new arrivals the same loving care and consideration he gave to his wife and daughter. As "Daddy" had decades earlier, a new and cherished nickname came into being for Earl Nolan – "Papa." He and his wife, Nellie, now christened "Gramma," were at the hospital for their grandchildren's births, and Papa protectively "baby-proofed" the Nolan house for safety, and kept high chairs, diapers, toys, and shelves full of baby food on hand for the daily visits. He had hundreds of photos of the youngest family members, and proudly displayed the up-to-date albums on the coffee table in the living room. As the children grew, he delighted in making their birthday cakes and buying surprises for them when he went to the store. His grandchildren truly were a constant joy.

Nolan was an intellectual man who was an avid reader. He seemed to read constantly and had a large library at home. A glance at his countless (actually, more than 1,500) volumes revealed in-depth interests in anthropology and the origin of man; archaeology; architecture and construction, from the building of the Roman aqueducts to the modern solar home; art, from Michelangelo to the Smithsonian book on cartoons; astronomy; biographies, mostly historical, military, and sports, from Alexander the Great to Stonewall Jackson to football star George Blanda and even comedian W. C. Fields; biology and anatomy; botany; chemistry; cosmology, featuring the works of Isaac Asimov and Steven Weinberg; ancient and modern cultural traditions, from the Native Americans to the Irish; ecology and the environment; electricity, energy, and alternate energy, such as wind, water, and solar power; engineering – civil, electrical, hydraulic, mechanical, and structural – as well as blueprints, sketching, and surveying; evolution, both physical and cultural; geography; geology; ancient and modern history, from the Roman Empire, Greeks, and Mayans to the writings of H. G. Wells, Winston Churchill, Dwight Eisenhower, George S. Patton, and John Kennedy, plus extensive studies of American history; military history of all eras; mathematics, from algebra, geometry, and trigonometry to differential and integral calculus, and logarithms; mythology; the nations of the world; natural wonders; oceanography; physics; psychic sciences and the paranormal, primarily astrology, color theory, ESP, handwriting analysis, magic, mystic places, numerology, telepathy, and UFOs; psychology; religions of the world, e.g., the *Wisdom of Confucius*, the Koran, the Book of Mormon, five different editions of the Bible and several studies of the life of Jesus Christ, as well as studies of Judaism, Buddhism, Hinduism, Taoism, and Shinto; sociology; Spanish; speed-reading; sports, with a focus on football, boxing, and the Olympics; warfare tactics and strategies; weather and the atmosphere; and wildlife, from the coral reef to the jungle.

He had a wide variety of books on all types of specific subjects, as diverse as the *I Ching*, body language and gestures, communication skills, etiquette, the history of entertainment and movies, explosives, mountain climbing, the history of the pipe, personality assessments, poker playing, railroads, shipbuilding and boating, chess tournaments, survival guides, western gunfighters and train robberies, weaponry, quotations and a dictionary of thoughts, the power of the mind, and yoga. After his retirement, two of the specific areas Nolan focused on were the desalinization of seawater and the disposal of solid waste. He sent away for and received voluminous information on the latest developments in those areas. He also had a large collection of classic and modern literature, from Homer, Charles Dickens, and Leo Tolstoy to Dean Koontz; numerous types of reference books, including ancient and modern world and historical atlases, such as the *West Point Atlas of American Wars*; and various encyclopedias, some of which were quite specific, e.g., science, electricity, inventions, international wildlife, United States history, football, medicine, the *Audubon Nature Encyclopedia*, the *Viking Desk Encyclopedia*, and even a practical handyman's encyclopedia. He once said that the best way to get a general overview of knowledge was to just sit down and read the encyclopedia from beginning to end; he had actually made it through all the volumes of his home set. In reality, it would be much easier to report what did not interest him. There could never be a doubt why Nolan built so many bookcases; books were as fundamental to his life as the air he breathed.

On top of all of this, he was a subscriber to several magazines over the years, most notably *National Geographic* since 1950, and *Smithsonian*. Of course, he also subscribed to *The Ring*! He kept up with current events, reading the two local newspapers daily, as well as subscribing to various weekly news magazines, and catching the television news each evening. One intriguing aspect of this was his ability to place these events into the context of history and the trends of civilization. Nolan's mind was incredibly active, his perspective insightful, and his comprehensive knowledge astounding. At one point, a multi-page IQ test appeared in the local newspaper; Nolan, his wife, and daughter took the test for fun. The highest IQ measured numerically on the test was 170. The number of correct answers he had attained surpassed that measurement by several. This was certainly not surprising.

Although he normally had his reading material with him, Nolan did watch television. He was a bit alarmed that TV seemed to be taking over American life and that we were all becoming too dependent on it. He did have his favorites, though: Westerns, sports, and programs about wildlife or nature. He enjoyed variety shows, comedy programs, such as *Hogan's Heroes* and *McHale's Navy*, and old movies and musicals, especially those starring Nelson Eddy and Jeanette MacDonald. You could also find him watching *Star Trek* and *Mission Impossible*. At the time, most families had one TV set in the house, and watching TV was a family affair, with a lot of interaction going on. Nolan made it fun.

Describing Michael Earl Nolan has proved to be a daunting undertaking. To say that he had varied interests and talents would be a definite understatement. He was a sensitive man who loved poetry, from Walt Whitman's *Leaves of Grass* to Omar Khayyam. He obtained the *Rubaiyat* on July 14, 1945, at Camp Tarawa, Hawaii, Territory of Hawaii. He deeply loved music, everything from opera to Western classics, and sang in a rich operatic-quality baritone. Some of his favorites were "Poor Butterfly," the famous "Serenade" ("Overhead the Moon Is Beaming") from *The Student Prince*, and the popular song "Mexicali Rose." When he sang, the glass in the house would vibrate. It is believed that Nolan had mentioned performing Handel's *Messiah* with the Oratorio Society at the University. Of course, it was a humorous story about slipping off the back row of the platform. He had a large record collection and would often tape his favorites to take with him to play in the truck on his long trips for the Forest Service. He was thoughtful and philosophical, and he had an amazing sense of humor – frequently pointing out, in a quiet and understated way, absurd and hilarious little details that other people around him would miss. And, as so many noticed throughout his life, he laughed easily, oftentimes at himself. Nolan greatly enjoyed playing chess – most memorably in foxholes – and observing human nature. He spent time collecting and identifying rocks and minerals, even had a portable test kit. He was an expert poker player, but also had a deck of tarot cards. He won a "Second Premium" ribbon in Education Class 417, "Hammered Copper – Best Book

Ends," at the First Southern Arizona Fair on February 19, 1932. His prize money was 50¢! There were many sides to this incredible man, and all of them were interesting.

Nolan was a unique individual who had definite likes and dislikes. He had a preference for the color purple and often wore purple shirts, a superstition he acquired after a particularly dangerous battle. He hated ties and felt that they made a man's head look as if it were floating above his body. He studied numerology and favored the number *1*. He had a true love for garlic. He thought strawberries were the perfect food. He favored a birthday lemon meringue pie or the amazing 12-egg pound cake his wife made. He would occasionally drink iced tea or water from a tin can, which he said kept it colder, but we later found out that the Marines in the Solomons often drank out of these cans. He was a saver and never threw away a letter from a friend, a card from his wife, or the homemade cards from his daughter. He had a pipe collection, and at times would cut up the Turkish cigars the local shop would carry for him, and at others would cure his tobacco with apple slices in his humidor. He once tried growing his own tobacco in the backyard, but decided that the company must have sterilized the seeds. He swore he could never learn to dance because each time he tried, there seemed to be an extra, unexplainable little hop involved in the steps.

Although Nolan was not much of a "joiner," over the years he did hold memberships in a few organizations reflective of his interests and his life history: the Marine Corps Association (1945-46), United States Marine Raider Association, Veterans of Foreign Wars, American Society of Civil Engineers, Arizona Alumni Association, Wildcat Club, Tucson High School Badger Foundation, International Association of Fire Fighters, Fraternal Order of Eagles (1949), Smithsonian Associates, National Geographic Society, Knights of Columbus, and Arizona-Sonora Desert Museum.

Along with his membership cards, we found others which showed more snippets from his life. In 1949, he held a Restricted Radiotelephone Operator Permit from the Federal Communications Commission. He held a Blaster's Certificate from the U.S. Forest Service Safety Service, certifying him as "Fully qualified all types of blasting," and a 1964 Fire Qualification Card for the Coronado National Forest, listing the fire qualifications of camp officer, equipment officer, and tractor boss. Nolan had a certificate in first aid from the American National Red Cross. He took the National Safety Council's driver course while in the Forest Service and had a USFS award license, qualifying him to operate up to 10-ton trucks and to issue incidental driver's licenses on the Coronado; that license showed him as operating motor vehicles since 1928, with no accidents on his record. In his typical sentimental fashion, he had also saved his October 25, 1944 USMC motor vehicle operator's permit from Camp Tarawa, Territory of Hawaii, and his international driving license from his days in Peru.

Throughout the years, his family heard innumerable anecdotes from Nolan's friends: tales of his feats of strength, like pushing a car up "A" Mountain; tales of his bravery, like rescuing a person from being carried away by the waters raging in the Santa Cruz River; tales of his compassion, like giving friends a place to stay if they were down on their luck; and tales of his generosity, like bringing back money from his boxing and football excursions and simply giving it to friends who needed it, usually arranging it so they never knew it came from him. His sister-in-law Adele Ahee spoke of Nolan's reputation in his hometown. She said that as a young woman, she would become unnerved if she was walking downtown and saw any unsavory characters. But if she saw Earl or his brother Clarence on that same street, she would all of a sudden feel protected and safe.

Michael Earl Nolan had a deep and abiding reverence for life and the dignity of human beings. He had unending strength of character and embodied the concept of honor. Whether it was to protect his nation, his family, his friends, or complete strangers, he was always the one to step up. He did indeed seem to "just appear" when someone needed help.

There were also fascinating stories about some unusual skills Nolan had. For instance, after a fall in 1989, he was in the hospital to be checked and was hooked up to a heart-rate monitor. He glanced over at the machine, and asked, "That's mine?" His daughter responded that it was, and almost immediately the rate lowered on the screen by approximately half. Nolan said, "That's better." When his daughter asked him if he had just done that, he simply nodded his head *yes*. On another occasion, she got out of her car one morning to run inside the house for a minute, and the car door jammed shut with the engine running. Her father, who had left for work hours earlier, again appeared "out of the blue" within just a couple of minutes, hit the lock once with the side of his hand, and the door opened as if it had been no problem at all.

At times, the family heard stories from people they did not know. After Nolan's passing, they received a July 14, 1992 letter from Geraldine Cox Wilkie, the daughter of Samuel J. Cox of the 3rd Division N.C.B., 1st Marine Amphibious Corps, 53rd Naval Construction Battalion: "You don't know me, but I knew your father when I was just a little girl and he worked on the same road construction crew as my dad. Dad was older than Earl, but they were the best of friends. They were separated for a while by the war, but, by an amazing coincidence they were assigned to the same theatre of operations in the South Pacific [Bougainville, 1943]. Dad never forgot Earl and often regaled us with their experiences in the service. We Cox kids never forgot him either. Earl was a hero to us when we were little. Your father was revered by three little kids and the entire Cox family. I'm sure you heard from many friends whom you knew, or knew of, but I wanted you to know that he is remembered by some folks you've never known." Mrs. Wilkie, having moved from the city during the war, wrote that she had come to Tucson and stopped by Nolan's house to see him again after all those years, but found the house empty. The neighbors, who had lived next door to him for thirty-three years, sadly told her that she had missed him, and then said wistfully that he "was the nicest man." Mrs. Wilkie added, "And I believe it. I cried when I got back in the car, and I was furious with myself for wasting so much time before I looked him up." She later kindly sent the family some sheet music she had saved from years earlier, when Nolan had been a guest at the Cox home and they had all sung together around the piano, memories she treasured. In addition, after locating his address in 1984, she had written to him, and graciously forwarded a copy of the response she had received, a letter she kept with her father's naval mementos. Nolan had answered in part, "Your father and I were friends. I had worked for him in the 1930s when he was the construction foreman for Pima County Highway Dept., and during the Solomon Islands battles, we worked together. What is not commonly known is that the U.S. Navy Construction Battalions and the Marines landed and fought together. The job of building airports, roads, etc., was the Navy's responsibility. The job of securing the beachhead was shared by both Navy and Marines." He enclosed photographs of her father and himself together on Bougainville. It would not be the only time that he mentioned the expertise and bravery of the Seabees.

It is obvious that Nolan had the same long-lasting effect on people he knew at all stages of his life. He was important to them and they never forgot him.

After his retirement from the USFS, Nolan penned several novels and novellas. The Jeff Dimond article quoted him as saying, "Having been all over the Pacific from Alaska to Asia helps out when you are imagining things." In a letter written in the 1970s to his brother Bob, he joked about getting his novels published, commenting that the "profession is harder to crack than the old Chicago Bears used to be." However, he did feel that writing fiction had helped him considerably in "adjusting to a less active life." Manuscripts by Nolan which are set in recent times, with descriptions in his own words, include *Grabbing the Brass Ring*, "leadership as seen through the eyes of a front-line fighter who secretly aspires for the leading role"; *Catanma*, "a dedicated woman's fight to raise her country from a state of starvation, foreign exploitation, moral degradation, and defeat on the battlefield"; *In Memory Of*, "wartime experiences of a front-line fighter and his efforts to salvage some degree of re-belonging to the human race"; *Richard Carver*, "one man's attempts to improve his social status in a world torn by depression, extreme racial consciousness, and the distant sounds of war"; and *The Specialist*, "a leader of an early international protection agency, who has his hands full putting his own internal affairs in order." Manuscripts which are set in historical times include *Rule or Serve*, "a medieval slave entrusted with propagating his people's most cherished desire – freedom"; and *Last of the Line*, "an ancient setting for world conquest and the actions of two brothers – one a king, and the other a common soldier." His imagination was indeed extraordinary, not to mention that a great deal of his personal philosophy found its way into these stories.

Nolan was the constant companion and caregiver to his beloved wife, Nellie, until her passing on March 15, 1985. Michael Earl Nolan passed away April 6, 1991. He used to say he figured that if he could live through Iwo Jima, he could live through anything. Those of us who knew him, and love him still, are forever sorry that time finally caught up with him.

Throughout his life, it was his inner power, his inner grace which caused him to be the inspiration to those he met, which encouraged them to strive for excellence in their own lives, which provided them with the strength to meet life's challenges and overcome them, which allowed them to believe that anything was possible. Whether it was through his determination in athletics, courage on the field of battle, profound respect for nature, fascinating imagination and ever-inquiring mind, devotion and loyalty to family and friends, or his intrinsic compassion and belief in the dignity and value of life, Nolan accepted responsibility; he protected those he met; he provided stability and security; he promoted creativity and the appreciation of beauty in life – he uplifted us.

Nellie Ahee, University of Arizona, 1933.

Beginning her teaching career. Nellie Ahee, 1938.

Engagement photo. Nellie Ahee, 1946.

Married At Nuptial Mass

Mr. and Mrs. Michael Earl Nolan, on their wedding day, June 12, 1946, followed by a honeymoon trip to the Grand Canyon. (Printed in *Tucson Daily Citizen*, June 15, 1946.)

The new daddy. Nolan and baby daughter, Jeannie, in front of the Nolans' first home, 1947.

A lighter overhead lift. Nolan and daughter, Jeannie, 1949.

Nolan, with life-sized snowman, 1958.

Ready to slice a favorite birthday treat. Nolan, 1968.

An amazing cook, Nolan grills shish kebab in backyard, 1964.

Papa Nolan with grandson, Michael, 1980.

Papa holding granddaughter Karin, 1982.

Papa and granddaughter Sara, 1982.

Enjoying Christmas together. Nolan with grandchildren, (from left) Karin, Sara, and Michael, 1986.

The Nolans' grandchildren, (from left) Sara Nolan McCallum, Michael John Nolan, and Dr. Karin Krygelski Nolan, 2013.

Great-granddaughter Jean Belle Nolan McCallum, 2013.

Great-granddaughter Mally Paige Nolan McCallum, 2013.